MW01030932

OF MASKS AND MAGIC

SARAH ZANE   M.K. AHEARN   S.L. THORNE

S. FRASHER   JES DREW   KATHY HAAN   JORDAN A. DAY

R.E. JOHNSON   JESSICA M. BUTLER

Copyright © 2023 by Jessica Butler, Sarah Zane, and Kathy Haan

Individual stories are of the respective authors.

All rights reserved.

No part of this book may be reproduced in any form or by any electronic or mechanical means, including information storage and retrieval systems, without written permission from the author, except for the use of brief quotations in a book review.

Cover: R.L. Perez

CONTENTS

Story X

THROUGH THE PAINTINGS DIMLY BY
JESSICA M. BUTLER

.

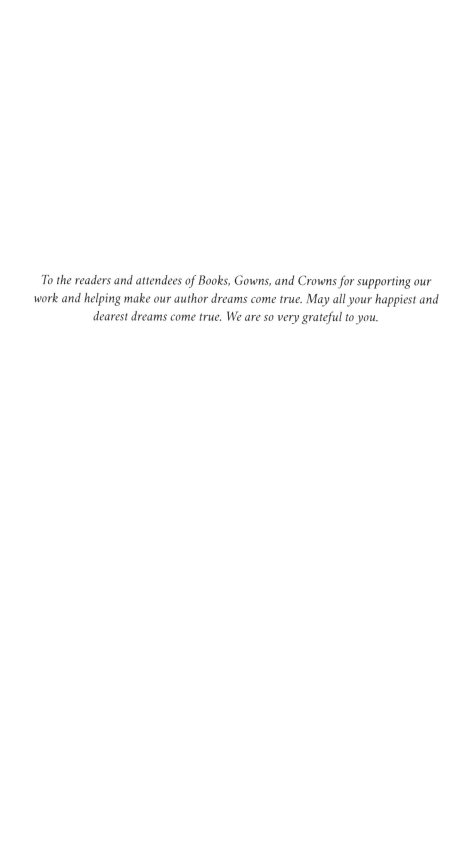

To the readers and attendees of Books, Gowns, and Crowns for supporting our work and helping make our author dreams come true. May all your happiest and dearest dreams come true. We are so very grateful to you.

FOREWORD AND A NOTE ON TRIGGER WARNINGS AND HEAT LEVELS

Dear readers and fellow Books, Gowns, and Crowns attendees,

We are overjoyed that we can now share with you *Of Masks and Magic*. The three of us decided shortly after chatting in the Books, Gowns, and Crowns group that the perfect addition to Books, Gowns, and Crowns Chapter 2 was an anthology that would represent some of the incredible talents and the beautiful creativity represented among the attending authors.

On top of that, we decided that we wanted our little anthology to make a bit of a difference in the world. So we decided to donate all profits that come from this anthology to Room to Read, an international charity that focuses on literacy and educational equality.

We writers of fantasy and fantasy romance can do quite a lot when we put our pens to paper, and it is such a delight to be able to share this with you now.

But we couldn't do it alone. A great big thank you to all the authors who contributed their talents to this anthology. They gave up their time and energy as well in sharing these stories, and they have made it such a simple task. Our thanks as well to R.L. Perez who provided her beautiful talents to crafting this gorgeous cover and the bookmark as well as some of the promotional graphics.

And an enormous thank you to you, the readers, for your reading and sharing these stories with the world. As much fun as writing is, it isn't half as much fun without being able to share it with people like you.

To help make sure that you get the best reading experience possible, we are using a heat scale for this anthology and noting triggers at the beginning of each story. The heat scale we are using is from FaRoFeb, a wonderful organization that supports and encourages authors in our genres as well as celebrates readers and lovers of all shades of fantasy romance. (Seriously, check them out FaRoFeb.com for fun events and reader opportunities. While February is their special time to shine, they are very active throughout the year.)

Their heat scale is as follows:

- Low heat: PG content
- Smoldering: buckets of heart wrenching tension; one (not especially graphic) sexual scene, not much coarse language
- Hot: generally one to three more extensive / detailed sex scenes, increasing use of coarse language
- Scorching: ALL the sex scenes, much description and detail, lots of coarse language

Hopefully this aids you in your reading journey, and you find the absolute perfect stories for your reading pleasure.

May you find much joy between these pages,
    Jessica, Sarah, and Kathy

STORY I
UNDER LOCK AND KEY BY SARAH ZANE

Heat Level: Low
(PG content)

Trigger Warnings:
Some violence and peril
Murder

CHAPTER 1

The first year of the curse had been an unbearable nightmare with Alanna's and Zara's murders never far from my mind. Thankfully, over the last year, I had formed a nice routine for myself. I didn't think about them as much and hadn't felt more than a stirring of the curse.

I wasn't happy per se, but I was content keeping to myself at my inn in its forgotten corner of Somerset. The inn wasn't busy and those that came to stay never stayed long, just the way I liked it. Some didn't even bother staying the night when they saw the inn was woman owned. Good riddance.

Had I known how different things were in Somerset, I might've picked another kingdom to run off to. The one thing Somerset had going for it was that no one paid too much attention to me or asked too many questions.

I had managed to keep a low profile, but I should've known my luck was going to run out.

What I didn't expect was that my peace would be shattered so abruptly.

CHAPTER 2

When she walked in the door, my mind couldn't form thoughts at the sight that was in front of me. A hint of jasmine, or maybe lilies, came wafting in with her. She smiled at me, and my heart stopped. I was instantly drawn to her. I could already feel the curse stirring. Yes, she was beautiful, but it was more than that. There was something about her that drew me to her. I wanted to be close to her, get to know her. I felt the thoughts warring in my mind; she needed to leave immediately, but I couldn't let her go.

She was in danger.

I wanted to scream at her to run. Leave now while you have the chance, while you're still happy and healthy. Get away from me before I ruin you.

I fought hard to make any of that come out of my mouth, to alter the smile on my face, but I couldn't. As my stare lingered on her, I couldn't stop myself from saying, "What brings a beautiful girl like you to a place like this?"

Her laugh was music to my ears. There wasn't a thing I wouldn't do to hear that laugh again. I could listen to it for the rest of my life. I tried to clear my thoughts. She didn't deserve anything about this.

There was still time to get her to leave, but

even the rational part of me was struggling. I wanted to get to know her, to learn anything and everything I could about her.

She faltered a moment when she saw my smile, seeming to sense something was off.

"Just travelling," she said with a shrug. "I needed a change of scenery, and this seemed as nice a place as any." She put down a large pouch on the counter weighed down heavily with silver.

I felt my eyebrows raise. "Will you be staying long?"

She shrugged "Maybe, maybe not." I continued to look at her, so she added, "I'll probably stay however long it takes the townspeople to run me out with pitchforks."

I laughed, and so did she.

I was a good deal taller than her, but even though she had to look up to me, I felt quite powerless in her presence. She could ask me to do anything, and I would. I had known her all of a few minutes and was already under her spell. I didn't even know her name. I wanted to blame the curse, but I knew this was different. This was me.

The curse had never forced any sort of feelings this strong on me before. It only encouraged the feelings and attraction that were there. But there was something about her, and whatever it was, was dangerous. Not to me, but to her. She needed to leave immediately, but of course, as luck would have it, she was staying indefinitely. Forever if I could get my hands on her. No. I had to leave her alone, do what little I could to keep her out of danger. The shorter her stay, the better.

The exact opposite came out of my mouth. "I'm honored you chose here for your stay. Please feel free, encouraged really, to stay as long as you like. Stay forever if you'd like," I said with a laugh.

"Who knows, I just might," she said, grinning.

Her smile would kill me. However this ended, that smile was going to haunt me for the rest of my days.

"Well, since you're staying for however long, I should probably know what to call you."

She adopted a look of outrage, placing her hand on her heart dramatically before saying, "You mean you don't recognize your princess?"

I quickly wracked my brain to come up with some image of what Princess Stella looked like but came up blank. I looked her over for a moment, wondering how the blonde and tan royal family could have a princess so opposite them. Her dark hair contrasted stunningly with her pale skin, but she looked nothing like the royal family.

Her laughter brought me out of my thoughts. "I couldn't help myself. Ignore me. I'm definitely no princess. I'm Loralie."

"Delphine, and it suits you. A beautiful name for a beautiful woman. Tell me, princess, what brings you to town?"

She looked uncomfortable for a moment before saying, "To tell you the truth, things ended badly with my ex-boyfriend. The whole thing was a mess, and I just couldn't stand to stay there."

I heard little after her saying ex-boyfriend. So much for her potentially being a problem, I thought, feeling both sad and relieved. "I shouldn't have been surprised. It's the same everywhere I go, really. The town before, it was my ex-girlfriend."

Hope shot through me at that before I could think about the consequences. "Things never go well. I don't know why I keep trying. I should know better than to get involved with anyone, really."

I couldn't help letting myself think there was a chance, though. Yes, a chance she would get hurt and broken by me like everyone else has.

It sounded like she had enough baggage for the two of us. There wouldn't even be room for my own problems. A girl like that wouldn't be able to trust me. The curse would claim her. There wouldn't be any way around it, so nothing could happen. But even if nothing could happen, I was dying to know more about her. I figured it couldn't hurt to keep her talking.

"Quite a heartbreaker, huh? It sounds like you left a trail of broken hearts a mile wide across all of Zanaria."

She smiled sadly. "Something like that."

She had a faraway look in her eye and I wanted to draw her back from wherever she went, but before I could think of anything, the curse intervened. I put my hand to my heart dramatically and said, "Well, do promise you'll go easy on me then, princess."

She smiled at that, but it didn't touch her eyes, and she stayed silent.

"Well, if there's anything at all I can do to make your stay more enjoyable, just let me know. I'm at your service." I couldn't stop myself, and don't know if I wanted to, from running my eyes up and down her curves before adding, "Really, anything at all." I licked my lips before adding, "It would be my pleasure."

She seemed too distracted to have noticed the cringey, blatant innuendo. She just thanked me, took her key, and went to her room.

Internally, I was kicking myself for not having made a better first impression. I should have been overjoyed she seemed distracted and not interested, but there was something about her and her sad smile that made me determined to get to know her, determined to see another genuine smile.

CHAPTER 3

The next couple of days, she didn't venture down into the lobby nearly as often as I would have liked. The first night she stayed, she slept well past noon and didn't emerge from her room until late into the day. The moon was rising by the time I finally saw her.

She smiled in my direction, but much to my chagrin, she didn't stop to say hello.

I should have been happy, but it was hard to stop myself from regretting that she didn't seem to want to know me. I had only known her a day, and I was already missing her when she left. This would end terribly.

I waited and waited for her to come back, well after the time I would have normally gone to sleep. I couldn't bring myself to leave the desk without seeing her back safe. It had been hours, and I didn't know her habits, but it seemed strange.

When the door finally opened, revealing her, I could have kicked myself. She wasn't alone. I don't know why I thought any different. Of course, she wasn't alone. Holding her hand was a short man who looked to be her age. Well, come to think of it, I didn't actually know how old she was, but they both looked to be in their twenties. I don't know why I just assumed she was around my age. From the way she looked and acted, she really could have been any age. She had a young-looking face, but a maturity about her that made me almost certain she was in her twenties. I would have to ask. Later, once she detached herself from the luckiest man in Zanaria.

I watched as she ran her fingers through his hair and laughed at something he had said. I could have killed him. I wouldn't have considered death too steep a price for his crime. He wasn't anywhere near worthy of her. He wasn't fit to be near her, never mind getting that sort of attention from her. I knew I could beat him in a fight, even before the curse, but especially now. All it would take was me wrapping my fingers around his neck and squeezing, squeezing until the struggling stopped and the light left his eyes.

"Oh!" she exclaimed, seeing me. "I'm so sorry. I didn't expect anyone to still be up."

He whispered something in her ear, and I watched as his lips trailed down, planting kisses on her neck.

Strangling was too good for him, too quick.

She giggled and leaned into him a moment before remembering me. A blush overtook her face, making her complexion match her crimson dress. The neckline plunged far enough that I could see the blush spread down to her chest.

I brought my eyes back to her face and saw her shoo him away from her neck, but not too far away. She still held his hand. She looked like she had been caught sneaking a suitor past her parents.

The last thing I needed was to continue to watch his lips on her neck. I don't think I could have managed it without violence. Thoughts of choking the life out of him came back. I clearly wasn't subtle about my mood, since she smiled apologetically before leading him up the stairway to her room.

I was stupid to have stayed up. She was a grown woman, and I didn't even know her. I didn't need to look out for her. No one had asked me to, and she clearly didn't care that I had.

I stalked down the hall, up the back stairs to my own room, praying to the gods I wouldn't hear them. Otherwise, I knew I would do something regretful, even if I wouldn't regret it.

Thankfully, the inn was quiet from my room. I finished getting ready for bed and slipped under the covers. Only then did it occur to me how weird it was that I couldn't hear them. She was only staying a couple of rooms down, and she didn't seem like the quiet type. At least they were being courteous to the other guests. The last thing I wanted to deal with in the morning, which, by the looks of the lightening sky through my window, was rapidly approaching, was unhappy guests.

CHAPTER 4

T he next day I rose far later than usual, rushed through getting ready, and practically ran to the front desk.

When I got there and nothing was amiss, I exhaled deeply. I hadn't meant to oversleep, but I had stayed up far too late last night, clearly for no reason. Normally, I was down checking on the rest of the staff and making sure none of the lodgers needed anything far earlier than this. Thankfully, nothing had fallen apart in my absence.

On the bright side, Loralie's nighttime guest would have left by now. Maybe it was for the better. I don't know that I could have calmly dealt with seeing him. The last thing I needed was him winding up dead at the Inn. That would definitely be bad for business.

I sighed, letting myself enjoy the thought of him no longer breathing, before sitting back down and checking my tasks for the day. There was always something that needed doing. Maybe today I would finally get around to fixing the door to the dining room. It probably wouldn't take too long. I considered it for a moment, but it could wait. It would be irresponsible to leave the desk unattended so soon after just opening it for the day. Besides, my book was calling out to me. I settled in, took my book from in the desk, and picked up where I left off.

It was a lovely tale about a wordsmith in a strange land. Whoever penned it had a wild imagination, though, with all the talk of dwellings stacked on top of one another so tall they touched the sky. The wordsmith was to be attending a ball, which I had gathered was less common-place there than it was here. She was meeting up with some of the other ladies attending when I heard footsteps on the stairs.

I stashed the book away quickly and looked up. Loralie's gust was still here. Why was he still here? As I watched, he stumbled his way down the stairs. I hoped he would fall and break his neck, but to my chagrin, he made it down the stairs without incident. He was holding on to his head and seemed dazed. It wouldn't be the first or last time a lodger indulged too much. I was surprised she hadn't bid him leave earlier, though. Maybe she had overindulged last night as well.

The afternoon faded into evening without her appearing. I was starting to get concerned. I thought about maybe getting her some water and a hangover draught. I twisted the idea around in my head, but it seemed too forward, so I fought to keep myself at the desk.

My body and thoughts were at war. I tried to focus my mind on my duties, but that didn't work. I tried reading but couldn't stop thinking about her. I knew I was going to cave.

I threw down my book in frustration and heard a laugh. "That bad, huh?"

I looked up quickly, knowing even before I did, that it was her. My suspicion was confirmed when I saw her standing in front of me in another crimson number that, if possible, looked even better on her than the one yesterday.

I just stared at her. How could I not? Seconds passed, but it could have been minutes. I had lost the power of speech. Her onyx hair cascaded over her shoulders and down her back in loose waves. I wanted to step closer and run my fingers through her hair. I wondered if it was as smooth and silky as it looked. I heard a noise come from her lips, drawing my eyes to them. I wondered if they were as soft as they looked. A moment later, it occurred to me she was speaking and that I should be mortified. I was just standing there, staring at her. I might as well have been drooling.

She paused and must have seen in my face I hadn't heard what she was saying. She laughed before saying again, "Clearly, I need to read that book immediately if it's gotten you that out of it. I've been meaning to pick up something new to read."

"I haven't read much of it yet, but you can borrow it if you'd like."

"I wouldn't dare leave you in suspense like that, but the moment you finish it, I'd love to borrow it."

I hadn't read much of the story, so I hoped it was one good enough to

OF MASKS AND MAGIC

recommend. I couldn't tell her the truth; that I hadn't even remotely been thinking about the book.

"If you're looking for something before then, we do have a library here."

Her eyes lit up and a smile stole over her face, making me wish I had brought it up earlier. "You do?" she asked.

I smiled back. Her excitement was contagious. "It's not as big as I'd like, but we have over a thousand books, so hopefully something will be to your taste."

Her jaw dropped as she looked at me with a mix of wonder and shock. "A thousand books?"

I nodded.

"Which way?" she asked.

I pointed down the hall, and she ran that way, before hesitating. I laughed, but before she could ask, I yelled over, "On your left."

She pivoted and saw the door, stopping for a moment in front of it and taking a deep breath before opening it. I heard her shriek from down the hall and couldn't help laughing. A few minutes later, she came back, a little sheepishly, holding a book. I strained to see which one but couldn't see the title.

"Would it be okay if I take this upstairs to read tonight?" she asked with a pleading in her voice that I knew I wouldn't say no to, even if it had been against the rules. It wasn't, though. Lodgers were encouraged to enjoy the library at their leisure.

I nodded and told her, "Of course. You're more than welcome to take as many as you like to your room."

Her eyes lit up when she smiled. She looked wistfully over her shoulder in the direction of the library. "I would love to, but I don't have the time to pick out any. I have to head out." She looked down, remembered the book in her hand, and added, "But first I have to run this upstairs."

"I can take that up-" I started to say, but she had already taken off back up the stairs. She moved more quickly than I would have imagined possible. A minute or so later, she returned, running down the stairs. I thought she was going to leave quickly, but she skidded to a stop in front of the desk. "Thank you," she said with a smile. "If it isn't too much trouble, do you think you could help me pick out some books for the rest of my stay?"

I jumped at the thought, literally. I was out of my chair in an instant, smiling widely. "I'd love to. Why don't we go look-"

She frowned. "I'm so sorry. I should have been clearer. I meant tomorrow." She, again, looked wistfully at the library and then sadly at me. I wondered for a moment if she regretted not being able to spend time with me, but that wouldn't make sense. She didn't even really know me. "I wish I could tonight, but I have an evening engagement."

I hoped it wasn't like her evening activities yesterday, I thought with a scowl that I had to fight to keep off my face. I nodded while attempting a smile. "Very well then, tomorrow it is."

"It's a date," she said with a grin, before turning and heading out quickly. "Don't wait up," she added with a chuckle.

I hadn't been planning to, but I couldn't sleep. I kept replaying our conversation over and over in my mind. I needed to know what she meant when she said it was a date. She couldn't have actually meant a date. If she did, I shouldn't do it. Every inch of me was screaming to be close to her after only a couple of days, but she clearly didn't feel the same. She had brought a man back to her room the night before. Just thinking about it made me want to hit something, strangle someone, but that had to be a pretty clear indicator she wasn't interested in me.

I desperately wanted to spend time with her, and she was only in danger if she caught any sort of feelings. She hadn't, and I reasoned she wouldn't. Not for me; not when she looked like that, and I looked like me. I had to be safe spending time with her. She seemed okay with the idea, too. She had asked me to help her. What kind of innkeeper would I be if I didn't indulge my guests' requests?

"Ehh hmhm". I startled violently, looking up to see a lodger standing in front of the desk.

I waited for him to say something, but he didn't, just stared at me, waiting. After a moment of silence, I asked, "Yes?"

He looked offended, puffing up his chest before saying, "Well, since you so politely asked how you could help me, we're out of towels, room 4. Bring some up."

He stormed off, but not quickly enough. Lucky for him, I had a stack of towels under the desk. Unlucky for him, I had good aim. I whipped two rolled-up towels at the back of his head, one after another. Both were direct hits. He stopped in his tracks before turning slowly, looking outraged.

I held in my laughter as best I could and smiled sweetly at him. "I found your towels and made sure to deliver them as soon as possible."

He looked at me in disbelief before scooping up the towels, muttering to himself about the treatment here and how he'd certainly be telling his friends about it. Good. The last thing I wanted was more people like him staying here.

CHAPTER 5

I stayed at the desk for another hour. I knew I shouldn't be up waiting for her, but I couldn't bring myself to leave and knew I wouldn't sleep even if I did. I occupied my time with thinking about what books she might like and what I could recommend to her. It would have helped if I had seen what she took up to her room earlier, but the longer it took to find suggestions and recommendations, the longer I got to spend with her. I was quite alright with that.

Another hour passed, and I decided to abandon my post. She might be out all night, who knows. I put away my things for the night and made my way up to my room.

I was turning my door handle when I heard laughter that was unmistakably hers, but from the sounds on the stairs, it didn't sound like she was alone. I opened my door quickly, not wanting a repeat of yesterday, not sure I could keep my cool seeing him with her again, knowing she picked him to spend the night with her again. I didn't want to see.

I went to close the door behind me and heard her musical laughter again, this time closer. I couldn't help myself. I left the door open a crack and stuck my head out. It turns out I didn't need to be that careful; they were so wrapped up in each other neither of them noticed me.

The anger spiked through me but was quickly replaced by shock when I looked at the man. He was taller and stockier than the man from yesterday. I pulled my head back into my room, pushing the door shut, not caring to stifle the noise.

I couldn't decide whether it was better or worse that it wasn't the same man. She wasn't letting him enjoy the paradise of a second night with her. But where was she finding these men? What was so special about either of them? What did they have that I didn't? My last thought before I drifted off to sleep was that the only thing they had that I didn't was her attention. What I wouldn't give to have her look at me like that.

CHAPTER 6

When her latest conquest came stumbling down the stairs the next morning, clutching his head like his predecessor, I made sure to loudly tell him to, "Have a great rest of your afternoon!" on the way out.

He clutched his head harder, making me laugh when he shut the door.

That helped a little to quiet the rage in me. I had no right to be feeling this way. She was her own person, and there was no reason she shouldn't be able to have fun with whoever she wanted, but I hated the thought of anyone getting to touch her. I wanted to run my fingers through her hair and pull her in close. I would kill for just a kiss, literally.

If I thought murdering either of those men would make her look in my direction, I probably would have done it.

Whatever she was doing with them, I hoped she was happy. I knew they were from how dazed they left the next morning. Whatever she was doing to them, I wanted nothing more than to experience it myself.

I hoped she would, at the very least, remember our talk from yesterday and still want to look at the library with me. I had been spending most of the morning, and a lot of last night, coming up with book recommendations for her.

I wanted to spend time with her. The curse was pushing me to pursue her faster and harder than I wanted, but the truth remained, I wanted her. Curse or no curse, I would have been trying to get her attention. But I was cursed, and I had to be mindful of that. I couldn't slip up like I did last time. I couldn't lose another person I cared about, especially not to my own hands.

After Zara, it had taken me weeks to be able to look myself in the mirror. I didn't want to face myself and know I was looking at a killer. I couldn't stomach it. Alanna's death had been in a fit of passion, but Zara's death was more calculated and even more devastating. She hadn't done a damn thing wrong besides meeting me, and now I had to live with the fact that she was dead, and I was to blame. There were no excuses, no one to pin the blame on or hide behind. It was my fault.

Sometimes when I closed my eyes, I could still see the life leaving hers. I could still feel my mind screaming at me to stop. I fought as hard as I could, but I couldn't control myself. I watched, internally screaming, as my own hands strangled the life out of her. The curse took control, only letting me stop after she stopped breathing.

I started compressions the moment I regained control. I could barely see her through my tears, but I had to save her. I tried to breathe air back into her lungs. I screamed and pleaded to every deity I knew the name of, but she was already gone.

I cried, sobbed, for the rest of the day over her lifeless body. I hadn't truly realized the horror of the curse until then. I hadn't really understood what it would mean. I had thought it would be easy to get around. If she just didn't open the door, she would be safe. If she cared about me, she would have listened when I warned her, but she hadn't.

She gave into temptation for whatever reason I'll never know.

In the early days of the curse, I had thought I would feel betrayed by anyone that entered. I had thought that if I was forced to entrust someone with the key and they ignored my warnings and went inside anyway that I would feel betrayed enough that I would have wanted to kill them.

I wished I had felt that way with Zara. It would've been easier if I had felt anything but devastation. I hated myself and still did. I wasn't worthy of being loved by anyone.

Alanna had been the first to show me that. She had only been with me for my connections. The joke was on her. I couldn't care less about my family or my duties to them.

I had run the first chance I got, longing for any sort of change. I just needed to get away. I travelled as far as I could, to this forgotten corner of Somerset, took a room at the Inn, and fell in love with the peace and quiet. I gave every last coin I had to my name to buy the place and never looked back, never regretted it, until Alanna and the curse. But the curse didn't change anything, not really. It just solidified what was always there. I wasn't loveable, and now I was a literal monster.

After Zara, I lost my will to live. I tried to hang myself, only to find I couldn't tie the knots in the rope. I tried to poison myself, only to find my hands wouldn't pick up the jar. I even tried to stab myself in the heart, but I couldn't turn the knife on myself. As a last resort, I tried to starve myself, but the curse forced food upon me. At least I wanted to think that it was the curse and not my own weakness. I had no will to live, and I deserved to suffer, but I couldn't end things.

I found out then that the curse kept me trapped in more ways than one. Not only was I essentially tied to the Inn, but I was tied to life, or, at the very least, couldn't end my life with my own hands or by starvation.

I kept trying new ways to end things, but none of them worked. I turned to novels for new ideas and found that burying myself in stories helped to bury some of my grief, despair, and loneliness. I was grateful for that small mercy.

After a while, it occurred to me to try to research the curse, but I couldn't find any reference to or mention of it.

I still hadn't been able to find a thing on it. It was useless. I was beyond saving and was content to stay away from everyone … until Loralie walked in.

There was something about her I just couldn't stay away from. The curse was part of it, but even in my own thoughts, I wanted to be close to her. I needed to get her to leave. I should have felt ashamed of myself for considering spending the day looking at books with her.

There was no way that was even remotely acceptable. The more time I spent around her, the more I craved her. At this rate, I would be forced to give her the key by tomorrow. I couldn't let that happen. I had no idea things would move this fast, that my own feelings would progress this quickly. With Zara, it had taken a couple of weeks for me to start feeling like this, and a couple more for me to have to give her the key, and that was only after we had slept together. I hadn't even kissed Loralie, and I could already feel the compulsion.

I knew it would be smart to avoid her, but I couldn't bring myself to. I could hardly think about anything besides her.

When she finally emerged, I knew it was her before I even looked up. I could hear her light footsteps and smell her jasmine perfume. I fought to keep my eyes on my work, wondering if she wouldn't engage with me if I didn't look up, but I heard her approach. My head and eyes raised of their own accord. She was wearing an oversized wool sweater and tights and was holding a book tightly to her chest.

She smiled at me and said, "I know you said to help myself, but I was hoping I could take you up on your offer to show me around the library."

Gods be damned. I couldn't say no to her. I raised an eyebrow at her, not able to resist teasing her. "You mean show you around the single room I overgenerously call a library?"

She laughed at that, her neck turning red as she blushed a little. I wanted to run my tongue up her neck and whisper in her ear about some other things we could do instead of exploring the library.

Before I could say or do anything besides stare at her, she explained, "I didn't mean show me around. I meant your offer from yesterday. I'm not sure what I should read next."

I wondered if I could make her blush deepen. I smiled and said, "If you wanted to get me alone, you could have just said that." I couldn't help throwing in a wink.

She laughed before saying, "You're quite stunning, but I really would like to see your collection and get some recommendations. I finished my story last night and don't know what to read next. I assume you're not done with yours?"

I looked down at the abandoned book in my desk. I hadn't touched it since yesterday and hadn't been able to read much then either. I hadn't been able to focus on much of anything lately with her under the same roof. A moment later, it occurred to me to be surprised that she had somehow found time to finish the book between when she came back with her nighttime guest and now. It couldn't have been more than a couple of hours since he left. That was impressive, even for me, and I normally read fast.

At least I did before she showed up. I couldn't stop the thoughts of her, of what I would love to do with and to her, and of what she might be doing when she wasn't standing in front of me. I'd never experienced anything like this before with anyone else. Even with Zara, she had never invaded nearly my every waking thought like Loralie had.

I smiled at her. "Well, I'd love to give recommendations, but first, what book did you just finish?"

She gestured to the book with her free hand. "This one."

"Which is called?"

She blushed again, which told me all I needed to know, even before she said, "It's not important."

"Well, it is if you want good recommendations."

She shook her head. "Never mind. I'll just look myself."

"Come on. It can't be that bad. Just tell me."

She shook her head again. I went to move from behind the desk, but she took off toward the library. Laughing, I gave chase, slowing my pace to let her win. If I timed it just right, her hands would be free.

I heard her laughing as I entered the library. She yelled triumphantly as she shoved the book back into its place. I noted the location so I could look later, but right now that wasn't what I had on my mind. I moved quickly, coming up behind her. She whirled around and jumped back in surprise when she saw I was much closer than she expected. She had her back pressed against the bookcase now. I leaned one of my arms over her head on the bookshelf behind her and watched her.

Her cheeks flushed. I loved how she reacted to me. She was breathless, but managed to say, "I win."

I watched her, bringing my other hand up to her shoulder and tracing my finger down her arm.

"You mean you don't think I know the book is behind you?"

She paled for a moment, before straightening as much as she could and saying, "You can't possibly know which of the twenty books near us is the one I just put back."

"Oh, but I do."

She didn't seem to believe me. She smiled. "You're all talk."

"Not quite. I just love seeing you squirm."

"Well, it's not working. You won't win. You're not seeing the book."

"I think we both know you're wrong."

"Prove it."

"I easily could." I let my fingers move from her arm, up to her neck, lazily tracing a trail of where I couldn't stop thinking about putting my lips. "But I might not look. I wouldn't want to offend your sensibilities as a lady."

"I'm no lady."

"You seem terribly proper, princess." I said with a smirk. "Are you worried someone might find out what you read?"

"No," she said defiantly.

"Well, I think you are." I started to move my hand to where I knew the book was, taunting her. "I think you're quite worried I might see that you-"

She cut me off, and caught me off-guard, spinning me so my back was against the bookshelf.

"Wow. Someone's feisty. If I had known you liked to be in charge-"

She cut me off with her lips. I lost all track of time, of where we were. I couldn't tell where my body stopped and hers started. She ran her tongue over my bottom lip before biting down, and I felt the warmth of the blood before her tongue captured it. I hadn't in my wildest dreams thought she would take charge like this, be rough like this. No wonder those men left so dazed. I couldn't have told you my own name. She was my world. Nothing existed outside of her. For once, my mind was quiet.

Until she pulled away and the horror of what happened hit me. The curse. My fingers were already itching toward the pocket I knew the key was in. I couldn't let that happen. I felt like panicking, but, thankfully, the curse kicked in enough to force me into some semblance of calm. At least until I saw her face. She looked how I felt. Fuck. As much as that couldn't happen again, I had foolishly hoped she would want it to.

"Wow," I said.

"I'm so sorry!" she blurted out. "I don't know what came over me, but I promise you it won't happen again."

I was stunned and, for once, me and the curse were at a loss for words. She bolted from the room before I could think of anything to say.

I didn't see her for the rest of the day, but when I went back to the library to see what she had been reading, the book and several others were missing. In the place of the book I had been looking for was a single lily. She couldn't have left it for me, couldn't have meant it for me, not after that reaction, but I took it anyway. I put it on my nightstand, unable to resist. It smelled like her.

CHAPTER 7

I only caught a glimpse of her coming down the stairs in a hurry the next day before she left. It almost felt like she was running from me. She was smart to stay away from me, but it killed me inside to see her almost seem afraid of me. I had no idea what I had done or what she had seen that would have made her feel like that, but it was for the best. If I didn't have to spend more time with her, she would be safe, protected. But I couldn't bring myself to be anything but miserable about it.

She went out wearing another barely-there dress, and by now I knew the drill. I knew I should go to bed before she returned. The last thing I wanted was to see her with anyone else. The last thing I needed was to rip out some guy's throat in the middle of the lobby because she preferred him. That would hardly help my case and would just push her further from me.

I was going to go to bed until I saw the flower. It was just a silly little lily; it didn't mean anything. It couldn't mean anything after how she had acted, after how she ran out on me, but I couldn't help hoping.

Against my better judgment, I put the lily behind my ear and without bothering to change, threw on my silk robe and descended the stairs. I couldn't decide if it was my idea or if it was another oh-so-subtle push from the curse, but I found myself waiting in the lobby for her.

I wasn't surprised when, in the middle of the night, she showed up with another new guy. I watched as she smiled at him, wanting to make him suffer for having done nothing to earn her smiles, for not appreciating what a gift they were.

Her smile faded when she saw me. I watched her eyes travel up the silk of my robe and shivered under her gaze. I was absolutely making a fool of myself, but I couldn't help but get some satisfaction out of the way she was looking at me. She pulled her hand out of his and whispered something to him. He went up the stairs, leaving us alone.

She didn't say anything, just continued to stare at me. The hunger in her eyes was a clear invitation. I sidled up closer to her and reached out my hand tentatively. When she didn't move, I let myself run my fingers through her hair, pulling her closer to me, caressing her beautifully soft hair. I was surprised she let me. She didn't bat my hand away, move back, or even tell me to stop. She actually leaned into my touch. When she met my eye, she looked surprised by her own actions and blushed. The blood rushing to her pale cheeks and the way she looked at me did me in. I melted.

She was the first person in a long time to look at me like that. She would be different. She had to be, because I couldn't let her go. The curse would always hang over my head, but she could be the one to stop it. It couldn't be broken, but as long as she didn't break my trust, the curse could be stopped. If she stayed, as long as she was here and the curse was attached to her, I could be free.

I saw it all flash before my eyes. Us sitting by the fire cuddled up together reading. Us holding hands and taking a moonlight stroll through the gardens. Us doing whatever it was she did with those men that left them so dazed leaving her room. I could see it all. Maybe she would be the one to save me.

I didn't say any of that. I just smiled down at her and told her, "If there's anything at all I can do to make your stay more," I licked my lips, "*enjoyable*, just let me know." I let my hand stroke down her hair to her face, and lifted her chin, moving her eyes to mine. "Just say the word. I'm all yours."

Her blush and the look in her eyes told me she understood my meaning and would be thinking about it tonight. *Good*. I sauntered back to the desk, swinging my hips more exaggeratedly than usual. I couldn't help looking back, and when I saw her watching, I winked before tossing my cobalt hair over my shoulder and closed the distance to the desk.

There was nothing I could do to stop her if she continued to take men to her bed, but from the hunger in her eyes when I saw her watching me, I was sure she would be thinking about me.

CHAPTER 8

I rose with a new purpose and a new hope the next day. I was going to make her notice me. Curse be damned, I wanted her. I couldn't bear to think of her not being in my life, especially when she seemed interested, at least physically. I was sure if she would give me a chance that she would see there was something between us. This couldn't possibly be one sided. I had to get her attention, and I had just the plan.

I rushed through my daily tasks that morning, making sure to give myself plenty of time in the kitchen. I pulled on an apron and got to work.

An hour or so later, I finished drizzling the icing on and took off the apron with a satisfied sigh. There wasn't much I felt like I could do right in my life, especially now, but no one made a better cinnamon roll than I did.

The scent of cinnamon wafted through the kitchen, and I couldn't help myself from having one. There were plenty anyway. I sunk my teeth into one with a satisfied groan. It had been far too long since I'd last baked anything, too long since I felt okay doing anything that might bring me any sort of joy. But I wanted to get to know Loralie, and what better ice breaker than my cinnamon rolls?

I used to make them all the time, back before the curse. The lodgers used to love them. I would make them fresh every morning, but I hadn't since that day. I couldn't stomach the thought. Just the smell of cinnamon used to bring me right back there. I was pleasantly surprised it didn't anymore. Pleasantly surprised I could let myself feel happy, feel some joy, without feeling too guilty about it.

I put a few cinnamon rolls into a basket and made the trek upstairs, willing myself not to think about how similar this felt to that day. It was a true feat of strength that I made it past room 13 without looking at the door.

A few doors later and I was at hers. I had written a little note that I attached to the basket since I didn't want to disturb her. I figured she might still be sleeping, based on her nighttime habits.

I put the basket outside her door and stood there, unsure if I should knock. After a minute of wavering, I decided to knock gently. If she was sleeping, I wouldn't disturb her, but if she was awake, at least she would know someone had been there and left something for her.

I tapped gently on the door for a moment before turning and going back the way I came. I was halfway down the hall when I heard a door open. "Hello?"

I turned around and waved sheepishly. "Morning, princess." She scowled, and I laughed. "Well, I should say Good Afternoon."

She grumbled and went to shut the door before seeing the basket. "What's this?"

I watched as she picked them up and tried not to blush as she read the note. Her eyes widened. She peeled back the cloth over the basket and gasped. "You made these?" She looked up at me with wide eyes. "For me?"

I smiled and shrugged. "I figured we had gotten off to a weird start, and I wanted to apologize for that. I would love to get to know you if you'd give me that chance." It was rare when the curse let me truly speak from the heart like I was now, rare for my wants to align with those of the curse enough. I had learned to highly appreciate those moments.

"I'm sorry for whatever I did to make you uncomfortable. I know I can be a lot sometimes," I said with a shrug.

She had still been looking at the treats, but her head shot up when I said that. "You're sorry?" she asked with surprise.

"Of course I am. I made a bad impression on you and I'm trying to fix it, if you'll let me."

She shook her head slowly, and my heart sank until she said, "You have nothing to apologize for. Me, on the other hand … I strong armed you into helping me in the library and then assaulted you and bit you. Gods, I actually bit you."

She was too damned adorable. The blush that crept up her neck was just icing on top of an already perfect cake. She didn't seem to see the humor in what she had said. Instead, she looked incredibly upset and serious, so I tried to hold back, but I shook with laughter. She looked up, startled.

"Princess, if that's what you consider assault, I would beg to be abused by you."

She smiled a little, saying, "I just got so carried away."

"You can get carried away all over me whenever you'd like. Ravish me, princess."

She chuckled at that, and in a flash, grabbed a cinnamon roll and chucked it at my head. I didn't even see it until it was in the air. Luckily, I had quick reflexes. I caught it a moment before impact. I glanced at it, thinking. I could take a bite, but where would be the fun in that? Looking her dead in the eye, I stuck out my tongue at her before slowly licking some of the frosting from the roll.

I felt her watching me and heard her utter, "Gods forgive me," before launching herself at me. I just barely had time to drop the cinnamon roll to catch her before she was in my arms with her lips on mine.

She kissed me with reckless abandon, like I was the air she needed to breathe. I hoped she would never stop. I wrapped my arms around her, but she pulled away from the kiss.

Anxious she was going to run like last time, I quickly opened my eyes, but she was smiling at me. She took a strand of my hair and twisted it in her fingers. "I love how it changes colors in the light." She twirled it one way. "Right now, it looks royal blue, but if I look at it this way," she twisted it again, "it looks sapphire."

I watched her, waiting for her to pull out of my arms, but she didn't.

"What?" she asked when she noticed I was still staring.

"You're not running."

She laughed. "I don't actually do that often."

I smirked. "Only with me then?"

Her gaze moved from my hair to my eyes. "What can I say? You bring out a feisty side of me."

"I love it."

She cocked an eyebrow at me. "There you go again, trying to make me run. It's a little early for you loving me, don't you think?"

I paled, and she burst into laughter. "Don't worry. I'm not going anywhere for a while. I planned to stay awhile, and I'm not changing my plans for you," she said with a grin.

I didn't feel I knew her well enough to ask what her plans were, but I would take any of the time she gave me.

CHAPTER 9

The next week flew by with her by my side. Her habits didn't change. She still slept most of the day away, but now she spent most of her nights with me. I started sleeping in later and staying up later, adapting as best I could to her schedule to spend more time with her. I didn't know what I had done to be lucky enough to capture her attention, but I was grateful for it.

One of the nights, I helped her pick out some books that I thought she might like. I still hadn't found out what she had been reading, but I recommended a few of my favorites to her.

I took my own book, closed the desk for the night, and went to the den to meet her. The nights were getting chillier, so I lit a fire and set up some blankets near the chairs by the fire in case she got cold. I settled in and started my book, waiting for her. She sauntered in with one of the books I had picked for her, forgoing the chair I had set out for her, and walked over to me.

"Aren't you going to make room for me?"

I looked confused at the other chair. "I put out a chair for you."

She looked at me pointedly before turning around. I thought she was going to the other chair, but she lowered herself into my lap. Not the most practical for reading, but far preferable.

I pulled her closer, making sure she was secure. "This is why you're in charge, princess."

She laughed at that, and my heart soared. "I do have good ideas, don't I?"

"The best."

I didn't get much reading done between her kisses and her jasmine scent clouding my thoughts, but the night was perfect.

————

We went for a moonlight stroll one night through the gardens. She led me to the lilies and jasmine, saying they were her favorite. No surprise there.

"They remind me of you," I had told her.

She squealed at that, and launched herself at me, wrapping her hands behind my neck, pulling me down and kissing me hard.

————

Another night, I took her to the kitchen with me and we cooked dinner. Well, for her it was breakfast, and when I say we cooked, I mean I cooked while I watched her watch in awe.

When she came into the kitchen, looking tired, I couldn't help but laugh. She rubbed her eyes, and told me she would help. I chuckled and, before she could protest, lifted her up and set her on the counter. I already had her cup of coffee waiting. When I handed it to her, she gave me a sleepy smile and was content to sit back, sip her coffee, and watch me work. I wanted to spoil her.

We shared the nights together, but she never invited me to her room, and I didn't dare invite her to mine. The last thing I wanted was to speed things up. I wanted to enjoy the beginning of this. The beginning of something so new, so fragile. We were so happy. I didn't want it to end. I didn't want the bubble to burst.

I was happier than I had been in a long time, and so far, I had somehow kept the curse at bay, but I could feel it hovering over my every interaction with her, waiting to strike. The more serious this got, the more dangerous it became. I didn't understand why the curse was allowing me the freedom to take things slowly with her.

Now I realize what I couldn't at the time; it was inevitable. The curse didn't push me further because her and I were already trapped. From the first moment I saw her, I knew she would be trouble, and I was right.

CHAPTER 10

It took another couple of days before I couldn't hold back anymore, couldn't resist the compulsions of the curse any longer. I couldn't fight any longer. Unfortunately for me, I couldn't have picked a worse day.

When she came wandering down the stairs that night, I was already waiting with her coffee and a cinnamon bun. Baking helped with my guilt, and I had been doing a lot of baking since she showed up.

If I was going to have to share this with her, curse her with this, then at least I would treat her to something delicious first.

She smiled, taking first the coffee and then the treat, her eyes sparkling. "How did you know?"

"Know what?"

"What today is," she said quietly.

"What's today?"

She smiled. "Yeah, okay, like you just have treats and coffee waiting for me right when I wake up every day."

"I could if you wanted it."

She laughed at that. "I don't know how you knew, but I'm glad you do. I never really celebrate. I've never really had anyone to share it with, but I'm happy to share it with you." She smiled and pulled me in for a kiss.

I racked my brain but couldn't come up with any explanation for what today was.

When she pulled back, she said, "Since you're too polite to ask the number, I'll tell you, I'm twenty-nine today."

Fuck. Fuck. Fuck. Fuck. It was her damned birthday. Of all days, her birthday had to be today. I tried to get myself to move, to run away from her, to leave the room. She'd be hurt, but she might understand eventually. I couldn't do this to her today. Not on her birthday. Especially not when she'd just been saying how badly she wanted to have a happy day.

Unfortunately, I had used up all my strength and willpower fighting the curse; I didn't have enough fight in me to stop it. It was already in motion.

A predatory smile crept over my face. I hated myself right now, more than I ever had. More even than in the aftermath of Zara's death. I despised myself.

"There's something I want you to have and something I need you to know about me."

"Ooohh, a present? You shouldn't have!" she said with a delighted smile.

"I've been holding myself back from doing this. I didn't know how things were going to go between us, but I know now that I can't hold back from you anymore. I need you to have this." I tried to say something, anything that might warn her, but nothing came out. I tried to stop myself, but my hand reached of its own accord for the key in the pocket it was always in. As I touched the smooth, cold metal, I felt my heart race. *Let go*, I kept telling myself, but my hand wouldn't listen. Against my will, my hand drew the key out and pressed it in her hand.

"Is this a key to where my present is?"

"No!"

She looked startled by my seriousness and laughed nervously. "Okay, okay, so the key is the gift." She looked at it perplexed for a moment before asking, "Is this what I think it is?"

I watched as her shoulders stiffened and her body tensed. A piece of her hair had fallen over her eyes. With a calm I didn't feel, I reached over and gently tucked it behind her ear. "What do you think it is, princess?"

"Are you asking me to move in with you?" I was so startled I didn't say a word. "I know we've been getting to know each other lately, but I'm not ready for that. We haven't even spent the night together."

"You mean the day?" I couldn't stop myself from adding. We both laughed and some of the tension eased from her body. "But no, that's not what that's for."

She looked relieved and perplexed, continuing to look at the key for any clues. "So, what is it for?"

"It opens room 13."

"What's in room 13?"

Now was my chance to scare her off, my chance to tell her, but try as hard as I might, I couldn't say a word. Instead, I felt my shoulders raise into a shrug and said, "A storage of sorts, for all my worst secrets."

"Ahh, it's where you hide the skeletons in the closet," she said, nodding.

Internally, I was screaming. How could she possibly know that? Why was she so nonchalant about it? Wouldn't that scare her off? A moment later, she started laughing. "So, what's really in room 13?"

"I hope you never find out. In giving this to you, I'm trusting you with my life and all my secrets. I need you to promise me you'll protect it and never use it, no matter what. If you truly care about me, you won't open the door."

She cocked her head with a smile, fingering the key in her hand. "So why give me the key at all? Is this a test?"

I shook my head quickly. "It's the most serious thing in the world to me."

"Okay, so I'm just supposed to hold on to this key for the rest of my time here, however long, without question? Without having any idea what it is I'm protecting?"

I nodded. "By protecting that, you are protecting me."

She watched me carefully for a minute, likely waiting for some sign I was joking, but she wouldn't find any. I was deadly serious. After a few moments, she rolled her eyes and laughed. "Okay, weirdo, I'll play whatever game this is."

My eyes followed as she slid the key provocatively near her cleavage before plunging it into her corset. When she looked up and saw I was still watching, her eyes brightened. "For safekeeping," she said with a wink.

A feeling of dread sank in that she might not understand the seriousness of this, but how could she? She didn't know what a monster I was. She had no idea, or she would never let me touch her. She pulled me close and kissed me deeply. I sank into her, savoring her, before she pulled away. "Next time, I do accept books or jewelry as gifts," she said, laughing.

"I'll take that under advisement," I said, smirking, unable to stay serious for too long around her. Maybe I was worrying too much. Maybe she would be the one to save me.

CHAPTER 11

Each new night that passed without incident was a small miracle. I thanked the gods every time I saw her safe and happy.

Maybe for once things would go my way. Maybe she would listen and things would be okay.

We had fallen into a blissful routine. Around nightfall, she would come wandering downstairs to see me. I greeted her with coffee and whatever I had been baking that day. It didn't matter to her that it was her first meal of the day or that they were essentially all sugar; she scarfed down whatever I made her.

She loved chocolate and was happy to have anything chocolate, but that was nothing compared to the way her face lit up when I made her my cinnamon rolls. Eventually, she told me it wasn't just because they were amazing, they were, but that wasn't why she was so excited for them. She loved them so much because she had decided they were our dessert. I hadn't known couples to pick and claim a dessert, but as long as she smiled like that, I would go along with whatever she wanted.

We passed most of our time together taking walks through the garden in the moonlight and reading by the fire in the den. With quite a few passionate kisses in between. Days passed into weeks with no mention of the room and no mention of her leaving. I stopped feeling as worried, stopped waiting for the worst to happen. I should have known better.

———

When she didn't come down at her normal time, I thought nothing of it at first. It wasn't until I noticed her coffee was getting cold that I started to get worried. Even still, I thought I'd give her a few more minutes before going to check on her.

That was when I felt it, and all the blood drained from my body. That little tingling in the back of my neck and the urge to go to room 13. This couldn't be happening... I had gotten too comfortable. Let my guard down too much, let her get too comfortable, and now I was going to pay for it. We both were. Her more so than me.

I couldn't do this. I wouldn't. I tried grabbing the desk with my hands to hold my body there, but my feet were already moving. I was internally kicking and screaming, trying whatever I could to stop myself. I couldn't reach the room. She would find some way to escape, and we could pretend this never happened. Things could go back to normal. Everything would be okay as long as I didn't open that door. But my feet wouldn't stop.

I was surprised when I felt tears coming down my face. Normally, the curse took complete control, stifling my emotions. But I was fighting with everything I had to stop my feet from moving. The curse must not have had the extra energy to force me not to cry. I let that give me a little spark of hope and redoubled my efforts to stop, but if anything, my pace seemed to speed up.

I was up the stairs and halfway down the hallway when a door opened right in front of me. Her door. I saw her raven hair and stopped dead in my tracks. She smiled until she looked up at me and her smile disappeared. She reached up for my face and wiped a tear away with her finger.

"What's wrong, love?"

"Nothing at all. You're here, you're safe, you're fine. Thank the gods. I'm alright now." I felt the pull of the curse again and knew I didn't have much longer. I pulled her close and kissed her hard, pressing her against me, before releasing her and pulling back. "I'm alright. I promise. I just have to go take care of something real quick."

I started to walk away, but she grabbed my hand. "Wait. What was wrong? Where are you going?"

"Everything will be fine. I just have to take care of something. In Room 13."

"13? But you said not to go in there."

I couldn't stop my legs from moving toward the room, but I was able to turn my head to see her. "I did, and you shouldn't ever."

"But how are you even going to get in? I have the key!"

"The door will open for me. I'll come find you once I'm done, once it's safe."

I could see the battle on her face about whether to follow me.

With one last burst of will, I added, "Trust me, please. Don't follow me."

She looked torn, but after a moment's hesitation, nodded.

Relieved, I stopped fighting and let my feet carry me the rest of the way there. I wondered what nightmare I was walking into, but I didn't really care anymore. Whoever it was, it wasn't her.

I grasped the doorknob and felt the handle's zap before it sprung open. I turned and closed it behind me as quickly as I could. Only after I had relocked the door and put the deadbolt in place did I turn around.

On the bed, sprawled out and waiting, was our maintenance man. Fuck. How many times had I told the cleaning crew in explicit detail to leave this room alone? I had told everyone that anyone who so much as looked at the door for too long would be fired. Most had been happy to not have the extra room to clean, others thought the request was weird, but they all stayed clear of the room, or they all had, until now.

I gaped at him on the bed. This wasn't how things were supposed to happen. I was supposed to make them fall for me, give them the key, and then murder them if they used it. He wasn't invited in; he shouldn't be here.

His eyes looked like they were about to pop out of their sockets and tears ran down his face. I heard muffled noises from him and realized he was gagged. That wasn't all. He was bound to the four-poster bed.

Either someone had done some of the work for me already, or the curse didn't like his being here anymore than I did. I watched as his arm almost broke loose only for the sheets to tighten around him; it was the curse. The curse apparently didn't take well to intruders. It was waiting for Loralie and wasn't happy that someone else had interrupted.

I'd only done this once before since the curse started, but I had thought I knew what to expect.

This was certainly new. I also had no idea how he had gotten in. There was only one key to the room, that Loralie still had. There wasn't any rhyme or reason for him being in here. Everyone on my staff knew this room was expressly forbidden. I had heard all sorts of rumors about what

I might be keeping in here or doing in here, but everyone knew it was off limits.

The pull of the curse had subsided a little now that I was in the room, thankfully. I took a minute to look around and noticed that next to the door at my feet there were a few metal tools and a sack. I leaned down to get a better look and after a moment, I pieced it together, but I wanted confirmation. The curse wouldn't let me leave, wouldn't let me spare him, but I hoped he might at least assuage my guilt a little.

Thankfully, I knew him well enough to know he was a loner. He always worked the odd shifts since he had no one waiting for him at home. At least I wasn't taking someone's husband or father away from them. I wouldn't enjoy this, but I was grateful the situation wasn't worse.

Honestly, it could have been anyone. As long as it wasn't her, I would have been grateful. I peeled the gag out of his mouth, and he started to scream in earnest. I knew it would do him no good. No noise ever seemed to escape the room. The curse made sure of it.

"I'm so sorry, but I'm going to need you to quiet down. I would like some answers from you, but I don't need them. If you continue screaming, I will put this back in."

He looked at me in horror and quieted down, but didn't stop talking. "Ma'am, thank the gods you're here! I don't know who cast a spell on this room, but the moment I entered and saw the bodies, I started screaming my head off, but the sheets sprung to life and grabbed me. I kept screaming, but then I was gagged. I'm so glad you heard me. Please help me."

"What were you doing in here, anyway? This room is dangerous."

"I can see that now, ma'am. I'm so sorry. I never would have come in if I had known."

"But you did know. I've told everyone on my staff numerous times that this room is off limits. What compelled you to enter?"

"I had forgotten. I thought this was room 12 and was just coming in to clean. Please help me." His voice was rising as he tried to get his hands loose.

"But the room was locked. How did you get in?"

"The door was open. You have to believe me."

I rolled my eyes and walked back over to the door, picking up the tools and the sack. If I hadn't seen the evidence myself, I might have believed his lies.

The curse took control. I couldn't stop it. I looked over at Alanna and

Zara's bodies, and laughed humorlessly. "What do we think, ladies? Do we believe him?"

He looked at me, horrified, terrified, speechless. I was disgusted with myself. I tried not to look at the bodies when I could help it. The curse kept them horribly perfectly preserved, and it was unnerving and always served to bring about feelings of guilt and grief.

More so with Zara than Alanna, but even with Alanna there was some guilt, and still some anger for her betrayal. It wasn't her fault, per se, but in a way she had ruined my life. Yes, I had taken her life, but the consequences were still haunting me, so most days I considered us even.

I sauntered over to him and dropped the tools and sack on his chest. "This doesn't look very much to me like cleaning equipment."

"Please, please. I'm so sorry. I only needed some money. I was hoping to sell whatever you kept so guarded, but I promise I never would have intruded if I had known, and I won't tell a soul about anything I saw. Please, please, please," he begged, on the verge of hysteria.

"So, the salary I pay you is worthless enough that you needed to resort to stealing from me. Whatever happened to asking for a raise?"

"I never meant to disrespect you, ma'am. Please help me, and I swear I won't breathe a word of this to anyone."

I shrugged. "Well, if I don't help you, you won't have the chance to breathe a word of it to anyone."

I was toying with him and hated it. I knew he wasn't going to be able to leave the room. The curse wouldn't let me let him. I hoped I could at least make it quick, but something felt different about this time. It wasn't like with Zara; there hadn't been much time allowed for talking or for goodbyes. I would have killed for the chance to have said goodbye, the chance to explain myself. At least I hadn't drawn it out with her, but I didn't know why the curse was letting me take things slowly this time. Why was he still breathing?

It wasn't until my hand started inching toward a lock pick that the realization and horror set in. This wasn't how things were supposed to go. I was supposed to strangle him like I did the first time with Alanna, starting the whole curse in motion, but nothing about this was normal. He wasn't even supposed to be here. I grimaced, hoping I at least wouldn't make too much of a mess.

All the while, he was still wasting his breath pleading for forgiveness and freedom, both of which wouldn't come. "Please, please, let me go. You don't have to do this! Please! Help me!"

I couldn't decide if his speech was for me anymore or if he hoped for some rescue, but none would come. I picked up the tool, holding it in my hand, spinning it around until it caught his eye.

His screams increased in volume as I ran the metal over his face, circling around one eye and then the other. I hoped the curse wouldn't really make me stab his eyes out. I felt a bit of relief when my hand took the tool further south and stopped over his heart.

I pulled it back and looked at him. "Be a good boy and hold still. You won't feel a thing." I winked at him. He started flailing and fighting in earnest then, but the magic held up and the sheets kept him pinned down. I shrugged. "Well, there you go, moving all about. This is really going to hurt now. Don't say I didn't warn you."

A moment later, I moved the tool back and plunged it into his heart. The blood spurted out quickly. All I could see and feel was red. I wanted to collapse in a heap on the floor. I felt like hyperventilating. I had taken two lives before, but never so violently. I would have been useless curled up in a corner if it wasn't for the curse. I couldn't be missing for much longer; I was sure Loralie would come looking for me if I was.

I also couldn't have any evidence leave the room, but the curse had already taken care of that. I knew I had had blood on me, and I could still feel its presence on me, but when I looked down, all the traces of blood on me were gone. A quick glance at the bed showed that the sheets and bed didn't get the same treatment. I had never stabbed someone before, so I couldn't be sure what might happen when I left the room. I wondered if the room would still look the same if I had to come back in.

A moment later, I realized the implication and shuddered at the thought. I wouldn't have to come back in. Loralie wouldn't open the door. She couldn't. But how could I ever really be sure of that? Visions of the past few minutes played out in my mind with her there instead, and I wanted to scream.

I had gotten so lucky this time that it wasn't her, but how long would I stay lucky? I had never thought Zara would open the door, and look where she was now, sitting with Alanna. But Loralie was different, right? She had to be. I had never felt this strongly about anyone before. She had to be the one, right? But was I willing to risk her life over being wrong? Even if I wanted to, was there any way I could get her to leave? I couldn't say for sure. But I cared too much about her to keep her in any danger if there was a choice.

If there was a choice, I would choose to be alone and miserable instead

41

of having her wind up dead. If I could get her to leave, I knew I should. No matter how wrong it felt, it was the right thing to do. I felt the tears running down my face and knew I would have to try, and soon, before I lost my nerve. But what could I really do or say to get her to leave? To get her to understand that she had to leave.

I knew I couldn't tell her any more of the curse, but maybe I could caution her away.

CHAPTER 12

I had to go find her. I stood and made my way to the door, feeling unsteady on my feet. A wave of nausea came over me at the sight of all the blood. I had to get out of the room and find her. I had to get away from the bloodshed. His death would haunt me just like the others' deaths had. Not because his death was particularly meaningful to me, like theirs had been, but because of how gruesome it was. I wouldn't soon forget how warm and sticky his blood felt.

I stumbled out of the room, taking care to shut the door tightly behind me. The last thing I wanted was someone stumbling on the door being open.

I headed for my room, wanting to change. I knew there wasn't any blood on me anymore, but I still felt like there was. A nice change of clothes might go a long way to making me feel more refreshed.

But when I opened the door, Loralie was waiting there for me.

She ran into my arms, but not before I noticed the tears streaming down her face. I hugged her for a long moment before pulling away.

"What's wrong, Lor? Tell me what happened?"

She stared at me in disbelief. "What do you mean, what happened? You terrified me!"

"What? Why? I promise I'm safe and fine."

She glared at me. "You can't just show up out of the blue terrified and crying and expect me not to worry. What happened, love? Are you okay?"

43

I nodded quickly. "I am. I swear I am."

"So, what happened?!"

I hesitated for a moment, trying to get the words out, but they wouldn't come. "I can't really explain."

"You can and you will! First you terrify me, and now you won't even give me an explanation. I just have to trust that you're fine and everything's fine now?"

"It's not that I don't want to tell you," I said carefully. I was at war with myself. I could try to warn her again, but then she would leave. But I still felt the blood on my skin, still felt sticky and like the stench of death clung to me. After all this time, I could still feel my fingers wrapping around Zara's throat as she pleaded with me for her life and I couldn't do a damn thing to stop myself. I couldn't do this. I couldn't do this to Lor. She deserved so much better than me and I would be even more of a monster than I already was if I let her stay. "It's that I can't tell you, but what I can tell you is-" I tried a few versions of the words and eventually was able to push enough past the curse to say, "I'm a monster."

She looked surprised for a moment, some of the anger dimming from her eyes, before she took my hand. "That's not true. I don't know what made you believe that, but there's only one monster in this room and it most definitely isn't you," she said with a sad smile.

I shook my head. "Loralie, listen to me. You could never be a monster. You don't know the first thing about evil. I..." Tears started streaming down my face as I tried to push out any words that might make her understand. "It's..." I was struggling hard. Fighting against the curse and my will.

I didn't want her to leave, but she needed to. Her life was more important than my happiness, and I had been a gods damned fool to let things get this far. It could've been her in the room today. Thank the gods it wasn't, but it was too close. I couldn't let her stay. "You're not safe here," I was finally able to get out.

"Not safe? What are you talking about? Are you asking me to leave?"

I bit my tongue hard; the curse was fighting back, pushing me to take it back. Tears still streaming down my face, I nodded.

"That's it? You just want me to pack my things and move on? Without a single explanation, you just don't want me anymore?" She sighed, and a tear slipped down her face. "I shouldn't really be surprised. This always happens sooner or later, once someone gets to know me. They always tire of me."

My heart broke into a million pieces. I was the worst type of trash in the Five Kingdoms. I let her get too close and now I was hurting her. I couldn't even stop myself in time before I said, "Lor, it's not like that. I will regret this every day for the rest of my life, but you can't stay."

She looked up at me, her face damp from her tears, confused. "Why?"

"I can't tell you."

She exploded. "You have to be fucking kidding me! You're just going to let us go and you can't even give me an explanation? You owe me an explanation!"

I did. I wished I could, but I just shook my head.

She glared at me a moment before something changed in her eyes. Looking determined and terrifying, she stalked past me to the door.

"I won't let you do this."

I watched the door close, debating whether I should go after her. I couldn't possibly make things worse, but maybe I should give her some space. I sighed and dragged my feet back to the bed, conflicted. I had hurt her, much more than I meant to, much more than I thought I would. I knew getting her to leave would destroy me, but I hadn't thought it would bother her as much.

A moment later, it occurred to me to be worried about what she might do, but when I felt the tingling on the back of my neck, I realized with horror that I was already too late.

I should have known. I should have known what she was going to do and should have stopped her. How could I have been so stupid? Of course when I wouldn't tell her anything, she would have thought about the key. Of course she would have thought that it might unlock not only Room 13, but my secrets. Of course when she saw me crying and entering the room, it would have stuck with her. And of course when, after shutting myself in there for a long while, I reemerged crying and urging her to go, she would assume the answers lied there.

I gripped the bed hard, trying to keep myself stationary, but I felt the itch start in my feet and felt them move of their own accord, felt my hands let go of the bed and my body betray me, getting up and crossing the room involuntarily.

It took far quicker than I would have liked to get to room 13. I was internally screaming at my body to stop, to slow, anything, but I wasn't in control. When I touched the doorknob for the second time today, it was still warm. I turned the door and burst inside, quickly closing it behind me.

I saw her sprawled out on the floor over the man I had just killed. She was making a weird noise in her shock. I cleared my throat. She whipped her head around, looking horrified, and then a moment later, relieved when she realized it was me. Her relief was like a dagger to my heart.

She was covered in blood. There was even blood on her face. She had more blood on her than the body did. I didn't have to look to see if any of it was hers. The curse would have sensed if she were weak. I knew she wasn't injured.

I wanted to ask her why she was covered in blood, but before I could say anything, she started talking hysterically. "Thank the gods you're here, love. I don't know what happened. One minute I opened the door and was turning to lock it behind me when I tripped and landed on whoever this was." She gestured to the body. "I tried resuscitating him before I saw where the blood was coming from. I have no idea what happened. He was like this when I came in. You have to believe me!"

"I do, princess. I know you didn't do this."

"Thank the gods you believe me. I know how this looks but-"

The curse took over. I couldn't fight it. A predatory smile spread over my face as I interrupted her. "You don't understand, princess. I know you didn't do this because I know who did."

"You do?" she asked, surprised. "Why haven't you called for help? We have to do something!"

I was trying to scream at her to leave, jump out the window, try to get out the door, anything, but I knew it was useless. Even if I could've gotten the words to come out, I was in front of the door, and it wouldn't be a pleasant fall from the second floor. She would at least break an ankle, only an ankle if she was lucky, and I would catch her before she could hobble away. There was no escape for her.

"You don't understand. There's nothing to be done."

She looked confused, before she took in the look on my face, and her own face paled more than usual. "You don't mean...?"

"Yes, princess. How do you like my handiwork?"

She stood up with a start and took a step back. "You can't mean that."

I took a step closer.

"Now you know my secret," I said with a grin. "There are no more secrets between us now. Actually, there is still one, what I'm going to do next, but I think that's pretty obvious."

She stilled. I advanced another step. *What is she doing? Run! Get away from me! Fight! Do something!* Another step. Only a few more and I would be within arm's reach of her.

She took a couple of quick steps back, hitting the bed and tumbling onto it. I sprung on her, straddling her body, and quickly pulled both her arms above her head. She didn't move, just stared at me in shock. *Fight me!* Didn't she realize what was happening? *Do something!* She couldn't over-power me, not usually, and certainly not with the curse controlling me, but why wasn't she fighting? Did she think I wanted to hurt her? That this was really me? I hoped she knew I would never willingly do this.

I leaned down and planted a couple of kisses on her neck. She shivered and leaned into my touch out of habit. "What a good little girl you are," I said with a purr. "Still so responsive. Even when you know it's not good for you, you still crave me. I wonder, will you even bother to fight me, or are you resigned to your fate?"

Fight me! I was screaming at her! *Fight me! Please, try anything!* I gestured with my free hand to Alanna and Zara's bodies. "They both fought me, little good it did them, but I'd love to see you try."

Try, gods damn it! Kill me if you have to! Stop me!

She looked up as a tear came down her face. "Why are you doing this?"

"Because, my dear princess, I'm a very bad girl." I tried as hard as I could to force out the truth, and was surprised when it came out. "The first time I took a life was Alanna over there. She was staying in this very room and was supposed to meet me for a romantic dinner, but she never showed.

"When I came upstairs to check on her, I heard her moaning from down the hall. I was terrified for her and broke down the door in two kicks, only to find her riding some man I had never met. I saw red. I grabbed her, threw her off him, and didn't think twice about strangling the life out of her. It didn't occur to me to remember the man she was with until after she stopped breathing, but he was already gone.

"Some man he was, not even trying to stop me. He must have really given a damn about her. She ruined everything between us and ended up dead all for a man who abandoned her to her fate. I hated her for that and couldn't bring myself to regret what I'd done.

"A day later, I was trying to figure out what to do with the body, when a face appeared in the mirror. It was the most beautiful man I'd ever seen. I couldn't stop staring at him. He looked at me judgmentally and asked if I was Delphine. I nodded. He looked at the body and asked if I regretted it, and told me he would know if I was lying. I thought about lying. It seemed like the right thing to do. Who kills someone in cold blood and doesn't even regret it?"

I smiled down at her. "Me, that's who. I was truthful and shook my head. She had deserved it, I told him. I wouldn't regret taking her life when she had deserved it. A smile so sad came over his face that I wanted to cry. 'Very well,' he had said. 'I take no pleasure in this, but know you brought it upon yourself. When the huntsman showed up and told us of you, he tried to strike a deal, but I told him I would only hold up my end if you showed no remorse. I had hoped you might, but you clearly lack any. You will remember today as the start of the rest of your life, and if you ever think of me with anger, think of yourself with more. This could have been avoided with any regret.

"From today forward, this room will be preserved for your eyes only. It will be your dirty little secret, a window into your soul and how much of a monster you are. You will want to keep this room a secret, but that's the curse. The moment you fall for another person, the moment you care about them more than yourself, you will have to give them the key to this room, the key to your soul and your dirty little secret.

"You will warn them to stay out, but you cannot prevent them from entering. Whether they trust your warning and listen will be up to them, but if they do enter the room, they will not be able to leave alive. You will be compelled to follow them and to mercilessly end their lives the way you did to her.

"The longer you go without caring about others, the more lonely you will become. You will be drawn to others and try to get them to be drawn to you as well. You will try to seduce them, keep them close, all so that one day, when you can't resist anymore, you will give them the key. There is no escape from the curse, not for you, not now, not ever. Although,' he had said with a sad smile, 'I know that doesn't mean you won't try. Here's a little reminder to make sure you can't go a day without remembering how much of a monster you are.' As he faded from the mirror, I watched in horror as my hair turned a vibrant shade of blue. It's been like that ever since," I said, using a strand of it to caress her neck. "So now you know my secret."

She didn't look nearly as horrified as I expected; she looked sad, for me or herself I couldn't tell. "Well, get it over with then, and know that, love, if you can hear me in there, I forgive you."

I was screaming at myself to stop. The curse wasn't strong enough to stop the tears from coming down my face. As I laced my hand around her neck, she didn't try to stop me. I forced out the words, coming out as a whisper, "I love you," as I tightened my hands around her neck. She looked at me with nothing but love until she stopped moving altogether, her eyes closing.

I started sobbing in earnest then as I slipped my hands from her neck, I kissed her forehead, still sobbing. "I'm so, so, so, so sorry. I won't ever forget you, Lor. I love you," I whispered, tears streaming down my face.

Half a heartbeat later, her eyes sprung open, and she smiled, "I love you, too," she replied with a wink.

I screamed, and before I could stop myself, my hand grabbed one of the leftover lock picks and plunged it into her heart. I screamed through my sobs. I had almost spared her, but I couldn't stop the curse. I moved away from her body, watching, waiting, hoping, but I knew she wouldn't move again. I could have sworn I had felt her stop breathing the first time, but I had run her through the heart this time. She wouldn't be moving again.

I tried to get my breathing under control; I needed to clean up the mess before I caused anyone alarm, but when I looked down, there wasn't any blood. The curse must have removed it already, but I didn't remember any in the first place. This was much more traumatic than killing the maintenance man earlier, but it felt different. I didn't remember any blood. There should have been blood.

I looked over at the bed and was shocked to find it empty. Had the curse moved her? It had never done that before. I looked over to where the other girls' bodies were, but she wasn't there. I was on the verge of hyperventilating. Had the curse really stolen the only thing I had left of her? I ran over to the bed, looking under it, thinking maybe she had fallen, but there was nothing there.

Then I felt a tap on my shoulder. I whirled around and saw her smiling at me. She took a step back, watching me cautiously. "Are we done with the stabbing?" she asked playfully.

"What? But you were…? What? How? Lor, is that really you?"

She smiled. "The one and only."

"But what…? How? You were just... you can't be. I have to be dreaming."

She smiled at me. "I'm better than a dream," she grinned, "but if you're quite done with the stabbing…" She looked warily behind me to the side table that held the rest of the lock picks. I waited to feel compelled to grab one, but nothing happened. I looked back at her in shock. She smiled.

"Well then, since you showed me your secret, it's time you know mine." She started to leave the room, but I couldn't move. She noticed I wasn't following her and doubled back, taking my hand. "Come on, love. There's something I need to show you now."

I couldn't think, couldn't breathe, didn't dare say a word, waiting for this cruel dream to end. She led me out the door toward her room, passing through the threshold without any trouble.

I had never been in her room before. Well, not since it had been occupied by her. She looked at me carefully and said, "This might be a bit of a shock to you, but I don't want there to be secrets between us, especially not now, and you've probably worked it out, anyway. You showed me yours, so I'll show you mine," she said with a wink and a giggle.

She took out her key and turned the lock. She looked over her shoulder, making sure the hallway was clear before opening the door and pushing me inside. She closed and locked the door quickly as I took in the room. The bed and furniture remained the same, but on every spare inch of the wall hung bags of a dark red liquid. I took a deep breath in, and the smell confirmed my suspicion. It was blood. I turned to look at her, only to see she had disappeared, but when I turned around again, she was in front of me, watching me carefully.

"So, now you understand?"

I gulped and nodded. This wasn't a dream. She hadn't died because she couldn't die. She was a vampire. I deserved a fate like this. "Make it quick if you can," I said to her.

She frowned. "Just what do you think I'm going to do?"

"Well, I just tried to kill you, so I would assume you're going to drain every last drop from me. Just do it. I deserve it."

She looked at me carefully, weighing my words. "You did just try to kill me." She ran her tongue over her lips, parting them a little. I watched as her tongue traced over an extra sharp tooth. How had I not noticed her two sharp teeth before? I wondered, not able to tear my eyes from her tongue. "I really should make you pay." She stalked forward, power in her walk, and I sunk to my knees.

She smiled hungrily at me. "I could get used to this." She approached me, grazed my neck with her teeth, and licked a line up to my ear, whispering in it, "Love, this changes nothing. I'm not going to hurt you. I love you."

My jaw dropped. I pulled away to see her face; she looked deadly serious, and happy. I started to cry, and she instantly fell into my arms. "I'm so, so, so sorry. I thought I lost you. I thought I killed you. I'm so sorry; that wasn't me. I never wanted to hurt you. I love you."

"I love you, too," she said, stroking my hair as I cried. I felt a few tears dampen my head and looked up at her from where I was still kneeling. She smiled through her tears and said, "Lucky for you, I'm more durable than that."

"Incredibly durable." Looking around at the blood, I couldn't help but ask, "How many people did you have to drain for all this?"

She looked at me in shock for a moment. "You should know me better than that! I would never hurt someone if I didn't have to. You remember those men I brought up here?"

"Like I could forget how jealous it made me. I wanted to tear out their throats for having the audacity to hold your hand."

"So violent," she said with a laugh.

I shrugged sheepishly. "You bring that out in me."

"Good. I can handle it." She grinned before continuing, "Well, obviously, none of them died. I only take as much as they won't miss. It usually takes most of the night to drain them as much as I can and let them sleep it off. I've only gone too far once and won't ever do that again. Controlling myself can be harder sometimes than others. You make it hard for me to hold back sometimes."

A laugh went through me as I remembered the kiss in the library, when she bit me. "The kiss?"

She nodded. "The kiss. I ran because I was worried I would lose control, worried I might hurt you, but I know better now. After the feeling I had today when you tried to end things, I know I would kill for you before seeing you hurt. I wouldn't ever hurt you and I would die before seeing you hurt."

Her words caught up to me. "You didn't know?" I said with a screech. "You didn't know if you'd survive, and you let me try to kill you?"

She shrugged. "I thought I might be fine, but I can't say anyone's ever actually tried to kill me before. At least not in the few years I've been turned. But if I tried to stop you, I might have hurt you, and I would've rather been dead than have hurt you."

I started sobbing again.

"Promise me," I started through my tears. "Promise me from now on, no secrets. From now on, if you'll have me, I'm yours, wholly and completely."

She grinned, tears still flowing as she leaned in and kissed me. She broke away far too quickly and said, "I promise. You are my heart and soul. Everything that I am is yours, wholly and completely."

I pulled her into my arms and held her close. From that day forward, I was never going to let her go. I don't know how I had known from the start, but I had. I had somehow known she was going to be different, and she was. She was my salvation, and I would worship her for the rest of our days.

EPILOGUE

A FEW MONTHS LATER

When Lor came rushing into the kitchen in a panic, my blood froze. I quickly glanced behind her looking for danger, a chill racing up my spine. My wife, an unkillable vampire, didn't scare easy.

She rushed into my arms. I squeezed her a moment, before pulling away and looking at her.

"What's wrong?"

"I don't know how they found me, but I don't know if I can trust them. I have to hide. They can't find me. I don't know what they would do."

"Lor, slow down. Who's here? Who found you?"

"My nephew."

"Your nephew?!" I exclaimed loudly. She didn't have a nephew. She couldn't have a nephew. She had never even mentioned her family aside from her missing brother. "Your brother had a child?"

She shook her head, looking over her shoulder. "No. No. Not my brother, his husband."

This was the first I was hearing of her brother having a husband.

"I guess he's technically not my nephew." She rushed out, fiddling with her hands. "He's my brother's husband's nephew."

Well, that was a whole lot for what had started as a normal day.

"How do you know it's him?"

"A few Somerset soldiers just breezed in telling us to prepare our poor excuse for an inn for the honor of housing the Prince for a night. Can you believe the nerve? Prince or not, he's lucky to be staying at our inn, especially if you make him some of your kingdom famous cinnamon rolls."

My mind was racing a mile a minute trying to keep up. Her brother's husband's nephew was the Prince of Somerset. But that wasn't possible.

"But that's not possible. The King only has one brother…"

It hit me then all at once. The King of Somerset's brother was the King Killer himself, King Damien of Bancroft. That would make her brother King Casimir. He wasn't just missing, he was dead. Killed by his own husband. But he couldn't be her brother, he couldn't be because that would make her a…

"Princess?" I breathed out. She couldn't be. She would have told me.

She still had her eyes on the door.

"What?"

"Princess." I repeated, not able to form other words.

Her eyes moved back to mine. "Yes, love?"

"No, you're a princess."

She looked surprised, and then seeing the comprehension on my face, resigned herself to nodding. "I tried to tell you."

"When?!"

She smiled sheepishly. "When we first met."

I thought back and glared at her. "You most certainly didn't!" *Technically, she had said it, but still.* "You didn't try all that hard. Gods Lor, you're actually a princess? You're the lost Princess of Bancroft?"

She gave me a small, sad smile "Technically, the hidden Princess of Bancroft. I'm not exactly lost. I'm so sorry love. I didn't know who I could and couldn't trust. I had been keeping my secret for so long I didn't know how to stop, but this doesn't change anything."

I just looked at her. "Doesn't change anything?"

She frowned and took my hands "Of course it doesn't. You have to know it doesn't change anything. I love you and I trust you, but with my brother gone, it wasn't safe for anyone to know. Plus, I loved being normal for once. I love our life here. This doesn't change anything."

"It changes a whole lot for me." She looked at me with a pain that startled me.

I rushed to finish my thought. "What are we even doing in Somerset if you're supposed to be in hiding? Being right here, under the nose of royal family?" I would have laughed if I wasn't so worried. "I mean, gods Lor, you couldn't have picked a worse place to hide unless you had just stayed in Bancroft."

Her eyes were watering, but I heard her musical laugh and couldn't help but smile.

"You're not wrong. I've been running ever since my brother disappeared, ever since I turned. I kept bouncing from town to town, running from my past... until I ran into you. I was just passing through Somerset, so really this is your fault."

She grinned playfully before looking over toward the door again, listening. I didn't hear anything.

She looked at me and said, "We have a few more minutes, and I don't think he would recognize me, but you should probably take over the desk until he leaves."

I couldn't help but laugh "Now that you're a fancy princess you're too good for desk work?"

She grinned. "If I had known there would be perks, I would've told you way sooner."

"Anything to get out of work, right, love?"

We both laughed a moment before it occurred to me that she said she had been running since her brother disappeared, not since he was murdered. "Wait, so what happened to your brother? He wasn't murdered?"

I regretted asking the moment I saw the smile drop from her face.

"We don't know. Him and I had always planned for something like this. Our family is powerful, or was. We thought this might happen. Most of our lives, we had always been looking over our shoulders. I don't know who got him or how to get him back. Gods I feel so helpless. If I still had my powers, I might be more useful, but that wasn't the plan."

"What do you mean?"

"Him and I had a deal." She smiled ruefully. "Whoever outlasted the other needed to be around long enough to avenge them. It was a sacrifice I never expected to have to make. I didn't think for a second anyone would be dumb enough to come after Cass. I always thought it would be me they hunted. Him and I made a pact that we wouldn't let them get us both."

She saw the confused look on my face and explained, "His magic was linked to mine, and mine to his. He could have been used to easily find me without even having to perform a spell. I could have tracked him down too. I should have, but I kept my word."

"But if he can track you down, then you're still in danger."

She shook her head sadly. "I'm not. I sacrificed any chance I had of finding him, of saving him, to keep my promise to him. I sacrificed a piece of me when I turned. Vampires and magic don't mix."

I looked at her in awe. "So you let yourself be turned knowing you would have to give up your powers?"

She nodded. "I had to. I promised him. He would never have forgiven me if they got us both, if they used him to get to me. I couldn't make him live with that even if it killed me. Giving up my powers damn near did kill me, because not only did I give up my powers, but my link to him. I used to be able to just know how he was doing, what he was feeling, but not anymore. It's like I lost a piece of myself."

Tears started to fall down her face.

"I don't even know if he's still alive, never mind how he's feeling. If I didn't miss him this much, I would curse him for that stupid promise. I know that he's out there somewhere, smugly satisfied that even though he couldn't protect himself, he was able to protect me. Gods, I hate him for it. It should've been me."

My own tears fell as I pulled her into my arms.

"I'm so, so incredibly sorry. I can't believe you've been suffering through this all on your own."

"Well, I'm not alone now." She said softly.

"Nor will you ever be." I agreed. "Me and you. Lor, you're mine and I'm yours."

"Wholly and completely." She pulled back and kissed me. Even now, her kisses still stole my breath away.

She pulled back, listening again. "They'll be here any minute now."

I looked around the mess of a kitchen, itching to straighten things up. I couldn't think straight and staying busy helped, but it could wait.

"I can't believe you've been dealing with this all by yourself. You're even stronger than I gave you credit for."

She shrugged slightly. "It's been hard, but I can't even imagine how bad things have been for Damien."

"The King Killer?"

She rolled her eyes. "Stop calling him that. He had nothing to do with my brother's disappearance. Although it seems like I'm the only one in Zanaria who believes that."

"How do you know he wasn't involved?"

She shrugged "I just do. You ought to have seen the way he looked at my brother, like Cass was a god among mortals." She laughed. "Damien worshipped him, like my brother needed any reason to have a bigger ego." She laughed before adding, "I haven't been able to speak with Damien since I ran. I don't even know if he would still speak to me if I tried. I don't know how he could possibly forgive me for abandoning him and throwing away our best chance of finding Cass. Even if I could safely contact him, I don't think he would want to talk to me."

"You mean you haven't heard?"

"Heard what?"

"King Damien is stuck in Sherbrooke."

"What? No. He can't be."

"He was supposed to marry Princess Serena."

She shook her head. "You have to be wrong. He wouldn't marry someone else, not with my brother out there waiting to be saved. It can't be him."

"Maybe I'm wrong, but I heard he went to the castle just before the curse struck."

"But that would mean…"

I nodded. "It would mean he's been in an enchanted sleep for the last few months."

She shook her head quicker now, "It can't be him. He's still out there looking for Cass. He would tear Zanaria apart piece by piece to find him if that's what it took."

Maybe I was wrong, but I didn't think so.

Before I could say anything else, I heard the horses. Enough hoofbeats that I knew they wouldn't possibly fit in our stables and that I was out of time.

I kissed her quickly before saying "Go. Quickly. I'll meet you in our room as soon as I can get away."

She hesitated a moment, so I added, "I'll be fine. I can handle a spoiled Prince and his entourage."

She laughed, "That's what I'm worried about. I don't need you being condemned to death for your special brand of customer service."

I laughed at that, protesting, "I'm not that bad!"

She just cocked her eyebrow at me, amusement dancing in her eyes.

I held up my hands in defense, "Okay, okay. I'll behave. I promise."

She laughed and stole one more quick kiss before rushing out toward our room.

I heard the doors barge open and took a deep breath, stealing myself for what was coming.

Well, this ought to be interesting.

I shouldn't have been surprised. Life with Loralie was proving to be many things, but boring wasn't one of them.

THIS STORY IS LOOSELY CONNECTED to *Off Script: A Book Ball Fantasy Adventure*, and will be expanded into a planned fantasy series in the near future.

ABOUT SARAH ZANE

Sarah is an author of happy endings for traumatized queers. She is a bisexual feminist and a licensed therapist. Her stories deal with themes of feminism, trauma, sexuality, and mental health.

STORY II
A CONTEST OF FIRE BY M.K. AHEARN

Heat Level: Low
(PG content)

Trigger Warnings:
Some violence and peril

THE DRAGONS

Dragon riders used to rule these lands. I grew up hearing stories of the mighty warriors who would tame the beasts and ride them into battles. Only the strongest willed were fated to be riders. Now, a rider hadn't been spotted in over one hundred years. Not since the Great War. A war that almost destroyed the kingdom of Alna. Between Alna and the kingdom of Gellia across the sea. Dragons still exist, but they are no longer tame or allies to our people.

"Leah, are you paying attention?"

I snapped out of the daydream I'd been in. The entire class had turned to look at me. Miss Elrod's head was tilted, awaiting an answer.

"Yes," I answered timidly.

"Then you have an answer for me?"

There were a few snickers from a group of girls to my left. She'd asked me a question, and I hadn't heard it.

"I'm sorry. What was the question?"

Miss Elrod only shook her head with disappointment. This wasn't my first time losing focus in her class. I hated having to attend school. This was my last year, and I couldn't wait to be finished soon. Then I could finally focus on training to be a warrior.

"I asked what the three most common trees found in Desall are?"

Such a useless question. Why did I need to know about trees when I was a fire elemental? Every person in our small town of Desall was able to manipulate one of the four elements. It pretty much determined your life. I resisted the urge to roll my eyes.

"Oak, spruce, and," I began, but got caught on the last one.

Maybe I really should've been more focused on the class. If I failed, they'd never let me become a warrior. The strongest of the fire elementals were recruited to become warriors. They'd leave town to travel to the capital, Crona and serve in the royal army.

"Maple!" an obnoxious girl with long, impossibly shiny blonde hair called out.

As she said it, she made a small maple sapling grow in front of her. Of course, an earth elemental would know the answer, but I couldn't stand Nalla. Always sucking up to the teacher.

"Thank you, Nalla, but next time wait until I call on you," Miss Elrod scolded. Although, I could tell she didn't actually care. Nalla was her favorite student.

Trees are of no use to me to learn. Only someone with earth abilities would need to know the different types. They'd finish school and work tending to the trees for lumber or crops for food.

"That's all for today's class. I'm afraid our time is up," Miss Elrod concluded.

"Thank the goddesses," I whispered. A small jolt to my shoulder startled me. Turning, I found my best friend, Finn, eyeing me down. His dark brown eyes set on me. By the look he was giving me, I knew he'd heard me.

"You can't blame me," I tried innocently.

"You really like pushing your luck, Leah," he said, frowning.

"I just have bigger aspirations than being cooped up in this place all day," I shrugged. Gathering my few belongings, I packed my bag and made my way out.

Every day after school, Finn and I walk home together. Our families live right next to each other. We'd grown up together and were best friends for as long as I could remember. He might be a pain in my side sometimes, but I knew he meant well. As a water elemental, it was a wonder we even got along. We were exact opposites by nature.

"Wait up," Finn called after me as I left the small school building. It was a stone building only a short walk away from where we live.

"I can't wait to be done with this place," I started, like I had many times before.

"I don't know whether you mean this school or this town as a whole," Finn answered with a slight laugh.

"Soon I'll be able to try for being a warrior. With all the training I've put in over the years, there's no way they'll deny me. Then I'm out of here."

Over the past few years, I'd trained harder than ever. Learning how to handle a bow and arrow, practicing my skills with a blade, and, most importantly, strengthening my fire. It wasn't a requirement to be a fire elemental, but the majority of those who tried to become warriors were. It was our first instinct to fight. We were natural born leaders and soldiers. Elemental abilities forged a person all the way to their soul. Before you were even born, your fate was decided by your element. Those with fire were bold and daring, perfect characteristics for a warrior. Air elementals were free-spirited and intellectual, they often became teachers within the community. The water elementals were very compassionate and creative. They took jobs as healers or caretakers. Lastly, those with earth abilities were grounded and practical. They handled most of the farming and growing trees for lumber.

"Yeah, except for one issue. You're a girl. They almost never take girls as warriors," Finn pointed out.

"Keyword almost," I reminded him. "I plan to be the exception."

"Of course you do." I caught Finn's eyes rolling as he said it.

Finn's words were true, of course. He was always the more realistic one. I, however, had no intentions of letting outdated views of women hold me back. They wouldn't deny me the right to participate in show-casing my abilities. All I had to do was prove without a doubt that I was the strongest fire elemental there. Which should be easy given I knew for a fact I was stronger than every other person finishing school this year.

"Do you want to train tomorrow?" I asked as we rapidly approached our homes.

Finn was the only person who willingly ever trained with me. There had been others in the past I tried to train with, but they were useless. Their abilities were weak or untrained, and they didn't make useful part-ners for sparring or working on new combinations. Anyone else who might come close to my ability had no desire to help me. It was every person for themselves, and there were limited spots available each year for warriors. Finn had no desire to become a warrior. His water abilities were better suited elsewhere. The moment school was done, I suspected he'd head for a port town and work with the ships there. I knew that was his dream growing up.

"Fine, only because I know you won't take no for an answer," he said, with a small annoyance in his tone.

Again, he was right. I wouldn't take no for an answer. There was limited time left to get the last training in before I needed to be ready.

"I promise I'll go easy on you this time," I grinned. Last time I'd sent him home with a few bruises from hits I'd landed.

"No need, I was going easy on you last time," he laughed.

We parted ways as we finally reached our houses. Tomorrow was a free day, which is why I'd spend it training. Every week we were given two free days where we didn't have to attend school. All of mine went to becoming the best warrior I could be.

Making my way to my small bedroom, I tossed my bag in the corner as I entered. Mother was in the kitchen humming an upbeat song to herself as she prepared dinner. She likely didn't hear me come in. Perfect, she wouldn't ask me questions about school. I always tried to lie, so she'd believe that I was keeping up in class but she always knew. My parents never understood why I wanted to pursue a warrior's path. They thought I should just accept that it was more probable I'd become a blacksmith or some other profession that catered to fire abilities, rather than waste my time on such futile dreams.

Of course, I never let their doubt stop me. I think it irritates them a bit how stubborn I am. I like to think I'm just extremely determined.

As the front door opened and shut again, I assumed my younger sister must've just got home. My sister and I were exact opposites. I was bold and outgoing, whereas she was more reserved. She was seventeen, making us only a year apart in age. Her short, blonde and wavy hair was in stark contrast to my long, dark brown curls. Our only similarity was our tan complexion and eyes that were a golden brown.

"Leah?" I heard her call out.

"In here, Aurora!" I called back.

After a minute, Aurora slid into the room quietly. I sat up on my small cot, where I'd been trying to relax.

"What're you doing in here? Dinner will be done any minute," she asked.

"Well, I was trying to rest a little before then."

I rolled my eyes and dramatically slumped back down into the cot.

"No studying to do?" she asked with a small grin.

Aurora loved reminding me how terrible of a student I was. She took pride in school. Every subject she learned, she'd ace. Beyond school, her abilities were strong. The small bit of land surrounding our house was always beautiful because she loved showing off her skills. With earth abilities, she was able to grow plenty of flowers and shrubs to decorate the property. Growing up, I always found it annoying. She was always creating things and all my fire did was destroy.

"Don't you have some tree to attend to or something other than bothering me?" I chided back.

With a soft giggle, Aurora joined me on the cot. She plopped right down next to me. Meeting my gaze, she raised her eyebrows.

"What?"

"There's only a month more of school. When are you going to start thinking about the future?"

"I do think of the future."

"Becoming a warrior is a fantasy. It isn't realistic," she sighed. "I'm only trying to look out for you."

"Aren't I supposed to be the one looking out for you?" I asked teasingly. She only shook her head in response.

"Joke all you want, Leah, but I seriously do worry for you. It isn't healthy to be so obsessed like this."

I knew she meant well. Aurora almost never started fights. Always level-headed and reasonable. I couldn't blame her for her concern. I knew I was aiming for the impossible.

"I'll be alright," I offered. It was the best I could do. Deep down I knew it wasn't enough, but I wouldn't lie to her. There was no chance I would just give up on my dreams.

"Now come on, let's go eat before father gets home and eats it all on us."

I sprang out of the bed and grabbed her hand, pulling her up beside me. Hoping this would be the last I had to have this same conversation, I focused on the priority ahead. Putting all my efforts into becoming a warrior.

∼

THE NEXT MORNING, I made my way over to Finn's house. If he was sleeping still, I was going to have to drag him out of bed. It wouldn't be the first time. He always tried to sleep in on our free days. I didn't see the point. Such a waste of perfectly good time.

Knocking on the door, I heard shuffling from within the house. I hoped it wouldn't be his mother to answer the door. She was always nosey, asking so many questions. Wondering why I wanted to spend so much time with her son, and if I had any men in my life who I might think about marrying. If I had to guess, she secretly hoped Finn and I would end up married someday. The idea was crazy. He was my best friend and neither of us saw the other that way.

As the door opened, Finn appeared, rubbing his eyes.

"Did you just wake up?"

"No," he replied, suspiciously.

"Yes, you did. You don't even have on actual clothes for the day yet," I waved my hand up and down emphasizing my point.

"Fine, I did, but I'll be ready just as soon as I change and grab an apple. You can come in to wait," he said, stepping aside for me. This was exactly what I wanted to avoid. "Don't worry, my mother is already off at the market today," Finn assured me, reading my thoughts.

"I have no idea what you mean," I said, unable to hide my small smile.

It didn't take long for Finn to get ready. I waited patiently, sitting in his kitchen while he changed. After only a few minutes, he reappeared.

"Ready?" he asked, grabbing an apple and tossing it between his hands.

Outside, we always trained in my backyard. It was more spacious than Finn's and I'd rigged up a few makeshift targets to practice with as well. We always spent time training both our physical strength and stamina, as well as our elements. Our opposite elements worked well for sparring. Finn was always able to pose a challenge to me. My flames needed to be stronger, hotter, and fiercer than ever to break through his water.

"What should we start with today?" Finn asked.

"Hmm, how about we work on core and then sparring?" I replied.

Finn groaned in response. He always put up such a fuss about core exercises. They were his least favorite, whereas I loved them. The feeling of my muscles burning as I crunched or planked. The way I felt more powerful all around the stronger my core got. As I held myself in a plank, I glanced to my left, finding Finn struggling to keep form.

"I really hate these," he complained.

Chuckling, I let myself drop on to my stomach after a few minutes. Rolling onto my back, I took in the warmth of the sun above. The way it kissed my skin made me feel relaxed. Closing my eyes, I found a moment of peace during training. That was, until a dark shadow hid the sun from my skin. Opening one eye, I realized Finn was hovering above me. Staring expectantly down at me.

"What?"

"Already slacking in training?" he scolded.

Grumbling, I pushed myself up off the ground. I was no slacker and I wouldn't be labeled one by Finn. I'd never live it down if I allowed it. With a quick movement, I let a whip of fire lash towards him. I wasn't aiming to hit him, only to knock him back and force him into sparring with me.

"There she is," he exclaimed. "Now that's the Leah I know."

Without hesitation, he jumped straight into throwing punches of water at me. Slowly, I began to circle my opponent. Finn may give me a hard time about whether I'd become a warrior, but he still took training seriously. I honestly didn't know if it was because he wanted to help me get better or he just didn't like losing.

Another stream of water flew my direction, and I dodged gracefully. I was light on my feet. Small and nimble, I was still stronger than I looked. With great force behind it, I returned the attack with a powerful ball of flame. It narrowly missed Finn, leaving a small singed spot on his shirt.

"Hey, I liked this shirt," he shouted, as he moved in closer.

A stream of water shot towards me, but instead of aiming for me it began to wrap around me, growing into a small vortex. Trapped in, I took a breath, thinking of a way through. Only a strong burst of fire would break this. If I didn't put enough power behind it, the water would douse the flame or it would be reflected back at me.

While considering if I would be able to muster enough strength behind a stream of fire, I came up with another idea. One that I'd been aching to try recently. It was a move I'd thought up over the last few days, but I had yet to use it. Concentrating on my fist, I willed my flames to cover it. Keeping them contained in this one area took a lot of effort. This wouldn't be very useful in a real battle until I perfected the technique.

Once I was confident the flames would stay in place, I was ready to make my move. Pulling my arm back, I prepared to land a punch on the swirling water before me. I swung as hard as I could, letting my flames grow wilder as they made contact with the water. My fist broke through, and as it did, water exploded all around me. The previously swirling vortex fell to the ground in a small rain.

"Wow, when'd you learn that one?" Finn asked.

"Just something I've been working on," I grinned.

After another hour of sparring and working on new element techniques, I decided to call it a day. I needed to get rest, or I was going to end up sore and burnt out. My flames always made me feel drained after using them too much. Lucky for me, Finn also seemed done for the day.

"I'll see you tomorrow?" he asked.

"Yeah, I need to go to the market for some new materials to make more targets back here. Want to come along?"

"Sure, why not?" he shrugged.

"Then I'll see you bright and early," I called out, as I made my way into the house.

I spent the rest of the day relaxing and briefly looking over some school work, which I begrudgingly completed. I knew that I had to at least finish schooling to have a chance at my goals. Once the sun began setting, the exhaustion from training really hit and I settled into bed early.

THE CONTEST

After finishing my breakfast, I met Finn right outside the short wooden fence that marked my front yard. A small tulip brushed my leg as I left our yard. This was a new plant. I didn't recall noticing it before. Aurora must've added this one yesterday, I thought.

The route to the market was practically the same one we walked almost every day to school. It was convenient living so close. That was one thing I would miss when I moved to the capital to be in the royal army. Living in the quarters provided for warriors, I doubted I would live so close to the center of the capital. It was more likely I would be living on the palace grounds, ready to be called upon at any moment.

From off in the distance, a loud rumbling noise sounded. Finn and I froze, listening. Every now and then, this happened. The terrifying sound that pierced the normal tranquility of our town. It was the roar of a dragon. Nearby there was a mountain that towered over our town and a few more towns nearby. At the peak of that mountain, named Fyr Mountain, lived one of the remaining dragons. It never bothered any of us, so long as we didn't climb the mountain or disrupt it. Few folks around town had claimed some nights they swore they saw the dragon flying over high above in the clouds. I myself had never seen it. Only heard the periodic threatening roars.

This was the only dragon I knew about. The rest were spread across the kingdom, or had fled across the sea. From the tales I'd heard, they inhabited many of the mountains and caves and were best left alone. Many hoped that someday the dragons would once again rise with fearsome warriors riding them.

As we approached the market in the center of town, I saw a large crowd of people forming. They were all focused on something right in the middle of the town square where a board for announcements stood. I couldn't see beyond the gathering heads. I was shorter for my age, and likely done growing. Even on my tiptoes, I still couldn't see what had caught everyone's attention.

"Come on," I said, grabbing Finn's hand and tugging him along. My curiosity getting the better of me.

As I hit a wall of people and dropped Finn's hand, I didn't check to see if he was following me. Pushing my way to the front of the crowd, I fought to see what the gathering commotion was about. As I finally squeezed to the front, I saw what everyone was staring at. A man dressed in a warrior's uniform had just finished hanging a flyer on the town board. I could just barely make out the words contest and reward.

"Her royal highness, the queen, has decided to hold a contest. All nearby towns are allowed to participate and the winner will be rewarded greatly."

A contest? Never in my whole life had the queen held such an event. I waited anxiously for the warrior to elaborate. If the queen was holding a contest, it must be important, and there was no way I would be missing out. This was my chance to be noticed and picked as a warrior.

"In three days, the contest will begin. The bravest fighters from each town will climb Fyr Mountain and attempt to tame the dragon that resides at the summit. Whomever is able to accomplish this task will be named the first dragon rider in one hundred years and will lead a regiment of her majesty's army," the warrior finished.

I couldn't be hearing this correctly. The queen wanted to bring back dragon riders? She had to know that was impossible. The beast at the top of the mountain was untamable. It'd incinerate anyone who dared approach the summit. Yet I couldn't help but be a little curious?

"You aren't seriously considering participating, are you?" Finn asked, beside me now.

"It'd be my shot at becoming a warrior!"

"You're delusional! You'll die!"

"Some faith you've got in me," I scoffed. Finn grabbed my shoulder, forcing me to face him.

"Leah, you know I believe you can become a warrior, but trying to tame a dragon, that's completely mad! There's a reason there hasn't been a rider in over one hundred years. Anyone who tries dies!"

He had a point. I knew there were dragons that still existed, including the one on Fyr, but they were completely wild and unpredictable. They were not the same dragons to serve warriors in the past.

"I have to try," I whispered.

Finn only shook his head. The look in his eyes pained me. I knew he was worried about me. He was the closest friend I had, and we cared deeply about each other. If any harm ever came to him, the pain would be unbearable. I could only imagine that's what ran through his own mind about me now.

"Your parents will never allow this. How are you going to convince them?"

"I don't know," I admitted.

"And Aurora?"

"She's even less likely to agree with this," I groaned.

Even though she was my little sister, she always acted older. Bothering me about school, or worrying about me. My parents had never put a stop to my training, but I had a feeling they were going to put up a fight over this.

PACING IN MY ROOM, I tried to find the right words to tell my parents about my plan to participate in the contest. Word had travelled fast around town, and when I arrived home, just hours later from the market, my parents were already discussing it in the kitchen.

"What if I lie and tell them I am going on a trip?" I murmured to myself.

No, that wouldn't work. Where would I say I was going? And what if I died? My parents would never know what happened. I was eighteen, an adult. I should just go out there and tell them I am participating, and that's final. I get to make my own decisions. Part of me knew they'd never agree with that. It was a hopeless cause.

A knock on my door interrupted my thought. Before I could call out, Aurora let herself into the room.

"What happened to waiting for an answer?"

"Were you going to turn me away?" she said, raising an eyebrow.

"Well, no. But that isn't the point," I replied, putting my hands on my hips.

"Did you hear the news?" she continued.

"About the contest?"

"Yes! It's insane. Everyone is talking about it. I heard that Kade from your class was planning to participate!"

I scoffed at this. Kade was also a fire elemental, but he couldn't do more than light a candle. He wouldn't even make it up the mountain, never mind tame the dragon.

"He'll die," I replied.

The look of horror in my sister's eyes made me feel a bit bad for being so blunt. It was true. Many would die in this contest, not realizing they aren't strong enough. I wasn't even so sure I was strong enough, but I had to try. My sister's eyes looked me up and down, and I realized she was catching on to my thoughts. I tried to train my face back to a neutral.

"No," she gasped. "You're not seriously considering this!"

"Aurora-" I tried.

"No, no, no! Absolutely not! You are not risking your life over a stupid and pointless competition. This is madness, Leah. No one is going to win this. It's a fool's errand!"

"I know, but I have to try. I think I can do it. I could be a warrior!"

"I knew you were serious about becoming a warrior, but I didn't realize how delusional you've become!" she shouted. "You are going to get yourself killed!"

"Stop yelling," I tried to shush her, worried our parents would hear.

"No! I will not stop yelling! You would do this to our parents? To me? How could you? How could you be so selfish?" she shouted, tears forming in her eyes.

"I'm sorry," was the best I could come up with. "I have to do this, Aurora. Please try to understand. This is my calling. My destiny."

"I know," she whispered.

"If I don't do this, I'll never forgive myself. All of my training has prepared me for this," I started to argue, when her words really hit me. "Wait, what?"

"I know," she repeated. "That's why I am so upset. I know you're meant to do this. I believe you can, but I'm still terrified. I don't want to lose you, Leah," she finished, looking heartbroken.

"You won't."

I rested a hand on her shoulder, meeting her eyes.

"I promise."

"Mother and father are not going to like this," she said, shaking her head.

"Yeah, I've been trying to think of how to tell them."

I bowed my head, worried they could still stop me.

"Don't."

"What do you mean?"

"Don't tell them," Aurora answered. "They'll only try to stop you and if you still go, it will only hurt them. They will be worried sick."

"But what if something happens? They'll never know."

"I'll tell them."

"I can't ask you to do that," I said, shaking my head.

"I will tell them, Leah. But that isn't going to happen. You're going to win this contest, and you're going to become the first dragon rider in years."

Meeting my sister's gaze, there was a new fire behind her eyes. She held my stare, and we both knew that this was my fate. I was going to journey up that mountain, and I was going to return on the back of a dragon.

THE JOURNEY

Three days after the contest was announced, I found myself at the foot of the mountain. My parents thought I was staying overnight with a friend from class. I couldn't believe they'd bought the lie, since I really didn't have any friends besides Finn.

Staring up, I couldn't help but feel intimidated. It was taller up this close than I'd imagined it to be. Looking around, I saw the many others gathering to participate in the contest. All men. Not a single woman in sight. I scoffed quietly to myself. It didn't matter, because I'd be the one victor at the end of this. I had to be.

"There are no rules to this contest besides being the first to tame and ride the dragon. You can use any means necessary!" the same warrior from town three days ago bellowed.

Any means necessary. That meant many of these competitors would try to knock out others from the contest on the journey up. I'd have to be careful. Vigilant. I'll avoid traveling too close to anyone. It may slow me down, but it's better than getting disqualified before reaching the peak.

"Hey." A gentle hand rested on my shoulder, and I startled.

Turning, I found myself face to face with Finn. What was he doing here? He wasn't supposed to be here. He had a small pack slung on his shoulder and looked ready to head up the mountain. Stunned, no words came out of my mouth.

"I can't let you do this alone. If you're going up the mountain, so am I," he said firmly. There was no time to argue as the warrior stepped forward ready to begin the contest.

"On my count the competition will begin. Three."

No backing out now.

"Two."

My breath caught in anticipation.

"One."

Multiple people rushed forward, pushing to be the first on the path leading up the mountain. I fell into place behind them. Plenty of stragglers also starting their journey behind Finn and I. It would take a total of two days to make it to the peak, if we kept a normal pace. Hopefully, we wouldn't need to make an unnecessary stop or detours. Others may make it to the top first, but I doubted they'd have what it took to tame the beast that awaits.

"So what's the plan?" Finn asked about an hour into hiking.

"The plan is to make it up this mountain and avoid others," I said, my feet already feeling a bit tired.

"I know that, but I meant once we get to the top. How are you going to tame the dragon?"

I'd thought about this a lot in the past three days. Every plan I'd come up with had seemed unreasonable, or bound to fail. I was only one girl going up against a wild beast.

"I don't know," I admitted.

He paused, staring at me. Forced to stop, I turned to face him. For the first time, Finn looked genuinely shocked. Usually he was so used to my antics and crazy plans, they never phased him. But this had stopped him in his tracks.

"You mean you have zero idea how you are going to win this, and we have only about a day before we make it up there?"

"Yeah, pretty much," I shrugged, pushing onward.

"Leah! You can't be serious. All the years I've known you, never once have you gone into something blind," he argued.

"I know, but this is different."

"How?"

"This is a dragon!" I snapped, as if he didn't know where we were heading. "No one knows anything about this beast. That includes me. I have no idea what we're about to face. So, no, I do not have a plan for us. You weren't even supposed to be here! We're just going to have to figure it out as we go," I said, crossing my arms and picking up my pace.

My anger was fueling me to push upward. Finn remained silent, not questioning me any further. For hours, we walked in silence. Neither of us wanting to speak first. I could tell Finn was frustrated with me. I was frustrated with myself. How could I be so stupid to think I could do this without a plan? On the other hand, I didn't ask Finn to be here. He chose to be here on his own. He couldn't blame me for not having a plan for us, when I thought it would be just me heading up.

Quickly, the sky grew darker above. We hadn't seen any of the other competitors in a while. I was thankful for that one small gift. I had yet to speak with Finn, after snapping at him earlier. It wasn't his fault I was unprepared. I shouldn't have been so harsh with him.

"We should rest," I finally said.

Finn only nodded, solemnly. He wouldn't even meet my eyes. I pulled out some sticks I'd thought to pack to make a fire. I knew we wouldn't find any sticks or twigs on the mountain. It was mostly rocks and dirt. I used my fire to light them and sat beside it. Finn copied, sitting opposite of me. His head hung, and his gaze remained on the dancing flames before him. I couldn't take it anymore.

"I'm sorry," I said. "I shouldn't have taken my anger out on you like that."

"It's okay," he said softly.

"No, it isn't. You're my best friend, and you're risking a lot being here for me. You didn't deserve that."

"I shouldn't have pushed you like that," he said.

"It's alright. I understand why you did."

"I'm just scared, Leah. I am terrified that tomorrow, you may walk in that cave up there and never come out."

"I know," I said softly, my foot pushing around a few pebbles.

"I will do everything I can to ensure that doesn't happen."

Finn's eyes finally met mine. I could tell he meant that. I would do anything to protect him like that, too. We were in this together.

"And I will do everything I can to ensure we both make it down this mountain," I swore.

Without another word, we both ate the food we'd packed before settling down to sleep. We would need all the rest we could afford to face the dragon tomorrow.

As THE SUN rose above us, the warm kiss of its rays woke me from my sleep. Shifting, I opened my eyes to barely a squint. I spotted Finn, also stirring across from me. At some point during the night, the fire had gone out. I groaned as I sat up. My back aching from sleeping on the cold, hard ground.

"Ready for this?" I asked, looking over at Finn as he also sat up.

"I'm not sure ready is the right word," he groaned, rubbing his own back.

There was no time to waste. We had to be the first ones to successfully reach and tame the dragon. I was counting on the first few people up to fail. There was no way everyone who tried had what it took. From all the legends and stories I heard, dragon riders were born destined to ride. Not just anyone would be able to mount the beast, or control him.

From what I could tell, we were already more than halfway up the mountain. It would take another few hours before we approached the peak. Beginning our trek for the day, we both snacked on fresh peaches I'd packed. Finn had offered up a handful of nuts as well, which I gladly accepted.

With each step we took, I felt myself growing more and more anxious. My body was tired. The hike up had not been easy on us. Our legs were sore, and we hadn't slept well on the mountain side.

Ahead, movement caught my eye. A man who looked a few years older was hurrying our direction. The wrong direction. Downward.

"Turn back!" he shouted.

"What?" I questioned, pausing.

"Turn back! Leave! It isn't worth it," he yelled.

"What do you mean? Did you see the dragon?" I asked.

"No, there's a group of men near the peak, stopping anyone from entering before them. From what I gathered, one of them tried and was incinerated on the spot. They're now grouped outside the cave plotting, but they also won't let anyone else try. They're using force to stop them. I didn't sign up for fighting other people. I'm done," the man finished, hurrying off.

I glanced at Finn, trying to read his face. He showed slight concern, but mainly remained neutral.

"It's your call," he said. "Do we keep going?"

I thought it over for a moment. I hadn't wanted to fight other people, but if it came down to it, I would. We had come too far to turn back now. We would just have to take them on.

"Let's go," I answered, my mind made up.

Another hour passed before we spotted the men the abandoner had told us about. There were three of them. We would be outnumbered, and at a disadvantage. I hoped all three would be fire elementals. This way, Finn's water would provide us with one advantage.

"Hey, you two. Stop right there!" one called out.

We listened, stopping in place. It was better to let them think they were in control. They'd play right into our hands this way. We needed surprise on our side.

"No one is to pass! We are going to go into the cave before anyone else. We are preparing right now," another chimed in.

"So no one else can try before you?" I asked innocently.

The realization must've hit them that I was a girl, because one of them started to chuckle. They all looked me over, clearly underestimating me.

"Go home, little girl," the first man said.

"I'm surprised you even climbed the mountain," the third and final man spoke up

I clenched my fists, trying to keep calm. I needed a clear and steady head. I could feel Finn's presence next to me, but I didn't dare glance at him. I didn't want to give away our plan of attack.

"Ready?" I whispered to him, barely even audible.

"Mhm," he whispered back.

Without another thought, I aimed for the man standing in the middle of their group and sent a stream of fire straight for him. Shocked, he barely dodged. My goal hadn't been to hit him. It had been to break the group up further. Together, they formed a solid wall. Apart, they left gaps to enter the cave. It worked as the other two men jumped away from the middle.

Finn followed my lead, taking on the man to the left. With a whip of water, he knocked him off balance. Before turning to my own two opponents, I noticed the man sent a fireball back at Finn. Thankful Finn had the advantage, I let out a small breath.

I didn't need to defeat these men. I only needed to slip by them and make it into the cave first. They wouldn't dare follow me in. It could mean their demise if they did.

"You're feisty for a little girl," one man taunted.

They were trying to get under my skin. They knew I was powerful. I wouldn't let them. Without another thought, I threw myself into battle. Sending bursts of flame at each of them. The two both ended up being fire elementals, like I'd hoped for. I could easily control and block their flames. I danced around them with grace. Taking any opening I saw, to strike.

My flames swirled in a great showing of power. I kept pushing myself harder and harder. Putting more behind my fire. I managed to knock down one of the men. While he was down, I focused my attention on the other. From beside me, someone called out.

"Go Leah!"

I lashed with flame at the man across from me and then looked at Finn. His water was keeping the other man busy.

"Go!" he shouted again, between attacks. "Take the opening, I've got them!"

I looked to the cave and realized with one man down, I could run and make it in. I didn't like the idea of leaving Finn behind. But once inside the cave, the men outside would likely back down, and there could only be one victor to this contest.

"It's meant to be you!" he yelled one last time, as I made up my mind.

I ran as fast as I could, putting everything I had into it. I wouldn't be stopped. No one would prevent me from claiming my destiny.

THE FIGHT

Bursting into the cave, I almost tripped as I suddenly stopped. The beast before me was huge. It stood, ready to burn anything that dared enter its cave. The dragon was a magnificently terrifying sight. Its black scales were as dark as the night sky, and its eyes piercing straight into my soul. I held its gaze, not daring to move.

It tilted its head slightly, as if challenging me to make the first move. I knew better. If I was going to claim this beast as mine to ride, I needed to wait and see how it would react. If I made the first move, it may view me as a threat.

Our standoff didn't last long. The dragon raised its head, and as it opened its mouth, it let out a breath of flame. I dove out of the way just in time. Rolling, I felt the heat of pure fire narrowly miss me. Standing, I raised my hands before me, ready to be on the defense. I didn't want to strike at the dragon just yet. I needed it to trust me.

A small black patch on the ground next to me caught my eye. It was a scorch mark. Little remained of whatever or whomever had stood there before. It might have been the men outside's friend. I could feel my anxiety creeping back in, but I pushed it down. Now wasn't the time to panic.

I circled slowly around the dragon, trying to place myself before it again. I would keep standing here until it accepted me. No matter what it took or how long it took. I was determined.

The dragon's eyes appeared to narrow a little as it spotted me. I couldn't tell if it was shocked I was still alive, or shocked I was willingly putting myself in its line of fire again. Its flames were much stronger than mine and more unruly. Could I possibly control them if they came at me again?

I didn't have time to decide as the dragon let out a roar, and again breathed hot flames in my direction. I sidestepped the attack and made a run for it. Not out of the cave, but further into it. I quickly passed the dragon, who already realized I was still alive. I saw a large chunk of rock ahead and made my way to it. Crouching behind it, I caught my breath. I needed a plan, and fast. How was I going to convince this dragon to trust me? The moment I attack the dragon, I lose. I had figured that much out. Yet, what could I do to prove to the dragon I was worthy of being its rider?

An angry bellow came from the dragon as it searched the cave for where its adversary had run to. I held my breath, fearing even the slightest of noise or movement would tip him off. I needed another moment to gather my thoughts.

Doubt filled me as I sat, my adrenaline finally fading. What would my parents think if they knew where I was right now? I had to succeed so that I could return to them. See them again before I leave for the capital. What was my sister doing right now? Would she be home worrying about me? I had to make it through this. She believed in me. Finn believed in me. Now it was time to finally believe in myself.

A moment later, I felt the dragon's approach. It was too close for comfort. If I kept hiding here, it would burn me alive the moment it sensed me. Jumping out from behind the rock, I came face to face with the beast. The moment its eyes locked on me, flames burst from its mouth. Again, I dodged the attack. I couldn't keep this up, though. I needed to make my move.

Going with my gut feeling, I made myself stand firm. I planted my feet before the dragon, awaiting its move. This just may be the most insane thing I'd ever done. I was right to believe the dragon would again attack with a stream of flame.

Willing all of my control and power to the surface, I didn't move. There was no dodging this time. Instead, I held my ground. As the flame approached, I raised my hands once more. I willed the flame to bend to my will the moment it made contact. Pushing it away so that it went around me. I could feel the immense heat from the fire and tried to remain focused. If I even faltered slightly, I would surely burn.

As the last of the flames made their way to me, I began to will them to swirl. Wrapping them around my body. They formed a small tornado of fire, with me in the center. I was the one in control now. The dragon watched, unmoving. I let the fire dance around me a little longer before dispersing the flames.

I stared down the dragon, refusing to break eye contact. The next move would be decided by it. No more flames came barreling my way, and I took that to be a good sign. I had the dragon's interest.

Before either of us could make a move, we both heard footsteps entering the cave. I quickly moved, putting myself between the dragon and whoever approached. A man appeared, and I recognized him as one of the three from outside. Soon behind him appeared the other two, with Finn also following but keeping his distance.

"I'm sorry. I couldn't keep them out any longer," Finn called.

So they'd finally made it through his water. I shouldn't be surprised. Three on one. It was impressive he'd kept them out this long.

"Move out of our way, girl. You had your chance," one said.

"I'm not going anywhere," I said, planting my feet firmly.

"Then we will just have to make you," another said, cracking his knuckles.

I prepared myself for whatever they'd throw at me. I had just tamed dragon's fire. These three's flames would be nothing. Although I was exhausted after what I'd just pulled off, and I wasn't sure how much more I could take. I tried not to let that show.

One of the men stepped forward, ready to fight. He pushed his palm out, flames leaping into action and barreling toward me. I readied to deflect the attack, hoping I had enough strength left in me. Before I was able to find out something, strange happened. Darkness. I was quickly swallowed into black nothingness. What was happening?

I looked around, trying to figure out where I was. Had I passed out? No, I still felt very much awake. That's when I looked behind me and found a dragon towering over me.

The dragon had used its own wing to shield me. It protected me from the man's attack. I hadn't even noticed it moving closer. I was in shock. Was this the dragon's way of accepting me and showing it trusted me? As the beast pulled back its wing, I found everyone was stunned. They all just stared at me.

I ignored their looks, turning to face the dragon. They no longer mattered. All that mattered here was this dragon and I. The beast knelt down, bowing its head in a sign of respect. I hesitated, unsure if I should approach. I'd never been this close to a beast of this size. I wasn't even sure how I would climb up on to its back.

It remained kneeling, awaiting my next move. I pushed my doubts aside, deciding this was it. This was everything I'd worked for. I made my way to the dragon's side. Using its hind leg for assistance, I pushed myself up onto its back. Up here I could see spikes ran along its head and neck. I moved myself all the way up until I was able to hold on to the spike at the base of the neck. The men below still looked stunned.

"Move out of our way, before we burn you where you stand," I commanded.

The men scurried from the cave. All but Finn, who remained unmoving.

"You did it," he said, shocked.

I only nodded. He remained pressed to the cave's wall as the dragon moved quickly by him. Heading for the entrance, I was sure the beast was about to take off into the sky.

THE END

Grasping to the back of the dragon, I held on for dear life. This was nothing like I'd dreamed. My stomach dropped as we took off, the dragon throwing us into the air. Luckily, it only took me a few moments to calm my nerves, and really take in what was happening. I was flying. Everything I'd ever imagined for myself was coming true.

"Do you have a name?" I asked, as if the beast could understand me. He only cocked his head slightly in response, as if looking back at me.

"I suppose I should give you one."

Racking my brain, I considered what name would be appropriate for a dragon. The name a rider gave their dragon was important. It bonded them for life. This dragon had grown up here the same as I had. We would both be moving on to a new and exciting chapter. I would give him a name to commemorate that.

"What about Fyren? Since you come from Fyr Mountain."

I was jolted a bit as Fyren sped up. With a loud roar, he let out a burst of flame from his mouth. I couldn't help but giggle.

"I take that as a yes, then."

Fyren soared even higher into the sky. I clung tightly to his neck, praying I just didn't fall off. I hoped that the rest of the competitors could see this. Still in shock, I couldn't believe this. I'd actually done it. I had won the contest. Even crazier, I had tamed a dragon. The first dragon rider in a century and it was me.

"We have to stop in town," I said, like Fyren would know what I meant. "I want to see my parents one more time."

Surprisingly, I think Fyren did understand me. We were connected now. Whether he understood my words or just knew my thoughts, I didn't know. But he changed course, heading straight for the town square. Hopefully, by now, the town would've spotted the dragon and gathered. My parents would've rushed to see who the winner was, like everyone else.

As we began our descent, I recognized some of the people gathered in the square. Ms. Elrod, some of my classmates, I even picked Aurora out of the crowd. They'd left a big opening in the middle for us to land. As Fyren's feet hit the ground, some of the people hurried back more.

He tilted his head up and let out a fearsome roar, shooting flames into the sky. I dismounted, feeling everyone's eyes on me. I could even hear some of the shocked whispers as people recognized who I was.

"Let me through," I heard someone shout.

Aurora pushed her way to the front of the crowd. No one dared approach the dragon. Fyren's eyes remained on me, awaiting my orders. I met Aurora's gaze as she took in the sight. Before I could say anything, she ran towards me. Not afraid. She hugged me tightly, unwilling to let go. I could sense Fyren tensing, unsure if this was a threat.

"It's okay," I said, comforting not only Aurora, but Fyren as well. "I'm okay."

"You did it," she said, pulling back. Her face was in disbelief. "I can't believe you actually did it."

"I know," I said just as stunned. "Are mother and father here?"

"Yes, they were with me," she said, straining her head to search the crowd.

We both spotted them at the same time. They were trying to make their way to the front. As they finally broke through, they paused. I was nervous. Would they be angry with me for going off without telling them?

"Leah," my mother began.

Before either of them could say more, I hurried to them. I was instantly wrapped in their embrace. My heart pounded as I realized I would soon have to leave them. Leave all of this.

"I'm so sorry," I said. "I'm sorry I didn't tell you."

"It's okay," my mother replied. "Finn's parents told us everything when he went after you."

Of course, he would tell them. I couldn't even be mad. Without him, I never would've been able to make it this far. He had my back when I need him, and I would be forever grateful.

"I have to leave," I said sadly, hanging my head.

I knew any moment the warrior from before would turn up, and I would be forced to leave my life behind. This was what I'd always wanted, but now in the moment I felt sad.

"We know." It was my father who spoke this time.

"You were meant for this," Aurora said from behind me. My parents nodded their agreement.

The crowd began to part as the same warrior from the mountain made his way into the square. I found myself face to face with him, ready for whatever would come next. I half expected him to scoff at me. To question how a girl had won. Instead, he reached out, handing me something.

"Here, take this scroll straight to the capital. You will be granted permission to see the queen when you arrive," the warrior instructed.

I nodded my head and prepared to leave. I gave my family one last hug goodbye. I knew this wasn't the end. I would be back to see them again soon. Climbing once more onto Fyren, I looked back down over the crowd. I found my parents and sister smiling proudly up at me. I gave them a small wave before setting my focus back on Fyren.

"Take me to Crona," I instructed.

Fyren understood, readying to take off. The crowd hurriedly moved back as the dragon expanded its wings. We shot into the sky. This time, I felt less nervous. I felt confident. Ready to take on whatever awaited me in the capital. As we flew away, I didn't look back. My focus was set on the future awaiting us.

ABOUT M.K. AHEARN

M.K. Ahearn grew up in Massachusetts as one of three sisters. She now lives in Maryland with her fiancé and three cats. When not writing she can be found planning her next travel adventure.

STORY III
THE YULE MASQUERADE BY S. L. THORNE

Heat Level: Low
(PG content)

THE YULE MASQUERADE: A SELF-CONTAINED EXCERPT FROM LADY OF THE MIST

The morning of Yule found An and Skye at the rath, slipping into the borderlands in the wee hours before dawn. Just beyond the gate, a carriage waited. It was gold with green trim and had the Gryphon King's sigil emblazoned on the door. The fey driver had four handsome bays hitched up and the page boy in green livery held open the door with high formality. An paused before stepping in. "I think ye can let me go from here, Skye. I thank ye fer what ye've done, but ye've things of yer own t' do. I'll see ye at dusk. Oh..." she added, suddenly worried. "The hedge! Are they goin' t' lock us in t'night?"

At this the page spoke up, "No, Mistress," he smiled. "Tonight no one rides out in force, and if we choose, we are welcome to come to the Masque. We have to abide by Hospitality, though. The King's gone once, a long time ago. They'll not put up the hedge tonight. And you'll not be late. ...So long as you arrive in time to the palace," he added pointedly.

An nodded and let him hand her up into the coach. She waved to Skye as he watched them ride off. Skye did not turn back to the gate until the carriage had entered the tree-lined avenue and faded from sight. Even so, he barely made it through before the door closed as the sun peered over the horizon.

She was right, though. He had a lot of preparation to do.

THE GRYPHON'S Rest was a huge, sprawling community, full of both the rescued Taken and mortal kin. It was not unlike the Irish villages of old, for all it lay smack in the middle of North Florida in the Suwanee valley. There were annual festivals celebrating each major solar event according to the ancient calendar, and while the magical portions were primarily for the benefit of those altered by Faerie, everyone attended. Yule was nearly everyone's favourite.

Outside of the obvious reasons for the celebration, Yule was one of the two most important of the year. As extra precautions, and to help bolster the magical protections keeping the Rest safe from Fey predations, the community followed an even older rite than the Solstice. That of the Oak King and the Holly King's annual battle for supremacy of the year. The evening began with a masquerade ball with the unmasking at midnight, and, as the page had said, the fey were allowed to attend provided they abide by Hospitality. They also had to leave shortly after the unmasking, before the 'war'. At that point, the forces of the Oak and the Holly would engage in a magical, non-lethal battle for control of the year and the claiming of the May Queen. During the Masque, both kings had to try to discover who the queen was before the unmasking in order to gain the advantage of her skills in the battle.

This year, the Holly King had been bragging that he'd know the queen by the power of her crown, amidst so many mundane costumes. So, the queen had gone on the offensive, enlisting the witch to make everyone equally magic and even the playing field. This was also why An had requested a favour of her former students, the Gryphon King's fey children, to help her fool Henry into thinking that she was the queen, Liberty.

Most of the festivals and rituals occurred outside, on the green behind the manor. Not so the Yule Masque. After twelve noon everyone was run out of the house, even Shannon and Martha, the housekeeper and cook, and Ian did something with his keys.

Skye stood back and watched as Ian, Henry, Sorrow, Liberty, Gabrielle and a woman named Magdelena, all gathered around the house. He had felt the expenditure of magic. It had a rippling effect throughout the gardens, and when Ian reopened the doors from one of the skeleton keys on his ring, the interior was no longer his house.

Skye walked through, gaping like a wonder-struck tourist. The outside of the house looked the same, except for maybe the garlands that draped the walls and windows and the absence of the roof on the veranda. The inside was one large ballroom with tall windows that glinted with frost at the edges. The floor glittered in whites and blues, and garlands of holly and evergreen draped the walls. The chandelier was made of icicles, and the fireplace at one end of the ballroom was large enough to have roasted an entire bull whole.

Ian strode across the tiled floor with Mikey, Skye and several others in his wake and threw open the French doors on the far side. "Well, gents," he began, "time t' fetch th' firewood."

They each grabbed an axe from where they gleamed against the wall and marched off into the wood to find a Yule log.

By the time they had returned, dragging the enormous section of tree trunk behind them, the greensward and the surrounding grounds had undergone a transformation. There was a light dusting of snow on the ground, making the trees pretty as a painting and the log easier to drag to the house. Sean and the others had been hard at work. Coach-And-Four followed the woodsmen, pulling the wagon with the rest of the wood by himself.

It seemed no time at all before it was time for everyone to get ready.

Skye had chosen his costume carefully, portraying something he most certainly did not see himself as: Prince Charming. He had acquired a glamour that made his hair fall in golden ringlets to his shoulder and a dashing black coat with gold braiding and the trousers with the red stripe of satin down the seam. His mask was black with a gleaming red and gold sunburst erupting from one temple, stretching across the bridge of his nose. He looked in the mirror and adjusted himself, very pleased with the results.

He stepped outside, not trusting the fey door to the manor at the moment. He had asked the chief if he might borrow a horse for the evening and waiting at his doorstep was a spirited white charger held by a rather short little grooms-man in green. As the groom handed up the reins once Skye was mounted, he gave him last-minute instructions. "Ride up in style. He likes showin' off. When ye dismount, toss th' reins o'er his neck an' he'll trot himself on home."

"Will doo," he said with a nod.

"An' lose th' accent, me bucko," the groom grinned. "That is unless ye want t' be known."

Skye nodded again, groaning to himself as he turned the horse's head. That would be the hardest part of all of this: losing his Scottish burr. As the only Scotsman currently at the Rest, it would give him away in a heartbeat.

SKYE'S ARRIVAL was everything he had wanted. He rode up, the horse prancing and high stepping up to the front door. He dismounted with flair and strode in, basking in the attention of those who were already present. He came off as dashing and devil-may-care.

The dancing lessons he had taken from Liberty had paid off. He had no shortage of dance partners as the sun began to set and more people drifted in. Very few arrived in pairs, but this did not confuse Skye. He knew why. There were a few couples: a Sonny and Cher, a knight and his horse, and Jack and Jill, the bucket merely a miniature dangling from Jill's wrist.

Even the musicians were costumed. The entire small orchestra was dressed as goblins in tuxedos. There were only a few servants, mostly to hold the reins of those who, like Skye, had chosen to ride, to help folk from sleighs and to hold the door. Food and drink was set up along a wall in one massive, unending buffet.

Skye was more than a little surprised when Jack asked him to dance. "Um... but... ye...you," he said, catching himself.

Jack laughed. "Tonight? Of all nights, one never knows what lies beneath. You could be a woman for all I know, or a goblin, a member of the Gentry. Or, more importantly, the Queen."

That made Skye stifle whatever objections he had been trying to articulate. If this was Henry, then dancing with him would delay his finding the real Liberty. He bowed over Jacks' hand, stopped short of kissing the air above his fingers. "So, who shall lead?"

Jack grinned. "Since you asked," he said, taking the lead and trying to sweep Skye out onto the floor.

The dancing was a little more awkward after that, as Skye kept unconsciously trying to lead and kept tangling them up. "And here I had thought you graceful as I watched you," Jack commented dryly.

"Perhaps it is my partner," he growled with a tight smile.

He was saved from a retort by the sight of a carriage riding past the tall windows. They turned, wandered over to the closest window and watched the arrival of a carriage made from spun ice. More impressive than the graceful swirls and delicate filigree which graced the vehicle were the four polar bears pulling it. When the carriage stopped at the front door, an arctic fox boy in pale blue livery jumped off the back and ran over to fold down the steps and open the door.

OF MASKS AND MAGIC

Skye could feel others pressing to the windows behind him, trying to see. He nearly missed the lion-man that descended the carriage in his attempt to keep from being jostled too much by a small otter in a ballet dress who slipped between him and Jack to get a better view. He did see the lion extend his hand into the vehicle and draw out a woman in flowing white.

There were gasps all around him at the sight of her. Even he had to admit the dress was beautiful and flattering. It clung to her waist and belled to the floor, slightly longer in the back. The neckline was swept across her chest, just to the edges of her ivory shoulders, and the bodice presented her feminine assets perfectly without being brazen. Pinned to the centre of the band was a huge diamond encrusted flower pin, and her throat was circled by a glittering, jewelled vine with snowflowers. Her mask was elaborate. It had white feathers that swept up and back, and small branches of silver leaves on the sides that followed the upswept line of her pale golden curls. The mask itself, which seemed to be made from pressed snow, caught the light and fragmented it. There was a line of ice crystals that dangled against her white cheeks. The red lips smiled up at her escort and suddenly Skye knew her, in spite of the perfectly normal eyes he saw within the mask. He smiled, kept his mouth shut, and turned to watch her entrance into the ballroom proper.

AN FELT her heart beating a rapid tattoo in her breast as Lion set her hand on his arm and led her to the now open doors. He purred a soft word of comfort and a reminder which caused her to draw herself up as the Snow Queen she was meant to be.

She almost lost that careful composure when they stepped through the door into the ballroom. It looked every inch a fey place, and she could see all of it. She closed her eyes, turned to look up at him as she opened them slowly. He smiled, his pride apparent. She strode into the room as if she owned it. She had seen this act before, enough to be able to imitate it, and felt herself sinking into the spirit of the Masque and the purpose that had drawn her here.

Lion let them gaze at her in awe for a moment more before he signalled the orchestra and led her across the dance floor. The dance was beautiful in its apparent simplicity, though it was as complex as it was serene. Others joined them on the floor, but none could follow the steps, and so dissolved into an easy waltz around them. The final flourish of the music came, and he spun her out and she sank into a deep curtsey before him. He kissed her hand and drew her up, whispered words to her in his rumbling voice. Those near enough heard only purring, but she heard the words he intended her to. "For one night," he said. "May it be all you hoped. It ends at midnight, Cinderella. Use your hours well."

With that he turned and strode towards the veranda doors, which for this evening only led to an uncovered patio at the foot of which waited his golden horse. He leapt from the top step to the saddle and, rearing, the horse spun on his heels and galloped off down the trod into the woods.

Left behind and feeling his absence sorely, An turned slowly, surveying the room. As she spun and the hem of her skirts swirled across the floor, snow began to fall from the ceiling. She looked up, watched the delicate, glittering flakes float down, evaporating before they hit the floor, and laughed.

As if this were some sort of cue, the goblin orchestra struck up a whirling, spinning melody that put one immediately in mind of swirling eddies of snowfall. She began to wheel into the stately steps, managing to put a more regal twist on what was essentially a peasant dance. One by one, the women took the floor, slowly spinning out to orbit around her, all of them like snowflake sprites dancing in the wind. Later, the men stepped in, one by one as they found the courage, floating up to a woman and joining her if she allowed it.

The first to so approach An was Jack. An smiled, allowed Liberty to take her hand and lead her into the graceful steps of the partnered portion, far less complex than the one the prince had put her through. Even her voice was slightly different, deeper. "Evenin', my Queen," Jack/Liberty grinned. "You've outdone yourself."

An conceded. "I had help."

"Who? The witch said..."

"I found a 'fairy godmother'."

Liberty's eyes danced, flitting through all the things that could mean. "I wish ye luck of it then, luv."

The dance came to an end, and she kissed the back of An's hand, bowing out and moving to another young woman, cutting in and sweeping off with the girl as the music restarted.

About halfway through, An noticed that the music was modern, something she had heard at Courtz, but, played by a full orchestra, it sounded far more high-culture. An found herself, for the moment, standing in the middle of the dancers without a partner, watching them move around her.

She was not the only singlet on the floor, but that one was a spritely young thing in a ballet version of a milkmaid costume. She was cavorting about the couples, taunting, encouraging, in a manner Liberty would have said reminded her of ballet. It did not take An long to realise that while the milkmaid was flitting about everyone, herself included, she had her eyes on one individual in particular.

The song ended, and An began to move off the floor now that it was safe to do so. She saw the woman pounce on her target and begin flirting in a shameful way which sent his current partner off, blushing. Before An could reach the safety of the resting area, 'Prince Charming' was looming before her and bowed, held out his hand.

"My Queen? Will you honour me?" he asked.

There was something deliberate in the way he spoke, as though he were trying very hard to cover an accent. She accepted and let him lead her back out onto the floor. He did not say much, just watched her with a smug look in his blue eye.

Finally, she could stand it no more. "Is there something which amuses you, Your Highness?" she asked him, using his costume's title.

He laughed, spun her around and bent his mouth to her ear. "Th' Prince out-did himself t'night. Or did his sister have more t' do wi' yer glamour?"

She gasped, pulled back and only with a great deal of effort resisted popping him. She put on her cold, Snow Queen demeanour, raised an eyebrow with convincing hauteur. "Cheat," she said flatly.

He just laughed at that. "Worry not, your Majesty. Your secret is safe with me." He sent her out into a spin, pulled her back in. "Hell, I might be convinced to run a little interference. Trip Henry in your direction. Though it seems to me, someone else has landed him... for a little while at least."

An followed his gaze, saw the milkmaid with her hand on the backside of a man with long black curls in a bright red pirate coat and hat. They were headed out the patio door into the night.

Skye escorted An over to the buffet tables, offered to get her something to eat or drink, and seemed surprised when she smiled secretively. "No need."

She reached across to a fountain of chocolate and picked up a strawberry, running it under the stream, and ate it delicately.

A raised eyebrow was his only response. He was thinking of saying something else, but whatever he had to say was cut off by the approach of a tall woman in a slinky silver evening gown patterned with snowflakes in tiny crystals. Her hair was the colour of a raven's wing and fell in ringlets beside her deeply exposed and heavily corseted bust. Behind the black and silver feathered mask were eyes the colour of ice.

She slithered up and wrapped her arms around his arm and pressed her breast against him, looking up into his eyes with an easy grace. "Ooo, Prince Charming. I have been looking all over for you," she purred.

She was beautiful, and she smelled like heaven, but the eyes were wrong. Skye knew they could be just a glamour, but still.... Something in his gut recoiled. Skye turned to An only to find her gone along with any excuse he might have had. He decided to do the polite thing, in case this was the witch for instance, and offer her a single dance.

"My lady," he said with deliberate formality. "May I have this dance?"

She flashed him a smile that would have melted most men and pulled back enough to curtsey and let him go through the rest of the little ritual. As he took her out onto the dance floor, he examined what he could see of her. Her jawline hinted at a perfect oval face and an aquiline nose. Her lips were full and pouty, perfect for kissing even though that was the last thing he wanted to do to them at the moment. Her breasts were bounteous over a slim waist, though she did not have much in the way of hips. She was most modern men's definition of beauty.

He glanced over at An, dancing again, this time with a tall, lean young man in a green suit. He had never thought her plain as he had heard her described at the army training camp where he had served in Faery, but tonight she was radiant. She truly was the most beautiful woman in the room. Even the beauty he danced with looked more like a goose than a swan compared to her tonight. It did not change his heart, however. His eyes did a sweep of the room, looking for someone with the dancing skills he knew Liberty possessed. So far, the only women showing that kind of skill were the milkmaid, Jill and someone who looked like she might be the Lady of the Lake.

He sighed, returned his attention to the viper he was partnered with. She made attempts at conversation, trying to draw out of him clues as to who he might be. He deflected them back at her, perhaps leading her on to believing he was someone he was not. When the dance was over, he bowed, excused himself and ducked out quickly as someone else came up to vie for the woman's attentions.

An spent nearly as much time sitting and watching the world dance by as she spent dancing herself. Occasionally someone, usually one of the women, would sit and talk for a while and then move on. Most of the conversations were about how their significant others were absolutely clueless. An watched the crowd, looking for someone herself, seeking some sign that might mark him from the others.

The pirate returned, looking very self-satisfied, and the milkmaid moved on to riper pastures. He spied An sitting across the room, looking every inch the regal queen of winter, chatting quietly with Jack, and strode purposefully over. Jack leaned back in the chair, crossing his legs in a manly manner and trying his best to look lazy.

The pirate bowed flamboyantly to An. "Captain Henry Morgan, at your service, My Queen."

An smiled coldly, nodding. "Your obeisance is accepted."

This threw him off a bit, and he straightened, eyeing Jack warily as if fearing he might be a rival. "Might this humble servant have the honour of this dance?"

"He might." An stood. "Though he is anything but humble."

The Captain laughed, taking her hand. "I would be less effective if I were."

As he drew her to the floor and swung her into position, she maintained her cool smile and aloof demeanour. "And what exactly would it be that you do for me?"

He pulled her uncomfortably close. "Keep your majesty safe from marauding Englishmen."

"And who is to keep me safe from marauding privateers?"

He laughed at that and loosened his grip, trotting her across the floor in what he thought was fancy footwork. "Ah, my queen, I protect you even now. You see that other pirate over there, the one in black, the Dread Pirate Roberts?"

An glanced in the direction he aimed their joined hands. There was a man there in a black pirate shirt, black pants tucked into tall, suede boots. There was a pouch slung at his belt and a strap across his unlaced chest. His hair and face were hidden by a scarf with an eye mask sewn into it, completely obscuring the upper half of his head accept for the piercing brown eyes that seemed to watch her as if she were an enemy ship on the horizon.

"That one, yes," he said, turning her away from him, blocking the man's view. "He's been stalking you. Circling you like a shark," he said, turning the pair of them in circles as if to illustrate his point. "I can't have that. I won't have gryphon-boy beating me to the punch. I must say though, my dear, you have led me a merry chase and damn near had me fooled. But I have found you, my queen."

"What makes you think…"

He bent to her ear, giving her once more a view of the other man. "Your crown is showing." He leaned back. "Metaphorically speaking, of course."

The man in black put An more in mind of a highwayman than a pirate, whoever this 'Dread Roberts' was. He was watching the milkmaid, was about to approach her when she grabbed someone's rear and he veered away, choosing instead fair little Jill. There was something about him which frightened her a little. She turned back to Henry, for she knew it to be him now, aware he had said something but not aware of what.

"Are we not?" he repeated.

She returned his leering grin with her coldest smile. "We are not."

He looked indignant. "Yer not even going to tell me I'm roight?" His eyes narrowed, and she began to see hints of holly beneath the rim of his hat. His accent of a British Gentleman-turned-privateer slipped. "Yer just doing dis because ye found out about de betting pool, making me lose. Well, I've already lost my slot, cousin dear. Ye could at least throw me dat bone."

She heard the song come to an end and tried to step back from him. He did not let her. "The only bone We are likely to throw you will be your own, if you do not unhand Us."

"Royal We's?" he asked, wide-eyed. "Really?"

She stiffened in his grasp, her expression ice. She did not raise her voice, but there was all the more threat for its softness. "Unhand Us, pirate, or We shall revoke your letters of marque and ye shall find thy next dance partner to be the ropemaker's daughter."

He let go immediately.

She took a single step back. "Come midnight ye shall learn if thy bet is won or lost. Not before." She then turned and walked away. An decided she needed a little air and went out onto the patio.

The sky was alive with stars, and she set her hands on the low marble rail to look up at them. They were not quite the ones she remembered, but they were real and she could see them and they were beautiful. There were tiny fey lights woven into the garlands of holly and evergreen that decorated the patio rails, and more scattered out among the low lover's maze she could see off to her left. From the flickering patterns of some of those lights, she guessed it was in use tonight. No doubt that was where the milkmaid had taken Henry.

She was aware of a few other people nearby, at least one couple cozying up in a corner of the patio behind her, and a few others walking not far away. Therefore, she was surprised to notice another presence, one with a bit more menace. She stood straighter, wishing she had her shillelagh, and slowly turned. The highwayman was there, by the door, watching her. It seemed the more he watched her, the angrier he got.

She decided it was time to go inside, remembering what she had been told, that sometimes the Gentry came. There was a chance.... As she passed him by, he reached out, stopping her without touching her. She turned, fixing him with what she hoped was a quailing stare. He seemed unaffected. "Dance with me, my queen?" he asked, though it sounded more a venomous demand than a polite request.

"I think it would not be wise," she began.

He cut her off, rolling off the wall and slinking up to her. He loomed behind her, close enough she could feel the heat of his breath on her neck, see it in the air between them. "Ye've a waltz for a filthy pirate, but not so much as a minuet for a lowly highwayman?" he accused.

She took a single step and stopped, unable to walk away from him. She was terrified, but there was something... something she couldn't put her finger on. He took that for ascent and slipped up behind her, one hand circling her waist to pin her back against his chest, and the other capturing her slender wrist. He guided her forward, out onto the floor to a fiery music that seemed to suit his mood. He was breathing down her neck and An was suddenly aware of the view he had. She flushed from the edge of her mask all the way into her dress-line, and she felt his anger grow. He turned her suddenly, a move full of suppressed violence as he swept her across the floor.

"When is a queen not a queen?" he asked.

She was determined not to allow this man to terrorize her, tried to maintain her cool. "When she takes off her mask."

"And when this mask of ice comes off, what will you be? Queen or tart?"

"Neither," she snapped, harder than she'd intended. This anger was beginning to ring familiar, though the last time she had seen it, it had not been aimed at her. Now it was. "Why have you been watching me? Stalking me?"

He scoffed. "Stalking? That the pirate's word? You didn't notice me until he pointed me out."

"You were skulking, and I was enjoying conversation. Answer the question."

"I was looking for someone. I was hoping you weren't she, but I fear I may be mistaken. If I am, then she is not the woman I thought her to be."

Her heart skipped, threatened to not start again. "And why would that be?"

"The woman I thought her would never be this shallow. This cold and heartless."

"Because she wanted for one night to be beautiful? What little girl would not want to be a princess for a single night given the choice?"

As their tongues sparred, the moves he guided her feet through also became combative, each of them fighting for hard won ground, and An feared she was losing and suddenly realised she wanted more than anything not to lose this one. He pulled her close, crushingly close. "I am no prince," he said in her ear.

Her temple was pressed to his cheek, and she whispered, her heart caught in her throat, "No, you are a Bard, and that is just as out of reach."

SKYE WAS DANCING with Jack again. They had finally sussed out who was leading, and Skye was dancing much better. "I take it back, you actually are a fairly good dancer," Jack said teasingly.

Skye smiled, remembering who'd taught him. "I had a good teacher."

Jack suddenly smiled with his whole face, "Awww."

Skye knew instantly who it was. "Gotcha!" he grinned.

"Oh, you're a right bastard," Liberty growled, but she was smiling. "Keep it under yer hat."

"What hat?"

His attention was suddenly diverted by bumping into another couple. He turned to apologise and saw it was An with the Highwayman who'd been lurking most of the evening. They did not even acknowledge the collision and danced off, and Skye thought he saw a tear glistening in the corner of An's eye.

He watched the pair, growing angrier the more he did, until Liberty had to snap him out of it. "Don't do whatever you are thinking," she growled.

An and her partner had stopped, even though the music had not. The highwayman started to walk away, and she reached out, touched him. Skye's sword almost dropped into his fist as the man in black whirled on her, backing her up as he approached. They stopped, their voices drowned out by the music and the chatter of the oblivious. She set her hands on his chest, pleading or explaining. He seized both wrists, driving her back again, turned her so that he was pulling instead.

"So you chose to be th' Snow Queen?" he was saying. "A cold-hearted bitch who collects hearts like trophies? I expected this of Serephina. Not you."

She gave a rueful laugh, tried weakly to free her hands from his iron grip. "It is a winter ball, a come-as-you-aren't. I chose something I was not, that would attract Henry."

His grip tightened. "Henry? You want his kind of attentions?"

"No! I wanted to help Liberty, to distract him so he couldn't find her. And I've done it. He's stopped looking for her. He thinks I'm..."

He growled suddenly and let her go, thrusting her hands away from him as if their touch burned. He was still frighteningly close. "Ye thought this layer of ice and snow would protect ye from those kinds of attentions? Foolish girl. You see this?" he snarled, indicating his costume. "This I so very nearly was, but that She heard me sing first. Something like this..." he indicated her exposed shoulders, "would have attracted my attentions, all right. As prey."

An felt her throat growing tight, fought back her tears with anger. "You can have any woman you want. How can I compete with that? Just once I wanted to be worthy of your attention."

He softened suddenly, a terrible sadness in his eyes as he reached out and brushed her cheek with the back of his fingers. "What ye fail to understand, Ceobhránach, is that ye already had my attention. Ye were already worthy. It was this," he stroked her cheek again as she flushed as he knew she would. "This blush of innocence."

"Innocence is lost," she said softly.

He continued as if she hadn't spoken. "...And yer high collars and yer hidden ankles... all of it, true modesty hiding such strength, such self-sacrifice. Aye, I have women throwing themselves at m'feet." His arm went out in a sweeping gesture to encompass the whole room. "I want none o' them. Nothing of them. Their beauty is only outward and inside they are shallow and still, or if there is any depth, it's either rotten and foul or an empty void. You..." he stepped closer, and this time she did not back away. "Yer pleasant enough to look on, but yer beauty lies here," his hand on the bare skin over her heart was so cold it burned, "and here," fingertips brushed her temple behind the silver leaves of her mask. "Yer a well, Ceobhránach. Strong and steady to last, fresh enough to slack any thirst, and deep enough for a man to lose himself forever. Yer heat is buried deep and heaven help any man what finds it."

He pressed his forehead to hers, closed his eyes, breathing deep of the scent of her. An felt a single tear run down her cheek, down her throat to her breast. Tonight he smelled of the open road, a snow-covered, blood-splattered road. "Ye don't deserve me. 'Tis I who are not worthy. Ye deserve better, more. I'll only break yer heart, Ceobhránach."

They were interrupted by two things. One, the sound of a church bell beginning to toll midnight in the distance. Two, Henry.

He approached, laid his hand on Jonny's shoulder and pulled him off An. "Here now, Roberts," he snorted. "I'm claimin' my queen. Ye've had more dan enough time wit' her."

Sorrow's lips narrowed, tightened, but he did not argue. He stepped back and allowed Henry to take his place before the Snow Queen, bowing sarcastically. "All yours, Morgan. Though ye may not find her all ye expect. And for th' record, yer majesty," he added to An, "that one's less worthy than any of them."

Henry started to growl something else, but the Highway-man turned and walked away. An wanted to go after him, but she could feel the magic fading with every stroke of the bell and her limbs weakening in response. Her vision was beginning to cloud over. The next thing she knew, Henry was untying the silk ribbons that held her mask in place and she reached up to catch it and lift it out of her hair.

Around them, everyone was unmasking with gasps of shock and gales of laughter and more than one wife smacking her husband. Henry stared down at An stupefied that he had been so wrong. He looked up, saw Liberty standing next to Skye, waving at him. Then his eyes lit on the milkmaid who, as she took off her mask and the last peal of the bell rolled away, became bent and haggard; her once lustrous dark brown hair becoming stringy, grey and coarse. Henry's eyes popped and his mouth dropped open in horror and revulsion even as the old woman cackled in true wicked witch fashion.

More than one person, An half-noticed, was having moments of horrified regret. At least one, though, had only a few seconds of 'eww' before contemplating the matter, then seemed all right, even impressed.

An's eyes cast about, looking for Jonny Sorrow. He was by the French doors, walking out, his mask still on. She ran, stopping in the door-frame, called after him.

He paused, slowly turned. He took her in, from her honey-brown hair, still elaborately dressed in a cascade of curls and sprays of crystals, to the faery damask gown that she still filled rather nicely, even though the artificial beauty had faded. Her eyes were once more dark voids swirling with mist and fog, and tears glittered in their corners. He crossed back to her, regarding her with a tip of his head, a very raven-like gesture. He looked up to the lintel of the door above their heads. Then, without warning or preamble, he seized her, crushing her against him and kissed her.

It was long and deep and passionate, full of his temper and his fire and something she dared not name. She was startled, shocked, and had no time to melt or stiffen or react. The kiss was a volcano erupting, and it took her breath away, devoured her. Everything stopped in the wake of that first kiss: the world, time, her heart, all thought. Then, just as suddenly, it ended and, with a rush of white feathers against her cheeks, he was gone and she was cold and alone in the doorway without a thought in her head. Quite reasonably, she slipped to the floor in a dead faint.

There was a roar from behind her as Skye rushed forward, pushing Mikey aside. He checked her over, glaring off into the night at the white raven winging away. Liberty was there, the voice of reason and control, ordering someone to fetch a couch and telling Skye to pick her up.

Skye obeyed, gathering her up easily, and growled. "Ah'll break his manky wings fer this."

Liberty popped his arm. "Ye'll leave him be is what ye'll do," she snapped, shooing people out of the way as they brought her to the fainting couch Mikey carried in.

"After what he just did?"

"All he did was kiss her under th' mistletoe, ye Highland ass!" she snapped, began to rub An's wrist.

"Ah may not be experienced in th' arts, but a kiss shouldna have that effect!"

Liberty put her hands on her hips and glared up at him, held up her fingers, counting off her points. "One, that was prob'ly her first kiss. Ever. Two, that was intense... passionate. Hell, it'd have curled even MY toes. Three, it happened suddenly and in public and she's Victorian. Add those up and faintin's a perfectly reasonable response. Now th' lot o' ye back off! She's goin' ta be mortified enough when she comes to."

Most began to move away, though Roulet trotted up, handed Liberty a small vial which she broke and wafted under An's nose.

An came to with a start, trying to escape the foul stench. She sat up slowly. Her vision was foggy. Not even Liberty was coming in clearly. It was like walking from bright sunlight into a darkened room. It was getting better, but very slowly.

Roulet was leaning over the back of the couch, smiling down at her. "Your coach melted, I'm afraid."

"What?" she asked, looking over her shoulder, confused.

"Your coach. It was out front all night. It just melted, polar bears and all." She glanced down at the 'ice' at her breast and on her throat. "Luckily, that's the only thing. You still got yer bling, girl."

Liberty fingered the pendant. "That is lovely. How do ye feel?"

"Embarrassed, heart-broken, tired and blind," she sighed. "I'll be fine."

Liberty laughed softly, elbowing Skye as he loomed too close. "After that, I imagine it will be a bit before yer 'fine'. Either way, we have to go outside shortly. Even th' orchestra is packing up."

Skye looked over at the band, was surprised to see they were still what they had seemed to be earlier: goblins in tuxedos. The man who had been dressed as a djinni, complete with blue skin and Arab clothing, was handing the conductor a bag. He turned around after the exchange and began to cross the floor, telling various groups to grab what food they wanted and head out to the Green. It was Ian.

Henry was suddenly there, glaring at Liberty. "You planned alla dis, didn't ye?" he accused.

"Well, I didn't plan on the Highwayman or have aught to do with what Baba did to you," she began, though a faint twinge told An this was not entirely true. She laughed as Henry shuddered at that. "But that's not to say I didn't enjoy it. Ye brought it on yerself. If ye'd not been braggin' ye'd know who I was by cheatin', I'd never have got th' idea to go to th' witch in th' first place."

Henry started to say something, reaching for Liberty's hand, but Ian's voice stopped him. "Not so fast, Henry. Yer forgettin' sommat."

He turned, glared over at him. "She's mine 'til ye win her, Green Man."

Ian laughed. "What yer forgettin', Holly King," he said deliberately, "is that neither of us found her, so... neither of us starts with her. 'Tis on even ground, we are, boi. No early spring, no long winter."

Henry growled, but dropped his hand. "Shall we battle, den?" he asked sarcastically.

Ian nodded. He took a moment to check on An. "Yeh all right, lass?"

"I will be. I can walk out on m' own," she said, standing. She was still flush, but managing. He nodded again as the group began to head for the door.

Liberty took An's arm, remembering she did not have her shillelagh with her for a guide. "What'd ye pay them with this year?" she asked her father.

He chuckled. "A handful of gold coin and a brace of Rubik's cubes. That ought to keep them happy some while."

As the others laughed at the joke which Skye did not get, he stripped off his jacket, and tossed it along with his shirt over the back of a rocking chair on the newly restored veranda. "Oi, Chief," he said. "Havya any paint?"

Ian looked back at him. "No, I've no woad. Not a real war."

Skye sighed. "Had to ask."

As he stretched, his naked chest rippling in the light of the newly kindled fires, he heard several whistles and calls of appreciation. The loudest was from the old woman who trailed behind, looking like the cat that ate the canary. She winked at Henry who could not suppress a shudder and hurried out to the field to round up his side.

Someone brought Skye the wooden claymore.

"Try not to break any heads with tha'," Ian called as he strode out onto the field.

Liberty led An and a handful of others, mostly women but not all, over to the bandstand to sit and watch the battle. One of the fires was near enough to provide sufficient heat, even though the night was warm for December as far as An was concerned. She found herself seated between Liberty and Solitaire, as Roulet had gone out onto the battlefield.

Henry came over to them as the final groups were lining up and got himself a kiss from Solitaire.

Liberty scowled at him, teasing, "Oi, gettin' kisses from someone other than yer queen in front of yer queen's bad form. Bad luck for you."

He growled at her, peeling off his coat and hat to allow his antlers free rein, "Takin' the kiss of an unwillin' woman inta battle's worse luck, wench."

The women in the pavilion laughed at that, and Solitaire shooed him off.

An could begin to see some of the combatants. Ian had gone full gryffon and, as he trotted up to square off against him, Henry went full stag. Ian was enormous. Even Skye standing near him seemed small.

Ian's voice was loud and clear as it rang out over the battlefield. "I, Ian the Gryffon O'Keefe, the Oak King, challenge fer sovereignty. The days are growin' long an' warm and yer time on this earth is done. Lay aside yer crown or I'll break it from yer head."

"And 'tis welcome ye are t' try, ye nut-headed antique!"

With that, both armies rushed forward, and the melee began.

An was still too absorbed in recent events to watch the battle with any interest. She was only just beginning to see more than the strongest magics, everything else was still a blur.

Something did click with her, distracting her thankfully from her moody ruminations. "Ye lied to Henry... sort of. Ye did have aught t' do with Baba and he..." she blushed, and didn't finish her sentence.

Liberty and Solitaire both laughed, and Solitaire leaned in. "Well, she made the agreement, but I had more to do with that bit of embarrassment. You see, her price for the charms was a bit of Henry."

"A button, a hair, anythin' from his person," Liberty grinned.

"So I got him alone in the maze and... got a ...hair," she said, leaving a great deal unsaid to preserve An's dignity. It had been bruised enough that night.

"So she used it t' cheat th' magics and find him?" An asked.

Liberty nodded. "He's been a mite rude of late, and she felt he needed some takin' down. Poor ol' girl doesn't get laid that often. She takes it where she can get it."

"Here, here!" Solitaire crowed, raising her glass in toast. An found herself blushing nonetheless.

Someone in the back cringed and made a sound of sympathetic pain at something that happened on the battlefield.

"You did a brilliant job with Henry though," Solitaire added, laughing. "That touch about removing his 'letters of marque' had him convinced. He thought you were referring to his gonads."

Liberty laughed. "That would seal th' deal."

"It was not what I meant," An blushed.

"Just as well. Not that he'd ever have considered I'd be dressed as a man," she chuckled.

They watched the war below for a bit, the only noise the sounds of battle and the cheering on of the people watching. An found her fingertips brushing her lips thoughtfully. Remembrance left her warm inside as she pondered what it could have meant.

"That was some kiss though, huh?" Solitaire's voice drifted in through An's reverie.

Liberty glared over An's head at her friend as An began to blush again. Solitaire put up her hands in surrender. "I wish I had a man would kiss me like that, just sayin'."

"Still not a conquest?" came the snide voice of the woman in silver.

An looked up to see Serephina lurking in the corner, watching her. She was surprised by the calmness of her answer. "Conquest implies seduction, not courtship. A 'love them and leave them'. One does not waste a great deal of time or effort on 'conquests'."

"So how long is long enough? Before you give him your other cherry?"

"Serephina!" Liberty snapped. "That is quite enough. Either comport yerself with some decorum or get off elsewhere. Woman's done naught to ye to warrant that kinda venom."

"You can't banish me from the Rest, Liberty, for all you're the ritual Queen and the Chief's daughter."

Liberty stood, every inch both of the things the woman had just accused her of being. "Oh, can't I? Th' ritual is in full swing, and I hold all power in matters of my court. As fer th' other, with yer reputation ye really think Da will even ask fer a reason should I ask?" She didn't wait for the woman's response before she continued. "And don't even think about bringin' that shite inta m' bar. I know what ye were tryin' t' do all last month. I even suspect yer goadin' her or any other o' my patrons an' I'll have ye thrown out like th' trash ye are."

An saw something flash in the woman's eyes and reached up, setting her hand on Liberty's arm to warn her. "Not on my account," she whispered.

Serephina humphed and stormed off, disappearing into the night back towards the carriage house.

Anything more was interrupted by a bellow like that of an elk being taken down and the cry of an eagle in triumph. Then the crowd was parting as Ian strode forth to claim his prize, filling in his wake. The wreath on his brow grew into a shining crown of Oak branches, the leaves a verdant green and subtle hints of mistletoe interwoven. He stood before the bandstand, mostly man again and looked up to his daughter who stood on the top step looking down at him. Vines of winter flowers and greenery had grown down around her Jack costume and formed a rough gown. The coronet on her shining brow was made of fir with bright holly berries and edelweiss.

"I am th' Oak King, and th' lightening year is mine," Ian announced, his voice deep and loud enough for all to hear.

She nodded her head regally, looking out over the two armies made whole, beaten and sore. "I am yours, my king, I and all my gifts."

Ian knelt before her, as Henry had six months past, arms spread. "Yer blessing, I beg, Bright May. For we are tired o' th' cold and th' dark and long fer Spring."

She descended the steps, stopping on the last, and placed the healing kiss upon her father's forehead. For extra measure, she plucked a snow-drop from her gown over her heart and tucked it into his crown.

Ian grinned up at her, even as the collective sigh of relief flowed out of the crowd as the healing flowed in.

Skye stood just back from Ian and Mikey, looking up at Liberty, his eyes bright. He could not help but notice the two women at the top of the steps flanking her: Solitaire, in her watery gown of the Lady of the Lake, and An as the now crownless Snow Queen. Both women were shining as the moon peeked through a hole in the clouds.

When Liberty stood again, and Ian took his place beside her, she was radiant and the fields began to smell more like flowers than sweat and churned earth. All around them, the magically placed snow began to melt, though the night remained near forty degrees.

Ian raised his arms and shouted for the after party to begin, and people began to stream towards the tables of food that had been brought out while they'd been fighting. Drink was more popular, as was the dancing area once it was cleared, and the Rest's handful of musicians brought out their instruments and began to play rousing country music.

An was not surprised when Cipín, her shillelagh, found her, slipping into her hand with a wooden sigh. She was grateful, having missed her once the masks had come off. She wandered around the gathering party for a little while, looking and hoping, but not at all surprised when she found no sign of Jonny. Well before two, she found herself passing through the woods back home, a quiet joy battling an incredible sadness in her heart.

This is an excerpt from Lady of the Mist. A story about a Victorian Irish woman who served as a governess for 3 royal fey children for 150 before losing her eyesight trying to save them. Once again in the real world, able to see only magic, she is swept up into a community of people who, like her, have left Faery changed. This scene is the yearly Yule ball, a masquerade event so sacred that even the Gentry sometimes attend. Considered a plain woman, An seeks for one night to be beautiful, with hopes of catching the eyes of the community's Bard, a man of impossible beauty. Having asked the children she once taught for a chance at 'the faery tale', they have granted her desire and wished her the best of it.

ABOUT S. L. THORNE

A Florida author, SL prefers historical or fantasy settings to modern ones and is a stickler for historical accuracy; often doing exhaustive research during the course of novel writing in order to present a believable, enduring world where things make real world sense along side the magical and the invented. She often refers to herself as 'a professional liar' instead of 'an author', as she is in 'the business of weaving a fantastic, unbelievable lie and presenting it in such a way that, at least within the confines of the pages, the reader wants to believe it is the truth.'

Fans of her novels tend to be somewhat rabid, often pushing her into publishing books she otherwise would have kept to herself. Writes because there is really no choice. The stories will just not leave her alone until she writes them. It all began as a way for a very small insomniac to fall asleep.

STORY IV
JACQUELINE AND THE BURROWING BEANSTALK BY S. FRASHER

Heat Level: Low
(PG content)

JACQUELINE AND THE
BURROWING BEANSTALK

I like that I had a unique upbringing, though it made me strange to my peers, it helped me become perfectly equipped for my destiny. When I was a child, my father taught me how to do many things, one of which was how to cut down trees with an axe. I had always been much stronger than the other children my age, and it wasn't long before I could hold and swing the axe well enough to fell a tree on my own. One day, when my father was away hunting and my mother was pregnant with my brother, a chill had settled deep into our house. I wanted to do something to make my mother happy, back when I still thought pleasing her was possible, so I decided I would chop us some wood and build her a big fire to sit in front of. With puffs of hot air slipping from my lips, I trekked up to an old tree and began chopping with my axe. After a few swings, the tree began to teeter over, and when it fell, it crushed a bird that had landed on the ground beside it. I couldn't hear the crunch of its bones, but I could see its guts shoot out from all sides of the fallen tree. Tears immediately poured from my eyes, and I ran from the tree, forsaking my original plan of cutting up wood and instead hid in my room under the covers until my mother came to wake me for breakfast. I still think about that bird from time to time, wishing I could have changed its fate.

ANOTHER DAY, *the same as the one before.* I thought to myself as the morning call of the rooster woke me from my slumber. I should have been born anywhere else than in that small provincial town, to a mother who barely had two widow's mites to rub together and hardly cared at all about me. I was tired. Tired of daily chores and my miserable mother. But I was used to it. I was nearly always exhausted, ever since my father's death. When he died, I was left to spend all of my days working on the family farm to keep us alive. And after the work was complete, while I should have been sleeping, I escaped into my books well into the wee hours of the morning. Sometimes I would pretend the stories I read were my own and my life was filled with great adventure and earth-shattering love instead of daily suffering and monotony. I miss my father every day. He was brave, strong, and kind, but he died young, leaving me, my mother, and my brother to survive in this unforgiving world without him. Dreaming of a better life.

I stand out in my town because I'm a dreamer, but I'm also different from the others around me in many other ways. As previously stated, I'd rather disappear into my father's old tomes than attend town events or court men. And instead of running around with my peers as a child, I spent most of my days with my father, learning how to shoot a bow and arrow, swing a sword, and research mythological creatures. Finally, the most obvious difference is that I don't physically look like the other women in my town. They all are petite, delicate creatures with fair skin and soft hair. I'm sturdy and tall, built wide like my ex-soldier father with thighs that touch, hands rough like sandpaper from working the fields, and tanned skin from hours under the sun. Every time I go into town, I hear people whispering about me,

"That girl, her head is in the clouds, thinks herself too good for us."

Or, *"Good thing she's buying men's work clothes. Doubt anything made for the ladies would fit her."* I'd be lying if I said the comments didn't sting.

"Jacqueline! Come down here!" My mother's shrill voice screamed up the stairs. I'm surprised it didn't crack the mirror I was looking into. I gave myself one final glance in our old funhouse mirror, and all I could see was a smattering of sun freckles across my nose and piercing green eyes like my father's staring back at me. "Jacqueline!" She snapped again. My mother was the only one who called me Jacqueline. Most people called me Jac. I took the stairs two at a time, each one creaking loudly from age as I stomped my foot down on them.

"Yes, Mother?"

"I need you to take Old Bess into town today." She gestured out the window to our aging cow.

"Why?"

Mother released an exasperated sigh. "Most children do as they're told without asking questions." I just stared at her, waiting for a response. She forgets that I stopped being a child long ago, after I had to sacrifice time and again to help this family survive. Not to mention I had passed eighteen a few years ago. "We don't have enough money for the seeds I ordered for this planting season. I need you to sell Bess and bring home the seeds from the town market." My heart cracked a little. We had raised Bess from a little calf, and she had lived on the farm nearly my entire life.

"There has to be another way. Maybe we—"

Mother interrupted me, a look of irritation on her features. She had once been beautiful, as lithe and dainty as all the other women in this town, but grief and age had taken her since then. "I won't hear of it, Jacqueline. Sell Bess and bring home the seeds." She pointed her bent, arthritic finger toward the door. "Go!" So out I went.

Bess moo'ed as I approached, blissfully unaware that this was our last morning together. Tears gathered in my eyes as I thought about giving her away. Why does life have to be so hard? "Come on, old girl." I lovingly scratched behind her ear before looping a lead around her neck. "Let's hope your new home is a kind one."

A mile or so down the road from my house, I began to make out a figure in the distance. A person stood on the side of the road, a large bag on the ground beside them. They looked as if they were waiting for someone. As I got closer, I could begin to see the features of a devastatingly handsome man, tall in stature with a broad, muscular build. His dark hair framed his face, a slight wave to it, and his jawline could have cut diamonds. He looked up and smiled at me.

You know those moments in life that feel utterly right? As if nothing else made sense before? That's how I felt when my eyes connected with his. For a second, I forgot that I was poor, that my life was hard, and that I didn't fit in — all I saw was him. And by the way he stammered his introduction, I wanted to think he felt the same.

"H-hello." He said with an awestruck smile. "Just the person I've been waiting for."

"Me?" I questioned, looking over my shoulder as if someone may be behind me.

This question earned me a laugh, "Yes." My heart hammered in my chest. "I have something I'd like to trade." And my hope deflated. He didn't want me; he wanted to sell his wares.

"Oh," I laughed nervously, hoping he didn't notice the burning blush that had settled over my cheeks. "What are you selling?"

"I have an object here with magical properties. Something that will give you your heart's desires." A devilish smile played on his full lips, and my mind ran through everything I desired. *Him.* No, stop. He's a stranger. What do I want? *Money, security, love.* I reached down in my pocket, feeling for the single coin in there, knowing I didn't have enough money to buy something magical.

"I don't think I can afford it." I began to walk away, leading Bess behind me as I went. A warm hand wrapped around my arm, sending a shiver down my spine. He had touched me, and he looked equally as affected by it as I felt. His eyes held a question in them. "Are you okay?" His brows were furrowed, his eyes yet to have left where our bodies touched.

He snapped out of it, ignoring my question to ask one of his own. "Would you trade your cow for what I have?" His blue eyes stared at me, and it felt like he was seeing my very soul.

"Would you be kind to her?"

"I give you my word. She will live her last days out like a cow queen." His voice contained jest, but he seemed sincere in his promise to care for her. I don't know if it was his ethereal beauty or something more profound, but he must have had me under some kind of spell because the next thing I said was,

"Okay." I handed him Bess' lead and held my hand out to take the magical item he had, the item that would grant me my heart's desires. Some may think it frivolous to hand over Bess for the promise of magic—but I could hear my father's voice in my head, urging me to buy it.

"Here you go." I felt three little balls fall into my hand.

"Beans?" I questioned. I had grown enough plants in my life to recognize bean seeds.

"Magical beans." His smile nearly knocked me over.

"What do I do with them?" I asked, holding them closer to my face as if inspecting them would tell me their secrets.

"Plant them," he said, though his smile didn't waver.

"That's it?" I asked suspiciously, wondering what the catch was.

"Plant them, and they will grow down into the ground. And overnight you will find yourself on the path to what you desire most." I swear his eyes drifted down to my mouth when he said desire, and my blush returned.

"What kind of backward beanstalk burrows into the earth instead of stalking up?" He laughed at my question.

"Soon you will see, Jacqueline." And off he went, towing Bess behind him, not even pausing long enough for me to ask him how he possibly could know my name.

I returned home, nearly giddy that I had managed to get my hands on a magical object. My father had told me of magic, but always said it was rare in the human realm and that if I ever happened upon it, I should snatch it up. What luck that I should find some!

"That was fast. I didn't expect anyone would be so eager to take an aging dairy cow off our hands." My mother commented when I entered the kitchen. "How much did you get for her?"

I smiled, excited to tell her of the bean's magic and the promise the stranger had made about their ability to make our heart's desires come true. I held out my hand, displaying the beans proudly. "Three magic beans."

"Magic beans?" Her face fell. "Where are the seeds I said to get from town?" When I didn't answer, her face contorted into rage. "You sold our cow for three measly beans?" She screamed, causing my brother to slowly step into the room and assess the situation.

"They're magic." I offered, hoping she would understand.

"Magic isn't real!" She slapped me across the face.

"Father said it was!"

"Well, your father was a fool, as are you." I could handle her insulting me; she had done it my whole life, but I hated when she spoke ill of my father. "Who sold you these?"

I couldn't help the dreamy look that crossed my face at the mention of my handsome stranger. "A man up the road, he said they would give me my heart's desires."

"You daft girl! You let a beautiful stranger deceive you." She looked at me mockingly. "Did he flirt? Did you think he would love you if you gave him what he wanted?" The laugh that followed was filled with cruelty. "Look at you." My mother had once come from money, and beauty had been her main commodity, so she detested our poorness and my appearance — this she always made abundantly clear. I often wondered what my father had seen in her. "Get out of my sight."

I ran up the stairs, hot angry tears spilling down my cheeks. When I reached my bedroom, I slammed open the window and threw the beans out, wanting them as far away from me as possible. Soft pings sounded when they collided with the cellar door, but I didn't look to see where they landed. Shame, rage, and another foreign feeling were all coursing through my veins.

"Jac?" My brother whispered. "You okay?"

"I will be." I sniffled and turned away, and he took the hint that I wanted to be alone. Maybe I was stupid, blinded by pretty promises and an attractive face. How foolish could I have been?

THE ROOSTER CRIED, and I awoke. Same as every other day. My mother refused to leave her bed, screaming through the door that my foolish decisions had ruined us. So, I did what I always did and took care of everything on my own. I fed my brother breakfast, tended to the fields, and gathered eggs from our hens. I hadn't forgotten about the magic beans, but I had forgotten the handsome stranger's promise that they would grow overnight. It wasn't until I went down to the cellar for canned peaches that I remembered what he said, *"Overnight, you will find yourself on the path to what you desire most."*

My mouth dropped open in shock at what was before me. The dank cellar had been transformed into a wonderland. Fireflies by the dozens flitted around, casting the room in a warm glow, and the once flat dirt floor was covered in vines and looked cavernous. A large hole, big enough for me to crawl down, sat in the middle of the cellar, right under the crack between the cellar doors. When I had thrown the beans, they had fallen through the tiny gap between the cellar doors and implanted themselves in the dirt floor, burrowing a hole into the ground and growing thick, ropey vines overnight. Just as the stranger had said they would. My heart quickened at the thought of him, almost as if he were with me. For some reason, the memory of him felt stronger in the presence of the burrowing beanstalk. Each thick vine reminded me of the thick veins that decorated his arms, and the soft hue flashing from the fireflies reminded me of the twinkle in his eyes as he smiled at me. Just the thought of him made me feel like I was floating. But I was snapped back to reality quickly when I heard a haunting, plucky tune emanating from the cavern beneath me. The music, though beautiful, vexed my soul. As much as I wanted to investigate the burrow and the promises made to me by my handsome stranger, the music compelled me to rush out of the cellar and slam the doors closed.

I could hear the haunting melody as I went through my daily chores — it was never ceasing. For days it could be faintly heard from all corners of my home and property. I couldn't escape it. Even as I sat at dinner days later, trying to listen to my mother discuss town gossip, I could hear the plucks of a harp in the background. Neither my mother nor my brother commented on the music, so I assumed they couldn't hear it and, thankfully, my mother had yet to venture down into the cellar. I didn't know how I was going to explain the unknowingly deep crevasse that had magically appeared under our house.

"…missing, all of them." Mother paused. "Jacqueline!" She snapped at me. "Are you listening to me?"

No, I'm busy thinking about the cerulean eyes of my handsome stranger and trying to drown out the plucky harp noises emanating from our cellar. "Sorry, Mother, what did you say?"

"Eight boys have gone missing from town." She eyed my brother nervously.

"What?" I was shocked. Nothing ever happened in our little town. It was many things, boring and predictable, but it was also safe.

"Up and vanished, all of them. The Town Council is thinking about organizing a search party later this week."

"Do they think they're lost or…?" I trailed off, not wanting to say what we were both thinking. That someone, or something, was taking or hurting them.

Mother looked somber and eyed my brother carefully. "Just be extra mindful of him until this gets sorted." I watched him as he shoveled way too many corn kernels into his mouth and then smiled wide up at me. I would go to the ends of the earth to protect him, my only true family member left. My mother watched him lovingly, for some reason she had always preferred him to me. She smiled sorrowfully, no doubt thinking about the grief she'd feel if he were among the missing.

"I will." And it was a promise I intended to keep.

THE NEXT DAY I was harvesting corn, plucking cob after cob from the stalks and tossing them into my gathering basket to the tune of that tragic harp song, when something caught my eye. My brother was walking ramrod straight and without wavering from the backfield. And he didn't have his gathering basket with him.

"Brother!" I yelled toward him. "Where is your basket? Don't tell me there aren't any cobs ready in the backfield because I won't believe you!" He didn't even flinch. He continued toward the house, marching his feet in a peculiar pattern. "Brother!" Again, he didn't stop. And suddenly, it clicked. He was marching his feet to the beat of the harp's tune. As I watched him march in a daze toward the cellar doors, I figured out with sobering clarity where all the missing boys had gone. "Stop!" I yelled futilely as I pumped my arms and ran as fast as I could. But he was so far ahead of me that he had already descended the ladder before I made it to the cellar doors. "Brother! If you can hear me, stop!" He got down on his hands and knees and disappeared into the burrow. I jumped from the ladder, the shock of the landing stinging in my feet, shins, and ankles. Assessing the situation, I could see the cellar was much like I last left it, dirty and covered in vines and fireflies. After yelling for my brother once more without a response, I got on my hands and knees and followed him down the hole.

I had never considered myself claustrophobic until that moment, though I had never faced a scenario to test it out either. Still, I could hardly stand the feeling of the tunnel around me, squeezing in tighter and tighter as I descended into the cavern. I whispered my brother's name a few times, hoping for a response, but got none. Had it not been for the faint light of the fireflies illuminating the tunnel, I might have gone mad, lost my nerve, or both. And once I thought I couldn't take anymore, the tunnel opened up, and I could finally see the beanstalk I had been promised. It was thick, nearly four feet in diameter, covered in hardy vines, and it hadn't stopped at burrowing into the dirt beneath my home. Around the stalk was another wide hole. Lying flat on my stomach, I shimmied to the hole's edge and looked down. Yet again, shock overtook me as I looked through fluffy clouds and down upon a village. It was as if I were standing in the sky.

"Brother!" I whisper-yelled once more and again received no answer. I didn't want to believe he might be climbing down the beanstalk into this unknown world, but there was nowhere else in the cavern for him to have gone. After several minutes of looking, I finally saw his mop of brown hair, and he was nearly halfway down the stalk. I remembered my promise to my mother, my promise to protect him. My hands grew moist as I considered my only option — I had to go down the beanstalk. I aggressively wiped my hands on my pants, grabbed firm to the closest vine I could reach, and began my descent. Over and over in my mind, I repeated that this was just like climbing trees to harvest honey, ignoring the fact that the trees I climbed were never hundreds of feet in the air or in another world.

I was about halfway down, descending more quickly than my brother, when a screech sounded somewhere close and pierced the air. Had I not been holding on for dear life, my first reaction would have been to cover my ears. Searching around for what could have made that noise, it didn't take me long to spot the hoard of giant birds flying toward the stalk. And when I say giant, I mean giant. Birds nearly ten feet tall, with wings double that, had made their way to the beanstalk, flying close enough to me that I could eventually see they weren't birds at all.

An image from one of my mythology books flashed in my mind. Beautiful faces and full breasts like a human woman, but the wings and talons of a falcon — known for destruction and kidnapping men. They were Harpies. Though not a man, my brother was still male, and it was suddenly clear why only boys had gone missing from my town. My brother had only just touched down on the ground when a Harpy swooped down and scooped him up with her talons, flying away with him toward the castle in the distance. Said castle maybe a mile away and was itself surrounded by swarming Harpies.

"No!" I cried and frantically climbed the rest of the way down the beanstalk. When my feet hit the ground, I immediately searched for aid, but taking in my surroundings gave me pause as I found myself in a nearly identical replica of my hometown. Though this one was covered in vines and cast in a magical hue, the resemblance was uncanny.

"As above, so below." A voice like honey and fire sounded from behind me. I recognized it instantly, and it simultaneously made me want to melt with desire and thrash with rage.

I spun on my heels and pointed an accusatory finger toward my handsome stranger. "You!" My face contorted in rage. This was his fault.

He pulled his lips in a pout and clenched his fist to his chest. "I thought you'd be happy to see me."

"I might have been a day ago, before my brother was taken and I found out your magical gift was a trap." I spat at him, and his face fell at hearing of my brother.

"It wasn't a gift. It was a trade." Such a strange point to get stuck on.

"You lied to me."

"I do not lie." He spoke calmly.

"You said I would have my heart's desire! I did not desire for this to happen! For a hole to open up under my house or for a Harpy to steal my brother."

"You know of Harpies?" He sounded shocked.

"My father used to read me books about such creatures."

"Of course he did." He nodded knowingly.

"How did that stalk even grow? It's not bean season." I gestured with exasperation. "And what did you do with my cow?"

Genuine laughter, despite the morose circumstances, spilled from his lips. I shot him a withering stare. "I'm sorry, you're just asking the most adorable questions, given the circumstances."

"Maybe I'm in shock." I deadpanned.

"Touché." He replied. "We had nature mages spell the beans to grow as they did, and your cow is safe and will be returned to you at no cost once you are back home."

"How can I believe you?" I eyed him suspiciously, even though my gut told me I should trust him.

"Our journey is not yet complete. You'll have to trust me on that. I'm sorry your brother was taken. You have to believe I didn't know the Harpies would take human boys. They've never done that before." My gaze softened when I sensed the sincerity in his tone. "I will help you save him."

"Human boys?" I asked warily. "You say that as if you are not also one."

That smile hit me like a ton of bricks. "Your father told you of magical creatures?"

"Yes."

"What did he tell you of Fae?" A coy smirk pulled at the corner of his lips, and I was very aware that he was slowly stepping closer to me. My whole body was aware of this, and I was responding to him in ways I never had before — heart racing, mouth drying, hands itching to caress him.

"That they are beautiful and not to make deals with them."

"He was right on two accounts." He winked. "But might I convince you to reconsider the no deals rule?" That smile and wicked look in his eye could convince me to do a whole lot.

I answered his question with a question. "Who are you?"

He didn't even hesitate. "I am Prince Theo of the Fae realm, and I need you." Those last three words were my undoing.

"Need me?" I asked, voice shaking. His piercing eyes appraised me, looking into my soul with softness and respect. That gaze told a thousand stories, all of which I wanted to hear.

"I cannot save the realm without you. I cannot save your brother without you." He gestured to the path. "Follow me, please." His gaze turned desperate, and, for some reason, my very soul trusted him. So, I followed. Something about him was safe and familiar, and despite all my logical thoughts to avoid strangers and fear this foreign realm — I couldn't resist him. My hesitance notwithstanding, something deep inside of me felt as if I would have given him the very breath from my lungs for the promise of more moments in his presence. And that was a foreign and frightening thought.

Deeper and deeper into the forest we trekked, basking in the warmth of the easy silence that had settled around us. I had a million questions, but no words to ask them. So, we carried on in stillness.

After nearly an hour, we came upon a fallen log, and without a second thought, he reached a hand out to me. I took his offering, noting the odd studying gaze in his eyes as I did so. The moment our hands touched, sparks flew, shocking both my hand and my soul. I stumbled and would have fallen had his strong arms not righted me before I hit the ground.

"Thank you, Prince Theo."

"Please, just Theo."

The look he gave me, one of shock and awe, made my mouth go dry, so I nodded in understanding and waited several moments before I asked. "What was that?" Gesturing about to refer to the sparks that had just danced before my eyes.

"Don't worry, that happens when you touch your—"

"When you touch your what?"

He cleared his throat. "Sometimes when people touch in the Fae realm. We're almost to camp." He changed the subject, and I allowed it.

"Camp? Don't Princes live in castles?"

A humorless smile pulled at his lips. "They do when said castle isn't overrun with Harpies who can easily put men in a trance and eat them."

"Only men?" I asked.

"Only men. Trust me. I wouldn't pull you into this if I thought it unsafe for you." And again, for some reason, I believed him. After walking in silence for so long, I was pleased the dam of conversation had broken, because there was much I wanted to know.

"How long have the Harpies been here?"

"Alive? Hundreds of years. Cursing my kingdom? Only a few." His face shifted, a mix of grief and anger. "But sometimes it feels like many life-times have passed since their arrival."

"They've brought great sorrow to your kingdom?"

He nodded. "Death of thousands, destruction of the castle, rot to our land," he paused before continuing. "The Harpy Queen killed my parents."

I had no words, so I acted. Grabbing his hand in mine, I used it to pull him close to me. His arms wrapped around me instinctually, as if they belonged there. My frame, which was anything but dainty in my realm, was easily encased by his girth and stature. His arms found their way around me with what felt like rehearsed ease, though this was our first embrace. His forehead melded to mine, allowing our eyes to meet as his hands worked their way to the nape of my neck and his fingers threaded into my hair. His gaze held grief mixed with pride, and somewhere deep within them an affection he had no reason to be looking at me with appeared as well.

As quickly as the moment came — it passed. And we found ourselves once again walking the path through the woods — though this time we were hand in hand.

"I feel I should have asked this earlier, but where exactly are we going?" He smirked at my question. I cursed that mouth of his and its constant upturning that continued to send my heart fluttering. He held out his hand again before answering, helping me over another fallen log — no sparks flew this time. After I traversed the log, he didn't let go just yet. He let his gaze and hand linger on mine before releasing me with a sigh.

"We're going to my camp, where those important to my kingdom, many of my citizens, and my army live as we prepare to battle the Harpies."

"And why is it so deep in the forest?"

"The tree coverage keeps the Harpies from being able to fly over and spot us."

"And in the winter?"

"We move around and go to the Evergreen Forest when the other trees lose their leaves." He looked at me, eyes full of hope. "But hopefully this is our last season in hiding."

The noise of camp drew my attention, distracting me from asking any more questions.

"Welcome to Camp Hope."

We stepped into a clearing, and a flurry of activity assaulted my vision. The camp was like a thriving nomadic village, with covered carriages, tents, and tabernacles scattered all around. I could smell bonfires and cooking meat, and children ran in circles around us laughing at the game they were playing. But what I saw next stopped me in my tracks.

I stood, slack-jawed, watching the army train. "Impressive, right?" I could hear the pride in his voice as we watched the all-female army engaged in practice combat. They moved as if they were dancing, slicing their swords through the air with rehearsed ease. Best of all, they all looked like me. Not a wispy frail thing among them — they all stood tall with broad chests and hips.

"They're incredible." My eyes filled with tears. I had never seen a group of women who looked like me. Women who didn't look like they were skipping meals to fit into their proper dresses.

"Best army in the entire realm." He beamed.

"All women?" I asked.

"Typically, it's evenly split, but since the Harpies prey on men, we gave the men different duties and transitioned all the fighting force onto our female warriors."

"And are all Fae women so…" I tried to find the words, but after being unable to, I decided to move my hands to represent their feminine curves.

Theo's warm laughter was a blessing to my ears. "Yes, thank God that most Fae women are blessed that way. Unlike the ailing, wispy women I saw in your village." He paused in consideration for a moment. "I don't know how men can lay with them and not break them in half."

My face heated in an instant blush. "Beautiful." I choked out.

He looked at me, eyes hungrily trailing up and down my body before he settled on my face. "Yes, you are." I didn't understand exactly what he meant. It was only happenstance that I looked so much like the Fae women. Our gaze held, as if unspoken promises were being passed between us, and we stayed that way for many moments. We only stopped when a warrior approached us.

"Your Highness." She nodded her head in respectful acknowledgment of me. "I assume this is the woman you've been waiting for?" Her words threw me off balance.

"What?" It was the Prince's turn to turn red. He rubbed the back of his neck nervously.

"We hadn't gotten to the prophecy yet, Captain."

"Prophecy?" I said this as a question, but it almost came out as a laugh.

"Shall we go to the strategy tent?" The Captain offered.

"Good idea." Theo held his hand out to me, seemingly desperate to have a hand on me again. "Please come with me." As if I'd stop following him at this point.

We moved further into camp, greeted by citizens as we walked toward the strategy tent. It was hard to miss, standing extremely tall and being draped in dark purple canvas. The Fae warrior, who was nearly half a foot taller than I, walked in without having to duck her head at all, as did the even taller Prince.

Once inside, the Captain and Theo made their way to a table, which was covered in maps and schematics of the castle and fields beyond. I half expected him to sit on a throne as we talked, but instead, he sat by me, thigh brushing mine under the table.

"So...a prophecy?" I asked, trying to focus on the task at hand rather than the tingling sensation that started where our legs were touching and was pulsating all throughout my body.

"Yes, well, before we get into that, I think it'd be good to tell you something about your father," Theo said.

The mention of my father caused a phantom pang of hurt to blossom in my chest. "What about my father?" It sounded more defensive than I meant it to.

"He was from this realm. Actually, he was one of my father's most trusted advisors."

My brain short-circuited. "My father?" I looked around the room. "Was Fae?" I think back to his obsession with mythology and knowledge of things outside our small town, as well as his abnormal size and ethereal aura — and it kind of made sense.

"Yes."

"Why did he come to my realm?"

"When the prophecy was told, it was long before they even knew what trouble would befall us. He volunteered to fulfill the first part of the prophecy."

"Okay...perhaps now is a good time to share the prophecy then." My voice had a level of demand to it.

The Captain laughed, "She has spirit. I like her." She clapped me on the back.

Theo smiled, "As do I."

Heat crept up my neck under his soft gaze. "The prophecy?" My ask was softer this time.

"Right." He cleared his throat. *"A half-breed female, loved by a full-Fae male, will journey here of her own fruition and save the realm from death and ruin."*

"A half-breed female," I was breaking it down piece by piece, trying to understand. "Loved by a Fae male?" I looked to Theo, whose nose bridge was slightly pink.

"Your father was full-Fae." Was all he said.

"I will save the realm from death and ruin."

"From the Harpies, yes. We hope you will draw them out and allow our warriors the opportunity to slay the Harpy Queen."

"And save my brother?"

"That is the plan."

"The Harpies," I drew in a shaky breath. "They're eating the boys, aren't they?" Theo nodded grimly. Anger boiled up inside me, "How could you give me those beans to open the portal when it would put others in danger?"

Horror and regret covered his features. "I promise you I didn't know the Harpy Queen would take humans. She had been satisfied by terrorizing the males of my realm for so long I didn't think she would even notice the portal."

"You didn't think she would notice a huge beanstalk that reaches from the ground to the sky and beyond?"

"Believe it or not, I haven't done this before. I am learning as I go. But I regret the human boys being in danger, and we will do everything we can to help rescue them."

"If they're even still alive." Dread filled my chest.

"My lady, it is likely that they are. The Harpies usually spend about a fortnight fattening up their prey before consuming them. When did the disappearances begin?" The Captain asked.

"About a week ago, give or take. If time works the same in this realm."

"It is relatively the same," Theo confirmed. "So we must move quickly."

"Okay." I considered my next words carefully. "My father said never to make a deal with the Fae. That's not an option right now. So, instead, I will make sure it is a fair deal that we both agree to.

The Captain laughed again, "I really like her."

Theo smiled again. "Agreed." His praise threatened to blow me over. *Focus.*

"So, I will help defeat the Harpies. What's in it for me?"

"The safe return of your brother," Theo said.

"And?"

His smile widened. "And daily gold, in the form of the rights to one of my Golden Geese." My mouth opened in shock. Even a single gold coin a day would change my life.

"Deal." We shook on it. "So, what is the plan?"

The Captain stood, placing her hands on the mapped table. "We will disguise you as a boy and covertly lead you to the beanstalk. Once there, you will need to act as if you're in a trance and, sooner or later, a Harpy will snatch you up and take you into their keep." She pointed to the castle blueprint. "Here is where the Harpy Queen spends most of her time," She pointed to the throne room. "And here is where they will take you." Her final gesture was to the kitchen.

"Okay, so I'm a prisoner, waiting to be Harpy food — now what?" Theo chuckled at my blunt questioning.

The Captain continued. "We will equip you with weapons, but you shouldn't need them if you can sneak out well enough. The Harpies are very connected to the moon. They'll take their daily slumber when the sun is highest in the sky, which we will enhance with a little magic. That's when you will escape."

"How will I get out? I'm sure there are cages or, at least, locked doors to contend with."

The Captain looked to Theo. "There is one more thing you should know. We have magic in our realm, each family passing down one power or another to their children. Your father was a metal mage."

"A metal mage? What does that mean?" I asked.

"It means he could control metal. He could bend open cell bars, unlock metal door locks, and even break enemy swords in half from twenty paces away."

I snorted. "And you think I can do this? I assure you I have never done anything remotely magical in my entire life."

"Magic can't live in the human realm, not unless you are very powerful."

"Like the sparkles that happened when we touched?" I asked, up until that point in my life those sparks of electricity were the most magic I had ever seen or felt.

The Captain spit out the water she had been drinking. "Sparks?" She sounded shocked.

Theo shot her a warning look and continued, "But here, you should be able to feel your magic. We will give you magic-enhancing tea after dinner tonight — it's what we give children to help them come into their powers."

I'm sure that I looked uneasy. "Sounds so simple…"

Theo patted my thigh encouragingly. "All you really need to do is pretend to be opening the locks as you normally would. Envision yourself having the key and go through the motions of unlocking the doors and it should work."

"So, half this plan is based on my ability to tap into magic I had never heard of before this moment? Excellent." An exasperated sigh slipped between my lips.

Theo chuckled. "I believe in you." And, somehow, that made me believe in me a little too.

The sun had already set once we made our way out of the tent, and I fell in line as my little group made their way to the dining pavilion. Upon entering the pavilion, the smell of stew hit my nose and instantly made my mouth water and stomach growl. Theo waited in line with us, talking with those around him, rather than stomping to the front of the line and demanding his food first as many human royals would have. It was easy to see that his people loved him, and it was even easier to see why. After only a day of knowing him, I trusted him. And after only a moment of being in his presence I was drawn to him.

We ate our food in easy conversation, Theo asking me about my life and, in turn, me asking about his.

"So, you didn't know my father?" I asked.

"No, I was a baby when we left this realm to find yours. But my father spoke of him often and missed him greatly." Something similar to pride swelled in my chest at the reverence he spoke of my father with.

"Why didn't he return here?" Though I was glad he didn't, I was curious why.

"Originally, he planned to go to the human realm, impregnate a woman, stay until the child was born to make sure it was female and healthy, and then leave. As things from our realm cannot live long in your realm."

"But?"

"But he loved you too dearly to leave and knew your mother wouldn't be right to you alone." My father was astute.

"Why didn't he pick a better woman then?"

"I think he chose the first willing." He shrugged. "I hope not to tarnish his memory for you."

"No, honestly, it helps to know. I always wondered how a good man like him could love her. Turns out he didn't." I paused, "So, he died young because Fae can't live in the human realm?"

"Yes, he thought since our lifespans here are several hundred years that he might make it in the human realm about as long as humans do, or he might make it until you were old enough, and he could return here and wait until you joined us, but alas, his theories were wrong. I'm sorry for your loss." His apology was sincere.

I placed my hand on his, "As I'm sorry for yours." Our eyes met across the table again, more silent communication seeming to pass between us. It was as if our connection was cosmic and eternal. It's weird to say, but it's the only words I could use to describe it.

"So, Fae beings can't thrive in the human realm? Can't live there?" I asked, although I knew the answer.

"Not for very long, no."

"What about me? Can I live there and be okay?"

"Yes, your father felt certain of that, or else he wouldn't have left you there."

I released a sigh of relief, both for myself and my brother. "What about here? Could I live here?"

"I'm not sure. You've been in the human realm a long time." And with that answer, Theo looked as disappointed to report it as I did to hear it. "Are you ready for bed? We have much to do tomorrow."

"Yes, that sounds great." I threw back the rest of the bitter, herbal tea one of the magic instructors had made for me and then followed Theo out of the pavilion. With practiced steps he led me through the twists and turns of his makeshift home, until we finally found ourselves in front of row after row of small tents, in the silent, sleeping area of camp.

"Here we are." Theo held back the flap to the small tent in front of us. I expected them to place me in a leftover tent, one with bare minimum necessities and maybe a cot, but this tent was lived in. Clothes were draped over a small chair in the corner, candles sat half burned on a desk, and the cot was covered in fluffy blankets.

"I'm surprised there's so much in here."

"Though I am a Prince of the people, I still like to have a few belongings to my name." He teased, and this caused me to tense.

"This is your tent?" I squeaked.

"Yes?" He asked, not understanding my confusion.

"Where am I to sleep?"

"Jacqueline, we don't exactly have a lot of extra supplies here, and with how important you are, I don't feel safe just putting you anywhere." I know he meant how important I was to the mission, but the romantic that was buried deep down inside of me longed to be important to him for other reasons.

"Jac."

"Jac?"

"Yes, I prefer to be called Jac." Though I loved the way his foreign tongue worked through the completeness of Jacqueline.

"Jac," Theo smiled, as if it felt right on his lips. "If you are uncomfortable, I will sleep outside the tent, but I wish to stay close to you."

"No," I choked out. "You can stay." My voice was barely above a whisper.

"The clothes there," Theo pointed to the chair. "Are all for you, something to sleep in and then your clothes for tomorrow." He grabbed the tent flap. "I will give you privacy to change." Then he left, and I found myself alone for the first time since seeing my brother get snatched up by that Harpy. I pulled off my dirty farm clothes, discarding them in the corner of the tent, and stepped toward the desk to use the water and washcloth left there. I was able to clean myself up a little bit before dressing in the clothes left for me, a pair of soft woven trousers and a sweater to combat the autumnal chill in the night air.

Everything had changed. I had learned so much in less than twenty-four hours, about both myself and the universe at large. It was overwhelming, and, before I knew it, I was crying. I plopped down on the cot, tucking my legs beneath me and covering my eyes with my hands.

The sound of the tent flap opening, and closing didn't even halt my sorrow. Suddenly, warmth wrapped around me, and without a second thought, I leaned into Theo's comforting embrace. I grounded myself to the sound of his steady heart and his smell of cedar, and I leaned in even closer when he worked a hand down my back and onto my thigh.

"Shh," He cooed. "Everything will be okay. The prophecy tells of your triumph." That did give me a level of relief, though I was unsure how exactly I was going to accomplish it all.

"I'm just overwhelmed and confused," I admitted.

"And that's okay." The thumb on my thigh started tracing small circles on my skin. "Remember, you won't be doing this alone." After a few more moments of sitting in his embrace, my tears stopped, and he released me a few more minutes after that. "Let's get you into bed." He guided me back on the cot and laid a fur blanket over me. "I'll be right here if you need me." He gestured to the floor.

"Thank you." He knew that I meant for everything, not just the blanket.

"Of course, I will do anything I can to help you." And he meant it.

As I laid there searching for sleep, I found myself unwell again — unsteady without his embrace. "Theo?" I whispered.

"Yes, Jac?" I loved the way he said my name.

"Tell me a story," I whispered, desperate for distraction. He leaned up, body resting on his forearms so he could meet my eyeline. Without pause, he began to spin a tale of adventure, magic, and star-crossed love. The romance of it all made my toes curl and heart ache with need. It was as if this tale had been on the tip of his tongue, just waiting for me to ask for it. If being Prince didn't work out, I was certain he could make a good livelihood as a storyteller.

During his tale, before the end, sleep began to find me. My eyelids were heavy, and even his voice seemed like it was growing distant. I was so tired that I didn't even flinch when Theo's gentle hand found its way to my face to brush a piece of fallen hair behind my ear. And though I did not flinch, I did speak.

"Will you…"

"Will I what?" His eyes searched mine as best they could in the darkness, and I could feel his breath on my face. "Jac?"

"Will you lay with me?" My voice was breathy and filled with sleep. I know it's foolish, and never would I have asked that with my full faculties about me, but I felt at ease when he was touching me.

He hesitated. "I don't know if that's a good idea."

"Just until I fall asleep?" I don't know when I became so bold.

He released a heavy sigh. "I find myself unable to deny you anything." My heart fluttered, unready but excited to be in close proximity to Theo. With more gentleness than a man of his size should possess, he laid beside me on the small cot. His hand found its way to my hip, his touch gentle and respectful as he nestled himself against me. "Is this okay?"

All I could manage was, "Mhmm," as I relished the squeeze of our bodies lying horizontally on the narrow cot. Though I was nearly asleep, his scent and touch were still intoxicating.

Out of nowhere, he produced a small harp and began plucking away a gentle lullaby on it. He continued his story as he played, and I continued to drift to sleep, his raspy voice reverberating through my body. And before I fell under sleep's spell, I swear I heard him say, "And legend says when the soulmates touched for the first time that sparks would fly…" But I couldn't be sure.

METAL CLANGED against metal as I joined in the dance of practice combat with the female Fae warriors. I had battled half the women in camp, using the sword skills my father had taught me to hold my own with them all.

The Captain's voice, filled with pride, echoed around the camp. "And that is why she is our champion!" Roars erupted from the warriors around me, causing my chest to swell with an unfamiliar sense of camaraderie, followed by a more familiar pang of sadness. Looking at these women made me realize that Theo wouldn't be the only one I missed when I returned to my own realm. Thinking of the Prince, my eyes began to search the camp for him, and a haughty sense of pride filled me when I noticed he stood on the edge of the training field, leaning against a tree watching me with a smirk on his lips. The distraction of his gaze threw me off kilter, allowing my sparring partner the perfect opportunity to knock me off balance.

I fell to the unforgiving ground with a thud, but my sparring partner was there with a helping hand in the blink of an eye. "The Prince seems to fancy you as much as you fancy him." My newfound friend whispered earnestly. "His eyes haven't left you."

"He watches me because I am of importance to the kingdom." I brushed her comment off and choked down a drink of my herbal tea.

"I'd say so." Her comment felt loaded, but she walked off without sharing any more.

"I thought a woman of the human realm wouldn't be ready for combat. It seems I've been proven wrong." The Captain remarked.

"My father trained me with swords since I was barely big enough to hold one up."

"As he should have." The Captain nodded approvingly. "I believe we could attack at midday tomorrow, if that's agreeable to you and Prince Theo." Fear gripped my heart. I knew the time to face the Harpies was fast approaching, and I wanted to save my brother, but hearing her say those words aloud shook me to my core.

I cleared my throat, noting Theo approaching behind her. "If that's the case, then perhaps it's time I put this tea to the test. No amount of combat skill will help me if I can't escape the castle. Who shall be teaching me that?"

"I will," Theo said. Two emotions warred inside me: desire to avoid him and desire to cling to him. Both scared me. And both came from a place of acknowledging our undeniable pull toward one another. I craved being in his presence, but it scared me, for I knew my time to leave this realm was quickly approaching.

"All right." I nodded, allowing him to lead me to a new area of the camp. Through the hustle and bustle of daily activities, we walked until, finally, we were directly in front of an old carriage.

"Taking me on a ride through the woods?" I teased, though the vision of the two of us curled up in that carriage together was not a bad one.

"I wish." He replied earnestly. "I want to practice moving the metal in a lock, and these are the only locks in camp." He gestured to the keyhole on the ornate carriage door.

I grimaced. "I don't feel particularly optimistic." I know I had only been in the realm a short time, but I hadn't felt any different than I had in the human realm. At least physically, emotionally was a different story. My eye caressed Theo's form and the way the wind was blowing his hair gently about. A pang of jealousy rang through me, jealousy that I hadn't gotten to grow up in this realm…with him. Our fathers had been close, so it reasons we would have been close as well. And with the amount of instant comfort and connection we already shared, what could years of being alongside one another have created?

My thoughts consumed me so much that I didn't see Theo had stepped into my space. "Jac?" My name fell from his lips like a promise.

"Hmm?" Why was I unable to form coherent sentences around this man?

"I asked if you were ready to begin?" His eyes were gentle, not at all irritated that I had dissociated into a fantasy world in my head as he had been talking to me. If anything, he looked amused by me. I nodded my head as an answer. "Your magic is an extension of yourself. Consider it another sense. Using magic should come as easily as smelling or touching something once you're familiar with the pull of it." The word touch triggered my dissociation again, images of his strong hands tracing the length of my body flashed through my mind as I subtly ogled him. "Jac?" Clearly, I wasn't subtle enough. His lips were twisted up in an amused smirk, and my cheeks heated with a blush. "What's going on in that head of yours?" He took another step closer, so close I could feel his warm breath on my face.

My blush deepened, and I avoided eye contact with him. "It's silly. You don't want to know. Trust me." My hand went up to brush an errant strand of hair from my cheek, but I was beaten to it by Theo. His calloused palm ignited a trail of fire on my cheek as it brushed upwards to tuck away the piece of hair.

His hand held my jaw, his fingers dipping into my hairline, and his gaze, now filled with heat and somber focus, pinned me frozen to the spot I stood in. "Believe me." His eyes dipped down to my lips before returning to my eyes. "I do want to know."

I struggled to swallow, a lump fully formed in my throat, and my voice came stuttering out. "I was thinking about what it would have been like to grow up in your realm." A flash of disappointment flashed across his face, only briefly, before a wistful smile replaced it.

"I curse your father for not returning you to this realm more than I curse those Harpies for existing." His tone was teasing, as was the smirk on his lips, but something in his eyes made me wonder if a level of truth rang in his words.

"Shall we unlock the carriage door then?" I interrupted our intimate staring contest, not knowing how much longer I could stand the palpable tension between us before I did something rash and out of character — like pull his body to mine and kiss him senseless. A hot blush had spread throughout my body, giving me the desire to strip out of my outer clothing layer despite the autumnal chill in the air.

"Of course." His face shifted, and he looked every bit like a powerful, stoic prince.

I turned my attention to the door, thinking about the lock and wishing it would turn. With the amount of focus I was using, I felt like I was going to give myself a migraine. But when I stepped toward the door and yanked, I found it still locked. A groan of frustration fell from my lips.

"I can't do this!" I stomped away like an insolent child, the pressures and emotions of the last few days weighing heavily on me.

"Jac," Theo's voice held a jovial tone. "That was only your first try. Come here." He took me by the hand, and in that moment, I felt like I would have let him lead me anywhere. Positioning us before the door, Theo took his place behind me and guided my right hand toward the door. It took all my focus to think about searching for the magic within me rather than focusing on the sensation of his body pressed against mine. "Imagine you're holding a key in your hand, and trust that the lock will move itself to unlock the door."

"That seems so easy." My words were leaving me in breathy wisps.

"Because it is. I know you are magic, Jac. Just believe yourself to be." His breath tickled my ear, and I could feel the warmth of his hand on my abdomen. "Take deep, deliberate breaths from here, and feel for it."

"I don't know what magic feels like." I tried not to sound frustrated.

"Keep focusing, Jac. I can smell the magic. It's working."

"You can smell magic?" I felt him nod. "What does mine smell like?"

He paused, mulling over the question thoughtfully. "Warm, like mulled cider and vanilla." He sighed. "You are intoxicating."

After a few steady breaths, and remembering his words of my being magic, I stepped forward and mimed unlocking the door. I thought it was my imagination, that I heard a click, but when the door fell open moments later, I knew it wasn't.

"I did it!" I jumped about gleefully, earning another smile from Theo.

"I knew you could." He stepped to the carriage door and locked it again with a key. "Now do it a hundred more times."

HOURS LATER, laughter filled Theo's tent as he regaled me with tales of his childhood.

"You set the ballroom on fire?" I snorted, an unattractive noise that somehow coaxed a smile from Theo.

"Listen, consider yourself lucky that you didn't have to go through puberty in the Fae realm — not only does it last longer for us, but also our magic is affected. I couldn't be around a pretty girl for years without my fire flaring up and doing some kind of damage." He placed his face in his palms and laughed at himself. "If that were still a problem, our whole tent would be aflame right now." He flashed me a flirtatious smile.

"I'm sure the girls were willing to risk third-degree burns to be in your embrace at a ball," I replied coyly.

"Would you have?" The question left his lips with ease, as easily as his eyes traced up and down my figure, pausing over my lips for many seconds before finding my eyes again. I had never found myself in close proximity with a male before, especially not with one who seemed as interested in me as I was in him. Being with him was like being tipsy, floaty and relaxed, and I loved it. And I don't know if it was my newfound heritage or magic — but I was feeling bold.

"You could sear the very flesh from my bones, and I'd say thank you," I attempted to eye him seductively, as he had me. *"Theo,"* I said his name like a promise, allowing my gaze to flick between his lips and eyes as he leaned in slowly.

"Jac, there's something I need to tell you." He whispered, still leaning in.

"Yes?" My eyes began to flutter closed, anticipating his mouth on mine.

"The prophecy—"

"Prince Theo! Jac! Come quickly!" A voice spoke urgently from outside the tent, not with fear but delight. A sigh escaped Theo's lips, but he willingly followed me out of the tent and into the night air. And I didn't need to ask what the commotion was all about, for as soon as I stepped from the tent, I could see it. Thousands of lights danced around the forest, flitting around quickly.

"Sprites," Theo offered from behind me. "They are celebrating tonight." One got close enough for me to see that it wasn't just lights darting around the forest but glowing little creatures.

"Mischievous creatures with a love of nature and power to create illusions, amongst other things." I quoted from my memory.

"Very good," Theo teased. "Star pupil." I shoved him lightly, causing him to teeter off balance. Before I could catch him, or watch him fall, a horde of Sprites appeared behind him. They used their combined strength to push him up, as more unseen Sprites pushed me forward — causing us to collide together, our bodies even closer than they had been in the tent or in bed the night before. It was Theo's turn to blush. "As you said, mischievous creatures." His hands were on my waist, refusing to let go. But my timing, as always, was flawed. A yawn escaped my lips, making Theo step away.

"Let's go to bed." He took me by the hand, weaving our fingers together with an ease that felt practiced. "We have a big day tomorrow."

❧

"I look ridiculous, I'm sure." I had been given a complete outfit of Theo's to wear, and I was distracting myself with the ridiculous details to avoid the nervousness swirling in my gut at the day's mission. I would be sneaking into the Harpies nest, acting as live bait, to free the boys from their keep. That, along with the fear of what I might find and worry over my brother, was nearly too much to bear. So I would focus instead on the inebriated feeling I got from the smell of Theo's cravat I was wearing. *Woodsy and masculine.*

"Good thing it's a rescue mission and not a ball. Though, there is something roguishly handsome about you now." He laced his words with teasing flirtation.

"You're incorrigible." This was something I had come to learn about him in our short time together.

"No," Theo stepped toward me and tucked a forgotten strand of my hair into the cap on my head. "I am distracting you." How had he known me for so little time and yet knew exactly how to comfort me? His hand trailed down my neck, shoulder, arm, and finally found my hand — sending a zap of electricity through me. "The sun has risen. We need to get out of the forest and to the beanstalk before the Harpies slumber for the day. Are you ready?"

No. "I have to be. For my brother." And for you.

"Then let's begin our journey."

Theo and I led the way, followed distantly by the entirety of the female army.

This walk through the forest was vastly different from the last one. Mere days ago, I had walked through these trees, but as I traversed this path again, I did it as a different woman. My past was clear. I knew more about who my father was and why I never fully felt at home in the human realm. But my future was still a mystery. As I clutched the hand of the man beside me, I couldn't help but wonder what it could look like.

Theo had told me his regrets for being powerless against the Harpies and having to sit on the sidelines while others took his kingdom back. But he didn't know just how much he was helping me. He told me stories to distract me, and his hand didn't leave mine the entire journey. It was a grounding force in the face of my fear.

The journey to the beanstalk felt short and seeing it filled me with a sense of dread that only Theo's steady hand could stave off.

"Remember, the prophecy speaks of your victory," Theo said with a confidence I wish I could steal from him.

"Repeat the plan to me," I demanded, my eyes never leaving the beanstalk or the swarm of Harpies in the distance.

His strong hands found my shoulders, rubbing out the tension I had been holding in them. He leaned over, still towering over me, and repeated the plan concisely. "You will walk toward the stalk in a fake daze, and when a Harpy swoops down for you, you will hold out your arms." I had worn armor beneath his clothes to shield me from the Harpy's talons. "You will take deep breaths during the flight and remember that I will not let any harm befall you, and the prophecy tells us of your victory." He repeated that part for my benefit. "Once inside the Harpy lair, they will likely lock you up. But don't panic, you will play this," Theo handed me his magic harp. "To lull them into a deep sleep. Once the Harpies slumber, you will use your magic to free yourselves and the males they've captured. You will silently sneak from the castle and lead the boys to the beanstalk while my army goes in and kills the sleeping beasts."

"Okay." I used the deep breaths Theo had taught me to remain calm.

"I will be waiting for you at the beanstalk to help get the boys to safety." He spun me around, giving me a final piercing gaze. "I believe in you. You were made for times such as these." I nodded, unable to use my words without crying, and began my solo journey toward the burrowing beanstalk that had led me to my destiny.

Mimicking my brother's tranced steps proved easy, as the image of him walking without consent toward our cellar was burned into my brain. I walked ramrod straight with my eyes trained ahead, waiting for the screech of a Harpy to tell me I had been spotted. And it didn't take long before that happened.

I heard the screech and the wind from her swoop threatened to blow the cap from my head and ruin my disguise. And I felt the pierce of a talon that managed to find its way between my armor sink into my flesh. I swallowed the scream that threatened to erupt from my mouth because you don't scream when you're in a trance — no matter what horrible thing happens to you.

I think I dissociated while in the air, forcing myself to focus only on

Theo's words instead of the drop in my stomach and the lightheadedness I felt from being so high above the earth. I only returned to the present moment when the stench of the Harpy den assaulted me. The stink of death filled my nose as horrors assailed my eyes. Blood, bones, and entrails littered the castle halls, and nothing could have prepared me for what I saw when I was carried past the throne room. Atop a pile of hundreds, maybe thousands, of bones laid a giant. The Harpy Queen was as tall as a house and had blood covering her muddy feathers and humanoid lips. An involuntary shiver worked its way through my body when I noticed the crown of bones that decorated her head. Some of which still had bits of flesh clinging to them. But despite the horror of it all, I couldn't look away from her. She was my enemy, and if my short time training with the warriors taught me anything, it was that one needed to know their enemy to be victorious.

I was jolted from my rage and thoughts by being thrown. Unforgiving copper met my cheek, stinging nearly as much as the Harpy talon had. I looked at my torn sleeve, which was now dripping in my blood, confirming the severity of my injury.

"Jac?" A shaky voice asked. And though the boy before me was dirty, plump, and nearly busting from his clothes — I would recognize my brother anywhere.

"Brother!" I whispered, engulfing him in a hug and immediately searching his body for injuries. "What has happened to you?" I looked around the cage, noting that every face looking at me was full and covered in grease.

"They want us fat." Tears filled his eyes. "They say boiled boys on toast taste better when they've been fattened with milk and cheese. He rubbed a grubby baby hand across his snotty nose.

Another boy began to cry. "They said they make the toast from flour made of our ground bones." I couldn't imagine the horrors these boys had faced in the days since their capture. But it would all be over soon.

"Listen to me," I whispered as I looked around the cage and made eye contact with each boy before me. "No one else is getting eaten because I am getting you out of here." I told them the plan, emphasizing the importance of silence when we finally made our journey out of the castle. The boys nodded and looked at me with reverence as I spoke. They understood. So then all we had to do was wait.

It had been nearly midday when the Harpy snatched me, so we didn't have to wait long before I took the harp from beneath my shirt, instructed the boys to plug their ears, and began to pluck the strings as Theo had taught me. The melody was rough but must have been effective because it wasn't long before I heard the sound of bodies hitting the floor echoing through the castle halls. I played on, maybe longer than I needed to, but I had to ensure they were asleep. Their slumber was the most important part of the plan because no amount of will or sword practice would allow me to take on a horde of Harpies and their giant Queen on my own.

I tucked the harp beneath my shirt again and confidently stepped before the locked cage. Theo's words danced in my mind. *You are magic, Jac.* My lungs shook as I took slow, deliberate breaths and raised my hand to the lock. In the fantasy stories I read, this was always where something went wrong. When the female needed to be rescued by a strapping knight. But this story wasn't like that. I am the hero of this story.

With more confidence than I had ever felt before, I turned my hand as if a key was within it. Time stood nearly still as I brought my hand to the door and pulled, but I didn't allow doubt to plague me, not when the lives of so many rested in my hands.

And despite all odds, the door opened. I wanted to jump for joy, but the time for celebrating was later. I could celebrate once everyone was safe.

"Hold the hand of the boy before and behind you, and silently follow me." I took my brother's hand and began the most important walk of my life.

Though the Harpies were asleep, it didn't make the walk through the castle any less horrifying. It still reeked, and the sleeping bodies of the Harpies littered the halls. But despite their fear, the boys did great. A few squeaked in fear upon seeing the Harpies up close, but that was the only noise they made, other than the collective sigh of relief we had after I unlocked the castle doors and let fresh air fill our lungs.

The plan was executed almost flawlessly. The only mistake I made was underestimating the weight of the castle door. I watched in slow motion, as the final boy stepped away from the castle and let the heavy door slip from his grasp. The door slammed, my breath caught, and the earth shook as a screech erupted from the throne room — followed by a haunting melodic phrase. I don't know if it was a command, a curse, or a spell, but the threat of it seeped deep into my bones when the Harpy Queen screamed, "Fee-fi-fo-fum!" And every Harpy awoke from their slumber.

"Run!" I pointed to the beanstalk and took up the rear of our pack as the short-legged, now fattened children ran as fast as they could toward the beanstalk.

Theo's army seemed to pop up out of nowhere. Nearly every tree, bush, ledge, and boulder had been concealing a Warrior, and now they were in battle mode. They didn't hesitate to run toward the castle, weapons drawn, as the groggy but enraged Harpies began to pour out of it. Archers using poison-tipped arrows aimed at the Harpies, taking several down with ease. Our warriors seemed a fair match for the dazed Harpies but not the Harpy Queen.

"Thief!" Their Queen cried as she flapped her massive wings and took to the sky — headed straight for the boys.

"Climb!" I yelled. "Faster!" But I knew my cries were pointless, those boys understood better than me the urgency of this situation, but their little arms and legs could only climb so fast.

I stayed on the ground, ushering each boy up the stalk and staying vigilant in case I needed to fight off anything threatening their escape. My brother was the last to climb.

"Jac! You have to come with me!" Tears filled his eyes.

"I will join you soon. You need to get home and lock the cellar doors. No one else can come down here. You understand?"

"But if I lock the doors, how will you get out?" His eyes searched mine for answers, not understanding exactly how I had unlocked our cage to free us from the Harpy lair.

"I will get out, trust me." I ruffled his hair and urged him one final time to begin his climb, and this time he didn't protest.

My brother was about halfway up the beanstalk when the Harpies and their Queen began to swoop and grab desperately at the escaping boys. Thankfully, most were concealed by the leaves and vines, but not all were. One boy, the son of the dairy farmer we bought Bess from all those years ago, was snatched up. I watched in horror as he flailed, unable to do anything to help him, and the horror turned to terror when I saw him slip from her grasp and plunge to his death. I had only seen one dead body before, my father's, but by the sound of the belligerent Harpies and screaming warriors — I was bound to see many more before this day was over.

"No!" I cried, drawing Theo's attention from the forest. I cried out again as the Harpy Queen began snatching at my brother, and without hesitation, Theo bolted toward the stalk, screaming as conspicuously as possible. "Theo! Stop!" I cried, knowing he was powerless if the Harpy Queen decided to control him, which she did.

"The Prince?" She cackled. "You're a little skinny, but my dinner is gone, and I'll take what I can get." A melodic song, not unlike the harp I had played earlier, spilled from her mouth, and Theo was instantly under her spell. He froze mid-sprint, his face devoid of all emotion it had previously held. The warriors were too distracted by the Harpies to notice their giant Queen was stepping toward the Prince with an unnerving look in her eye as she licked her lips.

Helplessness consumed me. I was no match against the giant before me. Desperately, I grabbed a sword from a fallen Warrior and ran at the Harpy Queen. I swung at her Achilles heel, but the skin on her falcon-like feet was so thick that my sword just bounced off of it.

I eyed the beanstalk, now empty, as my brother had made his escape. Relief that he was safe filled me, as dread for Theo replaced it. My eyes hunted frantically for help, and in an instant, my gaze focused on a forgotten axe beside a pile of wood. Images of a young Jac filled my mind, and the bird I had killed by felling an old tree. My eyes darted between the giant Harpy Queen, the axe, and the beanstalk, and with utter clarity, I knew what I had to do to save Theo.

I didn't have time to grieve the fact that chopping down the beanstalk might mean removing my only way home, because there was no time. Not to mention, the loudest voice in my head was urging me to save Theo above all else. Even above my own self-preservation.

After angling the beanstalk's fall as best I could, I began chopping, putting all my might into each deliberate swing. Sweat coated my brow, and blisters opened up on my palms, but I kept chopping. And I only swung harder when I heard Theo's strangled cry — the Harpy Queen had reached him. Lucky for me, she liked to toy with her food, giving me enough time to knock the final chunks of fiber from the stalk.

I felt the earth rumble beneath me once again as the ginormous beanstalk began to sway. Wasting no time, I ran toward Theo, pumping my arms and sucking in burning breaths of chilly air as I made my way to him. I had to time this perfectly. I had to pull him away from her, but not so soon that she would move out of the way of the falling stalk. Since she gave no care for females, the Harpy Queen didn't even notice my presence as she was preparing a fire to cook Theo over. She had stacked stick upon stick and used her melodic sway to force Theo to light the fire with his own magic. The earth shook once more as she plopped down and began to sharpen a spear to run him through with — but she wouldn't get the chance.

The shadow of the falling beanstalk was the only indication the Queen got before it fell right on top of her. Giants may have many advantages, but agility isn't one of them. Her attempts to move out of its way arrived too late. I grabbed Theo under the arms and pulled with all my might, a trail of blood following behind him as we went. The Harpy Queen only got a single squawk of indignation out before the girthy beanstalk fell upon her, cracking her skull, breaking her crown of bones, and squishing the guts from her body.

"Our Queen!" Her minions cried in a symphony of agony.

"We will be back!" One screeched. "You will pay for this!" These were their final words before retreating and disappearing beyond the mountains in the distance.

Ignoring the chaos around me, I fell to my knees at Theo's side, which had been cut open by the Harpy Queen's talons when she moved him.

"You're bleeding." He remarked, touching my arm gently.

A humorless laugh escaped my lips. "Theo, you're more gravely injured than I am. Let's worry about that."

"Don't worry, darling." *Darling, swoon.* "Fae heal extraordinarily fast. She didn't puncture anything vital. Harpies like to eat the organs whole." Though a horrid sentence, it gave me comfort.

"Let me see." I pulled up his shirt, inspecting the wound for myself. As he predicted, it had already begun to heal.

"If you want to get me topless, Jac, all you have to do is ask." A cocky smile played on his lips.

Though heat flooded my face, I responded in kind. "Someone is full of themselves now."

"Well, this prince just became King, and a fair maiden has saved me. So, I'm feeling pretty good about myself." I rolled my eyes playfully. Theo looked around, his face notably shifting when the gravity of what I had done sunk in.

"You cut down the stalk!"

"I had to save you," I replied honestly.

"How did you think you would get home?" His eyes flicked between mine, filled with earnest wanting.

"I didn't know anything except that I had to save you, Theo. I'm not sure why the need to save you was so strong, but it was — no offense." His lips tugged up. "I'm half-Fae, so I hope I can survive here."

"You want to stay here?"

I didn't have an answer for him, so I said again what I knew to be true. "All I knew was that I needed you safe."

In an instant, Theo was leaning up, both hands holding my face between them. His eyes searched my own for a moment, and then his lips were on mine.

Sparks flew as they did the first time we touched, and, in my mind, images flashed at a rapid pace. Us walking together in the forest hand in hand. He and I lying in a bed of clovers, looking up at the night sky. His hands on my body and his lips on mine. Us standing before a priest at a mating ceremony. Me swollen with child and his hand rubbing my stomach tenderly. The images that felt like memories flashed on and on and on. That, plus the kiss, was enough to take my breath away. His hands gripped me earnestly, as his supple lips ignited a fire in my soul. His tongue slipped out, running along the seam of my lips. I could feel his desperation to be as close to me as possible.

Despite my desires, I pulled away. His forehead found mine, and we rested there together, sharing air — our eyes never leaving each other. His gaze was telling me something, as if he knew what I would see when we kissed and hoped it told me everything I needed to know.

"The Fae male who loves me…it isn't my father, is it?" He shook his head no. "And the story you told me in the tent about the soulmates?"

"That was more of the prophecy." Too many thoughts were swirling in my head. Soulmates, prophecy, love. It was almost too much.

"Not all of it?" I asked. Theo's eyes shifted, a sadness filling them. "What is it?" My hands had found his, grasping desperately, clinging to them as if they would give me strength.

"You must return to the human realm, at least for a time." The pain of uttering those words was worse than the slashing of the Harpy talon against his body had been.

"What if I want to stay?" I asked, stubbornness lacing every word.

"We can't fight destiny, darling." His thumb brushed away tears that I hadn't even known had fallen. "But know our story doesn't end here, and you will see me so often you may grow tired of me before the next chapter of our story even begins." He was teasing, but something deep inside me said it wasn't possible for me to grow tired of him.

"How will I see you?" My voice trembled without consent.

"Remember how I promised you one of my Golden Geese?" I nodded. "They are Fae creatures, so they can't dwell in the human realm. I will have to hand-deliver your golden eggs every day." He smiled, proud of himself for having put a way for him to see me into our original deal.

"Clever boy." I conceded.

"That's Clever King to you." He marked his command with another kiss on my lips, causing them to twitch with the beginnings of a smile.

"What if I need you at a time other than when you come to deliver my gold?" His eyes darkened with desire.

"Keep the harp," Theo instructed. "And play it should you ever need me, *for anything.*" I gulped at his insinuation. "The magic within it, paired with the magic within you, will allow you to open a portal between our worlds." I nodded, taking it all in.

"Is that how I am to get home now?" He bobbed his head. "What if I'm not ready to leave?"

"I'm not ready for you to leave either," Theo admitted. "But you must, and I must work to get this kingdom and castle into order, so I can proudly show it off to you one day."

"Promise?" I asked as Theo guided us both to our feet and dusted the dirt and leaves from us as best he could.

"It'll take more than an axe or a thousand Harpies to stop me from bringing you home one day." His promise sent a shiver down my spine. *Home,* I liked the sound of that.

"I was told every Fae gift or favor comes with a price. What is the price of this?" I gestured to the harp. "My heart?"

Theo laughed, and the melodic sound found its way into my soul. "Is that something you're willing to bargain away?" A smile was the only answer I gave. "That smile alone could be the death of me." He groaned with Shakespearean angst. "Oh, that I could bargain for that heart, but I decree I owe you ten thousand favors for saving my life. Let the harp be the first of many."

Theo kissed me once more, a lifetime's worth of desire coming undone in a single moment of passion. And it was over too soon. His fingers reached down and plucked a single harp string, which opened up a swirly otherworldly doorway before my eyes. It was like looking through a window, and through it I could see the vine-covered cellar beneath my house.

After one more look of longing, Theo released my hand, "I will see you tomorrow, Jac."

∾

AND HE DID SEE me that next day, and the day after that, and the day after that. Theo came at sundown every night, appearing in my cellar after my day's work was finished and his Kingly duties had been sorted. Gone were the nights of me staying up reading in my room, and replacing them were nights in Theo's arms. As promised, he would bring me a single golden egg every day, along with another surprise. Sometimes it was a treat from his realm for us to share, other times it was a book for him to read aloud to me. But I was always gifted with his company. To say I loved him was a gross understatement, though I had yet to tell him so because what was between us was something more. Something that a simple I love you couldn't do justice. Something I had yet to fully grasp an understanding of. Something eternal and cosmic.

All day, every day, I looked forward to our nightly visits, and every day he fulfilled his promise of showing up. Until one day, he didn't.

After an entire year of Theo visiting and hand-delivering my golden eggs, he stopped coming. I had to physically rub my chest to expel the heartache that came with his missed visit. But I talked myself down. King's must be busy — perhaps something came up. But after a few more days without him, my melancholy over his absence turned to dread.

His words bounced around my head, *"Keep the harp and play it should you ever need me, for anything. The magic within it, paired with the magic within you, will allow you to open a portal between our worlds."* I bolted out of the cellar and into my renovated home, now only mine, as the money from the golden eggs had allowed me to build my mother and brother a house of their own on the other side of our thriving farm.

Without hesitation, I snatched the harp from its prominent resting place above my hearth and plucked out a simple chord with only Theo on my mind. The portal opened in front of me, and upon seeing him through it, I stepped inside and began the next chapter of our story.

ABOUT S. FRASHER

S. Frasher is an indie author from Cincinnati and she mostly writes fantasy romance.

STORY V
ENTREATY OF SHADOWS BY JES DREW

Heat Level: Low
(PG content)

CHAPTER 1

T don't think I was ever a child.

Being born the elder son of the Dusk Court meant I had responsibilities almost instantly. So mayhap I was a child, but no one let me in on that secret.

No one lets me in on a lot of secrets just now; even my own memory is hiding things from me.

Sitting at my bedroom desk, I pick up a quill and consider best how to answer my brother's correspondence. His letter is brimming with hidden meanings and riddles, that I can sense behind his words like deep magic.

But for once in my life, I know not what he's referring to.

I groan, set my quill down, and grasp my head, wishing I could just reach in, grasp the cloud of darkness swirling inside, and wrench it out.

"You'll never be rid of me. Not after what you did."

Tensing at the strange voice that sounds somehow like liquid night, I scan my bedroom. But there is no one here besides me.

That is, until my door bursts open and my valet rushes in, his dark face flushed as if he's been running for an eon and a half.

His *chiton* uniform is also in disarray, dipped in mud and covered in sand. I have never seen him in such a state or a single speck of dust on his Grecian attire.

I stand quickly, almost knocking my chair over. "Lateef, what is it?"

Lateef stands there panting, hesitating, as if it takes him a moment to register that I've spoken to him.

Then he quickly bows at the waist. "My lord, Miss Salma has escaped from her sickbed. We have checked the house and the grounds, but she's nowhere to be found. My father thinks he found a trail leading through the Desert In-Between, we fear toward the mortal realm.

I stare at him, waiting for his words to shock something into me,

But no memory returns, and I meet his horror with confusion. "Who is this Salma?"

"She is mine."

MY REFLECTION STARES BACK at me as I attach a cloak around my shoulders. As it is, my tunic, my breeches, and my boots are all black. I am dressed to disguise myself with the dusk.

Though I fear I will be forced to see the light of day in the name of this quest.

"Leave her be. I will attend to her."

I flick my nose. This voice is becoming quite a nuisance.

"You forget yourself, boy."

"She has long, black curls, brown eyes, brown skin . . ." Nubia, my housekeeper, wrings her hands together as she tries to remember how else to describe this member of my household that I'm sure I've never laid eyes on.

"Pretty," Lateef offers, chiming in to assist his mother. "She's quite beautiful."

"Ravishing, more like."

Nubia nods eagerly at this before frowning and glancing sidewise at her son.

But he's already moved toward me, trying to arrange my dark hair to cover my pointed ears, a tell-tale indication of my fae blood.

Sighing, he just grasps my hood and pulls it up over my head, obscuring my pale face, and more importantly, my pointed ears from view.

"Another thing," Nubia adds tentatively, her veil failing to conceal her unease. "Salma is under a curse. If she remains in the mortal realm for too long, it will become her tomb."

I shrug one shoulder. "That is the same with all mortals. They are dust living in sand and just as fleeting."

"She will perish more quickly than other mortals. The moment she steps into the mortal realm, she will only have a single turn of the sun in the sky, if even that."

Lateef looks rather ill himself at his mother's grim pronouncement.

"One final thing." Nubia gestures to my front tunic pocket.

I pat it, rather surprised to find something solid within it.

"Don't forget to read the instructions," Nubia adds cryptically. "The tome will tell you how to behave around her."

"I beg your pardon?"

"Please!" Nubia looks ready to drop to her knees before me and beg my pardon the old way. "You must go!"

"And remember the instructions," Lateef adds.

Studying my servants, I sigh and nod. "I shall return as soon as possible with this 'beauteous' Salma. I have done my best to strengthen the outer runes, but until I return, it may be best to remain indoors."

"And never leave our rooms at night," Lateef murmurs obediently.

"No, they most certainly should. I will take excellent *care of your pets."*

"Be inside before the first bell tolls." With that, I turn and stride out of my room, my cloak billowing behind me.

I WAKE with a start and find that I'm walking.

Glancing around, I see that I am still in the Desert In-Between, with dunes stretching as far as my eyes can see.

Ahead of me though, I see a slight haze. A tell-tale sign of another Realm. The mortal realm, if I stayed on course while I thought I was sleeping.

I turn my head to see a steady stream of footprints in the sand behind me. It would seem that rather than wavering back and forth, my sleeping self marched forward with almost military precision.

Turning back forward, I keep walking until I pass through the veil.

The mortal air smells so much more rancid than that of any other realm I've traveled through; the stench of death lingers everywhere. It is that welcoming scent that informs me that my steps indeed were sure last night.

Resisting the urge to hide my nose behind my sleeve, I take in the patches of grass growing up out of the ground and growing denser closer to a stream flowing ahead. Beyond that stream is a storehouse of sorts, with more buildings dotting the horizon. Like the grass, they grow in greater density the further from the Desert In-Between they rise up.

I suppose I will keep walking toward the mortal civilization so I can ask if anyone has met a strange, beautiful woman going by Salma. Though, whether she is truly lovely or just pretty in Lateef's eyes remains to be seen.

The poor lad seems to fancy my shrew of a cook, so his taste in the fairer sex is open to debate.

I take a step forward and notice two things at once.

There is a tug on my soul trying to pull me just to the left, toward the storehouse instead of straight toward the town. And a rolling sickness stirs in my gut, washing over my skin with a strange hot coolness.

I frown at the rare but disgusting feeling of weakness and then turn my steps toward the storehouse. The sooner I can find my quarry and rid myself of this cursed realm, the better.

Bounding over the stream, I come around the corner of the storehouse in time to see a rather pathetic-looking wiry mortal male wrenching someone out from inside the building.

An even frailer figure appears, lurching forward and just stopping herself from falling face-first into the sand, likely with some help from the male still holding her wrist.

Long dark curls fall over a form-fitting linen *kalasiris* that is primarily worn by the women of the mortal kingdom abutting the Dawn Court.

Though, as the Dawn Court and my own Dusk Court orbit each other in the fae realm. It is entirely possible that we are now the ones bordering the sunnier kingdom until the next orbital shift. A shame; I detest the scholarly mortals of the peninsula kingdom slightly less than those always battling to live here where the garish sun shines brightest.

As I watch, the woman reaches up with her other hand and presses her nails into the male wrist of the arm clutching hers.

He cries out and drops her, sending her crashing into the dirt and sand and grass after all.

The female creature immediately pushes herself to her knees and crawls backward, away from the man. As she does so, her hair falls back, revealing a clearer view of her face.

Her face bears gleaming dark brown eyes, light brown skin, and features that I can understand being described as beautiful. Intermixed with fear in her eyes is a determined sort of anger, the kind that wrath is born from. Her full lips do not quiver, and her chin is raised with regal pride.

"Mayhap your little servant boy has good taste in the female variety after all. At least we can agree that this one is indeed beautiful."

I tense at the return of the incorporeal voice. Since when must I agree with it on anything?

"Life would be so much easier if you stopped resisting, boy."

Beyond the voice, I see the mortal man steps toward the maid that my soul is sure is the Salma that I seek. He has one hand pressed against his arm where she clawed him, and his eyes are flashing with rage. "You're going to pay for that, you little *garbuua*."

Her back touches the storehouse wall, and she uses it to sit up against, and from this angle I see also that she is bracing as if to fling herself at him, to defend herself bitterly.

But if she is indeed my ward, that will not be necessary. I step out from the shadows cast by the storehouse, into the wrath of the garish sun, and between the man and the maid.

The man starts, but I have no patience to deal with his balking and begging this morn.

I make direct eye-contact and will him to comply. "Has a debt been incurred?"

"Who are you?" the mortal man demands, looking torn between wanting to flee and wanting to strike.

Both would be annoyances if I am to sever any bargains she has foolishly made in this realm. I try to illusion myself to appear somewhat less menacing, though I am still at least a cubit taller than he. "I am responsible for this '*garbuua*.' So, I'll ask again, has a debt been incurred?"

He juts his chin in an expression that seems somehow infinitely more annoying on him than it did on the woman behind me. "She slept in my storehouse last night and ate my barley."

"I ate no barley!" she cries.

"I was there. No barley was eaten."

I sniff. "There, so she took from you a good night's sleep alone." And I thought my fellow fae were *petty*. "That is something I can easily repay." Stepping forward, I close the distance between the man and me. Then I place my right hand over his face.

His startled eyes peer at me from between my fingers before rolling up into his skull. Then he topples backward onto the ground where he belongs.

Turning from the annoyance, my cloak waving over his fallen form, I face at last my quarry, who is now seated on the ground, as though her legs gave way beneath her.

She blinks up at me with wide eyes. "Wh-what did you do to him?"

"I gave him deep and peaceful slumber in return for yours." I step closer to her so that the toes of my boots touch the toes of her sandals. I do not feel like chasing her further into this mortal realm after the trouble I already sorted out.

"Speaking of trouble, you should kill him. Then I can take care *of him* properly."

As if the wretch unconscious behind me is even worth the trouble. No, it is the maid I came for, not vengeance.

Thankfully, rather than trying to flee, the maid presses herself closer to the storehouse, her chest rising and falling with erratic breaths. "Please leave me be."

"I'm afraid I cannot do that Salma, Daughter of the House of Orphydice."

"I'm a daughter?" She blinks at me.

And in her eyes, I see the same confusion I've been feeling more and more. As though the world turned without me several orbits and I have been left to catch up. "I am sure you are. I merely meant that you are of my household. And I have come to fetch you back." I reach out to her.

She stares at the ring on my hand. The ring I do not even remember acquiring, let alone what its crest represents. "Who are you? Are you going to . . . put me to sleep, too?"

"Nonsense, you are of my House. And I, Lord Adom, Lord of the Dusk and Master of the House of Orphydice, have come to reclaim you." I push my hand closer to her, trying to ignore that much of the smell of decay seems to be emanating from her. "In this instance, I merely want to help you to your feet. The curse seems to have taken its toll."

"Curse?" she gingerly takes my hand, as if still ready to flee at so much as a loud sound.

When our skin brushes, though, I can see the reason for her reservations. My hand feels branded by even her lightest touch, and the sensation of somehow pleasurable burning moves up my arm.

Ignoring the strange sensation, I tug her to her feet.

The weakened maid immediately totters into me, her face crashing against my chest, causing the smell of mortality to wash over me with the violence of a sandstorm.

I take hold of her shoulders and steady her even though the feel of her soft skin just outside the straps that hold up her *kalasiris* sears through me. "Will you be able to walk?" If touching her so briefly causes this reaction, holding her over-long will be torture.

"You should most certainly avoid touching her at all costs."

She steps back and I release her happily, though she totters once again. But she steadies herself and lifts that stubborn chin of hers. "I'm sure I can. Wh-where are we going?"

"Home, of course. Never fear; your curse will lose its grip on you once we step over the border between realms."

Salma glances around, as though the fae realm will open up before her. "I-I don't remember the way."

"Very well. Follow me, then." I walk around her and move toward the Desert In-Between. The sooner I can get out of this cursed sun and deposit this lost child into the waiting arms of my servants, the better.

I don't hear her behind me, though, and I turn.

She's on her hands and knees on the ground, looking almost as annoyed as I am at her inability to remain upright.

Biting back a growl, I march back toward her and proffer my hand I really should have gloved in anticipation for her touch. If only I could remember such things, like having met her before and the consequences of her presence.

The mortal throws herself back against the wall of the storehouse I'm beginning to think I'm cursed to never leave the sight of. "Please don't!"

"Don't . . . Help you up?" I raise my eyebrow at the quickly fading maid. Leave it to mortals to be repulsed by their only hope of salvation.

She lifts her gaze to mine, and I see a flash of unexpected anger.

Then her hand is back in mine, and I'm not sure how we came back to this point.

But I don't break eye contact with her as I tug her back to her feet. "Can you walk?" Such a basic mortal skill, and yet, mine seems to be assuredly broken.

"Of course, I can." She lifts her chin, throws her black curls over her shoulder, and takes a determined step.

And collapses once again.

Instincts take over, and I lunge forward, wrapping my arms around her frail form. Then I yank her completely up and against me.

As if her stench weren't enough of an annoyance, the foolish thing shrieks quite obnoxiously and clutches my cloak awkwardly as I twist her around so that one arm is under her bent legs and my other is wrapped around her shoulders.

"Your lifeforce is dissipating at an alarming rate," I mutter as I begin trudging toward the Desert In-Between, doing my best to ignore all the points of contact between her soft body and me.

She seems mercifully dazed for a moment. But then she has to open her mouth again. "I-I don't want to go back there." The mortal stares toward the Desert In-Between.

"I'm afraid, Daughter of the Manor, that if you stay in the mortal realm for another turn of the worlds, you will most certainly pass right from them in the mortal way."

She blinks up at me until her eyes begin to slowly close.

Then the roiling sickness returns, and grace and strength alike desert me. I lurch forward, clutching the mortal more tightly to keep from depositing her back to the waiting ground even as I fight to keep from crashing myself.

Finally, I straighten and then continue back on my way, trying to ignore the fact that my hood had fallen back during my fall. The sun beats mercilessly against the top of my head, and the maid's one-eyed stare feels just as hard and hot against my face.

I look away from her, not sure what to say to myself, let alone her, after such an uncharacteristic stumble.

"Y-you're a fae," she croaks.

Ah, so she has the intelligence to leave the stumble out of the conversation, at least.

Raising an eyebrow, I glance back down at her. "A fae lord, actually."

My words herald our arrival at the Desert In-Between, and I step us through, the air suddenly free of the stench of decay despite the half-dead thing in my arms. Though, now that I can smell her beyond the confines of her mortality, she has a sweetness about her, and I think I smell my roses on her.

I glance down at her, strangely curious to see her reaction to the Desert In-Between and watch her eyes widen.

And then roll back in her skull as she becomes suddenly heavier in my arms.

Frowning, I shake her slightly. "Did you *faint*?"

She doesn't answer, so deep has she fallen into her ridiculous death-like sleep.

I growl. "How frustratingly mortal."

CHAPTER 2

Night comes on swift wings, and with it will follow monsters. I must act while dusk still acts as a buffer.

Setting the still sleeping mortal on the sand, I remove my jambiya, curved in a crescent to match the form of the moon that shall soon be joining us.

I use it to cut off a corner of my cloak. Then I stretch the scrap until it extends enough to make a suitable tent.

The cooling evening air comes to my aid, billowing the growing fabric and curving it into a canopy over the mortal maid at my behest.

That done, I stoop into the canopy, check that this strange Salma is still sleeping, and then cup my palms together.

An orb both as silver and as bright as my jambiya blade grows between my hands. Then I pull back and let it rise to the top of the tent to keep the shadows at bay.

At least until I finish setting up the true protections.

"You really think you can protect her from me?"

"I don't even know you are," I mutter, ducking back out of the tent. I banish fear along with uncertainty since there is no safe place for me to process it. I focus on rounding the tent, stooping down, and beginning to trace the necessary hieroglyphic runes in the sand.

"You will remember in time, boy. All in good time."

I move as quickly as I can while still making sure I put the right lines and curves into the sun, all too aware of the way the sun is sinking quickly down the horizon. Thankfully, dusk is the time that my powers are strongest.

But should any of the Shades or Shadows roaming the sands catch a whiff of Salma's mortal scent, I will not be able to repel them all before she is tainted at the very least. Or, at worst, torn to shreds.

Finally, I come full circle, sealing the protections.

That done, I reach into my front tunic pocket for further instructions. I remove the small book from my front pocket and watch it expand into a full-sized tome.

I open the book and watch the pages dance magically below me until they fall open on a page with a sketch that looks keenly like Salma with her regal brows, round nose, and pert lips.

On the other page is a sketch that looks far too much like me, or perhaps Sef as I've never known such listless desire as this sketch depicts. Except, the sketch also shares my dark hair instead of my brother's gold.

Scrolling words around our illustrations simply say:

You must never begin the night in the same room as Salma. That is the way of death.

No further explanation is given, and I stare over the words again and again, but nothing new reveals itself.

Except the startling familiarity of my own handwriting. The pages are covered in my own scrawl. Flicking through the other pages, I see more of my etchings written in my finest ink.

Confused, I turn back to the first pages I read, the warning still present.

The warning written by me, a fae. And we cannot lie.

A sudden noise from inside the canopy has me pocketing the book and ducking inside. I straighten on the other side, all too aware of the few moments I have left before risking seeing the consequences of the warning in the tome.

Salma blinks up at me with bright eyes.

"Good, you have awakened." A thought of rebellion crosses through my mind, and I settle down and cross my legs.

"Yes, good. Test your boundaries. You have no need to live by a book."

My back stiffens.

"Wh-where am I?" Salma pushes herself up to a sitting position.

I prepare to reach forward and steady her should she collapse again, but she remains steady. Some color has returned to her lips, and new strength is gleaming behind her frightened gaze.

She looks annoyingly pretty. Mortals shouldn't be allowed to be so fetching. Even the roses in my gardens last longer than they do in their own realm. Beauty should not be so fleeting. "We're in the Desert In-Between."

"Between mortals and f-fae?"

I nod. "And your curse should be lifted by now. You should be strong enough to walk on your own come tomorrow."

"W-we're camping for the night?"

Night that is edging closer. Perhaps I should trust the warning that I wrote to myself in the past. "I may be the Lord of the Dusk, but it is far too dangerous for you to walk these sands after sunset."

She blinks. "L-lord of the Dusk?"

Her words carry only a taint of fear, and I realize her stutter doesn't appear to be caused by external circumstances so much as it is something she carries within her. Perhaps it is intended to disguise the strange melody I hear behind her words, the richness of her voice.

"Yes, and Master of Orphydice Manor. Hence my coming to collect a wayward . . ." I frown at her. Perhaps I should have asked Nubia what her position was in the household. Maybe gardener? That would explain why the aroma of my roses radiates so strongly from her now. "Whatever you are to the household. Nubia will know better than I."

"Oh."

Darkness reaches into the tent, emboldened now that the sun has ducked almost completely out of view. I glance outside before turning back to her. "You must not leave." But *I must* leave.

I'll obey a book in my handwriting over a voice in my head I don't recognize.

Salma starts. "Wh-what?"

I start to push myself up. "This tent. You must not leave this tent until I return to fetch you." I stand, looking down at the delicate figure.

"Y-you're leaving? I thought it was dangerous out there."

"For mortals. *I* am the Lord of the Dusk." I turn and duck out of the tent, dropping the fabric closed behind me.

I don't add that the Shades have been getting bolder as of late. While they are unlikely to attack a fae lord, there is a risk.

Still, I walk away from the shelter I created, remembering the pictures in the tome I don't remember acquiring, let alone filling with words. I sit on the quickly cooling sand and begin to trace a crude protection in a circle around me, utilizing a second orb of moonlight to illuminate my work until the moon rises to help me wage war against the night.

"It is a war you cannot win, boy."

CHAPTER 3

I awaken inside my circle, untouched by the darkness.

"That's because you always carry the darkness deep inside."

Rising, I make my way to where the canopy still floats in place. I stoop underneath.

Salma is lying somewhat where I left her, stretched out on the sands. I'm rather surprised that she hasn't curled up for warmth. Her *kalasiris* was intended for coolness under the hot sun rather than protection against the cold desert night.

"Awaken, mortal. It is time to return to the Manor."

She doesn't stir.

Growling, I kneel down on the soft sands beside her, grasp her cold shoulder, and shake.

Her body moves in an unnatural way, like her limbs must remain in perfect relation to each other.

Is she . . . paralyzed? Did a Shade get through somehow?

"Wouldn't you like to know?"

"What did you do to her?" I hiss, rolling her onto her back and scan her for a mark, but I see nothing.

Perhaps this is part of her curse? That she becomes paralyzed at night?

"How little you know of her. I know *everything."*

Reaching out, I shake her again, but still, she doesn't rise.

"Just leave her to me. I shall collect her, and she won't be your problem any longer."

"I don't trust you to take care of what's mine."

"You don't even remember her."

"What's mine is mine, and that is that."

Turning back to the girl in question, I sigh. Carrying her unconscious form was difficult enough. To do so while she is also paralyzed would be that much worse.

Salma is a particularly difficult mortal.

"Finally, something we can agree about."

Shifting to a sitting position, I whistle.

A moment later, a desert owl flies into the tent and perches on a sand dune that rises higher than the others.

"Fly to the House of Orphydice," I tell it. "Find Hager. Lead him here."

With a gentle hoot, the owl sleepily flaps its wings and flies out of the tent.

Groaning, I lay down onto my back and turn back to Salma's sleeping form. "Difficult. That's what you are."

"Perhaps you should kill her now. Save yourself the trouble."

I sit bolt upright. "Why have you changed your tune?"

"We were agreeing just a moment ago. Now I'm continuing to do so."

Scowling, I shake my head as further unease crawls over me at this strange voice in my head. "I don't want her dead. Why would I go through all this trouble just to murder she whom I am rescuing?"

"So, your servants will think you did everything you could."

"She is under my protection. I cannot kill her even if I wanted to."

"Would you like to test that theory?"

I clench my fists at my side. "I want you to be gone. Now."

"You have no power over me, boy. Nor shall you ever be rid of me. If you want peace, send the girl to the Duat.*"*

Drawing myself to my feet, I walk out of the tent flap. The hot morning sun is preferable to this.

"Kill her. Kill her. Kill her."

I cannot silence the voice, but perhaps I can drone it out.

Reaching into the music swirling around my soul at all times, I begin to hum deep and low.

"Kill her. Kill her now! I said kill her!"

The music transforms into words.

"The day deserted us.

The sun sets in the west.
My lover, where are you?
My lover, where are you?"

～

I WAS MOST DEFINITELY correct in my assessment that carrying Salma while paralyzed would not be an easy feat.

Still, I carry her stiff, still sleeping form into the carriage when Hagan pulls up. I situate her on the bench across from mine and then knock on the roof.

Hagan yells something at the horses, and they start, dragging the carriage behind them.

Leaning back, I stare at the girl for a few moments, but she doesn't stir, so I let my eyelids drift shut, far too exhausted for having a full night's sleep.

"Adom, my love?"

I look up from the paperwork on my desk to see the profile of a woman standing at my window. I forgot I even had a window in my room; the shades are always drawn shut.

But today they are open wide, and somehow the sun is gleaming through, painting the woman's silhouette.

The sun does not shine in full force in the Court of Dusk, though. Perhaps this is the moon?

Whatever the source of the light, it is beautiful. And so is the woman it illuminates, though the same light also disguises her features. But I take it on faith of a thousand memories I do not have that she is.

"Nothing, Adom," she murmurs. "I just wanted to call you 'my love'."

To my great and utter surprise, my lips move upward. I think . . . I think I'm smiling?

A sudden jolt pulls me out of the dream that felt so strangely like a memory, dragging me back to the carriage I'm crammed in alongside the mortal maid.

Whose body has responded to the jolt by sending her crashing to the ground.

However, her limbs finally move apart from each other, and before I can reach down to help her up, she looks up. Her expression is so wide-eyed and startled, it quite reminds me of the owl I was conversing with this morn.

173

Smirking, I bite back a laugh. "You mortals are a graceless lot."

Salma drops her gaze, but not before I see the slightest flush.

I shift on my bench in an attempt to get more comfortable. "Now, rise so I can make you look *somewhat* presentable."

She jolts at that and glances down at herself and her thin *kalasiris*. Then Salma finally manages to situate herself on the bench across from me. "Are we in a . . . carriage?"

I lean back on the bench. What an observant mortal she is. "Indeed. I summoned my driver at dawn when it was safe for him to come to us." I study her for a long moment, wondering if she's going to elaborate about what happened in the canopy last night.

She says nothing, though, so I disregard last night and glance down at her travel-worn *kalasiris*. "Now, to tend to your . . ." I wince; the other mortal kingdom truly has better styles. Their garments, which I have my staff imitate, are loose and flowing rather than tight and confining. "Nakedness."

"I'm . . . sorry?"

"If you find her so revolting, just kill her."

"Yes, yes, well, no need to shock the rest of the household." And since I have to do everything, I lean forward and brush my fingers across her lap.

She jolts, but that doesn't affect the enchantment. Rich, dark fabric begins to spread out from where I traced, consuming the rest.

I know that it will transform the appearance of her tight *kalasiris* into a loose *peplos,* but only the other mortals will truly see it as such.

Even though I see the new garment when I look at her from the corner of my eye, when I turn to her straight-on, I see right through my illusion magic.

Resting my chin on the palm of my hand, I just wait for the ride to be over.

As Salma continues to ooh and ah over the transformation of her clothes, though, I realize this may be the longest drive yet. So, I lie down and stare at my hands instead.

"If you find her so annoying, just kill her."

"Wh-what did you do?" Salma asks, breaking through the voice in my head.

"A simple illusion." I glance at her. "Any fae would be able to see through it easily enough, but as I have no guests at the moment, it will do its job to fool the mortal staff. But, yes, you are still . . . less than dressed. You just don't appear so."

"Oh."

"Now." I reach into my own tunic that I also glamoured to look a little fresher. Just because I'm traveling doesn't give me any excuse not to look like the Lord of the Dusk that I am.

I remove a translucent material from my pocket that I keep for enchantment purposes. I weave an enchantment into it to protect its wearer from deep glamours as it shapes itself into a gauzy veil.

Turning, I hold it out to Salma.

She gingerly takes it as if she's never seen a veil before. "What is this?"

This child truly knows nothing, does she? Why did Nubia employ her? "A veil. You must never leave the estate without wearing it. Or allow any other fae to see you without this covering."

Finally, she does something right and secures it around her face. "Wh-why?"

I snort. "This will give you some protection from glamours that they may seek to put on you." Glancing at her, I see again the *kalasiris* through the enchantment. "Not to mention that it is quite unseemly to traipse around with a bared face like yours. There are creatures who are spiteful that would take that as a challenge from one so mortal as you."

"Oh." She drops the gaze.

The carriage comes to an abrupt stop.

Finally.

Craning my neck, I look outside the carriage window. A familiar stone Manor rises up looking rather mismatched for all the towers and halls added over the centuries.

Still, it's *my* Manor.

"Our *Manor with* our *Salma.* My *Salma.*"

I swing my legs to the carriage floor and can't help but exhale in relief. "We're here; we're home." And I even managed not to slaughter Salma in her sleep.

We're off to an excellent start.

~

This is the prequel to the Cursed Fae of Orphydice Manor series.

ABOUT JES DREW

Jes Drew is the author of 40+ stories including the Cursed Fae of Orphydice Manor series, the Sunset at Dawn trilogy, and The Samurai's Student saga. She has three degrees, including a Master of Arts in Behavioral Counseling.

STORY VI
POEMS FROM BEDLAM BY KATHY HAAN

Heat Level: Low
(PG content)

Bedlam is the fae realm in all Kathy Haan's published novels. If you'd like to immerse yourself in a world of magic, Bedlam, and spice, you can begin your journey with Bedlam Moon.

The following four poems weave together a tale of a college-aged woman who receives an unexpected invitation to a masquerade ball hosted by the fae. Through a magical portal in a tree, she has been conversing with him for a year and has grown attached to him. But as she enters the realm of the fae, she realizes that the magic and mystery of the masquerade come with a dark and twisted edge, and once she goes back home, she yearns for what could've—and should've—been. This will eventually turn into a full-length trilogy, so stay tuned.

"THE INVITATION"

Through twisted trees, a portal glows,
A penpal's note, a secret shows,
A fae from Bedlam's wicked sights,
Invites her to his grand delights.

The girl with nerves, a heart abounds,
In dreams, she danced to fae's sweet sounds,
Now, 'cross the portal, she will meet,
Her fae penpal, at masquerade's feat.

The girl prepares, her heart aflutter,
Through portal's doors, she'll soon discover,
A world of magic, dark and bright,
And Bedlam's secrets, hid from sight.

The girl steps through, to unknown lands,
Where fae awaits, with open hands,
In his embrace, she feels at home,
And Bedlam's wickedness she'll roam.

The girl, now lost in fae's embrace,
Dances with him, in Bedlam's grace,

And as the night begins to wane,
The girl's heart fills with a sweet refrain.

For in Bedlam's realm of twisted dreams,
The girl found magic, or so it seems,
A realm of darkness, sharp and bright,
Where all is possible in the night.

"THE FAE OF BEDLAM'S MASQUERADE"

In Bedlam's realm of twisted dreams,
Where shadows dance and moonlight gleams,
The fae convene in secret shroud,
A masquerade of wicked crowd.

Each guest adorned in veiled disguise,
With twisted grins and furtive eyes,
All come to play in Bedlam's night,
Where dark desires take their flight.

The music swells, the shadows stir,
As laughter echoes in a blur,
The dance of death begins to twirl,
As magic weaves its wicked swirl.

The fae of Bedlam flit and prance,
In a game of wicked chance,
As each one seeks to dominate,
And rise above the masquerade's fate.

Their revelry grows evermore,
As they lose themselves in the lore,

A world of darkness, sharp and bright,
Where all is possible in the night.

The fae of Bedlam dance and play,
As the night turns into day,
And as the dawn begins to break,
They vanish, leaving not a trace.

The masquerade has come to end,
And Bedlam's realm begins to bend,
The dreams of darkness fade away,
As the light of day begins to sway.

And so the fae of Bedlam's night,
Disappear from mortal sight,
Leaving whispers in their wake,
Of a masquerade, they dared to take.

"THE AFTERMATH"

The girl had danced with fae that night,
In Bedlam's realm of twisted light,
The masquerade, a thrilling sight,
Had captured her, held her tight.

Her penpal, fae, had led the way,
To Bedlam's realm, where magic plays,
But as the dawn began to break,
The girl knew she must make her escape.

The memories of Bedlam's night,
Stayed with her, a magic light,
But as she left the fae behind,
Her heart ached for what she would find.

The girl returned to her own world,
Where colors paled and life unfurled,
The faes' memories still aglow,
In her soul, where magic flows.

But in her heart, the girl knew true,
That magic lay beyond her view,

And though the fae were out of sight,
She'd hold their memory in her might.

And so the girl, with magic's spark,
Lived her life, her days so stark,
But in her dreams, she danced once more,
In Bedlam's realm, forevermore.

"THE CALL"

The girl, a mortal, yearned to see,
Her penpal fae, where magic be,
For though she'd left the fae behind,
Her heart had been, with magic twined.

The Bedlam Moon had waxed anew,
And magic called, so strong and true,
The girl knew then, what she must do,
Return to where her magic grew.

With trepidation, she went back,
Through portal in the old oak's crack,
And in the realm of Bedlam's night,
Her penpal fae was in her sight.

The bond between them, clear as light,
Their hearts alight, their souls take flight,
As Bedlam's magic grows in height,
The two entwined, 'til dawn in sight.

And in the light of morning's sun,
The girl knew that her heart had won,

For she and fae were now as one,
Their souls bonded, magic spun.

And so the girl, with magic bright,
Lived life with fae, her soul's delight,
In Bedlam's realm, where magic's might,
Brought joy and love, forever bright.

As Bedlam Moon, with its sweet call,
Brought girl and fae, to each other's thrall,
Their bond, soul deep, they could not stall,
Together, they'd conquer all.

ABOUT KATHY HAAN

Kathy Haan believes the secret to telling a great story is living one. The second youngest, in a massive horde of children between her parents, she did her best to gain attention and kept everyone entertained with jokes and wild stories.

She lives a life of adventure with her hunky husband, three children, and Great Pyrenees in the Midwest, United States. While new to the fiction world, you might've seen her work in Forbes or US News, where she's a regular contributor.

.

STORY VII
THE LOST PRINCESS BY SARAH ZANE

Heat Level: Low
(PG content)

Trigger Warnings:
Some violence and peril
Magic torture

THE LOST PRINCESS

The Lost Princess has been found! The Imposter is on the run!
Come one come all to celebrate with the Crown'.

Just seeing the invitation made me nauseous.

Today was the day, and I wasn't ready.

I had barely been in the palace a month and didn't feel at all ready to be a princess. I tried to remind myself that the kingdom wouldn't expect much of me. They knew my past and would forgive my ignorance, but it was hard to quiet my thoughts. I didn't feel worthy. I didn't feel like some lost princess. I just felt lost.

Before the Queen had found me, I had been happy living in ignorance of my heritage, but now I was supposed to be a princess, next in line for the throne.

I straightened my back, pushed my shoulders back, and took a deep breath. *No; not supposed to be. I am a Princess. I always have been. I was born for this.* I wished I could make myself believe it, but deep down I knew this didn't feel like home.

I missed home. I missed my aunt, uncle, and even my unruly cousins. Our home was chaotic, but it was always full of light and laughter and warmth. There was nothing warm about the palace, and it wasn't just the stone that made the palace cold.

I had been overjoyed to find I had living family—a stepmom but still. It hadn't mattered to me that she was the Queen. I was just happy to have family. My "aunt" and "uncle" had taken me in from a young age, but they had never lied to me. I always knew that while they loved me fiercely like one of their own, I wasn't.

I had been overjoyed the Queen might have been able to tell me something about my father, about why he abandoned me. When the messengers came, I hoped she would truly be overjoyed at the reunion, but she felt a little dismissive. I suppose she was kind enough, overwhelmingly kind for royalty, but I didn't feel any warmth from her.

I wanted to like her, but there was something about her eyes, about the way that she looked at me, that made me shrink away from her.

She did everything she should and took time away from ruling to spend with me and make sure I was acclimated. She even made it clear that she had no expectations of me and would continue ruling in my stead for as long as I needed. I was grateful for that at least. These days, everything was so new that I hardly felt able to take care of myself, never mind a kingdom.

Today was the first step toward that unknown and terrifying future that lay before me. Today I was to be reintroduced to the kingdom as Miravale's Lost Princess finally home. I was the sole heir to the throne, not the Imposter, Ivy. The traitor "princess" who I had been told had impersonated me for most of my life. The traitor who had run away with half the kingdom's gold when the Queen had confronted her. Today I was to take my first step toward my destiny, and I was terrified.

I had a few panicked thoughts about running away, but I knew they were crazy. I knew I had to do this, so why did I feel so nervous? I looked around my chambers, desperate for any distraction, anything to take my mind off tonight, but the reminders of the night to come were everywhere. *Maybe a walk would help.*

One more glance around my bedchambers told me that even the cavernous rooms were too small to contain my feelings, too small to give me room to breathe. I fled from the room, not knowing or caring where I was headed.

————

I had hoped a walk would help calm me, but I couldn't think straight with all the hustle and bustle going on in preparation for tonight. The staff were in a frenzy and there wasn't a single place I could find that was left untouched.

I sought out the gardens to get some fresh air, but upon looking out the window, I noticed the gardens were not spared either. There were staff pruning trees and sweeping the paths clean.

As I watched in awe, I noticed they were hanging garlands on the hedges. I couldn't believe it, I knew the Queen liked extravagance, but decorating greenery with even more greenery was excessive even for her.

Seeing the spectacle that was already being made didn't bode well for the ball. The walk was a bad idea. I was more nervous than I had been. I silently thanked the gods for the small mercy that it was a masquerade ball and hoped my mask would hide some of my nerves from all those prying eyes.

It seemed there was nowhere on the palace grounds that had been untouched, nowhere I could enjoy any solitude today. I looked longingly toward the forest surrounding the castle, toward home, but I knew better.

I wasn't allowed off the palace grounds with the rebels crawling all over the forest. The Queen thought they were hunting for me and warned me more than once not to leave the grounds. It was a reasonable request that I knew better than to disobey, but my heart ached for the forest, for home. Even just to touch one of the pines would slow my racing heart, but today of all days, with tonight meaning so much to the kingdom, I couldn't risk it. With a sigh, I resigned myself to my fate and headed back to my chambers.

The closer I got, the more commotion there seemed to be. I picked up my pace, hurrying toward my chambers. I hurdled around the corner and collided with a wall of muscle. I jumped back a foot and quickly glanced up, relaxing when I saw it was Jace, my reluctant, stoic bodyguard. He was already scowling at me.

I couldn't help the laugh that bubbled up at his grumpy face. He had been assigned as my protector the moment I arrived, which he seemed to see as equal parts an honor and a disgrace.

He had taken one look at me, decided he didn't like what he saw and had been grumpy ever since. When I complained to a couple of my maids, they told me not to mind him. He would warm up to me in time. He had been slowly, but I had recently found out he had been close friends with the Imposter. I wondered from the way he was acting if they had been more than friends, but regardless of his immediate dislike of me, he took his duties seriously. Which was why his handsome face was frowning down at me.

"Just where were you all morning? There was another rebel attack and we have been looking all over for you! The Queen was beside herself when she couldn't find you."

No wonder he hated me. Just when I was making headway with softening him to me, I had to go and make his job harder by disappearing and worrying the palace and the Queen. *The Queen!* I thought with a start. *The Queen was looking for me!*

I paled. "Where is she?"

"Last I saw, she was pacing around your chambers."

I didn't wait to hear more. I picked up my skirt and ran in the direction of my chambers, not caring if Jace followed or not. When I rushed in, I found the Queen pacing in front of the window and immediately dropped into a low bow.

"Your Majesty!" I exclaimed. "I'm so sorry."

I picked up my head and saw her rush to me. She raised me from the ground, holding me at arm's length, scrutinizing me. "Helena, what happened to you? Are you okay? You had us all worried sick!"

I ignored my discomfort at her calling me Helena and quickly said, "I'm so sorry. I don't know what I was thinking. I just went for a quick walk. I didn't think I would be missed." I gulped, adding, "I didn't think."

She continued to examine me for anything out of place. Seeing nothing, she sighed, "Well, as long as you're okay," and pulled me into a hug. I was shocked and didn't respond quick enough to put my arms around her before she pulled away. "Well, no harm done. I'm just so glad you stuck to the palace and weren't off the grounds. They would have found you for sure."

She looked out the window toward the forest and said softly, "They're getting closer. I would cancel tonight, but we can't let them win. It's too important we show the kingdom and the rest of Zanaria that we won't back down or be afraid."

She looked reassuringly at me, saying, "We will fight and we will win." More quietly, she added, "We have to. I can't lose anyone else. I just found you. I won't lose you."

I fought back the tears that were gathering in my eyes. If she could be calm in the face of this chaos, I could be, too. At least, I could try.

"Well," I said with a smile, "it looks like we have a party to get ready for."

She smiled at that, before glancing down at us both and laughing. "We both have a long way to go."

With that, she called my maids and departed back to her chambers. I watched as she glared at Jace, who was stationed at the door, on her way out. "Mind that this doesn't happen again, or I won't be as forgiving the next time."

He bowed. "Thank you, Your Majesty. It won't happen again."

With a quick look back at me and a wave, she exited.

The moment she was gone, I rushed over to Jace. "I'm so sorry. I really had no idea anyone would miss me. It won't happen again."

His stare was ice. "I won't let it."

I gulped. "I promise I'll tell you the next time if I'm going anywhere. I won't go anywhere without telling you first."

He just nodded.

I swallowed hard, fighting tears, unsure why I cared so much about Jace and his opinions. He had been cold to me since I arrived, but maybe that was what I liked.

Since I showed up at the palace, it was hard to tell who liked me for me and who liked me because of my title. He made it easy; he just didn't like me. I think deep down, I hoped that if I could win him over like the Imposter clearly had that I would be worthy of being a princess, that I would belong.

Unfortunately for me, he didn't seem like he would be thawing anymore to me any time soon.

For the hours while the maids hustled about getting me ready, applying rouge and doing and redoing the curls in my hair, he just stood there stoically. I finally managed to get him to sit when I was brought in lunch.

I told him I wouldn't eat if he didn't. He grumbled about it, but proceeded to scarf down more than half of the finger sandwiches. I let out a giggle at the crumbs stuck to his chin. He scowled at me, but let out a small laugh when I pointed out his reflection in the mirror.

A much-needed victory for a big day. I needed it today, and I think he knew that. I had been so focused on Jace that I had forgotten to be nervous about the ball until one of the Queen's maids came rushing in to see if I was ready.

I looked at my maids, who scrutinized me once more before nodding. I rushed through the empty halls behind the Queen's maid, the only audible sounds the swooshing of my red satin gown and Jace's heavy foot-steps behind me.

I marveled at how quiet the halls were. A look out the window revealed it was already dark. Everyone would likely be gathering in the ballroom by now. The maid came to a stop in front of the Queen's chambers, knocking. When the door swung open, the Queen was waiting with a box.

She smiled at me. "I'm overjoyed to finally have you, the real you, home. I just wish your father had been around to see it, but I know he's so proud of you, Helena."

Again using that name that didn't feel like my own. It wasn't far off; I had been called Alina all my life. The Queen had told me my father's mother was named Helena and that he must have meant to name me for her, so she started calling me Helena. It was a kind gesture, a new name for a new life, but it didn't feel my own.

She smiled at me, slowly opening the box and revealing a breathtakingly beautiful ruby crown. The rubies were set in gold and seemed to dance before my eyes.

"It's beautiful," I breathed out.

"It's going to look even better once you put it on."

I stared at her in shock. I couldn't have heard her right. "You mean for me to wear that?"

She nodded. "Of course! It's your day." She leaned closer, adding conspiratorially, "Besides, it's heavier than the crowns I prefer."

I gulped as a passage from my favorite story raced through my mind. *'Heavy is the head that wears the crown.'* I used to fantasize about living in the palace, about having a life that was more adventurous than my own. Leave it to me to have had my dreams come true and to be missing home.

I smiled at the Queen. If she trusted me with this, if she wanted me to wear this crown and one day take over the kingdom, then I would. She believed in me, even if I didn't. There must have been a reason she did.

She gestured to the mirror, moving behind me and stretching her arms to place the crown on my head. The weight, even having been warned, caught me by surprise, as did the sharp tang of metal in my mouth.

The crown seemed to dig into my very skull and take root there. I felt like I was being pulled to the ground, but I stood tall.

A glint in the mirror caught my eye. I almost gasped when I looked up and saw a beautiful man with a glinting ruby necklace staring back at me. I was mesmerized by the sight and stared for what felt like ages, before I heard the Queen make noise behind me, breaking me from my reverie.

I blinked, and just like that, the man was gone. I must have been more stressed than I thought. I was an avid daydreamer, but I had never halluci-nated before. I turned back to the Queen and saw her watching me with a feline smile.

"How does it feel, darling?"

I swallowed. My mouth felt incredibly dry, and the taste of metal still inexplicably coated my mouth. I forced my spine straight and smiled at her, hoping it didn't look like a grimace.

I can do this. I was born for this.

"Wonderful. Thank you, Your Majesty."

She smiled again. "I think it's well past time, dear, that you start calling me 'Mother.'" My heart warmed at that. "Of course, Your-" I stopped, laughed, and started again. "Of course, Mother." It felt weird on my tongue, but I smiled anyway.

"That's better. As the closest I have to a daughter and the sole heir to the kingdom, I hope you'll take some advice from your dear mother."

"Of course. Anything you have to say, tonight especially, would be more than welcome."

"Well, dear, there will be many vying for your attention, but there's a gentleman in particular that I want you to pay special attention to. He has my utmost respect and approval, and I hope you'll be as taken with him as I was." She leaned close and whispered, "If you're lucky, he might even be compelled to ask for your hand."

I was surprised but kept that off my face as much as I could. "Of course I'll dance with him, Mother."

She looked startled for a moment before laughing loudly. "Dear daughter, you misunderstand me. I believe he means to offer to marry you."

Marriage? I hadn't given it more than half a thought. In my old life, I hadn't planned to ever marry. We were well off enough that, thankfully, there was no need.

I had never wanted to explore romance any further than reading about it, but I was a princess now and I had to come to terms with the new expectations.

Of course I would be expected to marry. I would be expected to give the kingdom a king and expected to produce heirs with the king. I gulped. I had given some thought to ruling eventually, years down the line. I was grateful the Queen was willing to bear the burden as long as I needed, but I knew it was a burden I would have to shoulder eventually. It was a reality I was working to coming to terms with, but I had never given a thought to having someone rule at my side.

She saw something in my eyes that had her saying, "Don't worry, dear. I'm sure he'll love you." She straightened my crown, which dug further into my skull. I bit my lip to hide the grimace. She smiled, satisfied, and added, "I'm sure you'll love him as much as I do."

I tried to let that reassure me, but it shattered any peace I had found with Jace earlier.

Satisfied I was ready, she spared herself a quick glance in the mirror and swept out of the room, bidding me to follow. I did, and was more startled than I should have been to see Jace's frowning face waiting outside.

The Queen's ladies were waiting as well. They had been giggling and were staring at Jace. No wonder he was uncomfortable. Maybe, for once, that wasn't my fault. Her ladies fell into place around her and they started toward the ballroom.

The Queen looked over her shoulder and said in parting, "Be ready for your entrance when the bell chimes eight times." With that, her and her entourage were gone.

I looked at Jace, and saw him watching me, frowning. That wasn't unusual, but it seemed deeper, so I asked, "Is something the matter?"

He gestured at my head. "That crown."

I touched it carefully, concerned. "You don't like it?" Even as I asked, I tried to tell myself it didn't matter, but I couldn't lie. It did matter. In the month I had been in the palace, he was the closest thing I had to a friend, the only one I trusted with my life and trusted to be honest with me.

He sighed, shaking his head. "It's not that. You look good, I guess."

I laughed before saying, "Gee thanks. Such high praise. You might have a future as a poet if you keep that up."

He laughed for the second time that day, shoving me lightly. I wasn't expecting it and started to fall to the side. Before I could move to stop myself, he had me in his grasp and righted me. He laughed again. "I didn't realize you were so clumsy."

"Hey!" I said, grinning. "I'll have you know I'm as graceful as any royal when a brutish guard isn't shoving me."

"I take offense to that. I'm sure you meant a handsome guard." He wiggled his eyebrows at me, in what might have been a suggestive way had he been anyone else. But this was Jace, and the look was too hilarious not to laugh at.

"I suppose if I can be a beautiful princess for the day, you can be a handsome guard."

"Ah. SoSo, when it snows in Santerra then."

I laughed at that. "I knew I would get through to you sometime."

"I…"

I froze at his pause. I had ruined it. He was warming up to me and I had ruined it. "I'm sorry."

He sighed. "It's just, you're not her, and-"

I cut him off, "I know."

He stopped mid-sentence, looking surprised. "You know?"

"Of course I know! She trained her whole life for this. I've been here for hardly a month and feel more at home in a forest or on a horse than I do in the palace. There's so much I don't know. So much no one is willing to tell me. You're the only one that I know is being real with me. I know you're sad she left." He looked about to interrupt, but I rushed on, wanting to get my point across. "Whether or not she was real, she was real to you and if she hadn't left, she would've likely made a better princess, a better ruler even, than I will."

He just stared at me before uttering, "The crown, though."

"I know. I know. It was hers, right? It doesn't look nearly as good on me as it did on her, right?"

He shook his head, frustration seeping into his features. "There's nothing wrong with how you look. It was hers, but it wasn't always. The Queen gave it to her a week or two before she disappeared. She wasn't acting herself. I know you'll think I'm crazy, but that crown is bad news."

I just blinked at him. That wasn't at all what I expected.

"You said you trust me. Only the gods know why since I've been pushing you away as hard as I can. It's hard seeing someone in her place, hard to have to act like she was never here and forget about her. I'm sorry. Taking that out on you isn't fair, but I can't take how fake everyone is around here. Just a couple of months ago, the maids and the Queen's ladies were cozied up to Ives, and now they act like she was nothing to them. I'm glad you at least can see through that. I just... I don't know, really, but something doesn't feel right. You said you trust me, so trust me in this. Be careful with that crown and be careful who you trust."

I just nodded. "Thank you."

"I will do better by you than I did by Ivy. I swear to you, I won't fail to protect you."

I couldn't even begin to understand what he meant about her, and it seemed too personal to ask.

"Thank you. Although a friend would be more agreeable than a guard," I said, knowing I was pushing my luck.

Relief coursed through me at his smile. "Well, the guard part is non-negotiable, but I might be open to a friend. The gods know how hard it is to come by a real friend in a place like this."

I couldn't tell if he meant the palace or the kingdom, and kingdom and didn't ask.

"Friends, then?"

He nodded. "Friends. I can do that, but don't expect me to be all friendly and everything."

I put my hand to my heart and dramatically gasped. "My good sir, I would never. I know grumpiness is your nature and would never seek to change that."

We both laughed at that before he said, "I suppose I could stand to light up a little."

I looked skeptically at him. "I don't know. It really might kill you to be nice."

"I'll have you know, I'm quite nice most of the time."

"I believe it," I said, thinking back to the small kindnesses I had seen him bestow on maids and their children and his comradery with the other guards. Even to me, he had never been unreasonably cold.

"Well, friend, we should probably be going."

I looked at him questioningly. "We must have some time before the eighth bell?"

He nodded in agreement. "Just enough time to sneak in and raid the dessert table."

"You can't be serious?" I asked, giggling at the thought of him sneaking pastries into his pockets.

He grinned. "I don't joke about food."

I gestured wildly at my crown and dress. "And how exactly am I supposed to be sneaky in this?"

"I have just the thing." He reached into his coat pocket and produced my mask. *My mask! Of course!* I had completely forgotten it was a masquerade and had forgotten my mask.

"Okay, I'm in, but if we get caught, you're taking the blame."

He smirked. "If we get caught, it won't be my fault. Try to keep up."

With that, he headed in the direction of the ballroom, leaving me to quickly follow.

_____

He led us outside through the garden, and I gasped at the floating lights strewn along the path. I still wasn't used to the casual displays of magic.

It wasn't that magic was discouraged anywhere, but with the disappearances, people didn't feel safe practicing out in the open. It used to be safe, but over the past few years, magic users had been slowly, unexplainably disappearing. Children taken from their homes, parents from their children, lovers from one another, all without note or explanation. There was no pattern, only that those who were disappearing were known magic users and hadn't been heard from or seen since. The rebels were suspected, but in all the raids of their camps, none of the magic users were ever found.

Had I given any thought to it, I would have realized things would be different in the palace with magic, where there was safety in numbers and guards ready to defend those inside the palace, but it hadn't occurred to me how different it would be.

Even before the disappearances, magic was only used sparingly, certainly not for tasks like lighting a garden that could have been easily accomplished with fire and torches. As I took in the twinkling lights, I couldn't bring myself to be upset about the careless magic use. It was a breathtaking sight.

Jace noticed I had stopped, turned, and put his hand on my arm and dragged me toward the ballroom.

"Come on. We're running out of time before they'll be looking for you for your grand entrance. Plus, we want to get the good pastries before they're all gone."

I laughed at that, checked that my mask was secure, and picked up my pace, hurrying side by side with him. He didn't let his hand fall from my arm. I was glad of it. For the first time since my arrival, I didn't feel so lost and alone at the palace.

_____

Jace hadn't been exaggerating about the dessert table being worth sneaking in for. There were almost a hundred different types of pastries and desserts, most of which I had never seen before and likely had never heard of never mind tasted. The chocolate and coffee aromas hit my nose first, making my mouth water. I surveyed the table, immediately laying eyes on and grabbing a chocolate tart.

I looked over at Jace and saw he already had crumbs on his face and his hands full of fruit covered pastries. I grinned at him, scarfed down my tart, and scanned the table, looking for the delightful looking strawberry pastry he had, when I heard a male voice from somewhere behind me mention the princess.

I froze where I stood, hoping he and whoever he was talking to hadn't noticed me. I risked a glance over at Jace to see his back was rigid but he hadn't made a move to leave, so I stayed where I was. I was sure there was chocolate on my face, and tried to lick it off my lips, thinking I might be forced into conversation sooner than planned and not wanting a chocolate-covered face to be anyone's first impression of their princess.

I glanced at Jace and saw him stifling his laughter. He gestured to his cheek. I copied his gesture and blushed when I came away with chocolate. I mouthed my thanks to him.

Satisfied I was at least presentable, I took a couple of steps toward Jace, closing the distance between us, and slowly turned to see who was talking about me. My heart stopped when I saw *him*.

It wasn't just that he was handsome, he was, but that wasn't what made me stare. He was the man from the mirror. Well, the man I had imagined in the mirror. He was every bit the same man. The same sweeping dark hair. The same burning, passionate eyes, the same muscled figure, he even had on the ruby necklace.

I gasped, unable to help myself. Jace shot me a confused look, followed my gaze, and then looked concerned. He went to take my arm, but I pulled it away. I needed to hear what the man was saying.

I sidled closer to the table, within earshot of the stranger, and heard him say, "I do hope she hurries up. I don't like to be kept waiting. I hope she'll be as beautiful as the last. She was feisty, and I would have loved to bed her. Sad she got away."

I felt Jace stiffen at my side, and instinctually grabbed his arm, not knowing what he might do. His callous way of referring to the Imposter made *me* angry, and I hadn't even known her. I imagined Jace was feeling tenfold what I was, so I gripped him tightly.

With my attention on Jace, I had failed to notice that I had the stranger's attention. When I looked back in his direction, his dark eyes were locked on mine.

"Hello there," he said, staring at me.

His companion turned and stiffened when he saw Jace glaring at them. He pointed to his empty glass as an excuse and practically ran from us.

"Jace, what a pleasure."

"Amir," was all Jace said.

I watched as Amir's eyes raked over my body and asked, "Who's this beauty on your arm?"

I considered a moment what to say, but Jace pushed me behind him and said, "She's no one."

Amir's lip curved into a smile, delight coating his features. He licked his lips, and I couldn't help it as my gaze dropped, tracking the movement of his tongue across his lush, alluring lips.

His grin widened. "Well, well, well, someone's quite protective over 'no one'. And here I thought you were still mourning over that Imposter, Ivy."

Jace stiffened even more. I dug my nails into his arm. Whoever this was, this clearly wasn't the time or place.

"A pity you seem to be spoken for. You seem like the entertaining sort. You must be if you already have Jace on this tight a leash." I blushed and Jace strained forward, but I tightened my grip on his arm, trying to force some calm and sense back into him.

Amir grinned at the display. "A real pity, but I'm sure the princess will keep me well entertained."

I froze. He couldn't mean it. I had only just met the man, but Jace's lack of recommendation, and this man's own words, had done him no favors in recommending himself to me.

Amir looked around Jace at me, and said, "I don't recognize you, but from the attire, you must be one of the Queen's new ladies?" he asked.

I nodded, feeling strongly that I didn't want him to know the truth. "I am."

"So, you must have met this new princess then. Tell me what you know of her, my intended. The Queen hasn't let me within fifty feet of her since her arrival. I doubt very much the Queen wanted to share me." He grinned at that. I blanched further.

He couldn't mean what he seemed to be implying. I was certainly not his intended, and the Queen had never mentioned taking a lover.

He continued, "She hasn't told me much of anything about the new princess. Although she didn't have to for me to agree, the throne being on the table and all." He couldn't be serious, but he seemed alarmingly so. My blood ran cold at the thought, but I reassured myself the Queen wouldn't allow that, before second guessing myself.

She had been kind enough to me, but I hardly knew the woman. It seemed he knew her a good deal better than I did. I didn't know what I would do about the situation, but I had to get away from him and get to the bottom of this. The Queen had never mentioned Amir to me. Maybe he was wrong about her plans. She had mentioned a man to me, but it couldn't have been him. He was too much a of brute to have her recommendation. At least I hoped that was the case.

Amir was still watching me expectantly. Jace said quietly, "You don't have to tell him anything."

Amir laughed delightedly at that. "There, there, Jace. I promise I won't scare your little friend, but what's the harm in telling me about the princess? What sort of lady is she?"

I thought for a moment before saying, "She's a loving person, kind to most, determined to do right by those she cares about and quick to care for others-"

He cut me off, shaking his head in annoyance. "No, no, no. I asked what she looked like. Is she as beautiful as they say? She can't be more beautiful than the last, though, could she, Jace?"

If I didn't get Jace out of here soon, Amir would be dead and the ball would be ruined, but I couldn't bring myself to move quite yet. I stepped in line with Jace, trying to move him behind me, but he wouldn't move and tried, unsuccessfully, to push me back behind him. Unfortunately, Amir noticed the exchange and grinned. "Now, now I'll play nice. No need to defend him. I promise I won't hurt a hair on his head. Not tonight anyway. I would never hurt a beautiful woman's plaything. But are you quite sure he's satisfying you?"

I couldn't help the rage that coursed through me, and gave into it.

"Positive he does more for me than you ever could. Speaking of which, we must be going. There's a private corner of the garden calling us both." I looked at Jace, pleadingly. "I know it's only been a few hours, but I need you."

Jace didn't respond, still glaring at Amir. Amir looked at us both in interest. "Well, if you want a third, don't be shy to summon me. I'm sure I have some time before the princess deigns to arrive."

I threw all my weight into tugging on Jace's arm and was awarded with him staggering back into me. I shot him a warning look and tugged him toward the garden doors. We were running out of time and the sooner I got him out of the ballroom and away from Amir, the better.

The moment we crossed the threshold in the garden, I whirled to face Jace. "Who was *that?*"

"Bad news. I would avoid him if I were you. I don't know how you managed to be here a month without seeing him, but it doesn't seem likely you'll be that lucky again. He's the Queen's right hand man. Say whatever you must to her, do whatever you must, but don't let yourself actually become his intended."

I shuddered at the thought. "As if. I'm about as likely to marry him as I am a dragon."

He snorted, but the serious look didn't leave his face. "He had been after Ivy for ages. I honestly sometimes wonder if he wasn't the reason she left." He looked away for a moment, adding almost to himself, "The reason she left me."

I didn't know what to say, but I felt I should do something. I put my hand on his shoulder. He turned to me, watching while I again apologized. "I'm so sorry. I know I'm not her. I know I'm a sorry excuse for a princess and am barely a friend, but I'm here for you if you need to talk."

He smiled a little and thanked me before saying, "We'd better be going. It's almost time and we both know better than to keep the Queen waiting."

With that, he took off through the garden and I followed closely behind.

Standing outside the ballroom entrance behind the closed doors with Jace and two footmen in front of either door, my nerves came back but I also felt a rush of excitement. I had seen a small portion of the ballroom when we snuck in earlier, but I had been so focused on the tarts, and then on Amir, that I hardly registered most of the room. I was excited to see the true opulence and grandeur of a Miravale ball. All my life I had heard about them, but most commonfolk never received invitations. I was excited to see what all the fuss was about for myself.

I tried to ignore my nerves and push away the thought that the ball was in my honor. Ignore that I was symbolically and literally facing and greeting my future tonight.

The Queen had even mentioned marriage and her approved suitor. I would be on my best behavior of course. The Queen had been nothing but kind to me and she deserved that respect.

I hoped the man she had spoken of would be good company and a good dancer, but I would silently suffer through his company and dancing if he wasn't. However, I wasn't willing to agree to anything more than a dance or two. I didn't know what the future held for me, never mind what I wanted in a partner, what I wanted in a King to my Queen, in a ruler for Miravale, and I didn't feel I would for a long while. I knew I was of marrying age, but twenty-five hardly seemed old enough to know what I wanted out of the rest of my life. I was already tied to the throne; I didn't want to be tied to anything or anyone else right now. Fortunately, from what I knew of the Queen, I believed she would respect that and not push me.

I glanced back at Jace, and he smiled gently at me, leaning forward to say, "Don't worry, you just have to manage to walk down the stairs. I'm sure you can manage that. Especially if you're as graceful as you say."

I laughed at that, swatting at him. "I'll manage just fine, thank you."

I would. All I had to do was make it down the grand staircase and then people would stop staring. They would go back to what they were doing, and I would be able to breathe again. I was a princess. I was going to have to get used to dramatic entrances, but I was nervous.

"I'll be right at the bottom of the stairs waiting for you," he said seriously.

I looked at him, surprised.

"I'm your escort for tonight, obviously. Tonight, and every night, although how I got so unfortunate to have that job is beyond me," he said with a teasing smirk. "I mean, really, who did I offend?" I rolled my eyes, but he must have seen the anxiety in them since he added, "I'll make sure nothing happens to you, Helena."

"Alina," I said softly.

He looked at me, confused.

"Thank you, truly, I don't deserve your kindness, but please call me Alina."

"No thanks needed, *Alina*." He tried it out, rolling the sounds slowly over his tongue, and nodded decisively. "I like it. Much better than Helena. As I was saying, no thanks needed, Alina, it's my job, and really not such a terrible one."

I flashed him a smile and watched as one of the footmen gave us a warning that it was almost time. I turned and nodded to him, but quickly turned back when I saw something red glinting out of the corner of my eye. I turned and was surprised to see it was my own reflection that had caught my eye.

The Queen loved mirrors. The whole palace was full of them. The reflection was no surprise, but what did surprise me was my appearance. I hadn't had a chance to see the full effect of the gown, crown, and mask, but I was utterly unrecognizable. I looked beautiful, every part the princess I was supposed to be.

My dark hair looked beautiful with the crown and the red satin contracted in at my waist before jutting out in waves and pooling all around me. When I had first saw the dress, I was sure with all that fabric that I would look and feel like I was swimming in it, but somehow it suited me. The simple gold necklace I wore perfectly matched the shade of gold of the crown. I watched Jace come up behind me.

"If you're quite done admiring yourself, you have a ballroom of people to charm, *princess*."

I rolled my eyes, but took his proffered arm and moved back to the door. He surprised me by dropping my arm and stepping away when the footman nodded to him. A moment later, he started to walk away.

"Where are you going?" I called after him.

"I'll see you at the bottom," he said over his shoulder as he rushed around the corner.

I gulped. I had forgotten I would have to make the entrance on my own. The bells started to chime. I took a deep breath and squared my shoulders back. I could do this. *I am Alina Miravale, Princess of Miravale and future ruler of the kingdom. I was born for this. I can do this.*

On the sixth bell, the footmen nodded to one another, turning the door handles in unison on the seventh bell. On the eighth and final bell, they swung the doors open into the ballroom. I heard the music swell in anticipation for my entrance and stepped inside.

My jaw dropped at the sight. The chandeliers sparkled overhead, the glass ceiling opening the room to the glittering stars above. Candles and floating lights joined the chandeliers in twinkling throughout the room. They had been brighter earlier; they must have been dimmed for my entrance. I wondered why for a brief moment until I saw a spotlight materialize and was hit with the full force of its light. I blinked, once, twice. Trying to regain my vision.

I heard the footman announce, "Presenting Her Royal Highness, the recently found and universally adored Princess Helena of Miravale, sweetheart of the kingdom and future Queen, forever may she reign."

"Here, here," responded the crowd in unison. "Long live the Princess, forever may she reign."

A barely suppressed shudder ran through me at their proclamations and their faith in me, but I would strive to live up to them. I forced my legs to move, and nearly stumbled off the landing onto the first stair but felt it just in time to catch myself and started my descent.

After a few steps, I regained enough of my vision from the blinding spotlight that I was able to see the room again.

The spacious ballroom was packed with what seemed like every noble from the entirety of the kingdom. It seemed like the whole kingdom was here tonight. I scanned the crowd for familiar faces before I caught and stopped myself. I knew better. The commonfolk wouldn't be in attendance. My adoptive family and my old friends had never been invited to the palace before, and tonight would certainly be no different.

I saw movement at the bottom of the stairs, and was impressed to see Jace moving into position. There must have been a shortcut I didn't know about for him to have made it there so quickly. I took a breath. He was there waiting and would make sure I didn't make a fool of myself. I just had to make it to him first.

I could do this. I would impress the kingdom and the Queen. I hadn't seen her yet, but knew she must be watching like everyone else was.

I scanned the room again, looking for her. When I found her, my steps faltered. I caught myself and forced my feet to continue their descent, but knew the color had drained from my face. The Queen looked happy enough. It was her companion that made my blood run cold.

I should have known. Jace had warned me that he was her right-hand man. It shouldn't have been a shocking sight, but she had grinned up at me in a way that seemed to imply he was the man she had been telling me about.

He couldn't be. Maybe I was mistaking her signals. Maybe she was just talking with him and would introduce me to her favored suitor for me later. I clung desperately to that hope as I finished my descent and clung on to Jace's offered arm a bit too fiercely to be proper.

He looked at me questioningly, but I shook my head. I couldn't explain right now and hoped I was wrong. It felt like I would be speaking it into existence if I said it now. I had to be wrong.

He leaned over and asked, "Where to now?"

I looked around the ballroom, for what or who, I wasn't sure, but found nothing. When I didn't respond, he took another look at me and said, "Drinks it is," and steered us toward the tower of glasses and fountain of wine by the wall.

Wine was pouring from the mouth of a stone lion's head on the wall and into a pyramid of overflowing glasses until it reached the surrounding pool below, which looked far deeper than a fountain pool should be. Deep enough to swim in even. I wondered if anyone had ever tried.

Before I could ask, Jace leaned over and said, "You're going to want to be careful around that. If you fall in, you end up swallowing enough wine that it gets hard to find your way out."

I looked at him skeptically. "And you know this because?"

"I wasn't as careful as I should've been."

I laughed at the vision of him floundering around in a pool of wine, floating on his back and spitting wine out of his mouth.

"I'll take that under advisement," I said, grinning. The grin dropped from my face a moment later when I saw the Queen headed this way on Amir's arm.

Thankfully, Jace saw them as well and moved us quickly to the fountain, taking and filling a glass for himself and me. He handed me mine, and with a look that said drink up, turned me to the wall, out of the Queen's line of sight. I took the hint and downed the contents in two big gulps. I turned back and handed him the glass. He looked impressed and handed me his own still full glass before refilling my old glass for himself. A moment later, the Queen was upon us.

"My dear daughter, just the royal I was looking for," she said, smiling.

I fought to smile back at her, but it was hard with her choice in escort.

"Your Majesty," I said, but at her stern glass, quickly corrected, "Mother, you look beautiful."

She nodded her head and smiled. "Thank you, dear. As do you. I didn't want to waste any time in introducing you to a dear friend of mine, Lord Amir Valence."

"Amir, darling, this is Princess Helena, my daughter."

He had the decency to look embarrassed at the revelation and dropped into a deep bow. When he looked up, he lightly grasped my hand and planted a soft kiss to it. I met his eye and was disgusted at the butterflies I felt in my stomach. I couldn't deny he was handsome... when he wasn't speaking anyway.

"A pleasure to meet you officially, Princess."

Unable to hold my tongue, I said, "The pleasure is all yours, I'm sure."

Amir looked amused, but the Queen looked stunned. I gulped.

"I beg your pardon, Amir. Please do help yourself to a drink while I have a quick, private word with my daughter."

He bowed his head. "Of course, Your Majesty. I won't be far."

She looked at me, confused, and stepped closer to me. She was about to say something when she noticed Jace was by my side.

"Captain, consider yourself relieved of your duties for the rest of the night. Do go and have some fun. You are dismissed."

Jace's shocked look mirrored my own. I hoped he wouldn't stray far. He looked around, unsure, before his eyes settled on something in the far corner of the ballroom. He bowed, backing away, and quickly made his way in that direction.

I gulped.

The Queen turned to me. "Mother, I'm so sorry. I didn't mean to be rude, but I already had the misfortune of making Amir's acquaintance and I can assure you he was anything but a gentleman."

She looked at me, concern and disapproval battling over her face, but she listened as I briefly recounted our meeting.

More concern washed over her face as she reached out and stroked my hair before adjusting the heavy crown.

"There must have been some misunderstanding, darling. That doesn't sound like him. Maybe it was someone else, or if it was him, he probably recognized you and was acting in jest. You can hardly blame him. You weren't supposed to be in the ballroom yet in the first place." She sighed. "I don't want you miserable tonight, but do promise me you'll give him a chance and at least a dance or two." I started to protest, but she said, "I swear, just a dance or two, with an open mind, and then you can spend the rest of the evening however you'd like, agreed?"

It was a highly reasonable request from someone who had been nothing but kind to me. As much as I wanted to refuse, I knew I couldn't. I could manage a dance or two. I nodded. "For you, Mother, I will give it my best shot."

She smiled. "That's all I ask." A moment later, Amir, at some signal I didn't notice, flounced back over.

"Our apologies for sending you away. I can assure you, you are most welcome back."

"I thank you, Your Majesty," he said, taking her hand and kissing it like he had mine. However, unlike me, the Queen let out a small giggle.

I suppressed my nausea and tried to smile.

"I was just telling my daughter about how skilled a dancer you are."

He laughed amiably. "I should hope you haven't been telling tall tales, your Majesty. I should never live up to them."

The warmth in his voice was jarring. This was miles from how he had acted earlier. The complete personality change was giving me whiplash, and I was stuck wondering which was the real him and if it even mattered to me to find out. His looks were disarming, but I knew I would have to keep my guard up with him.

He looked at me with a pleading look and said, "If you'll do me the honor, I can try to live up to the promises Her Majesty has made. I promise not to step on your feet."

I couldn't help the laugh that came out of me.

"We shall see if you're able to keep that," I said with a small smile of my own.

He offered me his arm, and I placed my hand in the crook of his elbow and let him lead me to the dance floor. I looked back a moment and saw the Queen grinning at me. Seeing her happy warmed my heart. I hoped she was right about Amir, or at the very least that the dance would be quick and painless. The crowd parted before us, clearing the dance floor to watch as their princess glided into her first dance.

He laced his arm around me, pulling me close, and quirked an eyebrow at me, seeming to question if this was okay. I was surprised and grateful for his manners. I nodded.

I would give the people their show. I wouldn't just look the part; I would act it. I was their princess, and all eyes were on me. I would give them a show.

He laced his fingers through mine and whirled us off. With him leading, I felt incredibly light on my feet as I followed him through the steps. He coaxed me gently and never took his eyes off me. It was like we were the only two in the room.

I felt the heat rise to my cheeks when he whispered to me how beautiful I was. At least I wouldn't have to worry about faking a smile. Maybe the Queen was right. He was quite charming when he wanted to be. Maybe he was just trying to get a rise out of Jace earlier. Jace could be prickly. Maybe that's all it was. I was probably just a casualty in whatever was between him and Jace. I would have to ask Jace, later, after this dance, but the music faded away and my mind was screaming when he moved his hand from my waist too soon.

"Would you care for another?" I asked quickly before I could think better of it. A surprised smile overtook his face. "I didn't have the nerve to ask for the honor, but I would be grateful."

With that, he laced his arm back around me and pulled me in close. The embrace felt more intimate than our first dance, and I felt myself breathless when I looked in his eyes. I tore my eyes away from him long enough to see the Queen on the edge of the dance floor grinning at us. It warmed my heart further, and I let myself get lost in the twirls and spins of the dance.

When again the music ended, I reluctantly pulled away from him, curtsying to him while he bowed. He had such an adorable look of wonder on his face when he saw my smile that I giggled.

He sidled closer to me, took my hand, and kissed it, causing us both to blush. "I hope you might consider saving another dance for me later, but I know better than to think I could have you all to myself tonight. I'm sure there's a line a mile long of nobility wanting to dance with you."

I was about to protest that highly unlikely fact when I saw Jace trying to get my attention over Amir's shoulder.

"It seems you are right in a manner of speaking. A friend of mine is looking for me, but you have my word I will save you another dance. It would be my pleasure."

I started to walk past him, but not before he said, "I can assure you the pleasure is all mine."

I made my way through the crowd as quickly as I could to where Jace was standing. He was just on the outskirts of the dance floor and had a worried look on his face.

"Is everything alright?" I asked hurriedly.

He stared at me. "I should be asking you that. How you managed to put on so good a show while being stuck on Amir's arm is beyond me, but it was thoroughly convincing. You are apparently quite skilled in deception."

I blushed at that and looked down toward the floor. "Well, actually…" I started before trailing off, unsure of what else to say.

"A phenomenal performance, because I'm sure after the way he treated you earlier that it was just that, a performance. It seems the Queen bought it, so that should buy you some peace, likely for the rest of the evening at least."

"I mean, it actually wasn't all bad."

He looked at me in shock, and I watched a flash of hurt cut across his face. "You can't be serious!"

"I'm not sure what happened between the two of you, but there wasn't a hint of arrogance or hostility when he was with me."

"Convenient, of course, that now that he knows you're the princess, he's nothing but nice."

"Come on. It's not like that."

"Isn't it?"

I was contemplating what to say when a nobleman interrupted to ask me to dance. It wasn't an unattractive proposition in and of itself, but I was too focused on Jace to truly want to dance right now. Unfortunately, I didn't have a choice. Not wanting to seem rude, I shot an apologetic look to Jace and turned back to the nobleman to agree, but didn't get the chance.

Jace cut in, saying, "Apologies, sir, but Her Highness has promised this dance to me."

Without waiting for a response, he took my hand and led me further onto the dance floor. I was grateful for his quick thinking. I expected him to lead me through the throng of people to the other side, but to my surprise, he stopped, straightened his posture, and held out his hand for mine. I hadn't for a second thought he actually meant to dance with me, but accepted his hand and laced my fingers through his. His fingers were warm, and he felt familiar in a way I couldn't explain. I relaxed against him as the swarm of bodies pushed us to and fro, waiting for the next dance.

The music that started a moment later was a lively dance. I would've preferred something more intimate so we could continue our conversation, but at least I was on the floor with him.

We pulled back in time to the music, pressing our hands together and apart, spinning and repeating. The next time we pressed our hands together I heard him hiss, "You can't be serious."

I didn't know what he meant and had to wait since we pulled apart and executed another spin before coming back together, giving me time to ask, "Serious about what?"

We repeated the steps, and I grew increasingly frustrated with the interruptions.

"You actually buy his act?"

The hurt on his face was alarming and speared me through with guilt.

"He really was nice to me," I said sheepishly when we met again.

"I can't believe you!" he exclaimed.

My heart dropped at that, and I didn't bother hiding the pain from my expression, doubting I could if I wanted to. Unfortunately, at that moment, the dancers shifted and I was in front of a new gentleman. I watched Jace, barely paying attention to my own steps or my own partner. Willing Jace to look at me, to understand. Willing the dance to hurry up so I could be reunited with him and explain. I shuffled through a couple more partners, not taking my eyes of Jace, but I noticed someone else had caught his eye and when I let my curiosity get the best of me and followed his gaze, I couldn't blame him.

I may have been the princess, the guest of honor at the ball, but she had every eye glued to her as she made her way from the garden into the room. Her auburn hair glittered in the candlelight, her silver and midnight blue mask obscuring most of her features, except her blood-red lips that were curled into a smirk.

Her dress was the same midnight blue as her mask and clung to her tightly, loosening a little at the bottom to form a small train behind her. From her shoulders hung a silver cloak embroidered with dark constellations that trailed behind her when she walked.

She glided over to the dance floor and inserted herself between Jace and his partner, making a spectacle of herself. I saw his jaw drop at the brazenness of the move. I watched in amazement as they had a whispered exchange through the dance.

I felt a tug of emotion that felt an awful lot like jealousy, but that made no sense. I didn't care who Jace danced with. We were friends, just that, friends, and that was enough for me. That was all I wanted from him. So why was it bothering me seeing their hands touch? Seeing their whispered conversation? Was she a lover of his? Or an ex-lover? What did she even want with him? I had to find out.

We switched partners again, and I was appalled that she followed him, bumping the next woman out of line as well.

She did this once more. I would be next. I wondered if she would try that with me as well. I wondered if I would let her. By now, everyone in attendance should have known who I was, I doubted she would cut into my dance on my night, but she had already been bolder than most women would have ever been. Her auburn hair fanned around her as she spun, her mask glinting in the candlelight and her mischievous smirk still playing across her face.

One more swell of the music and I was surprised that Jace was back in front of me, surprised she hadn't intercepted.

He looked surprised and startled to be back in front of me, too. I met his hands, and whispered, "Who *was* that?"

He didn't reply before the music ended. He ceremonially bowed to me, and I curtsied back. I went to step closer to him but saw him stiffen. I stopped my progress before I noticed he wasn't staring at me, but over my shoulder.

I turned around and was surprised to see Amir, and even more surprised at the lack of ease and friendliness I felt from him this time. He glared at Jace, ignoring me. "I should've known. Already making moves on the new princess, I see. Sniff around all you want, you'll never be more than a glorified guard dog. Helena needs a real man."

My mouth dropped open at the complete change in his personality and his callous disregard for me and how he was treating my friend.

I narrowed my eyes at him in warning, but he either didn't see or ignored it, continuing, "What a rotten trick, trying to make me look bad in front of Helena. An honest man would have warned me it was her."

I didn't know what had happened between Amir and Jace, but it didn't matter anymore. Jace hadn't done anything to incite him, and Amir's behavior was unacceptable. I hoped the Queen would forgive me, but I wouldn't let him continue to talk to my closest and only friend in that manner.

"A good man wouldn't have needed a warning. But since you apparently require one, here's mine: You won't win my favor if you continue to abuse and mistreat my friend."

Amir met my eye, looking almost startled and dazed to see me there. He considered for a moment, and in taking in my resolve, he nodded in what looked like contrition. "Of course. My apologies, Your Highness. I didn't mean to offend you."

I nodded, not trusting anything kind to come out of my mouth.

He looked like a kicked puppy when he met my eye again and said, "I do hope you will still honor your word to save me another dance."

I was about to tell him exactly where he could shove his 'another dance' when the Queen made her way over to us.

Jace quickly made his exit, making a beeline for the wine fountain, where I saw his mystery woman waiting.

The Queen put her hand on both mine and Amir's shoulders, saying, "My two favorite people. It warms my heart to see you both getting along so well. You make quite a handsome pair, you know," she said, grinning at us both.

I swallowed my unease and smiled at her. "Mother, I hope you're having a wonderful evening."

Her eyes watered for a moment. "Of course I am, darling. There's nothing quite so right with the world or magical as seeing your daughter finally home and taking her rightful place where she belongs."

I swallowed hard at that. I really should have been showing more gratitude than I was.

"I'm delighted to be…" I paused, stumbling over the word and the wrongness of it before forcing out, "Home."

She beamed at me, lacing her hand through Amir's arm. "If you wouldn't mind excusing us, Amir and I have a few things to discuss."

He bowed lightly, before righting himself and leading her away.

I hadn't expected to be alone, and looked around, not knowing who I was looking for or what to do now. I knew I should have been making new acquaintances and dancing with nobility, but I couldn't bring myself to bother.

My eyes had found Jace and the auburn-haired woman without knowing I was looking for them. Jace was leaning precariously against the fountain, and they were awfully close, their lips mere inches from touching. I held my breath, watching, waiting, but they continued to talk at that distance.

Unable to fight my curiosity and compulsion anymore, I made my way through the crowd over to them.

I heard the woman's voice asking Jace hurriedly, "How long has she been wearing it?"

I craned to hear his response, trying to stay out of sight for a moment longer.

"Just tonight. A few hours at most."

"And can she be trusted?"

"I think so. She seems to trust me."

She was about to say something else when her eyes landed on me.

I moved forward, awkwardly, trying to seem casual, like I hadn't been standing there listening, like I wasn't now wondering who and what they were talking of.

"I'm sorry to interrupt," I said, looking from her to Jace and back again, surprised at their closeness and intimacy. "I was looking for Jace."

He smiled, but it felt forced. "Well, you found me." He moved away from her, closing the gap between us. "Unfortunately, not in the best of company," he said pointedly to the stranger. "But I'm sure she was just leaving."

The abrasiveness he said that with reminded me of how he used to talk to me. It was odd seeing him use that tone with someone he was so clearly intimately acquainted with.

Even more surprising when instead of being hurt or offended, she laughed. She turned to me and bowed deeply. It was odd seeing a woman bow. I hesitated a moment, wondering if I was supposed to curtsy back, wondering who she was. I was frozen for long enough that she righted herself and said, "Robyn of the Mirawood at your service."

I had never heard the forest referred to like that, as if it were its own small kingdom. Coupled with her bowing instead of curtsying, it was clear this Robyn was quite a strange woman. It only added to her air of mystery.

"Jace is an old friend of mine."

"We're not friends," he gritted out. "We clearly never were and certainly aren't anymore."

Now she looked wounded, but hid the expression a moment later, saying, "Oh hush. Friends quarrel. So we're having a quarrel. We're still friends." She turned back to me. "You know how he can be when things don't go exactly his way," she whispered loud enough for him to hear.

I was inclined to agree, but held my tongue at the anger on his face. I didn't know what to say.

A moment later, she sighed happily. "I love this score." She looked at Jace, pouting when he didn't say anything. She turned her sights to me and exclaimed, "I know! How about a dance? That will give him some time to reconsider."

I looked at him, waiting with bated breath to see if he would accept, before I noticed she was still looking at me.

"You want to dance... with me?" I asked after a long pause, sure I was misunderstanding.

"Of course. You're the royal of the hour. The new princess and all. It would be my honor." She grinned and added, quietly but loud enough for him to hear, "Plus, it will give the big grump over there time to cool off, and might make him jealous."

I didn't know how she meant that, but before I could ask, she took a step closer to me and her hand reached up toward my face. I startled and moved back a little before she gently brushed a loose curl from my face. Her touch was feather light and warm.

"What do you say, Your Highness? Grace me with a dance? I'm sure there isn't a better, more fair partner than you here tonight, or really in all of Zanaria, if I'm being honest."

Before I knew it, I was taking her hand and shooting an apologetic look at Jace, who simply nodded at me and continued to glare at her. I was grateful for the mask obscuring not only most of my confusion, but also the blush that warmed my cheeks.

When she stopped us on the dance floor, it occurred to me I didn't know where to put my hands. Thankfully, she was more than happy to take the lead. She put my hand on her shoulder, lacing her arm around my waist, pulling me close. It was a more intimate dance than I had danced yet, and my cheeks heated further at the closeness.

"Tell me, *princess*, how are you finding the palace?"

The way she drew out 'princess,' like it was some secret nickname, had me flushed and breathless. "I-" My throat was too dry. I swallowed and tried again. "In all honesty, I haven't been here quite long enough to have much of an opinion."

"You must have one, though, fully formed or not."

There was something about her and the way she was clutching my waist and delicately holding my hand as she led me through the steps that made me feel safe. Not giving myself time to think better of it, I told her the truth. "It's quite beautiful, and I know everyone says I'm lucky to have been found at all, to be returned home, but," I sighed, "It doesn't feel like home. I miss my village and the life I had there."

She looked forlorn at my admission and asked, "And the Queen, how do you find her?"

That was harder, and more dangerous to answer. "She's nice enough. If anything, it's me that hasn't really been pulling my weight in the relationship. Probably because I miss my adoptive family. I'm probably imagining things. Really, I must be."

She cocked her head to the side, asking, "Imagining what?"

"I can't really put it into words, not well anyway, but every once in a while, I get the feeling she's watching me a little too closely. She probably just wants to make sure I'm adjusting okay, but," I shuddered before I could stop myself, "there's something about the way she looks at me sometimes that makes me worry if it might be more than that."

Robyn pulled me tighter to her, my body flush against hers. I could feel her curves pressed against my chest. My heart pounded in my ears so loudly I almost missed her whispering, "You're right to be worried. Stay vigilant, don't trust anyone, especially her, and don't wear that crown a minute longer than you have to."

I blanched. She was the second person to tell me that today. That couldn't be a coincidence. Was I actually in danger? I took a calming breath, trying to slow my racing heart, and thought for a moment. She was friends with Jace, or used to be anyway. Maybe he told her to say it. Maybe. Something told me this wasn't just his influence, though.

She pulled back, her lips inches from mine, and said, "Do be careful, princess."

I couldn't quite read the look in her eye, but she seemed to be saying she would hate for something to happen to me. As kind as it was of her to warn me, I was a little over the cryptic warnings. How was I supposed to be careful when I didn't know what it was I was supposed to be cautious of? I almost asked her, but she spun me around in a tight circle, stealing my breath and balance, before catching me in her arms and dipping me low.

I had a quick thought that I would rather like to feel how soft her cherry lips were, to see how they tasted. Feeling emboldened by the wine and the masks and her being a stranger I was unlikely to meet again, I laced my arms around her neck. She tightened her grip on me, holding me suspended over the ground. I pulled her face to mine and kissed her. When our lips touched, I felt her gasp in surprise and felt her come alive a moment later, pulling me closer as she deepened the kiss, stealing my breath.

A few moments longer than it should have, it occurred to me we were still in a ballroom full of people, and I had only just met her. I pulled away a little, and she took the hint, righting me on my feet. We had attracted some attention, but everyone had the decency to look away when I looked around. I was sure my face matched the crimson of my dress. Thankfully, the mask obscured some of that.

I curtsied to her, not sure what else to do. She licked her lips and bowed with a smirk. When she righted herself, she said, "You're not at all what I expected, princess."

"I do hope that's a good thing?"

"Most definitely."

I felt a hand fall onto my shoulder. I turned more quickly than was proper, confused and alarmed, before seeing it was Jace and relaxed.

He was looking from me to her in disbelief and addressed her, "If you are quite done putting on a show, we have some things to discuss."

I couldn't decide if he meant for me to go with them or not. I was about to ask when the ballroom went black. There were shocked gasps, and I felt two hands immediately grab mine. I felt sure one of them was Jace, but could only hope the other was Robyn. I stayed frozen, not sure if I should pull away, not sure what was happening, when the candles started to light up one by one in an eerie green. I saw it was Jace and Robyn who had me in their grips, and was calmer, until I noticed the alarm on Jace's face.

"He's not supposed to be here. Alina, you have to get to the Queen and, *Robyn,* you have to get out of here before anyone is smart enough to notice you and who you are."

I would have to ask him later for an explanation. I needed to know more about Robyn. Hoped I might see her again. I scanned the room for the Queen and saw she was already headed for me. Jace saw, too.

He looked at me questioningly, seemingly unsure if he should stay or go. I had no idea what kind of danger was coming, but I hoped the Queen could handle it. I knew I would be protected by the Queen and the guards. They wouldn't be. "Go!" I said decisively.

They both just looked at me. "Quickly!" I urged.

They looked to one another and said in unison, "The gardens," before running off toward the back of the ballroom.

I turned back to where the Queen was coming from and scanned the room for her, squinting to see in the eerie green light.

I felt a hand on my shoulder and didn't bother turning. "Go, Jace! I'll be fine. Just make sure she stays safe."

"I'm not so sure you will be fine, *princess,*" a deep voice I didn't recognize said with a drawl.

I turned around slowly and saw a pair of glowing green eyes and feline like grin. I took a step back and then another, almost tripping on my gown. He was as handsome as he was terrifying. His hair was dark, but nothing compared to the darkness of his robes. They seemed to suck the light out of everything around him.

His eyes were glowing the same green the candles were, and I didn't like the look in them.

I took another step back and tripped over my dress, falling on ass. I pushed past the panic and quickly slipped out of my shoes. I jumped back to my feet, holding one of the shoes in my hand and kicking the other behind me. I foolishly had no other way to defend myself. Thankfully, I just needed to hold my own until the Queen and her guards got here.

I clutched the shoe tightly, ready to use it in any way I could at the first sign of him advancing, but he only watched with amusement.

"Who are you?" I asked.

"King Damien of Bancroft. You must be the new princess."

I stifled a gasp. I had heard of King Damien; everyone in Miravale had.

He was ruthless, diabolical. He had killed his own husband to take the throne for himself.

"King Killer," I breathed out, tightening my grip on my makeshift weapon.

His expression darkened to murderous, and he took a step toward me. I threw my shoe at him hard, and backed up another step to get the other one, only the first one didn't hit its mark. I watched in horror as it burst into green flames inches before his face.

Before he or I could move further, the Queen showed up with Amir and her guards flanking her. I risked a glance at her, and saw her look between the two of us. She moved in front of me. I tried to stand my ground, but one of the guards pulled me back. Why weren't they pulling her back, too?

After a tense stare down, the Queen sighed and said, "Come now, Damien, must you insist on the theatrics?"

He grinned. "Narcissa, looking lovely as always. You must know by now, I can't just walk into a room. Besides, you should know better than to not invite me to your little soiree."

She sighed impatiently. "And you should know to let my messengers across your borders. If you had, you would've received the invitation."

At that, the green flames sputtered out and were replaced by the normal soft candlelight. "Apologies, Cis. There, your candles are fixed. Happy?"

"I will be once you explain yourself. Helena looks scared half to death."

"She should be. You know I have a special taste for princesses."

I blanched, and he laughed. The Queen rolled her eyes. "Damien, I insist you stop scaring my daughter."

He looked at her with surprise. "Daughter? So, you're claiming this one, too?"

She narrowed her eyes at him. "The Imposter was just that, an imposter. She certainly was no daughter of mine."

He considered. "I see. Well, a pleasure to meet you, Princess." He wiggled his fingers at me in a way that felt menacing.

"Apologies, Your Majesty," I said. "I didn't know you were invited."

He let out a hearty chuckle. "Well, Miravale is certainly going to be a more interesting place if you have started assaulting uninvited guests."

I blushed upon seeing the Queen look at me in shock for an explanation.

"I'm sorry, Your-" Majesty almost slipped out before I corrected,

"Mother. I'm sorry, Mother. I thought we were under attack."

She nodded thoughtfully. "I suppose I should have warned you, and I might have if you had deigned to respond to my invitation," she said, glaring at Damien. "I can assure you no one else will be assaulted tonight on my watch. Amir, why don't you take my daughter for a stroll in the gardens? Get to know each other a bit more."

Amir stood rooted to the spot, staring at Damien. Damien didn't spare him a passing look, still staring at me. I shivered under his gaze. I didn't want to have to walk with Amir, but it was better than continuing in the presence of the King, and I didn't want to further embarrass the Queen.

Amir still hadn't moved. The Queen looked back and caught his eye. "Now," she said.

I took his arm and turned him away, noticing with wonder that as I did, his necklace was faintly glowing.

————

The gardens glowed with magical light illuminating more flowers than I could ever hope to name. It was a magical sight that I couldn't bring myself to be excited about sharing with Amir.

I tried to slip my fingers from his grasp now that we were out of the ballroom, but he held firm.

I excepted him to head to the roses, so we could sit on a bench and talk. I felt I needed to catch my breath anyway, but he steered us toward the hedge maze. Before I could protest, he hurried us down the darkest hedge path, practically dragging me.

I tried to get him to slow down, tried to pull away from him, but all my energy was focused on not tripping or injuring myself. Without my shoes, I was having to be more watchful of my steps, avoiding rocks in the path.

I was confused about the hurry. Were we still in danger? Was the Queen wrong about the King of Bancroft? Did he come here for me? I shuddered at the thought and then shivered at the cold. The night air had turned cool. I was just wondering how far we might go when he mercifully came to a stop.

I looked around, unsure of what I was expecting, but seeing nothing. We were utterly alone and likely lost. I sighed. "What are we doing out here, Amir?"

He looked at me with a grin that put ice in my veins. "This is what you wanted, right Princess? A private corner of the garden? Why don't we have some fun while we aren't missed. We probably have an hour or so before Damien leaves and anyone starts looking for us. Plenty of time to have some fun."

He crossed the gap to me and pulled me tight, crushing his lips to mine. I gasped in shock, and he took the opening, shoving his tongue in my mouth. I gagged on it, pushing against him hard enough to dislodge him and move back.

I tried to breathe through my panic. He must have been confused. "I'm sorry. There must be some misunderstanding. This isn't what I want. I hardly know you. Contrary to what you might believe, I'm not in the habit of kissing strangers."

His eyes darkened, the only light in them reflecting from his ruby necklace. "I see. So only strange women then."

I blushed. "She kissed me, and I told her the same thing," I lied.

"Well, you might not want me yet, but I can change that." I could've sworn he hadn't moved, could have sworn I felt something push me, and then I was in his arms again.

His lips crashed against mine, and I pushed against him again, to no avail. He didn't loosen his grip. Again, his tongue forced its way into my mouth. I tried harder to push him away, but pulled my hand back in pain when it touched something hot. My hand felt inexplicably burned, and he still hadn't budged. I felt his tongue stroke mine and bit down on it, hard. I tasted blood, but he pulled away quickly.

I moved back, quickly glancing around for anything that I could use to defend myself, but found nothing. I cursed myself for not being better prepared. Two attacks in one night and here I was shoeless and at the mercy of this Lord, but I wouldn't go quietly. I straightened and made to run, but felt a strong wind push me back right into the hedges. The hedges dug into my back as I strained against the inexplicable wind. It only clicked how much danger I was really in when I noticed him strolling toward me, unaffected.

He closed the small distance between us and stroked his finger down my face before pulling back and slapping me hard. I gasped. A moment later, I started to panic when I couldn't catch my breath. The wind stopped and my hands immediately clutched my throat, trying to force some air into my lungs.

He laughed at my efforts before using my distraction to come closer to me and kiss me again. I felt air rush back into my lungs and sighed in relief. I pulled away after regaining my breath, only to find I couldn't breathe again.

I choked, trying to force down air, but none came. He grinned. "I'd love to help, princess, but apparently you'd rather suffocate than kiss me."

Bastard. I would survive this. I would, and I would make him pay. I did what I had to do. I stepped back to him and kissed him greedily, taking in the air he offered. After a few moments, I pulled away, hoping he would tire of his sick games, but I still wasn't able to breathe.

I choked out a, "What do you want?" and felt tears rolling down my face.

"I want you, and the throne really. I want to rule with you beside me, well trained. No time like the present to start. Of course, I could just let you die. I might. You're not making this fun. Show me you want this. Convince me to spare you."

My vision was starting to go hazy, so I kissed him again, sweeping my tongue into his mouth, forcing his mouth open wider, forcing the air into my lungs. He started to pull away, so I took his hands and pulled them around my waist.

He pulled his mouth away from mine, taking away my air with it. "You'll have to do better than that, princess." I laced my hands behind his neck and pulled his lips to mine. I would have rather laced them around his neck, but I doubted very much that I could have killed him before dying myself.

He pulled away again, despite my efforts to keep him still. "I don't know. I'm not really convinced you want me."

Internally screaming from lack of oxygen and outrage, I grabbed him again and put his hands on my ass. Before he dipped his head back down to mine, he started groping it and whispered, "That's more like it."

Any relief I felt dissipated quickly when he pulled me closer, groaning as his body pressed against mine.

I heard a shocked gasp and, "Alina?"

Jace! Thank the gods! I caught Amir off-guard, pushing away from him, and whirled around to see Jace starting wide eyed at me. I clutched my throat with one hand and gestured to Amir with the other, hoping he would understand, but he continued to stand there confused.

With the air left in my lungs, I yelled at him to, "RUN!" but it was too late. Before he could make a move either to help me or retreat, the wind took hold of him, dragging him to Amir. I clutched his arm, trying to pull him to me, but it was no use.

Thankfully, Amir seemed to have lost some interest in me and was allowing me to breathe. I screamed for help as loudly as I could. Pulling on Jace, trying to pull him away from Amir, but it was no use. I couldn't weather the wind any better than he could, and my screams were drowned out by the roar of the wind.

Amir stepped closer with a predatory grin. "No one can hear you, princess. Scream and cry all you want. No one is coming for you."

I locked eyes with Jace and hoped he read my thoughts in them. If this was the end, at least we'd go down fighting. As one, we launched ourselves at Amir, only to be blasted back by the wind into the hedges. We were pinned there.

I tried to move but couldn't move more than my hand. I inched my hand toward Jace's and was able to grasp it. I couldn't turn my head to see him, but at least I could feel him. He squeezed my hand. I squeezed back, hoping he knew how sorry I was that he was meeting this sort of fate.

Amir stalked closer, but out of the corner of my eye, I saw the hedges behind him start to move. I looked closer and saw it wasn't actually the hedges at all, but vines of ivy. They raced out of the hedges right for Amir. I held my breath and watched in awe as they wrapped around his throat and squeezed. The wind instantly stopped restraining us as he turned all his attention to the ivy. Jace and I sunk to the ground. A moment later, I felt him pulling me up.

He looked around and fixed his gaze on the hedge where the hedges were parting. Out stepped Robyn. One hand raised in greeting, one hand directed toward Amir. She started to tighten her fist and he choked.

I stared at her in wonder.

She shrugged. "Seemed a fitting punishment."

Her ivy circled him, coiling around him like a snake, constricting him. I noticed the ruby necklace was glowing more insistently and was about to say so when the ivy brushed against it.

Robyn recoiled, wincing in pain. She moved the vines away from the ruby, making sure she was still keeping him occupied before rolling up her sleeve. Her skin was raw and red and looked burned.

I looked down at my own hand, and saw the matching burn from earlier.

"Robyn, can you get the necklace off him?" I asked quickly.

She carefully used the ivy to tug at the chain holding it, but no luck. "Gods help me," she said before using her vines to wrap around and squeeze the ruby. She cried out in pain, and I immediately told her to stop, but she was determined.

Amir's form started to shift, his face changing, growing more rugged, scars appearing from nowhere. "The Queen," he gasped out. "Get away from her while you can." Robyn loosened her hold on his neck and let him gasp out, "She figured out a way to control me. I-" His features contorted into the face we knew and back again. "I can't hold her off much longer. Get out of here, all of you! And if you see Damien, tell him I love him. I never stopped."

Robyn screamed in pain and moved her ivy from the ruby. His features contorted again, bringing back the familiar face. Robyn again tightened the ivy around his neck, when he started to fight in earnest.

"I'm sick of him," she said, squeezing tighter until he dropped to the ground and the wind stopped.

I looked at her tentatively. "Is he?" I couldn't finish, but she shook her head.

"I should. I probably will regret leaving him alive, but there's some powerful magic working on him and my ivy wasn't able to actually strangle the life out of him. We're lucky I was able to knock him unconscious in the first place."

"So, what now?" I asked hurriedly. I felt a squeeze and looked down, surprised to find I was still holding Jace's hand. I didn't let go.

She grinned. "Well, now you two come with me. You don't really have much of a choice, do you?"

"Just like you to find some way to get your way, Ives," Jace said with annoyance.

"I didn't know things would play out like this. But I came here to see if I could convince her to meet with me. I can't help that things worked out."

He looked at me. "We should go, but if you say you want to stay, we will."

I looked at Robyn, or Ives, whatever her name was, whoever she was. I thought for a moment, knowing it would have to be a quick decision. Despite there being no reason for me to feel like I did, I trusted her, and she had saved my life. At least that's what I told myself. It wasn't about the kiss, or about how sweet she tasted or about how I wanted to run my fingers through her hair. It was the rational thing to do.

"We'll go. I don't know what to think of you yet, but I know enough about the Palace to be okay with being anywhere but here."

With rogue Kings and powerful masochistic lords roaming the palace, it was clear it wasn't safe.

Jace squeezed my hand reassuringly. "I'll make sure you're safe."

Robyn rolled her eyes. "Quit being so dramatic. I wouldn't have saved her if I had some evil plan for her."

I hoped that was true, but I trusted Jace to keep his word and something in me trusted Robyn.

"Come on," she said, stepping through a new person-sized hole in the hedges. We followed through, and I gaped as a path cleared through the hedge maze straight to the forest.

The moment we stepped through the last hedge, she looked back and said, "Wait."

I worried she might be changing her mind, that she might have decided I was more trouble than I was worth, but she gestured to the crown. "That cursed thing stays."

"Done and done," I said, happy to be rid of it. I chucked the heavy crown as far back into the maze as I could.

At the boundary to the forest, there were people waiting with torches. I stiffened until Robyn grinned and waved to them.

She tried to pick up the pace, but almost tripped over her dress. She crouched down and pulled a knife from her boot, and I watched in horror as she turned it on herself and proceeded to cut the skirt of the gown away, revealing breeches that I refused to believe she had fit under her dress.

She glanced back at me. "I don't suppose you're hiding breeches under yours?"

I shook my head, lifting my gown enough to show her I didn't even have shoes.

She groaned. "What happened to your shoes?"

"I threw one at the King Killer."

She looked at me in a way that insinuated she was impressed.

"It didn't actually hit him," I felt compelled to add. "It would have, but he torched it before it could."

She laughed, grinning like a mad woman. "I like you, Helena."

"Alina," Jace and I corrected her at the same time.

She laughed. "Okay, *Alina,* I like you. You're going to fit right in with us."

"Who is us?" I asked curiously, but she didn't answer. I looked to Jace, and he shrugged. "Hard to know what she's going by these days or whose company she keeps."

"Just wait. The Queen has ears everywhere. It's not safe yet, but once we get there, I'll tell you."

We traveled through the night, Robyn taking the time at first to make me a path of grass to walk on, but the longer we walked, the more tired we all became. Eventually, she stopped and after I stepped on the second rock, Jace took me in his arms and carried me. I protested lightly, but he insisted, and Robyn said it wasn't much further.

When we stopped in front of a pine tree fifty feet wide, I was thinking I had made a mistake. I was longing for my bed at the palace, thinking wandering off with a stranger probably wasn't my smartest move. I gasped when a door formed in front of my eyes and Robyn opened it. The others poured in, talking and laughing, clapping each other on the back for accomplishing their mission.

I didn't know whether to be happy or worried about that. There was so much I still didn't know, but something told me to trust Robyn. Jace put me lightly on my feet, and I stepped through the door. It was a short tunnel to another door, and when we stepped through the door, I gasped.

There were fifty huge tents, and dozens of campfires roaring to life as people started to prepare breakfast and the dawn light creep through the trees. I looked around, wondering how secure the place actually was and noticed that we were surrounded, enclosed on all sides by huge trees. The tree canopies converged, blocking out all but a small fraction of the sky. I gasped as I noticed the trees had stairs coming out of them. I followed the stairs with my eyes up to the treetops and saw houses built into the trees. There were lights strung from the tree branches, emulating the stars.

I looked around the camp and saw little children happily racing around the tents, playing. I saw families sitting by the campfire and watched as the others who had come to the palace were greeted warmly on their return.

Robyn doubled back, saying, "I'll show you where you'll be staying. Jace, too, since I'm guessing he won't let you out of his sight," she said, rolling her eyes.

I looked at him, but he was looking at her, nodding grimly.

"Some things never change. Very well. Come this way."

"Wait," I said. She turned back, waiting. "Where are we?" I asked.

She smiled apologetically. "I can't tell you, I'm afraid. Top secret."

"Well, what do you call this place? Who are you?"

"My dear princess, I'm Robyn of Mirawood, and this is my ragtag band of rebels."

"The truth, Ives," gritted out Jace.

"That is the truth."

"The whole truth."

She sighed. "I was Ivy Miravale, Princess of Miravale, recently deposed now, I suppose."

"But Ivy, you," I amended, "ran off, with the rebels," I said, looking around. That would make this a rebel camp, but that couldn't be right. The people hardly looked dangerous.

She nodded. "I did. After the Queen let her pet Amir take an interest in me, the palace wasn't safe for me anymore. I escaped, much like you did, and was lucky to stumble into the rebels. I've been helping them plan and keep hidden." She blushed a moment before adding, "I didn't plan for it to happen, didn't even want it really, but they look to me as their leader."

"How convenient," Jace deadpanned.

"Jace here is still skeptical, but even he knew there was something not right about the palace, about the Queen, something going on with that crown. I started losing parts of my day, small gaps in my memory. I thought I was going crazy. When Amir came after me, it was the last straw. I struck out and ran as far as my legs would carry me. I was lucky the rebels found me when they did. They took me in, made me feel at home for the first time in a long time. I hope to do the same for you, Alina. I swear on my stolen crown, my kingdom, and all the names I go by, I am on your side, and I will fight for the people of Miravale."

One of the rebels heard her and took up the cry, "Long live Robyn of Mirawood, Princess of the people. Down with the Queen."

The cry was taken up by the others until it echoed throughout the entire compound. She grinned sheepishly at me. I looked around in awe at the people staring at her with such hope in their eyes that my own started to water. Even Jace looked begrudgingly impressed.

She opened her arms wide, gesturing to the safe haven, saying grandly, "Alina, short lived Princess of Miravale, my former impersonator and new friend, welcome to the Mirawood and welcome to my band of rebels. May chaos reign."

I grinned back at her. She went by many names and was a lot of things, but boring wasn't one of them. If her rebels were anything like her, I could already tell I was going to like it here.

THIS STORY IS LOOSELY CONNECTED to Off Script: A Book Ball Fantasy Adventure, and will be expanded into a planned fantasy series in the near future.

ABOUT SARAH ZANE

Sarah is an author of happy endings for traumatized queers. She is a bisexual feminist and a licensed therapist. Her stories deal with themes of feminism, trauma, sexuality, and mental health.

STORY VIII
SOLSTICE BY JORDAN A. DAY

Heat Level: Hot
(generally one to three more extensive / detailed sex scenes, increasing
use of coarse language)

Trigger Warnings:
Underage alcohol consumption
Older teen protagonist
Explicit language
Consensual sexual content

SOLSTICE

Only sixteen, and my life was about to end. I wouldn't get to do all that I wanted in this world. I wouldn't get to have adventures or experience life's greatest wonders. I wouldn't get to spend the days ahead with my best friend as we shoved aside all responsibilities and lived life to the fullest. I wouldn't get to—

"Dashiell," my father gritted forcefully, "are you paying attention?"

Nope. Absolutely fucking not.

The day I turned sixteen, my father decided it was time for me to fulfill my duties as prince and heir to the Kingdom of Caelum, despite my many, *many* protests. And thanks to his choice, I was now dying slowly from utter boredom. Was I being dramatic about it? Sure. Did I care? Again, nope.

"Of course," I lied cheerfully.

My father's jaw clenched in disapproval, but before he could reprimand me, the door to the council room opened, and my savior entered. Felix threw me a glance as he strode to my father—a look only I knew meant he had the means to bust me out of this Gods forsaken room.

"Your Majesty," Felix announced in the ass-kissing tone I loved to give him shit for. "King Harbin and his court have arrived."

I perked up at the news with hope-filled eyes. They weren't supposed to arrive until this evening, and it was early enough that lunch hadn't even been served yet. I straightened in my seat as the taste of freedom danced on my tongue.

As one of my father's advisors, Felix usually attended these meetings with me, but today he was instructed to oversee that my father's orders were being carried out as we awaited the arrival of our guests. The solstice celebration they came for wouldn't take place until tomorrow evening, but given that they showed up early, it looked like the fun would be starting sooner than later.

"I should go and greet them," I announced, quickly rising from my chair.

"Stay seated, Dashiell," my father announced, and I groaned as I sank back down.

He wanted me to die. There was no other reason he'd force me to sit in that meeting and do nothing but stare at the ceiling and contemplate how exactly I'd end my misery. I didn't have to look at my best friend to know he was trying to devise a clever way for my father to let me go.

"My king," he started, and I had to bite my lip to stop from laughing at the ridiculous way he said the words. But I also knew Felix well enough to know he did it on purpose just to get that reaction from me. We often played games like that to see who could trip the other up first. Most of the time, I won. All of the time, we ended up in a world of trouble for it. "King Harbin's court was interested in a tour of the grounds," Felix explained. "The king himself hoped Prince Dashiell would be kind enough to escort the princess and ladies in her company."

I fucking loved my best friend.

I heard my father's teeth grind with annoyance, and I held my breath as I waited for his response, not daring to take my eyes off the ceiling.

"Fine," he said, and I pushed myself out of my chair and hurried out of the room before he had the chance to reconsider.

"Was any of that true?" I asked the moment we entered the hall, and the guards shut the door behind us.

"Nope," Felix said, flashing a devious grin. "You ready?"

"Absolutely."

~

WE HURRIED through the corridor to our rooms to change clothes and then carry out the plan Felix devised while I was in the meeting from hell. We had almost made it when a high-pitched voice called out from behind us, halting our journey at once. I threw my head back and swore under my breath as Felix prepared to plaster on his tight-lipped smile.

"And where are you two sneaking off?" Cordelia asked, and my hands tightened as we spun around to face her.

The Princess of Ministro and I had never once gotten along. She had been in love with Felix since we were children, and the only thing stronger than her feelings toward him was her hatred for me. She had always harbored jealousy towards my and Felix's friendship, and there was no sign of that stopping anytime soon.

"Somewhere as far away as possible from you," I said sweetly, and she clenched her jaw hard enough to crack a tooth.

Cordelia shot me a look that told me she was probably playing my murder on repeat in her head, but I didn't give a fuck. She was annoying, and Felix and I had somewhere to be. She sliced her gaze to my best friend before fixing a pout on her lips.

"But I haven't seen you in so long. We need to catch up," she said, reaching out to touch his arm. Felix smiled politely and layered on the charism he was so known for.

"I would love to, darling Cordelia, but I promised His Royal Highness the pleasure of my company," Felix announced, and I suppressed a gag at his sickly sweet, fake-ass tone.

"Well, then I'll just come along too," she said, but I cut in immediately.

"The fuck you will."

"You get him every day of the year, you little shit; it's my turn! Let me join!" Cordelia ground out, and I smirked as her face twisted with rage.

"Not a fucking chance. It's Felix and I—always has been. There will never be room for someone else in our friendship," I told her, throwing my arm around my best friend just to rub it in. Felix placed his hand over his heart in exaggerated appreciation, and I rolled my eyes at the display.

"Sorry, Cordelia. I can't defy an order from my prince," Felix said as he dipped his head and backed away toward his room.

I knew he had just as much desire to spend time with her as I did. The fact that she always tried to make a move on him creeped us both out. There was always something about it that just felt *off*—wrong. Cordelia stomped her foot and huffed in irritation before stomping thunderously down the hall in the opposite direction. Problem averted.

∼

I TOSSED my shirt to the ground, my back muscles flexing with the movement, and shook out my arms to prepare for the fight. Felix's brilliant idea was to come to the training ring and show off our skill with the sword. We had been training relentlessly every day for months and had gotten pretty damn good. The fact that the grass surrounding the ring was filled with eager onlookers raking their eyes up and down our bodies told me Felix was definitely on to something. He cocked a brow in my direction and smirked in a way that said *told you.*

My fingers gripped the hilt of my sword as I sliced the open air to get a feel of the movement and weight of the weapon. Several people giggled and cooed as I went through my exercises to limber myself up.

Okay, this definitely was a brilliant plan.

I didn't want to consider myself a pretentious asshole, but I couldn't deny I liked the attention I was getting. It had been a couple of weeks since I spent my time with anyone, and my hand just wasn't doing it for me anymore. Tonight would be different.

"Ready?" Felix asked from the opposite side of the ring, tossing the hilt of his sword between his hands.

"To kick your ass? When am I not?" I jabbed back, and Felix smiled before lunging at me.

I dodged and deflected his attack before offering one of my own. The clanging of metal and our gentle laughter rang in the space around us as we sparred, determined to put on the best show we could for our audience.

Gasps and applause broke out intermittently during the fight, and Felix and I made a silent bet about who could make the crowd cheer the loudest. We both knew it would be me simply because of my title, but that would never deter Felix from accepting a bet—even a losing one.

He swung his sword, hitting mine hard enough that the metal reverberated through my body, and my features flooded with confusion. We constantly sparred, but Felix was going harder than usual, relentlessly striking over and over again until I was forced to push away from him and compose myself. I glanced at him questioningly, but he simply arched a brow in challenge.

I smiled wide, accepting his offer of a more exciting fight, and ran for him. Our swords repeatedly collided until we gasped for breath, and sweat dripped down our brows from exhaustion, but we still didn't stop. We wouldn't yield until one of us was the clear victor.

Felix swung his weapon in my direction, and I spun around quickly to avoid the hit, but I was too late. My skin stung as his blade sliced through the skin along my ribs. He smiled victoriously, and I swore under my breath, pissed that I had lost the damn match.

All at once, our audience rushed for us, crowding me as they looked at my injury with fearful eyes. My gaze dropped to my skin and the small trickle of blood that rolled down from the even smaller scratch. Felix had barely punctured the skin, yet everyone acted as if I had been flayed in half with no chance of survival.

"Are you okay, Lord Felix? You must be so guilt-stricken," someone said, and I looked up to find a red-haired girl gently rubbing his back. My best friend's stare slid from the girl to me, and our eyes widened as a new idea occurred to us.

Felix pressed his fist to his mouth as he closed his eyes and shook his head, giving the best damn performance of remorse I'd ever seen. He choked back a sob while I groaned, playing up the barely there scratch.

"I'm so sorry, Your Highness," Felix said, wiping away an expertly crafted fake tear as the girl clutched his arm tight. "Please forgive me."

I nodded, running my fingers through the blood to make it look worse than it was as three people tried to coddle me. Hands ran through my hair and over my body as people yelled for a Medicus to come and heal their prince.

"Try not to move, You Highness."

"It'll be okay."

"We'll get you healed in no time."

Constant waves of reassurance washed over me as Felix pretended to cry while his face was pressed into the chest of the red-haired girl. She dragged her fingers through his silver strands as she shushed him soothingly and promised to make everything better.

A soft hand brushed across the thin cut on my skin, and I looked over to see a beautiful girl with long black hair staring back at me. I had spotted her before and recognized that she was one of the visitors from Ministro. She leaned in, her lips grazing the shell of my ear as she spoke.

"Would you like me to take care of you later?" She whispered, and my cock instantly went hard, knowing she was sure as fuck not talking about my cut.

"Only if you let me return your kindness," I replied smoothly, and she bit her lip before nodding. It looked like I definitely wasn't going to be using my own hand tonight.

"You have to fuck her," Felix declared from his spot on the couch in our private room of the library that we dubbed as the Sanctuary.

"What is your obsession with my dick, and where I put it?" I joked, pouring each of us a serving of the amber liquor from the bottle I stole from the guards.

Felix had sex for the first time over a year ago, and ever since, he's been trying to get me to do the same. It was like I didn't want to have sex, I just…. never went for it when the time came. And apparently, knowing I had many opportunities at my disposal and still never did anything about it only infuriated him more.

"Because there is absolutely no reason for you not to use it to its full potential," Felix answered. He wasn't wrong, but that still didn't mean I was going to fuck that girl this evening. "Just promise me this," he began, and I arched a brow, ready for some term I was not going to do, "if the chance arises, you'll take it."

Okay, that actually wasn't that bad and something I could agree to.

"Fine. But if I do, then you have to stop being concerned about what I do with my cock," I reasoned, and Felix rolled his eyes.

"Never," he responded, and I threw a book at him, barely missing his face. "Okay, now drink up. We need you good and drunk, to get rid of those nerves."

I swallowed the liquor in my glass, letting it burn all the way down, and watched Felix pour us another serving. He was dead set on getting me wasted, but there was no way that was happening. I was nervous as fuck for some reason, and I didn't think alcohol would help for once. I needed to get through this night with her stone-cold sober.

Two hours later, Felix was passed out on the couch and thoroughly plastered. I managed to get rid of my drinks whenever he wasn't looking, and it was finally time to start my night. I stood, threw a blanket over my best friend, and headed from the library to where I planned on meeting my date for the night.

The halls were quiet, but it wasn't too late that people weren't still mulling about. My gut twisted with nerves though I wasn't sure exactly why. We probably weren't even going to have sex. Us *taking care* of each other could simply mean pleasuring one another in other ways, especially because that's always what it's meant for me. I was getting ahead of myself and just needed to calm the fuck down.

I rounded the corner and found her standing with her back pressed against the door that led to the throne room, with guards flanking her on either side. Her head perked up, and a seductive smile lit her face the moment she saw me approach. I nodded to the guards before grabbing her hand and leading us inside the room to be alone.

"So this is the throne room," I said nervously as if it wasn't completely fucking obvious, thanks to the giant throne in front of us. Smooth, Dash —real fucking smooth.

Before I could say some other dumb as shit thing, she shoved me, my back hitting a pillar hard. Her lips crashed to mine, and she jumped up, wrapping her legs around my middle. I kissed her back, my tongue slipping in and claiming hers as I spun us so she was the one now pushed against the marble pillar.

She moaned into my mouth, and my Gods, if that sound didn't taste fantastic. My hand trailed down her side until I caressed the soft skin of the leg hooked around me.

"More," she pleaded, and I was happy to oblige.

My fingers trailed higher up her thigh, and I slipped my hand beneath her dress, finding her wet and ready. I may not have known what to do as far as sex went, but pleasuring someone in other ways was something I was well versed in. Granted, I'd rather have used my tongue, but given that she was practically riding my hand before I even slid a finger inside her, I wasn't about to change our position.

My mouth claimed hers as I shifted her underwear aside to give her more of what she wanted, and she gasped as I pushed two fingers inside her. I relished the way she tensed, already close to unraveling for me. I worked her, moving in and out in a slow, methodic rhythm to bring her close to the edge just to hold off and pull back. She whimpered against my mouth, and I smiled as I continued to draw out her pleasure, refusing to give her the release she desired until I knew she would break without it. That was always the key to making them come harder than they ever had before.

She panted hard, grinding herself against my hand faster and faster until I finally stopped holding back and let her have what she was so desperate for. My tongue swept over hers as she screamed her pleasure, her body convulsing from the orgasm rocking through her. I didn't stop, though. I kept working her until she was primed and ready to fall all over again.

My cock was hard enough to cut fucking glass, and I would combust if I didn't deal with it soon, but I needed this first. I needed to have her coming hard again before I even tried to take care of myself.

"Your Highness," she breathed, her voice shaky.

Gross.

I never shied from my title, but hearing her beg for me with it just left me feeling like a pretentious asshole. Sure, it could be hot as fuck, but not right now... not with *her*.

She clenched her thighs tighter around my middle, and her nails bit into my shoulders like they would keep her body from giving what my fingers demanded. This was a losing battle for her, and I wouldn't yield until I got what I wanted. She moaned even louder, breaking our kiss and throwing her head back as she came undone for the second time.

My lips found her neck, kissing and nipping her soft skin as she caught her breath and climbed down from her high.

"Holy Gods," she whispered, and I smiled in satisfaction against her. I'd never get used to the victorious feeling of hearing my partners shatter for me so thoroughly.

I probably would have chalked it up to them just trying to boost my ego because of my princely status if it wasn't for the reputation I had garnered regarding my.... *Skills*. Even Felix, who was far more experienced than me, had begged me to explain exactly what I was doing. When I declined, he threw a bitch fit before trying to get me to draw a diagram for him instead.... Which I, once again, declined.

Fuck. Maybe I *was* a pretentious asshole.

Whatever.

She tipped her head forward, and I moved my mouth to hers again, tasting her desire for more—a desire I'd gladly fulfill. This time though, I'd do it from my knees. I kissed her one last time and pulled away, but before I could set her down and kneel, she reached between us and began unbuckling my pants.

Even though I was planning on pleasuring her again, interrupting her would have been completely rude, and I was nothing if not polite. Obviously.

Her hand dove into my pants with more force than was probably necessary, but before I could comment on the terrifying form, she gripped my solid cock. The moment she started to stroke me, all words left my mind, and I instead just focused on the feel of her hand gliding up and down my length. The way she squeezed my dick as she worked wasn't exactly the best, but it definitely wasn't the worst I had experienced.

Nothing could ever compare to that horrifying time with Lola….

ABOUT A YEAR AGO, Felix had practically thrown this girl, Lola, at me after going on and on about how amazing she was with her hands and mouth. It wasn't unusual for Felix and me to have spent time with the same person at some point, especially since he was on his way to going through the entirety of the residents in our age group. Often we gave each other notes on what to expect and if it was worth pursuing them for an evening. So when Felix told me I'd be a *'fucking idiot'* if I passed up a night with Lola, I trusted him and went for it.

Big fucking mistake.

At first, I thought the worst thing about her was that she kept her eyes wide open when I kissed her, never once blinking. And yeah, it freaked me the hell out, but I also couldn't look away, which made the whole scene just weird. But that wasn't the worst thing that happened with her. Not by a long shot.

When she dropped to her knees and freed my barely hard cock, I thought my time with her would turn around for the better. Nope. Instead of lowering her mouth to me like I assumed she would, she gripped me at the base and began to wave my cock back and forth like a fucking flag in the wind, slapping her face with it as she went.

I sat there gaping at her because what the fuck else was I supposed to do? Say, *'Umm, perhaps you shouldn't smack yourself in the face with my now extremely flaccid dick, but feel free to deep throat it instead?'* My jaw dropped as I watched the horrifying scene before me, completely frozen and my mind blank.

"Do you like this?" Lola asked seductively.

Absolutely the fuck not.

"It's….. so great," I lied, shifting myself to try and take back control of the situation. "But how about I do something for you first?"

Yes. That was my way out. I could halt the dick assault on her face and focus on getting her off before making an excuse to leave the second she was finished. Foolproof.

"That's okay. I'd much rather have you instead," she explained, gripping my shaft even harder as she ceased waving and instead began to move her hand up and down my length vigorously.

Fuck.

And not *'fuck'* in a mind-blowing, 'yes, keep going' sort of way. No. In a 'holy shit, this girl is going to rip my fucking dick off' sort of way.

Her nails bit into my flesh as she moved, undoubtedly leaving marks on my sensitive skin. I clamped my lips shut as I threw my head back from the pain. I needed to get her the hell off of me before I lost the ability to use my cock ever again, but I also didn't want to be a complete asshole about it.

Wet warmth spread over me, and I glanced down to find Lola gripping me as her flat tongue roamed over my cock in fast, desperate strokes. There was no rhyme or reason—no pattern, to how she moved. Drool trickled down her chin as she slobbered all over me, and I suppressed a gag at the sight. There was no way she could be enjoying whatever the fuck this was, and my limp cock should have been a clear indication that I wasn't either.

She moaned loudly as she took me into her mouth, and I cringed at the sound. She was definitely playing this up because who in their right mind would have been turned on by this exchange? But what if she was? What if she was actually into this? If that was the case, I figured there was no harm in letting her continue. Maybe she'd get her fill and decide she had enough, and I could be free of this exchange. Free to leave and beat the ever-living shit out of Felix for setting me up.

Lola dipped her head up and down as she slid her mouth along my shaft when something sharp grazed me. Holy shit. She was using her teeth.

Nope—absolutely the fuck not. I was not about to let this girl chomp on my fucking dick like it was a late-night snack.

"I have a meeting!" I exclaimed, pushing back from Lola so fast I almost fell backward in the chair I had been sitting in. I got to my feet quickly and carefully tucked myself back into my pants, too terrified to look at the damage though I could feel how sore it was.

"At this hour?" She asked, and I nodded.

"I ummm…." I started, buckling my pants back up as I tried to devise a reasonable excuse without sounding like a jackass. "I was supposed to go earlier, but it completely slipped my mind. My father will be furious if I don't attend," I added, knowing full well everyone was scared shitless of their king and wouldn't give his demands a second thought.

"Of course, Your Highness. Maybe we can pick this up another time."

I gave Lola a polite smile before hurrying for the room and heading for the Medicus facility downstairs. My Unda Gift immediately rushed forward, coating my hand in ice, and I pressed it to myself, instantly feeling some relief from her assault. Because my magic was strictly elemental, I couldn't care for my brutalized cock alone and would have to have one of our trained healers do it for me. Which meant I was going to have to tell them exactly what happened tonight. Joy.

The walk felt so much longer than usual, and it seemed like every resident in the palace was awake and strolling the corridors. I didn't miss the concerned looks and whispers that flooded the space as they watched their prince stride through the halls, his ice-coated fist grasping his dick through his pants.

Fucking great.

When I arrived at the Medicus facility, Felix was already there, resting his back against the wall like he had been waiting for me. His head picked up as I approached, and a shit-eating grin spread across my best friend's face, clearly knowing exactly what had happened to me.

"How was your night?" Felix asked tauntingly, and the only reason I didn't punch him was that the ice against my damaged cock felt so fucking good.

"Once I'm healed, I'm going to kill you," I said through my teeth as I pushed past him and stormed into the Medicus facility. If I wasn't terrified of losing my dick at that moment, I would have applauded him on the prank.

After several shocked glances, two tonics for the pain, and an awkward ten minutes of our Medicus trying desperately not to make eye contact while he held my dick to heal the damage, I was as good as new. As much shit as I had experienced, nothing would ever be as embarrassing for me as that night with Lola.

Or so I thought….

As forceful as her grip was, it was nothing compared to what Lola had done to me, so I could at least enjoy it. My head lulled back, and my eyes closed as I sucked in a breath through my teeth while she continued to work me. I was all for offering her another round of pleasure, but there was no way I was going to stop her from what she was doing.

She shifted higher, positioning me at her entrance, and my eyes snapped open as realization hit me. Holy Gods, she wanted me to fuck her. This was really going to happen. I was going to have sex with…. Wait…. Oh my Gods, what the fuck was her name? Talia? Seraphina?

This could not be happening. There was no way I forgot her fucking name.

I absolutely, without a doubt, was a pretentious asshole.

Fauna? Lily? Okay, it was *definitely* something flower related—that much I was positive about. I could not fuck this girl without being sure of her name…. Or that she even wanted me to.

Holy Gods, was I reading the situation wrong? Maybe she was just trying to adjust, and placing my dick only a breath away from her entrance was prime comfort level. If she so much as breathed too deep, she'd be impaled on me. Maybe she liked the danger in that? Panic began to rush through me like an ocean wave as I struggled with what to do next. First things first, check in with her.

"Are you sure?" I asked, and she nodded, pushing herself onto me. However, my grip on her waist held firm, so only my tip slid in before I halted her movements. But fucking Gods did just that little bit feel like pure bliss.

She whimpered as she tried to move again, demanding more of me, but I couldn't give it to her. Not until I figured out her name, because if I didn't, then I definitely was an asshole. I quickly ran through every floral name I could think of, hoping one jumped out at me, waving a flag of familiarity. Daisy? Rose? Ivy? Violet? YES, VIOLET! My mind swam with the memory of that name, and I sighed in relief as I sank deep inside her.

Oh. My. Fucking. Gods.

Why in the world did I put having sex off for so long? She squeezed and clenched around me, making every thrust of my dick feel like ecstasy. She was warm and wet and so Gods damn welcoming that I could imagine doing anything else ever again. It felt like….

Oh no.

It felt like it was about to be over way too fucking soon. No, no, no, no. This wasn't happening. I didn't just slide my dick in her to be done three pumps later. I needed to get my head on straight and focus on anything but how it felt to be buried inside her. I stopped my movements, but Violet didn't seem to like that and instead took it upon herself to rock against me at a relentless pace.

Dear Gods, please no.

I needed to think of something else—*anything* else. Just not the way she moved while she rode me and how tight her body clenched around my dick, coaxing me to come before I wanted to. I needed to think of the boring ass meetings I always had to attend. I needed to think of all the responsibilities I had to see to this week. Hell, I needed to think of Felix taking a shit—anything that would help take my mind away from what was happening.

Violet ground her hips again, and I knew nothing I did was going to help. This was going to end before it even started. My fingers dug into her waist as she rocked forward, pushing me entirely over the edge. My head fell to her chest, and I groaned her name as I came hard.

As I came not even one minute after entering her.

Yup, that definitely happened.

I couldn't pick my head up as I slowed my breathing, too embarrassed to look at her. Her body stilled around me like she was trying to figure out if what she thought just happened actually happened.

It did.

"Did you just…." She said slowly, not bothering to finish that question. I nodded, unable to admit the words out loud. There was no way this situation could possibly get any worse. "It's Andria, by the way," not Violet said.

Of course, it fucking was.

I pulled my head back from her, ready to offer the apology she deserved when she spoke again.

"Was Violet a previous girlfriend?" Andria asked, and for some fucking reason, I nodded at once. It wasn't like pretending I had a reason for calling her by another name made me any less of a douche head. "Well, she was a….. lucky woman," Andria offered awkwardly.

Kill me now.

She wiggled in my arms, and I pulled out, setting her back on the ground as we both adjusted ourselves. This encounter needed to be over quickly. I fully planned on locking myself in our private room in the library for the remainder of the week. There was absolutely no way I could face her or the other ladies from Ministro, who she would undoubtedly tell about what happened here tonight. Perhaps I could somehow get her to keep the events to herself….

"Could you not mention what transpired between us to anyone?" I asked, tucking myself back into my pants.

Andria met my stare, and I could see the wheels of her mind working as if trying to get out of agreeing to my request. As the Prince of Caelum,

I could simply order her not to utter a word about it, but I didn't want to have to go that route.

"It's just that," I began, deciding to take a page from Felix's book and lay on the sympathy thick, "tonight with you has been amazing—one of the best I've ever had." Pink rose to her cheeks at my false claim, and my heart thumped wildly at the possibility of this actually working. "But it also made me realize how much I care for Violet. We could never be together with you being from Ministro and me from Caelum. I don't want to throw away the chance to experience with her just a fraction of what I had with you tonight, and if she catches wind of us, I know she'll never take me back," I explained, forcing my voice to break on the last words as I let my water Gift surface to my eyes to line them with tears.

Andria pressed a hand to her heart as she looked me over, seeming completely moved by my bullshit story. She lifted onto her toes and kissed my cheek softly before nodding vehemently.

"Of course, Your Highness. This night will forever stay just between us."

Fuck. Yes.

FELIX'S back was pressed against the door to my room as he flipped through a book he was reading while waiting for me. I definitely didn't want to share what happened tonight, but I knew there was no way he would let it go. I would have to lie my way out of the truth, though that would be near impossible, seeing as his Gift as an Empathi allowed him to detect the emotions coursing through my body. And right then, I was flooded with guilt, regret, and embarrassment.

"So, what happened?!" Felix asked excitedly as he followed me into my room. I strode for the bed, flopping face first and speaking into the mattress so my words came out muffled.

"Not much."

"Bullshit," he countered, and I groaned.

"We fucked…. Sort of."

I felt the mattress dip as Felix climbed next to me with all the excitement of a puppy, and I knew he was hungry for every last detail. There was no point lying to my best friend, so I might as well have just gotten it over with.

"What do you mean by *sort of*?" he asked, and I flipped to my back and threw an arm over my eyes to shield myself from him. I was going to tell him what happened, but I didn't need to look at his smug as fuck face when I did.

"I mean, I don't even know if you could call it that," I explained.

"The ass still counts as—"

"No," I interrupted. "It had nothing to do with *where* I stuck my dick, Felix. It was how long it was in there for...."

Felix was quiet for long enough that I removed my arm and glanced in his direction to find him biting his lip to suppress a smile. I groaned as my best friend basked in my misery.

"How long was it in there for, Dash," he coaxed like the arrogant asshole he was. I shook my head, instantly deciding against confiding in him. "You have to tell me. It's against our code as brothers to keep secrets from one another."

Gods dammit.

Felix and I may not have been related by blood, but we were family to one another, and there wasn't anything I'd keep hidden from him. By the cocky twitch of his lips, I knew he was thinking the same thing.

"Less than a minute," I admitted remorsefully.

Felix bellowed with laughter as he threw himself next to me, and I couldn't stop my own smile from forming. His laugh was always infectious and had this way of bringing me out of the darkest places I found myself in from time to time. Soon, my stomach cramped from just how hard I laughed alongside him.

I guess it wasn't so bad after all, and I'm sure there were ways I could prolong the experience now that I knew what exactly I was getting myself into. Both figuratively and literally. Thanks to my sob story, I was sure Violet—fuck—*Andria* wouldn't announce to anyone just how terrible tonight had been. Everything was going to be fine.

But there was no way in hell I'd ever tell another soul that I only lasted one Gods damn minute.

$$\sim$$

You can read more about these characters in Jordan A. Day's *A Ripple of Power and Promise.*

ABOUT JORDAN A. DAY

Jordan A. Day currently resides in Virginia with her three kids, husband, and six pets. When she's not thinking of ways to emotionally damage her future readers, she can be found bingewatching The Office for the billionth time or some reality show of no substance. She's a huge lover of Star Wars and all nerdy yet totally awesome things. Also, she massively enjoys coffee and wears a size floor seats in Taylor Swift.

STORY IX
THE MACABRE DANCE OF THE SANGUINE SIX BY R. E. JOHNSON

Heat Level: Scorching
(ALL the sex scenes, much description and detail, lots of coarse language)

Trigger Warnings:
Blood play
Biting
Doms/subs/Domme with a very dark Dom
Sadism
Degradation
Multi-POV
Poly/Why-Choose/MMdemiFFFMdemiM
Claw play
DubCon
Impact play
Restraining with arms
Whip play
Cum/spit play
Multiple penetrations
Class dynamics
Mild self-loathing
Repressed sexuality coming out

Violence
First time
Anal
Oral
Orgasm denial/edging

CHAPTER 1: EVE ARKWRIGHT

I'd been chosen. Me, some penniless no one from one of the smallest hamlets surrounding the great Blood Elf territory of the Vraxsite Empire. Of course, we all paid our dues to the Blood Elves that ruled over our nation, even my tiny village of Saugues. Still, it was highly unexpected that a participant for the centennial ball would be chosen from our lowly ranks, let alone that it would be an orphaned candle smith who'd inherited the business from said deceased parents and could barely keep it afloat amid all the fines, taxation, and meager success.

And yet here I was, choosing a gown with an appointed representative who would ready me for presentation to the Royal Court at their High Masquerade this night.

What in this realm has possessed the mayor of my village to send me to represent us? Although as I let that thought permeate my brain, it occurred to me that I was likely chosen because of the very *intriguing* reputation the ball maintained. Villagers and townsfolk had been sent for eons, and none so far had returned- not man nor woman nor the many shades in between.

I was unlikely to be missed by anyone, and depriving the village of my candles would hardly cause so much as a hiccup in the daily flow of trade. There were far better and far more liked chandlers in town.

And stranger still, I couldn't believe that I was actually looking forward to it— to being pampered and primped and primed, made ready for the ball like some sort of doll. But looking at the beautiful gowns that littered the space around me was like being a child in a chocolate shop. For the first time in years, I felt like I was doing something special for myself, even if it was just to make me more presentable for what was likely to be my new captors.

The small shop I had been guided toward was warm and cozy compared to the frigid air that greeted us outside. It smelled of dust, age, and fabric, but all the gowns it showcased were beautifully maintained. How on Earth my guide thought I would be worthy of wearing any of the immaculate dresses was beyond my comprehension, but the attendant who the mayor had forced to oversee my delivery to the ball simply shuffled me off to a back room where I could change.

The older woman brought dozens and dozens of gowns, each more fantastical than the last. There was a great handful that I could barely squeeze into, my hips stretching the fabric to near tearing. I couldn't afford to be what one might consider *well-fed,* but I had never been a small woman, at least not when it came to my sizable hips. Griselda, the woman taking care of me, had quickly figured out that she needed to amend her choices in gowns.

We cycled through dress after dress before she threw one over the top of my changing screen, which actually made me gasp. It was a dark red with black lace coating it from head to foot. Tiny black gems were sewn here and there throughout the entire garment, which weighed nearly as much as I did. Underneath the lace, the front neckline of the dress was cut very low, and the open back that came to a point right at my sacrum would expose my skin to the air. The long lace sleeves that trailed down from the shoulders came to a point over the top of each middle finger. It was breathtaking.

When I studied the lace closer, looking at the larger pieces of intricately sewn material as they sat against my arms, I noticed that what I assumed had been roses were, in fact, skulls. Flowers did appear throughout some of the material. Still, the darker motifs continued as I took in more and more of the lace work, finding snakes and what I believed were thorns embroidered into the swirling patterns. It seemed fitting for a ball hosted by Blood Elves, but looking at the dark fabric against my pale skin made the reality of what would soon happen press in harder like a fist around my throat.

"Well," said Griselda, "Come out then and show it to me."

I stepped out from behind the screen, hands shaking, and waited for her to tell me that, yet again, it would not do.

"My, my. I think we've got ourselves a winner. Now we'll just need to find you the right slippers to wear. You'll be dancing for quite some time, I hear. And who is to do your makeup and hair this evening?"

"Oh. I don't know. I assumed I would."

"No, no, no. Not for Royal Court's Tribute Masquerade. I shall guide you to the proper assistance as soon as we finish here."

Griselda quickly flitted off, like a mother hen clucking about the shop, until she found a pair of velvet slippers she deemed appropriate. As she surveyed my attire, I fidgeted with my fingers, running them across the edges of the delicate lace.

"Would you desist, child? Ugh," she stamped a foot down on the old wooden floor, "What is it?"

"Where am I to place my things? I've no satchel or bag." I stared down at my hands as I spoke.

"You aren't to bring anything with you."

"Oh."

I didn't speak more for fear of aggravating her further, but it worried me that I'd leave all my possessions behind. Not that I had much in the way of belongings. The only tangible reminder of my parents was the candle shop, and I supposed I wouldn't see that again. Being chosen seemed to simply be a quicker act of fate, parting me from the shop a month sooner than my declining rent payments would.

Griselda walked me down the line of shops in the center of the village toward a woman I knew was famous for her beautiful face painting and exemplary work with hair. Would this woman be as tired of my presence as my shopping partner was?

"Hello, Eve. Welcome in. Come sit, please." Though considerably younger than Griselda, the older woman gestured at a chair just in front of her and across from a large gilded mirror.

I did as instructed and was grateful for the time off my feet. While the shoes I'd been given were lovely, they were not comfortable, and my toes ached.

"I'll be doing your hair and makeup for the Ball. Now, I'm unsure if you've ever had this type of service, so if you agree, I'd like to do my work and then show you the results. I'll face you away from the mirror until the end."

"I've not. And yes, that's fine. Will you be staying, Griselda?" I didn't want the woman to stand and watch me be painted.

"No. I have the duty of collecting your mask. Apparently, it was sent over by the Elves themselves and designed especially for this ball. I'll see you when you are finished in front of the town hall. Your carriage will be there waiting to take you."

"Very well. Thank you, Griselda." I tried my best at a grateful smile.

"Uh-huh."

And with that, she stomped off. While the weight of the air lessened some without her gloomy attitude, I could still feel the pressure of the evening lingering over me. I was supposed to make a good impression at the ball, but how precisely would the town know if I'd succeeded? We rarely heard anything from the Elves besides new proclamations and vague rumblings from the gossip-centric members of the Court who enjoyed spreading rumors. By the time any news or intrigue reached Saugues, it had become not so much fresh-off-the-fire reports but luke-warm leftovers.

My mind wandered as my makeup and hair were styled into something fitting the masquerade. At least that's what the woman, Penelope, had said. I thought about all the times I'd been too poor to afford a decent meal, when weather or old age would cause a crack in the shop roof, and my inability to fix it. The buckets perfectly placed under the leaks were still there, waiting for me in my dank attic room.

And now every inch of me was covered in garments and decorations so fine I would never have been able to imagine them. They felt heavy and odd atop my skin and bones. So much was suddenly changing.

I silently bit my lip as I remembered that the ball had already affected my life a month or so back when the order for candles became so great that even our small village was tapped for assistance. I was one of the few merchants with supplies left, and I'd stayed up for several nights trying furiously to keep up with the Elves' demands.

However, I'd been paid handsomely for my service, and it had been the best I'd eaten in quite some time. I had even afforded fruit. I could still remember the taste of the ripe strawberries on my tongue and the crunch of the apple as I chewed.

Wondering what food I might find at the ball, I noticed that Penelope had gathered my long, black curls at the back of my head and was pinning the unruly waves in numerous places. She'd allowed a few tresses to fall down my back, likely standing in stark contrast with my especially pale skin. I rarely had time to enjoy the outdoors, stuck in my ironically dimly lit candle shop as I worked. After all, I couldn't burn the merchandise.

"Eve, I believe we're done. Would you like to take a look?" Penelope asked kindly.

Her presence was far more comfortable than Griselda's, and I smiled. "Yes, thank you."

Penelope turned my chair around to face the long mirror I'd seen before, and it took my brain a few moments to process what I was seeing. Was that indeed me?

Whoever was sitting in the mirror before me looked like a queen. Black curls had been piled around a sharply pointed tiara and resembled dark rapids at midnight. There were even black and red gems woven through them that caught the light. The tiara was slim, but a large metal skull was in the center. Two large rubies had been stuffed into the eye sockets, giving the face an eerie look.

Below the intricately styled hair was equally impressive makeup, which did strike me as a bit of a waste, considering I would be wearing a mask. Regardless, the work Penelope had done matched the red and black of my gown. Sharp black wings stretched past the corners of my eyes, and striking red had been blended into my skin both above and below my eyes. There were even small gems that sat under each wing. Their red color and slightly scattered arrangement made my mind conjure up the image of blood splatter, and I stifled a shiver.

Penelope has also used no rouge, so my pale skin stood out all the harder against the striking contrast of black and deep red.

"One last thing."

My kinder attendant stood before me and painted a shining coat of matching red on my lips. When she stepped back again, I took in the deep color on my mouth.

"Is it true that the Elves... drink blood," I asked.

"I'm not sure, but I suppose you'll soon find out."

I'D COMPLETELY FALLEN into the well of my thoughts, and so suddenly, I was in front of the town hall waiting for my carriage— and my mask. Grisela appeared before me, almost sneaking up and causing me to jump. In her hands was a small black box that shone in the fading light of the afternoon.

"Here you are then. Your mask." Griselda thrust the box into my hands, and I hastily scramble to take it without letting it land in the dirt.

"Thank you. Is it fitting for the dress?" I asked.

"I don't know. I didn't open it."

"Oh. I supposed I should check then?"

Griselda just shrugged, so I made the decision for myself to look into the box and be sure that the mask wouldn't look odd paired with my attire.

What I revealed had me frozen in place. It was impossible, but somehow the mask was perfect, like it had been designed precisely for me, for exactly this night.

It was constructed from two separate parts. The top portion connected to a bottom piece that would cover my entire face, creating an eerie porcelain doll image. The lips were painted in a small, heart-like shape in black, and the "skin" was a pearlescent white. Just beneath the cheeks and hidden through a tiny mechanism was where the halves attached. The area framing my eyes was drawn similarly to the wings of my makeup, black and red, with touches of gold. There was swirling filigree across the pale skin that mirrored the skulls and snakes of my lace. A large plume of black feathers was affixed to the side of the mask and secured with another skull head with two ruby eyes.

How could it so perfectly match? As I took in the mask, utterly shocked, I looked to Penelope.

"Did you know?"

"I did not, but the Elves are powerful creatures. Perhaps they did and saw fit to ensure everything looks exactly as they want it to?" She cocked a coy smile.

Swallowing hard, I turned my back to her, "Would you assist me with securing it?"

She tied the mask in place, and while I could still see, it was as if I was completely gone. Nowhere was the small-town peasant who could barely afford to eat. Suddenly in her place was a Mistress of the High Masquerade Ball. And with that, I was escorted into the carriage and carried off toward my new life and, potentially, my death.

CHAPTER 2: EVE ARKWRIGHT

The carriage ride was bumpy and long, the road seeming to drag on into eternity. Night had fallen when the driver's voice startled me out of my dozing. I looked out the cab's window and took in the incredible sight of a sky full of stars. Their tiny pinpricks of light punctured through the deep navy above me, winking like silent observers.

When we'd reached the edge of the Blood Elves' Vraxsite Empire, I noticed it was much darker than the evening had been outside the nation's borders. I remembered that the Blood Elves lived in a realm of permanent midnight. The sun never shone here; only the stars and the moon, strangely decorated with red splotches, lit up the sky.

The carriage passed through a thickly wooded area that sat above the castle, which was sunk low in the next valley. The trees were massive, their looming shapes blanketing the carriage in an even deeper layer of darkness. Strange howls and gnashing sounds sporadically echoed out from the forest, and I shivered. It was much cooler here, and the weight of something ancient and malicious hummed through the woods.

As the wheels bumped along the uneven road to the palace of the Blood Elves, my mind wandered, landing on what my future might hold in store. There was a reason we were called Tributes. When individuals were sent to the ball, we did so with the knowledge that we were sacrificing our old lives in service of the Elves that protected us and held dominion over the land. The history was murky. The Blood Elves' rise to

CHAPTER 2: EVE ARKWRIGHT

power or long-held control was hotly debated. Whichever camp you landed in, we all knew one thing— they demanded Tributes for their balls every few decades, and those sent *belonged* to them- in every way possible.

My ride ended, and the footman opened the coach door wide for me to disembark. He held out his hands so I could navigate the steps, and as my feet hit the pristine stone before me, I gasped. The palace was breathtaking and terrifying.

Seemingly matching my attire, or rather my attire it, the castle was black and gothic and immense. Large fearsome gargoyles perched on every ledge and tower that crested the building, which stretched into the night sky. Red curtains and drapery peeked out from the massive windows, all featuring thick wrought iron bars that crossed through them. A pair of gargantuan double doors sat before me. I was guided up to them, where they seemed to open by magic as I approached, and then I was left alone, standing at the entry like a fawn before a wolf.

I was supposed to enter immediately, but I shook so hard I could hear my teeth rattle. I stared at the marble floor, which looked like a chessboard, and couldn't bring myself to look up. My heartbeat was like rattling booms in my head, and my stomach twisted and churned. That's when an unseen servant cleared his throat from behind one of the large doors.

"Oh! Apologies."

I quickly hustled inside and felt heat pool in my cheeks. I'd not been here for more than a handful of minutes and was already making a fool of myself.

When I finally took my eyes off the floor, the sight of the immense ballroom stopped me dead in my tracks, yet again, though at least I'd made it fully in the room this time. Looking around, I realized I stood on a massive, curved staircase that flooded into the room below me. The stairs showed that black and white chessboard and deep, blood-red drapery hung around the vast archways and windows that circled the large ballroom floor. There were candlesticks on the tables as big as a person and large posts of them that put mighty oaks to shame.

It smelled like cinnamon and wine and something else I couldn't quite place, something that seemed to pinch with its metallic quality. The air was surprisingly warm, and the lack of coverage that my dress afforded me no longer felt so out of place. Everyone in the grand hall, no less than one hundred, wore varying shades of red and black, and no one was covered up much. Except, of course, for the masks.

I could see no faces that weren't a beautiful construction of a master crafter. There were white masks with striking red gems and black masks with perfectly etched white cracks, making them look like shattered glass. Nearly everyone wore long black gloves, and I saw several masks covering their wearer's eyes. Many of those people, I realized, wore nothing else, their naked forms draped over couches and chaises.

The walls of the room were deep, blackish stonework, and several tables were scattered about the edges of the room and covered in deep red and black tablecloths. Massive fountains were perched on top of them, surrounded by rows and rows of exquisitely made goblets. The liquid that rained down the fountains' tiers was no doubt blood. The thick sanguine fluid rippled slowly as the Elves filled their cups.

I swallowed hard. The amount of blood rushing through the large wells was enough to make up armies of townsfolk. How had they acquired it? My hand instinctively went to my neck, and I had to quickly school myself so that I didn't offend my hosts and risk my life all the quicker.

Having little idea of what lay ahead of me, merely speculations about the Elves' eating habits, I wondered if I'd even need to remember my dance lessons or if, in moments, I'd be nothing more than a meal and died shortly after that. I heard my mother's voice in my head, her grim warning about the power of the Blood Elves' creeping down my spine.

They'll catch you in their cage, and you'll be glad to be there. When you should fear your demise, you'll instead be a puppet under their control, willingly bleeding out for them.

I was startled out of my thoughts when the shimmering from a large silver tray caught my eye. A handful of attendants walked through the room, delivering beverages and hors d'oeuvres as they checked on the guests. They wore fascinating and terrifying black and white costumes, split equally down the middle. Their masks covered the entirety of their faces, but somehow their eyes seemed to glow from within them.

Many of the Elves' clothes reflected a similar style, with large cuffs and billowing sleeves that poked out of form-fitted suits for those masculinely presenting. The ball gowns I saw were equally as lovely, intricate lace and velvet constructions that would have made me feel out of place if it weren't for the gifted attire I currently wore.

There were also statues made of a shiny black material positioned throughout the space that also wore masks. Their frozen forms were eerie, and the black, highly detailed masks they wore, which couldn't be made of fabric like mine, only offered tiny slits for the sightless eyes and no mouth or nose holes. The combination created an impassive expression that sent a chill down my spine.

I slowly descended the stairs, the music of the space swelling around me and creating a blanket of dark sensuality that licked across my skin. It was intoxicating, and between the Blood Elves' reputation for magical skill and shameless behavior, I imagined that the music could very well be enchanted.

Massive chandeliers of candles hovered in the center of the ballroom. Their weight seemed impossible for their thin chains to hold up, and that's when I noticed that thick wrought iron chains dangled from various places throughout the room, and some of them were occupied.

Moaning, masked people of every gender and color were strung up by their wrists, ankles, and occasionally both, creating the look that they were meat on a spit. I wondered what it might be like to be so ready for the taking and immediately chastised myself. How could I have let myself think something so…? I didn't know what.

Clearly, dancing wasn't the only activity on the roster this evening. I shuddered. I'd never had the opportunity to enjoy intimacy. Being a poor girl from the edge of town didn't lend itself to carnal interactions. I *had* thought about it, however. With so much time spent alone, entertaining myself with the power of my vivid imagination had become one of my few enjoyable pastimes. I also loved to read about it, smuggling the frowned-upon literature into my home whenever I could purchase some from a traveling salesman.

Gods, was that what the Tributes were for? Blood and… sex?

I trembled. I would have no idea what to do in that situation. Though the idea of being taught and told what to do, heated my blood and caused me to flush everywhere. I had barely dared to think such thoughts alone. Now I was in a crowded room full of exquisite Blood Elves in varying levels of undress, and I could scarcely contain the moan trying to break free from my throat.

A balcony surrounded the ballroom, overlooking it, and the people there laughed and drank heavily from their silver goblets. From what I could tell, there was lounging furniture up there and more of the massive red drapes that hung in graceful curves from the ceiling.

Paying closer attention to the dance floor, I saw a group of Elves in quite possibly the most beautiful, most sexual, and most terrifying finery.

I couldn't help but stare. Behind their masks, it looked as if there were no eyes, simply pools of blackness I could see myself falling into.

One of the women's masks was a large crown-like structure with a large half-circle shape protruding from behind her hair. It was covered in carvings of snakes and dripped with thin metal chains. She was one of the Elves who wore a mask with no eye holes, but her mouth was on full display, her full, pouty lips painted a deep red. She also wore little clothing; black straps of fabric hanging loosely from her gorgeous body were the only thing between her creamy skin and the room.

Her nipples peaked from behind the lace strips, and red curls between her legs echoed the color of her long hair. She somehow sensed me and turned to "look" straight at me. I gulped.

Her movements caught the eye of her companions, and they, in turn, stared at what had stolen her attention—me.

One wore a long black frock coat and held a long black cane in a gloved hand. It appeared to be for aesthetic appeal because they used it to gesture toward me as they whispered to their other companions. Their mask also covered their entire face and was composed of a simple and pristine white base with intricate blackened gold filigree swirling around the eyes and nose.

Another masculine figure among them wore a sleek velvet suit with incredible gold stitching and a corseted back. I admired the lacing until the Elf turned around, after which I quickly ducked my eyes to the ground.

Unable to keep my gaze from returning, I saw the man smiling at me. His jovial expression was noticeable behind his half-mask. But the most striking thing about his smile was the sharp teeth that peeked out from between his full lips. I thought of them piercing my skin, and something bloomed within me alongside my fear.

As I reached the bottom of the steps, several gloved hands reached out to take mine, as well as my arms, and floated me down to the ground. I felt light as a feather and studied the masked faces around me. It was the group who'd noticed me, and they were even more immaculate up close. It was nearly painful how beautifully styled they were. And not all of them wore full masks. With them, I could see the most lovely skin I'd ever laid eyes on, shades of cream and tan and umber sparkling in the candlelight.

There were six of them. As I'd noticed, a few were obviously masculine or feminine, but two were ambiguous. None of their hands left my skin, and for some utterly foreign reason, I didn't want them to. They circled around me like panthers, guiding me down the steps and toward a dark corner near a collection of low chaise couches and hanging manacles.

As I was set down on top of the pillowy cushion, an androgynous Elf among them sat next to me, lifting one of my curls from my neck gracefully. Their fingers were slim and feminine, and on each tip was a strange and beautiful decoration. They were blackened metal rings of sorts that created claw points on each digit out of swirling filigree.

Their mask covered half their face, but instead of revealing only the bottom section, this one split their wearer's face into two halves vertically. It, too, was intricately-designed metal filigree that resembled black lace. The warm-skinned Elf's lips were full and painted black to match. Most interesting was how the visible eye, deep brown and inviting, was painted to look like it was crying gold. The shimmering metal highlighted the sunny yellow in their skin, and I wanted to run my fingers across it.

Similarly, their outfit was a long black coat with edges that dripped with gold threading and metal accents. They wore no shirt beneath the jacket, and their gently muscled chest and warm tan skin glowed in the candlelight.

Another Elf quickly took up the space to my other side. He was exceptionally tall, and his dark umber skin looked positively velvet in the soft light. I wanted to run my fingers across the firm muscles of his bare arms. His long vest coat was the only thing between us all, with no shirt or tie beneath it, and the fabric of his tails swept across the floor as he moved. His tightly fitting black trousers were made of shiny leather, and as he sat next to me, they stretched around his muscular legs.

Tearing my eyes away from the impressive bulge contained within his leather pants, I took in the design of his mask. It looked very much like a royal court jester, but this one featured a long red tongue I was sure was reserved for demons. The crimson coloring was slightly shimmering, and his eyes glowed from behind the delicately cracked white face.

I felt the others I'd seen before slide behind me on the large round settee, the warmth of their presence leaking into me like a hot bath.

And that is when I saw the last of them.

He stole the group's attention, snapping their gazes up toward him as he loomed over us all. My eyes traveled the extended distance from his simple black suit, which made him look like a walking shadow, to his mask. His dark eyes stared at me through the eye sockets of a gruesomely realistic silver skull.

I was sure my heart had stopped.

He walked toward me, standing inches before my seated form and forcing me to look up into his eyes. My blood chilled and heated simultaneously. The deep voice that filtered out from behind his chilling skull mask had heat pooling between my legs and goosebumps rippling across my skin.

"Well, hello there, little mouse. And who are you?"

CHAPTER 3: ALOK BRYRIE

T took in the terrified woman, drinking in the taste of her fear and warring arousal. The bitter bite of it traveled down my skin and straight to my cock. The others had seen her first, but as soon as they'd alerted me to her arrival, I knew our long-awaited mate had arrived.

Ordering them to pursue through our shared bond, I relished how she played out her role as our prey, eyes darting to each of us as she took us in.

"I… I am Eve. Arkwright. Good evening, sir."

I nearly growled, the panicked attempts at civility only serving to make me that much more excited to destroy her.

My other mate's desire raked across them, and a hungry malice pooled in my gut. It had been centuries waiting for her arrival, and now, with Eve inches away from my grasp, I nearly came from the thought of breaking her alone. The chase was here, and it would be earth-shattering.

"Eve. We've been waiting." A devilish rumble infiltrated my voice as my Blood power surged to the surface.

Letting the magic snake out of my words and straight into her bloodstream, I pulled her heat and desire forward. I found it supple and wanting, already willing and ready for the taking under our grasp. Eve's eyes were nearly shut behind her mask, and she struggled to contain a moan from breaking free of her lips. Watching her fight, it was intoxicating.

"Eeevvvee," Paeris, the youngest and most flirtatious of us, dragged out her name from between his teeth, and I held back the desire to smack his delicious pink mouth so that I could appreciate the pleasure he got from pain. *Soon.*

As it was, the others couldn't help growling at her and tugging on his corset strings. Siraye pulled him down to their mouth with a biting kiss, drawing blood and lapping it up. They let some of the crimson fluid dribble out of their mouth, enjoying a mess like they did, and their Domme claim on Paeris sung through our bond.

"Oh, Eve. We have been waiting. Siraye. You may call me, Siraye. This," they yanked on Paeris's hair, "is our sweet, Paeris. He's positively weeping at the thought of that pretty cunt of yours on his mouth."

Eve flushed a deep crimson, and my cock hardened all the further. Siraye leaned in toward Eve, pulling off the bottom half of the mask we'd sent to her village free, exposing her supple lips. They laid a gentle kiss on Eve. Still, as nicely as it may have started, I felt Siraye's decision to let their fang scratch Eve's lower lip, bringing out the faintest taste of her blood.

"Siraye. You naughty thing," I spoke into their mind.

"Promises. Promises." They responded, *"Make me your good girl tonight. If you can."*

I internally lit up. So, they wanted to play it that way. They *would* pay their own penance for acting out of turn, but I could hardly put it past them. The rampant desire to fuck was already a heady mixture floating through the room. Adding Eve took it to entirely new levels.

Our Coagulate was finally complete with her here.

Siraye looked back to Eve, blood coating her lips, and smiled at the shocked expression decorating her face. Devdan, our resident oral wonder, couldn't help himself at the sight and quickly discarded his tongued mask so that he might use his own. He bit down and lapped at Paeris's neck, turning to Siraye and mixing the fluid with them as he pressed closer to Eve.

They both shoved Paeris's face down into the cushions, holding him draped across Eve's lap, dangling onto the floor as he writhed for more, begging us to ruin him through our bond.

Both Corym and I had been content to watch their shenanigans unfold, as we usually were, but he surprised even me as he pressed in tight to both Eve and Amedee, gripping his cane hard enough to send a delicious wave of pain through our bond.

The evening was picking up steam quickly, and as much as a part of me wanted to see how far Eve might let the experience go without so much as a pause, I wanted to torment her a bit more.

"Eve, our little mouse. Do you want to run? Do we frighten you?" I lowered my mouth to Eve's ear, kneeling on Paeris's prone form.

Her eyes darted down to Paeris, who made no move to escape his predicament, and then back up to the others, landing squarely on me. I held back the need to drag her by the hair to our private sanctum. She needed me, my cruelty, and I was chomping at the bit to give it to her.

"You… You do frighten me… but I don't want to run, at least not for long." Her fingers shot to her lips, taken aback by her own words. Our blood magic had pulled the truth from her lips, and thanks to Siraye, we all had a claim on it now.

Amedee circled to my back, clinging close to my leg as I kneeled on Paeris's delicate, pale skin, stroking it. She looked up at me as she flicked out her claws and dragged them through his skin, seeing clear as day through the opaque mask she wore, thanks to her gifts.

"Alok," she whined, "She needs you. We can all feel it. Take her down below. Let us watch— and play."

I gently stroked her gorgeous red curls and smiled down at her through the skull mask.

"Amedee," I yanked her hair back, arching her back and lowering my mouth to her exposed breast, "Say please."

I bit down on her creamy skin, piercing her nipple with my fangs and tasting the ecstasy that roamed through her.

Eve stared in wonder. She never broke eye contact with me as I feasted on Amedee, and I could *feel* the pulse of lust shoot through her like an arrow.

"Please!" Amedee cried out through a tearful smile, and I released her to Corym.

He stroked a gloved hand through her blood and trailed it up to her mouth, dipping their finger inside and relishing the way she sucked the leather clean. I could feel it all through the bond, and though our connection with Eve was still new, I sensed her fascination and wonder.

Corym was tightly buckled up behind all that fabric and false civility, and I watched as Eve tried to piece together who he truly was. Corym, our demi-male mate, was far too complex for a single night's investigation. I looked forward to watching him use Eve, providing her with a very harsh lesson in their tastes.

Eve looked back to me as I wiped Amedee's blood from my lips, allowing Siraye and Devdan to lick it off my gloved hand.

"Are you sure this is right?" Eve asked, "I'm just... I'm just me. I couldn't—"

I grabbed her around the throat and gently squeezed, drawing Corym from his torment of Amedee as he sensed this new pain.

"Do not tell me or any of us what we want or should be. We have claimed you, Eve. And tonight, you shall break apart beneath us and become one of the Sanguine Coagulate."

As heat bloomed from within Eve, I felt the first of what were sure to be many orgasms slice through her like a knife.

"Now, tell me, our little mouse, how long do you think you'll last against this pack of predators?"

CHAPTER 4: EVE ARKWRIGHT

I've never experienced an orgasm so blindingly intense. Still, the moment my skull-masked captor seized my neck, all the tension of the past few moments overflowed within me, and I came in a great wave. My little experience alone paled in comparison to how this group, this Coagulate, made me feel. Any hope I had of maintaining my wits was obliterated.

In fact, I believed wholeheartedly that I wouldn't be able to keep anything from them even if I tried. Siraye, as they'd called themselves, had tasted my blood when they'd allowed their fang to pierce my lip, and the tether I felt bonding us spread to the others, if less intensely for the moment—except for him.

My Skeleton had a hold over me from the moment we met eyes. I trembled as he held my throat, moving his thumb to drag it across my bloody lip. If this beautiful, horrible creature asked it of me, I'd do anything his words demanded, and I think he knew.

The warm tan skin of his nose touched my neck through the hole in his mask as he inhaled me. Wetness gathered between my thighs yet again, and I worried I might drip. Sensing the thought, my Skeleton's dark eyes flashed to mine.

"Little mouse, the thoughts that must be filling that dirty little mind. Your scent," he breathed me in again, "is so thick with arousal. You filthy girl."

I blushed all the harder, and then Siraye and Devdan were at my back again, trailing claw-like fingers up and down my spine. Tiny pinpricks of pain scattered through my skin as the sharp points danced across my flesh. I moaned; I couldn't help it.

As the sound escaped me, the Coagulate pushed in tighter. I should have felt trapped or claustrophobic, but I didn't. If anything, I wanted all of them nearer to me, touching, tasting, *devouring* me.

My Skeleton's hand never left my face, and he slid it around to the back of my neck and pulled me forward. I was moved off the soft cushion and planted right on top of Paeris, who only groaned in approval when my weight settled on him.

"What are you doing? Umm…" I didn't know My Skeleton's name yet.

He grinned. Somehow I knew it was there behind the mask, and then he yanked and fluffed up my dress so that my bare skin was up against Paeris's.

"Giving you a proper seat. And it's Alok." His hands snaked up my sides and found their way into my hair, squeezing just enough to make my scalp burn. "But you will address me as Sir, understand?"

"Yes, Sir."

Another felt, but unseen grin reverberated through me. I *loved* pleasing Alok.

"Corym, bring Amedee to her."

The intriguing figure with the black frock coat and cane pulled the gorgeous redhead toward me by her hair.

"You all get two minutes. Don't disappoint." Alok's words left him with a growl.

Suddenly, Amedee, Siraye, and Devdan set upon me like wolves, ravenous and greedy. My arms were quickly pinned behind me, held in place by Devdan's strong arms, muscles bunching under his dark brown skin. Siraye's tongue slid out from her deep maroon lips and found my neck, and they trailed their fangs across my thundering pulse. Amedee's bite on my nipple drew my gaze downward. She'd punctured my gown's fabric, and I quickly went from impressed to boiling with lust.

The surface beneath me shifted as Paeris moved under my thighs. He rotated and lifted my legs over his shoulders, burying himself under the layers of my skirts. My face must have turned the brightest shade of crimson as I was angled back to fall into Devdan's chest. He smiled down at me, his long tongue swiping over his own bloody lips and swirling with promise.

"Paeris love, what say you take this to the next level?" Devdan asked. His deep voice was like molasses dripping over me, coating me in rich sweetness.

From beneath my dress, I felt Paeris find his way between my dripping lips and lick up a long, slow trail. I shuddered. The things the beautiful Blood Elf could do with his tongue were positively sinful. Arching up and thrusting my breast further into Amedee's mouth, I felt Siraye slide onto the floor, kneeling beside Paeris.

"Give me a taste, boy," Siraye demanded, and Paeris quickly pulled his mouth back and presented it to them.

Siraye licked my cum from Paeris's tongue and sighed. A gush of wetness surged from me at the absolutely hedonistic sight. Devdan reached a hand around my side and dipped his long fingers inside me. I squealed lightly as he worked my clit, pinching it as he took his hand back to lick his fingers.

Amedee trailed her claws up to my shoulder and pushed the sleeve of my dress down, exposing my breast. Siraye pushed Paeris back under my dress and smacked him hard across the ass, the bright noise barely standing out against the collective sounds of pleasure filling the room. As Paeris's tongue dove back inside me, I kicked my head back with a gasp.

"Oh, that's nothing, love," Devdan spoke in my ear. He lifted me, Paeris's mouth instinctively following, and I hovered in the air, my legs draped over Paeris's shoulders.

The free space allowed Paeris to dive deeper, and I cursed.

"Fuck. Oh, Gods."

Siraye replaced Devdan at my back, whispering, "Show her your tricks, Devdan."

With that, he sank beneath me. Before my mind could piece together what was happening, his wickedly long tongue was stuffed inside me as Paeris tongued my clit. I came instantly, liquid spilling from me as I writhed against the joint effort of their tongues.

I tried desperately to look at my fellow companions, longing to see them for a reason I couldn't place. Amedee was kneeling under me and just before Siraye, who held me. Her face was between their legs, and I watched as her head bobbed up and down. Siraye moaned in my ear.

"Do you like watching her taste me? Do you want to share my cum with her?"

I squirmed against Devdan and Paeris, whose efforts had yet to cease, and vigorously nodded. When I looked forward, I saw Corym and Alok relishing my torment. They looked at each other, and Corym nodded. When their eyes met mine again, the evil look in their eyes sent me over the edge.

Another orgasm raked through me, and I cried out, thrusting my cunt against my mates' faces.

Wait. Mates?

But as the thought rippled through me, I truly felt it. The tether I'd been aware of vaguely was alive and throbbing between us, gaining strength with every moment of bliss. As I looked back at Corym and Alok, I understood. This was Act I, and there was far more in store.

CHAPTER 5: SIRAYE HOLASATRA

"Time's up. Set our little mouse down," Corym said. We obeyed and draped the near-liquid form of our final mate across the round settee we'd claimed.

Devdan, Amedee, and I circled around her, with Paeris saying right between her legs, albeit seated on the floor before her. Our mouse was an exquisite feast, and Corym's timing had been enough to allow us to bring Eve to orgasm more than once while leaving all of us desperate for more.

Tasting Eve off Paeris's tongue had been intoxicating, the bitter and sweet flavors mingling in my mouth and making my core weep. She was completely new to everything we offered, and I could sense her lack of experience with both Blood Elves and sex. Eve was untouched, and our Coagulate would have the supreme honor of claiming her maidenhood for ourselves.

I wanted that reality soon. Taking hold of Eve so that Devdan and Paeris could work her over with their tongues had only served to rev me up. Amedee's tongue, while talented, wasn't what I had a taste for this evening. We all wanted a piece of our Eve's fresh blood, welcoming her into our Garden of Sin.

The fragility she demonstrated was just too mouthwatering, and I wasn't the only one desperate to destroy her. Alok's blistering arousal for the little mouse pulsed so hard through our bond that I was actually taken aback by the level of darkness swimming through his veins.

We all fit into each other's hearts and lives differently, if entirely. The Sanguine Six, as we were called, were a family, a depraved one. Still, while many of us allowed both Corym and Alok to Dom us frequently, none of us were entirely submissive to them. Aside from Paeris, and his submission was tinged with a delightful brattiness. What's more, Corym and Alok's constant cock fighting was delectable to watch, particularly when said cocks were rubbing against each other in a dance of deep tan and dark brown, but they both needed someone to top after their dueling.

Eve was pure submission, a penetrating need to serve and please, to be commanded and pushed past her limits. It was exquisite, and even I couldn't put it past Alok when I felt his intense desire for her. Eve truly was the missing piece.

As Corym approached, Amedee reached out a hand to stroke his long, black sleeve, smiling. They turned toward her for a moment, eyes penetrating her from behind his full mask, and then returned his gaze to Eve.

"Shall we play our favorite game?" He asked, never breaking eye contact with Eve as she struggled to regain her breath. "Are you up for it?"

Corym, the slightly warmer of our two Doms, waited patiently for her response, though I could sense their desire to pounce rumbling through our bond.

We understood much about each other and related in a way the others didn't. Corym and I both considered ourselves both a part of our assigned genders and not. Notably, we both felt they didn't matter. We were us, and that was all that was necessary.

Choosing to accept both "he" and "they" references, Corym was far more than that which could be defined by a simple pronoun. I adored them for that. I preferred "they" on most occasions. Still, as I watched the hunger build behind Corym's eyes, not to mention Alok's, I remembered why there were only the two people in this world I allowed to make me their "good girl."

They earned it, and one of my favorite ways they did so was through playing *our favorite game*.

The raw need that echoed through our shared bond as Corym brought it up felt like being in a splendid magical loop, where each person's desire fed off of and fueled the others. We all froze as we awaited her response.

As Eve shifted onto her elbows, she looked into Alok's and Corym's eyes, searching their stares and the new bond connection for his meaning. When she found it, her eyes went wide, and another lustful assault ripped through the Coagulate.

"Yes."

"How long do you need?" Corym asked softly.

Eve's stare darted around the room until she found the large black doors at the back. They revealed stairs that went down, and my mates and I internally hummed. She'd found our special place quickly.

"A few minutes? Five?" Her wide-doe eyes begged Corym for a positive response, and heat pooled in my folds.

Corym stood back up, standing near Alok, who nodded. Their eyes went to ours, and we gave Eve the space she needed to move quickly.

"Go."

As soon as the words left Corym's lips, Eve bolted for the dance floor and toward the door. The Chase was on.

CHAPTER 6: CORYM PABANISE

The little mouse ran fast, and she quickly dodged through the crowded ballroom. I counted internally, eyeing my mates as I waited for five minutes. I was one who adhered to rules, after all. Even if I set them myself.

My pet, Amedee, crawled toward me on the floor, her strips of fabric she called a dress hanging off her and revealing her fabulous breasts. She leaned down as she reached my leg, raising her perfect ass in the air. She was a tiny but curvy thing and nearly as much of a brat as Paeris.

I slid my cane between the curves of her ass and rubbed it teasingly against her slick pussy. Amedee moaned and dragged her tongue across the shiny leather of my boot. I smiled, hidden though it was, and tapped my cane against her slit.

"Hungry little thing."

"Has it been five minutes, Sir?" Paeris crawled up next to Amedee, Siraye hot on his tail and standing above him to rest their foot on his back.

"No."

Evil arousal surged through our bond, and I looked back at the source.

"Alok? Would you care to vocalize what's got your cock twisted?" I adored pushing his buttons.

"Fuck you. You're well aware that it's Eve. I want... The things I'm going to do." Alok's voice sounded pained, which of course, got me hard as a rock.

"Are you claiming First Bite? You may have to fight me for it." I smirked behind my mask, all too aware that Alok could tell.

"Corym." He dragged out my name, gloved knuckles squeezing the fabric of his gloves as he gripped his hands into fists.

"Loves, put them away. We've dallied too long; others could have noticed Eve's arrival. You know many of the fringe Coagulates will give a fuck if she's our mate." Devdan's smooth voice cut through my tussle with Alok, and I frowned.

"He's right. I noticed Vinchenzo eyeing her."

Alok growled so low and so primal that we all hummed through our bond, even me.

"So let's go then! I'm desperate for another taste of her cherry pussy," Paeris squealed.

I rolled my eyes but began stalking across the dance floor, moving people out of the way with my cane as necessary. Alok was hot on my heels, and the fury boiling off him at the thought of someone outside our group touching her was palpable- bond or not.

We followed her path through the doors and down the stairs to our hidden sanctuary, a room we'd discovered and stolen for ourselves centuries ago. Only the Coagulate could enter, and while Eve was undoubtedly one of us, it was still possible she might not head directly toward it.

I sniffed the air. Among our group, our gifts were varied. I possessed the best sense of smell of all of us, especially when it came to blood, and Eve's delicious scent traveling down the long dark hall pulled me forward like a dog on a leash.

It diverted from our familiar path to our private space, and I shook my head. I should have realized she'd get a bit lost, and if it weren't for Devdan's warning, I might have enjoyed the prolonged hunt for her. But as it was, something almost prescient about his comment struck me. Someone would try to fuck with our little mouse, and I'd have none of it.

"This isn't the way to the room," Siraye noted, and I simply nodded.

I felt the tension bristle up through our group and did my best to open my senses up all the more to follow her trail quickly.

That's when we heard it.

A piercing scream cut through the endless hallways, making my blood cold. As one, we all shifted to the left and took off running. Our steps against the cold, stone floor echoed around us as another cry, clearly for help, ricocheted through the chambers. The pitch was unmistakable.

Someone was harming Eve, and that someone was about to die.

We arrived at a smaller rounded chamber set into a corner near a left-forking hall. It was dark, and several arched doorways went in and out of the room. Low-burning torches barely lit the space, but our Blood Elf eyes were a match for the darkness. In the center of the floor, one of Vinchenzo's pets held Eve by the hair as she knelt on the ground. A large blade was pressed to Eve's throat, and her mask had been discarded. Eve's welling eyes were as large as saucers. The terror on Eve's face knifed through my heart, through all of ours, and we collectively growled.

"What the fuck are you doing, Contessa?" Alok roared at the woman restraining Eve and threw his mask to the ground.

Contessa was a large enough female that holding our human mate was easy for her. Her gaze was bloodshot and furious as she made eye contact with our group.

"He wants her! Her! Hasn't stopped talking about the fucking *human* since she arrived! It's an insult to our entire Coagulate! I will not let this trash tarnish the name of The Sabbath Coagulate!"

Contessa's blade pressed into Eve's neck, and a trickle of blood started to drip down her skin. At speeds I didn't even know we were capable of, Alok and I were at the Contessa. I squeezed her arm, forcing her to drop the blade. Then, I twisted it back, relishing how it snapped with a sickening crack. Alok gripped her by the face and tore through her with his claws at the exact moment, diving into her prone neck and biting hard.

I heard him gulp her blood as the life slowly drained from Contessa. Pulling Eve away and toward the others, we huddled around her.

"I- I'm sorry. I didn't hear her behind me. The things she said…." Eve's eyes fell to the floor as her words trailed off.

"Hush. She's dead. No harm will come to you." I did my best to comfort her. Thankfully, Amedee and Devdan were there with soothing words.

"Our sweet, Eve. She has long been an issue. You're safe. We will always come for you," Devdan soothed.

"And don't listen to that cunt. Contessa has been a jealous hag her whole pathetic life," Amedee chimed in, and Paeris snorted in response.

"Are you okay? Do you want us to take you somewhere else?" Paeris asked.

Eve looked toward Alok, who was letting Contessa's body fall to the ground in a heap, thick blood dripping down his mouth and chin. It was the first time she'd seen him without his mask, and I could sense the lustful intrigue flooding her.

"Oh, don't look at that, love." Siraye tugged Eve's chin back toward the group, but it didn't last. Our mouse was quickly looking back at Alok and meeting his eyes.

"You killed her."

"She threatened you," he responded, "Does that upset you?"

Silence hung for but a moment before Eve stood up and walked toward him.

"No." She put her hand on Alok's chest. "Show me how to be brave. Show me how to break free of my old life. Teach me… how much I can take."

Alok's pupils blew wide at her words, and our Coagulate was hushed with awe. So, Alok would have First Bite of Eve, but this dangerous little mouse would experience us all tonight, and the ruination of her innocence would be bliss.

CHAPTER 7: ALOK BRYRIE

E ve's words struck me to my core, my heart if I had one, and the look in her eyes only served to silence any apprehension I may have had. Not that I did. I was a fucking sadist, and everyone knew it. I was going to ruin her for anyone else but me and enjoy every tear I forced from her doe eyes.

But our little mouse, our tempting Eve, looked at me like I was a savior. Worse, she looked at me like she saw me, the *real* me, and wasn't running away scared. She wanted my darkness, needed it, and she was going to fucking take everything I gave her until she fell apart.

"Strip," I commanded.

Her clothing was already in disarray, and shrugging the rest of the way out of the dress took but a moment. The lacey black fabric hit the floor in a billowing heap. I pointed behind me toward Contessa's body without breaking eye contact with Eve.

"Move that."

The Coagulate quickly discarded the fresh corpse, licking the blood off their fingers after ditching it down another hall. Dead bodies weren't an entirely odd occurrence, particularly at a masquerade, and the laws among Blood Elves differed from those of mortals.

Eve shivered in front of me. The ice and fear crawling up her skin thrummed through our shared bond, and for a few moments, I simply stared at her, watching her stare track my movements. Her skin was pale, and the dark hair between her legs matched the long waves piled on top of her head. The chill and arousal hardened her nipples, and I could hear her heartbeat speed up as I fucked her with just my eyes.

In many ways, improved hearing was a blessing.

"Take your hair down."

Reaching up to her curls, Eve pulled free the pins holding her locks in place and let them drop to the floor. The midnight wave came tumbling down her shoulders, creating a blanket of gorgeous black.

I walked forward slowly, relishing how she struggled to hold back a flinch. As I came within inches of her, I pushed Eve's hair behind her shoulders, exposing her breasts once again. I trailed a gloved finger down her neck to her nipple, pinching it between my fingers until her knees buckled.

A rush of desire shot through our bond from the others. They loved watching me break our newest mate and turning face to her and breathing in her scent, I could tell that Eve was enjoying it as well. As I dragged my other hand down her side and reached between her legs, I gathered Eve's growing wetness on my fingers.

"Open."

She did as told, and I stuffed her mouth full, choking her just long enough to have tears streaming down her pretty face and ruining her makeup. I retracted my hand, and Eve gasped for air.

"Last and only warning. I will not be kind. I will not be gentle. Your screams will belong to me, and I will demand them often. I will use every part of you. I will command them to use every part of you. The others, our mates, call me the Devil, and that's exactly what you'll get."

I held her delicate throat in my hand, squeezing but leaving her room to speak.

"I have been waiting for this my entire life, Alok. I am yours to do with as you please, Sir."

Oh, she was a quick study. The doors caging my inner animal were flung open, and I took her hair in my grip. I gathered the long waves, twisting them around my hand and forcing her to the ground. Eve's knees hit the floor, and she groaned. I towered over her, holding her hair taught and pulling up just enough to keep her off balance.

Leaning over her, I took Eve's chin in my other hand, gripping and forcing her jaws apart.

"Keep your mouth open unless you're told otherwise."

Eve relaxed her jaw as much as possible and took a shuddering breath.

I sniffed the fragrant perfume that had been used on her hair and skin, dragging my nose down her neck. Her pulsed thundered under the thin skin, fast as a hummingbird.

Squeezing her hair tighter, I angled her head to the side, bringing her neck close to my lips.

"Scream for me."

I bit into the tender flesh and pulled her blood into my mouth. Eve's cries were sharp and echoed in the small space. Her taste was better than any wine and infinitely more rich and intoxicating. The surge of arousal it ignited traveled down our bond, and I heard the others groan and hiss.

Forcing myself to stop before I drained her too much, I pulled back in a rough arch, tearing my fangs free and eliciting another scream. Eve's head fell forward as she panted. Her mouth was still open as I took off my gloves.

Standing, I looked toward my Elf mates. They'd torn what little fabric covered Amedee free and stripped Paeris. Devdan and Corym feasted on Amedee's creamy skin. At the same time, Corym pressed Paeris into the ground, forcing him to lick his boot. Siraye was behind Paeris, stroking his cock as they fucked his ass with their hand. I grinned, relishing the depravity of my mates.

I circled around behind Eve and smacked her ass hard. She jumped and yelped as the pain zinged through her. Her blood trickled down her neck to her breast, creating a thick, crimson trail that coated her nipple. I licked the wound closed, causing Eve to moan and arch. I flung my coat to the ground and rolled up my sleeves, revealing some of the tattoos I'd collected from spelled ink merchants.

Eve's breathing was ragged, and she swayed on her knees. I dragged my fingers down her spine, stirring goosebumps that rippled across her flesh. She shook under my touch, and I again snaked my hand through her hair.

As I pushed her head toward the ground, I revealed her slick pussy and tight ass. Her mouth was still open, and saliva dribbled down her chin, mixing with her blood. I wiped the fluid across her face, smearing it into her once-pristine makeup and hair.

Landing another smack across her ass, I quickly followed with one across her wet cunt. Eve cried out, but it flowed into a throaty moan as she ground her face into the stone floor.

"Little mouse likes the pain, doesn't she? Do you want more?"

"Yes, Sir. Please." Eve's words were desperate whispers.

I removed the sash that decorated my waist and formed a crude whip. I brought it down over Eve's skin, slapping her ass until the cheeks burned a bright pink. Eve muffled her scream, burying her face in her arm.

Targeting her folds, I whipped across the skin hard. "Do not keep your screams from me."

She slid her arms back, pulling them into her side, and let the full force of her screams reverberate through the stone chamber.

After a few more lashes, I could feel the heat of her swollen pussy pulse through our shared bond. Eve was inches from an orgasm. I draped the makeshift lash over her back and traced my fingers over the welts on her ass. She hissed and arched up, pushing her ass higher and seeking relief for the ache in her cunt.

Coming down on one knee, I slid my fingers through her crack to her pussy, toying with the deliciously slick and tender skin. Eve moaned. Slowly, oh so slowly, I slid two fingers inside her. She was beyond tight, and I lit up like a fire knowing mine were the first fingers inside her.

I stroked in slow pulls, finding that trigger spot inside her and rubbing it back and forth. Eve curled up, embracing and trying to avoid the intense pleasure working through her.

"Oh, Gods, Alok. Oh, Gods," her words tumbled out, nearly incoherent.

I reached for her hair, yanking her head back as I continued to fuck her with my fingers.

"The only God you need right now is me."

At once, I picked up speed, pummeling her untouched cunt until she writhed around my fingers and sprayed hot cum all over me. I pulled back. Eve's pussy dripped onto the floor, and the desire was too much to restrain. Licking up in a long slow motion, I finally got a taste of her and couldn't stop. Sucking and swirling my tongue around Eve's clit, I pulled another orgasm from her, and Eve flooded my mouth with cum as she screamed.

She trembled as I moved in front of her, pulling her onto her hands and shoving my hand into her mouth, forcing her to taste herself. Eve sucked my fingers before I claimed her mouth with my own, biting at her full bottom lip.

I mentally messaged the others, bringing them closer so they could aid in her ruination. Paeris and Siraye were on Eve like feral wolves in seconds, drinking up the blood and cum covering Eve's face and body.

Eve hummed with raw arousal as their tongues caressed her and slid between her ass and pussy. Devdan's impressive tongue quickly joined the action, and he slid it deep inside Eve, making her cry out.

Corym had quickly come to kneel beside me and expertly caught on to my next idea. As Devdan continued to reach incredible depths inside Eve's delicious cunt, he forced another orgasm through her, and this time as she screamed, Corym and I stuffed her mouth full with our cocks.

Her eyes went wide, but then she surrendered to our thrusts as we rubbed the heads of our cocks across her tongue. I pushed further in, gagging her and coating my length in a glistening layer of spit. Allowing Corym a turn, I wiped my dick across Eve's face, smacking it against her cheek.

I looked up. Siraye and Amedee had draped Paeris across Eve's back as she knelt on all fours. Then Amedee slid underneath Eve to suck on Paeris's cock, joining her fingers with Devdan's ravenous mouth and working Eve's clit. It all sang down our bond with an intensity that made my mind spin.

Siraye continued to torture Paeris, edging him to orgasm with their fingers in his ass and then backing off. He whimpered as Amedee popped his glistening cock in and out of her mouth.

I fucked into Eve's mouth harder. Grunting, I bit down on my molars as the feeling of Corym's thick head rubbing against my own heightened the sensation of sliding in and out of Eve's mouth. It was incredible.

My own orgasm was building, but I demanded Eve's tight pussy for that— at least the first one.

Mentally commanding Devdan and Amedee to give me and Corym room, I circled behind Eve, admiring how she dipped. Siraye pulled Paeris to them, demanding his shaft in their folds as Corym shifted beneath Eve and seized Amedee's cunt, tasting her as she hovered above his head.

Devdan helped to position Eve, quickly flipping her over and grabbing her by the hips to seat her ass against Corym's pelvis as he lay on the floor. I stared at her wet and wanton before I descended and whispered in her ear.

"Say goodbye to everything you were, little mouse."

CHAPTER 8: EVE ARKWRIGHT

I could barely think. The strange humming power that radiated through me and from my newfound mates was intoxicating. It was as if I could *sense* their passions, their desires, and the joy they experienced by succumbing entirely to them.

As Alok's words hit me, I felt Corym's cock nudge at my ass, and I couldn't help the gasp. I'd been doing my best to keep my mouth open as instructed, and the screams they tore for me helped me to ignore the ache building in my jaw. Devdan's dark skin was a gorgeous contrast to mind as he took Corym's equally deep brown cock and covered it in the slick juices leaking from me.

Then Alok's hard shaft was at my pussy, pushing in and stretching me wide for him. I cried out at the intrusion, unsure I could take him, let alone both of them.

"Alok, please! It will be too much!" I still vibrated from the arousal pumping through me, and despite everything, it wasn't backing off.

He grabbed my hair, yanking my head to the side as Devdan rubbed Corym's head against my asshole. "Shut the fuck up and take it like my good little whore."

As he growled into my ear, Alok thrust his cock into my weeping pussy, and I came so hard I saw stars. Fluttering around his shaft as Alok pumped in and out, Corym rammed into my ass, stretching me slowly as he fully seated me on his dick. My ending climax quickly launched into another and another as they fucked me ruthlessly.

Amedee leaned forward over my shoulder as she rode Corym's face and bit down on my neck. I screamed, more spit dribbled down my chin, and new blood mixed with it as Amedee tasted me. Thanks to the angle Amedee had shoved my face in, I saw that Devdan had gone to Siraye, who was being furiously fucked by Paeris, and stuffed his cock into their mouth, the immense, dark brown wonder disappearing down their throat.

Paeris's screams broke through the moans and grunts, filling our small space.

"Please, Siraye! Please!"

Devdan slid free, allowing Siraye to speak. Her words were tinged with exertion.

"Not yet. Let Devdan take that ass of yours."

In a flash, Devdan was behind Paeris, burying his cock deep inside the gorgeous, pale Elf.

"Please! I can't!"

"Yes, boy. Fill me up." Siraye rasped.

His release flooded through our bond, and I relished how it raked through me. I was seconds from coming again, the feel of my two mates' cocks utterly filling me up, and Amedee's teeth deep in my neck was beyond bliss. Then she tore her fangs from me as Corym sent her over the edge. Devdan and Siraye were quickly reaching their own release. The pound of it through me seemed to draw out my ecstasy into eternity.

Alok pulled my face to him, smacking me across the cheek as my vision glazed over with lust. The pain bit into me and sent sparks down through my cunt.

"Scream, Eve. Scream and make us fill up that tight pussy of yours with our seed," Alok growled.

Suddenly, Corym's cock was gone, and I whimpered at the loss. But in just a handful of moments, it returned, now pushing alongside Alok's into my throbbing pussy.

I screamed.

The stretch, the fullness, was nearly too much, and a blinding orgasm ricocheted through me into the others with world-ending intensity. Corym and Alok fucked into me with everything they had, grunting and clawing into me as they filled me with ropes of hot cum.

It seemed to last forever, but as the frenzy died down, the sound of all our ragged breathing echoed through the halls. I was unseated from Alok and Corym by Devdan as he scooped me up and cradled me against his chest. I couldn't keep my eyes open, soothed by the feeling of fingers sweeping across my arms and legs.

"You did so well," Siraye whispered in my ear as they stroked my hair.

"I must have more of a taste next time," Paeris added. I heard him yelp as someone's hand slapped across his ass, but I was too exhausted to figure out who.

"Here," Amedee's tongue swiped across the still open bite she left on my neck, "That'll stop the bleeding."

I hummed as her warm, soft tongue ended any remaining twinges of pain, and then Corym's words were in my ear.

"You're mine next, Eve. So rest up." The raspy sound of their voice sent chills down my spine.

"Rest, indeed," Alok spoke to us all, "Let's get our mate home. You'll need to care for her, so she's ready for our Claiming Ceremony."

"The what?" I tried to ask.

"Shh. Get some sleep. We'll explain later," Amedee said.

So I did. I let myself drift off into sleep, carried in Devdan's arms and not missing my old life in the slightest.

Be sure to follow R.E. Johnson to see what else they do within this world and with these characters!

ABOUT R.E. JOHNSON

R.E. Johnson is an author and copywriter with a major in Professional Writing and a minor in Creative Writing. Johnson has been a passionate storyteller and fantasy fan since they were in kindergarten. In fact, they wrote their first novel in fifth grade.

Now, when they aren't working, they're passionate about creating stories that profess love, respect, and triumph over evil and contain strong female characters who are always ready to throw down – both in and out of the bedroom.

Currently, R.E. Johnson resides in Las Vegas, Nevada, where they spend their free time playing Dungeons & Dragons, wrangling their two rambunctious children, and reading all the smut, fantasy, sci-fi, and mythology they can get their hands on.

STORY X
THROUGH THE PAINTINGS DIMLY BY JESSICA M. BUTLER

Heat Level: Smoldering
(PG content)

Trigger Warnings:
Suicidal thoughts
Depression
Some violence and peril
Death
Fear of death
Grief

PROLOGUE

S moke. Oil. Blood. Those are the first things I smell. My eyes sting and burn, my throat chokes. Everything is dull and thick. Pain courses through me, bright and spiraling. It's getting hot. Too hot. I can't breathe.

Forcing my eyes open, I squint. It's hazy, dark, and red, everything streaking and blurring together like a nightmare. I...I don't know where I am. I start moving out of instinct.

Pain slices through my hands and knees and thighs. Metal? Glass? Knives? My body resists every step as I clutch and creep forward. Some horrid impulse for sleep claws at me. I could stop...just lie down for a bit, hide my face, and disappear.

But some other part of me, some stronger part, wants to live. It drags me forward. Everything burns. Something hot and wet streams down my face. My vision turns red.

It feels like eternity, and then somehow, I'm free. Cold wind stings my face, and the air clears though I splutter and cough and gag. Bile drips from my mouth. My entire body is wracked with pain.

The memories eke back, slowly, painfully. The border collie running into the middle of the road. The headlights illuminating it for a fraction of a second before the car swerves with sickening force. Then the black ice. Then crashing. Falling. Tumbling. A sheer drop of almost fifteen feet.

The guardrail up to the left has been sheared clean through. The back end and driver's side took the full force. Flames lick the crumbled vehicle I just managed to escape. A trail of blood follows me from the passenger seat where I crept out.

Passenger...

I wasn't alone! I was the passenger.

Desmond!

Desmond had been driving.

"Desmond!" My voice croaks.

I can see him, hanging in the car. The flames are spreading faster and faster, the smoke building in massive black bulges.

"Hang on down there!" someone calls from above. The voice is distant, snatched up in the wind. "Help is on the way."

It'll be too late. I dash my hands at my face and start back for the car, crawling through the snow.

"Desmond!" I scream. "Desmond!"

My body won't move as fast as I will it. It creeps and creaks along, the pain hitching me at every aching breath. I'm so slow. In the back of my mind, I know I won't make it.

"Desmond, come on! Please." I twist my head up. There are small lights on the overhang near the guardrails where people are gathering. "Help him!"

The heat from the fire swells. Desmond starts struggling with his seat-belt. It isn't unfastening. His motions are clumsy, awkward.

I keep moving forward, digging my hands into the snow and frozen earth and pulling myself forward. My legs aren't working. The heat grows. Sirens wail.

Everything slows. "Desmond!" I gasp his name out.

His hands jerk and pull against the beige strap. Then he stops. Looks at me. He knows...

That moment lasts forever. I want to reach him. I try. But the heat stops me. I'm too far away. And I know too. I can't break past the heat.

It's too late.

His mouth opens as he starts to say something. I see the fear. The knowledge.

Someone grabs me, lifts me up roughly, drags me away from the car.

It all lights up. The flames engulf the car, and Desmond vanishes in smoke and flame.

Gone.

My head swims, and darkness closes over my eyes. The one thing I see is Desmond staring back at me.

CHAPTER 1

A *few weeks later*
There was nothing anyone could do. At least that's what the medics said. By the time the ambulance and the fire truck arrived, it was too late. For Desmond.

One of the EMTs snatched me from death, but I wish he hadn't.

Every time I close my eyes now, I see Desmond staring at me. See the shock. The horror. The realization that he is trapped and I am free. He's asking why I didn't save him. I'm asking that too. Why couldn't I save him?

Everyone is asking that.

It's dark out now. The sun set almost an hour ago, but I haven't bothered to turn on the lights as I sit here with my back to the blue-curtained casement window.

Most days I don't turn the lights on. It doesn't matter. My life is the same now, lit or dark. The only reason the heat is on is because it was on before the accident.

Maybe the furnace will go out. Maybe it'll get so cold out I'll freeze to death.

It's all so still. The shadows have engulfed everything from the long light curtains to the blue corduroy couch. When I was little, I used to be afraid of monsters hiding in the shadows. Now I wish that the shadows would swallow me up and consign me to oblivion.

I'm not that lucky though.

Sniffing, I press the back of my hand to my face, trying to push back the tears and the great sagging weight that chokes my breath. The seconds sludge into minutes, but all too soon it will be a new day.

A new day.

It's wasted on me.

I wish I could stop time. I don't want any more of it.

Desmond's funeral is the end of this week, the day after tomorrow. Most funerals happen within a week, maybe two or three if there's an autopsy to be done or suspicious circumstances. But occasionally funerals are delayed for other reasons such as family abroad. That's what happened here. His mom was in some part of Bhutan on a mercy mission, providing medical supplies and treatment to the sick. Desmond was following in her footsteps. If he hadn't died, he would have been on a mercy ship weaving through the islands by now, making ports of call in city after city, tending to the sick and providing much needed care.

Supposedly his mother is getting in tonight. Some small part of me is afraid she'll come to the house. Knock on the door. Ask to talk to me. At the funeral, I'll have to face them. His father. His mother. His sisters. His cousins. His friends.

My throat knots. His friends? They were my friends too, and I had let them down as much as him.

In every accident, someone must be blamed. If the accident had been because of a drunk driver or a careless trucker, there would have been a villain on whom to focus all the pain and rage.

But there is only one villain: me.

It is my fault Desmond is dead. I know it. He knows it. Everyone knows it. And everyone knows that it would have been better if I had died instead of him.

Some nights when I sit wakeful against the window, I imagine that I could return to the site of the crash and trade my life for his. He had plans. He had achievements. He was...wonderful.

How could he be anything else? He'd been that way since I met him twelve years ago. The kind of friend you always wanted but never knew if you could find. Never cruel. Always kind. Always listening. Always ready to smile. I remember someone saying once that once you knew Desmond, you loved him, and he was the easiest person to know. One of those people with the easy smiles and that way of making every person feel like someone. He volunteered at Puppy Love, our animal shelter, and from time to time, he had been known to adopt a dog who had been deemed unadoptable, take it home, and find a way to reach whatever terrified heart beat in that furry little chest. Those dogs loved him. Everyone did.

I would have adopted his dogs, but they had already been taken in. Everyone was happy to help. They didn't need me, and, truth be told, even his dogs would hate me now.

I wish I weren't to blame, but I hadn't known who else to call that night. The night of the accident. It had been stupid to meet Rick at a place I didn't know. Even stupider to not drive myself. But that's me. Stupid. And it had been stupid to call Desmond and ask him to pick me up on the side of the road.

I shouldn't have. Whatever would have happened with Rick wouldn't have been nearly so bad as what happened next.

The doctor tried to comfort me by saying that the accident wasn't my fault. The driver's side had been crushed in. Even if I got back to him, Desmond would have been pinned. And I wasn't the driver. Desmond was.

Besides, the doctor said, as if this somehow made it better, you shouldn't swerve to avoid a dog on an icy road. You've got to hope the dog gets out of the way. But Desmond would never hit a dog. He wouldn't even hit a squirrel. One time he stopped the car to rescue a snapping turtle from the middle of the highway. Of course he swerved to miss the dog.

No matter how many times the doctor said it wasn't my fault, I knew it was. Saying I wasn't to blame is the sort of thing doctors are supposed to say and so it doesn't count. They want to keep you alive. And guilt is a cancer that can eat out your soul before the stitches heal.

I took a taxi home from the hospital when they were finally ready to release me. It'd only been a couple days. Everyone else was busy or didn't answer when I asked for a ride.

It's all right. It's true. They're completely right to blame me. If I hadn't called Desmond and asked him to come get me, he wouldn't have been in the car at 1:10 AM on a Saturday morning. And if he hadn't been in the car at 1:10 AM on a Saturday, he wouldn't have swerved to miss a dog. A dark-eyed border collie with a broad white band across its chest. And if he hadn't swerved to miss a dog, the car wouldn't have fishtailed and crashed off the embankment. And then I wouldn't have been disoriented, and I could have —

Why am I lying to myself? Tears burn my eyes, but I can't cry any more.

I could have saved him. Some way would have appeared. If I hadn't been so afraid.

I should have ignored the pain...moved faster, called for help, cut him down, saved him first...so many things could have been different.

It's playing through my mind again. The searing hiss of the fire as it spreads. The thick black smoke. And that awful, awful sound of the car igniting. The look in his eyes. They're so wide. Scared. Frightened. Horrified.

My friends won't forgive me. How can they? I wouldn't. I start blubbering again, sobbing into my dampened cardigan sleeve.

It's so dark right now. Some small part of me hopes the night never ends. I deserve this. The isolation. The darkness. The silence.

As I sit here, I twist and turn my yellow-orange pill bottle about, sometimes flipping the cap open and then shut with a reassuring *pop snap*. The little triangular tabs to mark the correct opening position grate on my still healing fingertips. It hurts, but what does that matter?

A sharp knock sounds at the door.

"Iscah."

It's Lydia. A friend I've known almost as long as Desmond. She's using her no-nonsense voice right now. Not a good sign.

"Iscah, I know you're in there." She knocks again, harder and faster this time. "Listen, you can't hide in there forever."

Yes I can. I've tried going out a few times. Nothing good comes from it. And I'll stay in here until my vacation days and sick leave are all used up.

"Iscah...listen, you haven't been answering my texts. You haven't been talking to anybody, and this is ridiculous. You haven't even helped with any planning of his memorial."

I wasn't aware that I was welcome.

Lydia continues. "Now I'm going to pick Desmond's mother up at the airport. You should come too."

She continues to drone on, but I tune her out. I pull my grey cardigan up higher and bury my chin in the scratchy wool.

"I'll pick you up for the memorial. All right? It's really important that you're there." Lydia is using her teacher voice now as if I'm some sort of willful toddler who pulled her friend's hair and broke her purple crayon in half. "After everything that's happened, Desmond and his family deserve at least that."

I can almost see her face pinching with concern, her hazy grey eyes even darker. She was always the reasonable one. "It'll be good for you too," she says. "You'll get some closure."

I snap the pill bottle open and then closed again. Yeah, closure. That's exactly what I'm going to find there.

"Iscah..." Lydia's voice trembles as if she's about to cry. "Iscah, can you at least tell me if you can hear me?"

Silence falls, becoming more awkward by the second.

Lydia strikes her fist on the door. "You're a selfish bitch, you know that? I'll pick you up at three. You better not make us late."

Off she storms. Her boots click on the snow-covered sidewalk, slowly fading into the night.

I don't think I can do it. Face everyone. See them staring at me. One time I went online to read the news story, and I reached the comments. That had been a mistake.

The mail slot clicks and something slides in with a soft *shoop*. What could that be?

I peek out the window.

A woman is leaving. She's crossing in front of the skeletal lilac bush in the front yard. As if she feels me looking at her, she stops, turns, looks at the window, and smiles. My hand falls away, and the curtain slides back in place. I saw her clearly enough, and I'm certain I don't know her.

Her dark brown hair is straight and cropped above the shoulders, and her dark eyes are large, round, and elongated at the edges, the length and angles of the eyes exaggerated by eggplant eyeliner. She wears an olive pea coat and an autumn striped scarf. Who is she? And what is she doing here?

Tucking the pill bottle into my pocket, I slip to the door and pick up the letter. The shaft of moonlight that cuts through the window is bright enough to illuminate the ecru envelope. An indigo crescent moon is stamped in the upper right-hand corner in lieu of a stamp, and the letter itself is addressed only to "Iscah."

The letter inside holds a small card with a holographic moon on a black velvet night sky next to a silver barcode with a series of numbers at the base.

An easy to read but calligraphic script flows across the page.

Dear Iscah,

You do not know me, but that is of no consequence. I am Claudia from Mab's Catering, which is catering Desmond's memorial. We have not met, but I have seen you from time to time, and I have heard the stories.

I can only imagine that this time is an incredibly difficult one for you. So I want to make you an offer.

My family owns a cabin up north. (You'll find instructions to reach it if you can enter the barcode into your phone.) It's sort of an ongoing project. We're always adding to it, you see. And there's lots and lots of room with all the luxuries and comforts of home. The perfect little getaway.

If you would like, then you can come and stay in one of the rooms. There will be other people there, all going through similar griefs and struggles. But you should not be disturbed if you don't want to be. The cabin is for you and for those like you.

Now you might be asking why I would give you this since we do not know one another and there are many sorry people in the world, many of whom you might think deserve this more. My family does this in honor of a kind person who surprised my family with an all-expense trip to the mountains after my grandmother's death. It certainly felt like the wrong time to go on vacation, but it helped us keep our sanity. Getting away, escaping from all the day-to-day agonies, was the only thing that saved us. So we decided that we would pay it forward so to speak.

My family has done quite well for themselves and so, though we initially intended to rent the cabin out, we soon realized that it would be better to show the same kindness that was shown to us.

So I have chosen you. I know that you are not actually a member of Desmond's family, but I believe that you would benefit the most. Everyone loved Desmond. He was probably going to win the Nobel Peace Prize and who knows what else. I have to admit, I was a little in love with him myself. And the one thing I know about him is that he would not have blamed you even if he is dead because of you.

I flinch at those words, but the letter continues.

If anyone ever needed to get away and recoup, it's you. And that's not going to happen here. You know it. I know it. Stay here, and you'll be two steps away from an overdose. So just take this. If you decide you want to come, then come. Stay as long as you like. A week. A month. Two months. Three. It doesn't matter.

All expenses have been taken care of except the gas to get you up here. Meals are included. Kitchen is always open.

We only ask for two things. First, when you do leave, whenever that might be, find a way to pay it forward. Make the world a better place. Second, don't leave within three days of the full moon's passing. The locals say it's bad luck but really, there's nothing more beautiful than a full moon over the mountains in winter. It'll do you good.

It's going to be all right eventually, Iscah. It might not feel it, but trust me. Within two weeks, you're going to be in a much better place. Please come. Do it for Desmond.

Sincerely,

Claudia

More tears trickle down my cheeks. A few spatter onto the letter. It's a generous offer, but how can I accept it? I don't want to leave, but staying isn't doing any good.

Still...it is incredibly generous.

Maybe...maybe after the memorial I'll go. But it'll make everyone angry if I don't —

Someone pounds on the door, deep thundering blows.

"Iscah, open up the damn door! Iscah!"

TJ. I cringe against the wall. He was Desmond's best friend.

"Open up, Iscah. Come on now! Open up! You think you can treat Lydia that way? You're just going to hide out in here until you rot? Well fine then, you little piece of shit. It's your fault Desmond's dead. You should be the one apologizing to his mother and his father and everyone else. If it hadn't been for you, you filthy piece of trash, he'd still be alive. And what are you worth? Huh? It's not like you're going to do anything with your life. He was gonna be somebody. He already was somebody!"

"Come on, man." Another softer voice, Mik, I think, comes alongside him. "You don't have to do this."

"I want to make sure she knows!" TJ shouts. His words slur. It sounds like he's on the verge of tears. "Do you know what you did, Iscah? You should kill yourself! Drink bleach and die, you whore."

I curl up in the nook by the door and shield my head with my hands.

The shouts and bangs on the door continue. I'm shaking. Little gasps and cries tear out. I can't stop them. This isn't the first time TJ has been by. I don't know what he'd do if he ever saw me.

"Hey, hey, come on, let's go," Mik says.

"She's not worth it, TJ," Mona, his girlfriend, says.

"Come on," Mik says. "Let's go before someone calls the cops."

"Kill yourself, Iscah. You'd make the world a better place." TJ hits my door again. "You're nothing. You're the one who should've died, not Desmond."

"Let's go, TJ," Mik says, firmer this time.

TJ's crying now. It's a disconcerting thing to hear someone like him sobbing like a child, blubbering, snorting, wheezing. "You killed him!" TJ shouts again. "It should've been you!"

"It's all right, baby," Mona says, her voice gentle. She's probably wiping the tears away. "She's the one who has to live with herself."

Their voices fade into the darkness, swallowed up in the dullness that is the night.

My chest feels like it's going to explode. Everything is crashing around me.

This is it. I can't do it.

No.

Claudia is right. If I stay here...no, I'm not even going to think about it.

I don't care what's in the cabin or why they picked me. Whatever is there, whatever else I find, it has to be easier to deal with than this.

CHAPTER 2

I t takes me less than half an hour to slip upstairs, jam a few things into an old overnight bag, and jump into my beat-up navy Ford Explorer.

A quick scan of the card with my phone loads the GPS with directions. A ten-hour drive up north into the mountains on a cold snowy night. No problem. Anything is better than staying at my house.

It takes a little longer than the GPS states because I take the winding roads and hairpin curves slow and stop once for a coffee at a 24-hour McDonalds. The over-bitter flavor stings my tongue and burns my throat, but it keeps me going.

At least I'm not crying. There are no more tears left to cry. At least for now. And I know deep inside, that it isn't going to do any good. I'm of no use to anyone right now, and I really shouldn't be at that memorial. The only reason anyone wants me there is to make sure I feel properly sorrowful. To make sure I know what a tragedy it was. That it was me who should have died, not Desmond.

If Desmond was alive, what would he say about all this? He'd probably insist that I had something great to do. He wasn't the sort to cast blame. And he'd tell everyone to give me a break, but that would make it worse because it would remind everyone how wonderful he was and how worthless I am.

Why did you have to die, Desmond?

A faint haze blurs my vision, but I dash it away. So much for being done. There's no time for crying now. And it isn't safe. Not while I'm on the road. Once I get to the cabin, I'll have a good cry.

After hours on the road, I am miles away from the nearest city, town, village, or settlement. All is quiet and clear as the sun rises. The road is quiet. An eagle swoops along the currents of the wind, sailing the gulf between these majestic mountains.

For once, breathing is easier. The air is lighter here. Already my mood is lifting. My phone lies facedown in the seat beside me. No one will notice I'm gone for a good bit longer, but that doesn't mean I won't get texts. Particularly tomorrow. I'm expecting a barrage of well-meaning questions to ensure that I am where I belong: center-row, center-seat, present and ready for Desmond's memorial.

It's going to cause quite a stir my not being there. But I don't care. I can't bear any more of the silent judgment or the bellowed rage or the shrouded pity or the murmured statements about how it should have been me.

People want to know how I can live with myself?

I don't really know how, but being around them certainly doesn't help it.

I pull up to the cabin at about eight o' clock in the morning. The pale pink sunlight has become a soft gold, but the ice and snow on the firs has not melted even slightly.

The cabin looks more like a lodge with little evidence of multiple building projects. It appears to be a solid four-story cabin constructed of red-brown logs with a cheerful green door and white trim. The overhanging rafters protrude out a good four feet, and the roof has a dusting of snow on it. Whoever Claudia's family hired to make this look like a single construction, they outdid themselves.

A minivan pulls up alongside me, tires crunching over the snow and leaving deep treads. The door whirs open and a skinny-faced teenager slides out, clutching a knit purse to her chest. She waits for her mom to get out before moving.

Both look as if they have been crying, the mother's eyes red and her face flushed, the teenager dead eyed and downcast. They walk hand-in-hand toward the cabin.

There are nine other vehicles parked in the narrow rectangular lot. Perhaps some are visiting.

My phone flashes again with a message, *Welcome. You are in Hawthornes 310.*

Picking up my bag, I slip it over my shoulder and slowly make my way forward.

There's not nearly so much snow up here as I expected. A couple inches in some places though the temperature is well below freezing. My breath frosts against my purple coat. The cabin is exquisite though. The closer I get, the more entranced I become.

Underneath the overhang on the porch are willow rocking chairs and a swing. There's even an upturned barrel with a checker game in progress and two pitted stools for sitting. It is idyllic.

There's even a ring of gold and silver mushrooms forming a broad circle around the cabin. No dustings of snow frost their smooth caps. They look nothing like the mushrooms in my own yard which are so delicate an errant brush would uproot them. These look almost as if they are made of stone.

Stooping down, I examine one. It wasn't carved, the texture is all wrong, and there are neither pour nor chisel marks. In fact...I press my hand upon the thick cap. It's a little warm. No wonder they have no snow on them. As I rise, I notice that upon each cap is carved some text.

Leave your sorrows behind all who enter here and do not overstay your welcome or else your grief will keep you here and you will be forgotten.

What a bizarre message. If I could leave my sorrows behind, I surely would.

More snow crunches behind me as a Range Rover parks near my car. Someone else?

Standing, I shift my bag on my shoulder.

Yes, it is. Claudia wasn't joking when she said her family invites a lot of people.

A young man in a sky-blue jacket slides out of the driver seat. He sets his arms akimbo and draws in a deep breath, tilting his head back and blinking rapidly as if suppressing tears. His face is blotchy, and his nose is red.

What a merry bunch of travelers we all are.

I enter through the green front door. A great warmth rushes out as soon as I open it, and my mouth falls open.

The foyer is broad and open with a great, double mouthed, river-stone fireplace in the center. Brown suede couches and easy chairs are arranged around it with glass coffee tables and end tables at intervals. Deer, elk, moose, bear, cougar, and other heads are mounted upon the rustic wood walls along with the odd tool or hand-painted sign. Two polished wood staircases cut into the log walls and coil upwards, and large arched door-ways open into other rooms.

But what holds my attention fast is the tree.

Yes, a tree.

There's a living oak growing in this foyer.

It's not in the center and not in the corner. It's off a little to the right as if it one day decided to sprout up and they decided to build around it.

Something about it fascinates me. I always have loved trees. There's something so peaceful and calming about them. When I was little, I used to climb as high as I could and hide in the uppermost branches. I often ran out to the woods, and there I found my favorite tree, a sway-branched maple, and I climbed it until I felt safe. From within that nestled perch, the crisp wind twisting my hair, the branches swaying, the leaves rustling, all had been right. Whatever promises had been broken, whatever vows unmade, whatever nightmares taking residence in my home, always among the trees was I at peace.

Reaching out, I place my hand on the tree's coarse bark. It's an oak from the looks of it though it is of a richer color than most I have seen. The deep ridges and protrusions are like a hidden message. Each tree is unique in this I like to think, no pattern of bark exactly the same. Little bits flake beneath my fingers, and...just as with the mushrooms, there's warmth.

Pulling back, I frown. Could it be the fire?

The fireplace is quite warm, but it's a fair ways away. There's no sign of blistering either.

Another strange thing.

I circle the tree. It is so thick I can't wrap my arms around it. Its branches extend outward, skeletal but strong. Its uppermost sections disappear among the rafters through closely cut holes. The roots likewise are invisible. The floorboards cover the tree up to its very trunk, and they don't show even the slightest hint of buckling. The tree has to be quite old, but if the cabin was built around it, then modifications had to be made regularly to keep the tree from breaking apart the cabin's foundation.

Slight cracks in the floorboards allow me to peer down. There appears to be a large gap to allow for the roots. The roots are even odder though.

They creep about in large arching spirals. More like a mangrove than oak. Almost as if the tree had tried to leave...

Wait...what am I thinking?

I almost laugh, but the sound dies in my throat.

Along the lower portions of the tree, the bark is scuffed and broken with mud in the grooves. People have been scraping their feet on it. And there's barb wire.

Several pieces actually. The wire is embedded deep in the wood. A sharp spur of pain strikes my spirit. That shouldn't be in there.

Kneeling beside the tree, I work at the wire. It twists in my hand as I take care to avoid catching myself on the barbs. It comes free, surprisingly easy. Bits fall away, exposing the deep red-brown wood. Large globs of red-gold sap seep from the gouges.

It's hurt. A jagged pain cuts through me again. Opening my purse, I pull out a notebook, tear out a page, tear it into strips, chew up the strips, and then stuff them into the wounds.

Some small measure of peace spreads inside me as I move on and do the same with the next bit of wire. Whoever did this was just being cruel. I can't imagine the reasoning for such an act.

"What are you doing?"

Losing my balance, I fall back, catching myself with my elbow. A woman in a puffy coat stands behind me, her face sealed in a scowl. One hand is on her hip, and the other languidly holds a pair of black Oakley sunglasses.

"Uh..." Bits of paper are still stuck to my mouth.

The woman shakes her head, an expression of disgust breaking across her perfect features. "Freaking psycho," she mutters. She turns to walk away and slings her grey leather computer bag over her shoulder.

My cheeks burn. Well, so much for not being noticed. Then again, Claudia probably didn't expect me to attempt emergency tree surgery with my bare hands and spit paper.

Standing, I readjust my own overnight bag and hurry up the polished staircase to the third floor. The painkillers have worn off. Snaking pain runs along my back and shoulder, and the cuts under my bandages itch. I didn't take time to dress them before I left.

It only takes a couple minutes longer before I reach Hawthornes 310. Each of the doors has a different name, but the numbers are consecutive: Marchcrest 308, Loontrace 309, Pinedunes 311. The paneled oak door opens with a soft click when I scan the barcode under the door with my phone.

Once more, I am stunned.

This bedroom is open, airy, and pleasant. The cream-colored walls have no decorations on them except for a single turquoise and green necklace woven with beads. Long ivory curtains flow from the floor-length windows, bound back with a single sash. The double bed in the center of the room has more than a dozen pillows, crisp tan sheets, and a down-filled comforter. The bed appears to have been made from aspens, the distinctive bark brilliantly streaked.

This is the perfect peaceful haven.

Nicely done, Claudia.

The door clicks shut behind me. My bag falls to the ground. This is beautiful. And...

Well...that's surprising.

The oak from downstairs is in my room as well. One branch arcs up from the floor and enters the ceiling, continuing upward. There's no draft though suggesting that the roof is open, and I don't remember seeing any similar openings.

I'm not sure what they do to keep this tree alive. But I feel comforted that it is here.

This place is perfect. And now it's time for my meds.

The bathroom is as nice as the bedroom with a deep whirlpool tub and a layered marble sink. Three opalescent teacups in primary colors hang from brass hooks beneath the medicine cabinet. There's a covered dish with salted almonds and a message that says, "Eat. These are changed regularly." One cup of water, a few almonds, and a palm of pills later, and the pain is already easing.

The experimental meds the doctor prescribed work quickly and well. Unlike other meds, I don't have to worry about as many unintended side effects. Supposedly addiction isn't such a problem either, but I suspect that so long as pain is a problem, addiction is a possibility. Not to the pills themselves but to escaping the pain.

Focus on the small blessings though.

I take the time to unwind the gauze and bandages over my many scrapes and cuts. Most look worse than they feel, and the sight brings horrible memories to mind.

No.

No.

I won't let them in.

What good will it do? At least bathing them makes me feel better. As if I'm somehow washing away my sins with the dried blood.

I lean closer to the mirror to clean the stitched up gash in my forehead. It slides from my hairline across my forehead and down my cheek as if the dashboard had tried to open me up. Several other cuts, far closer to healing, accent my otherwise pale complexion. They're like bloody freckles.

I was lucky to get out with so little damage as I did. The doctors said so. Desmond...

Suddenly the tears are in my throat again. They're like a Gordian knot. I know I said I could cry now, but I don't want to. Not again. Not now. But the tears don't care. They well up, my throat and heart swollen.

Whimpering, I slide onto the ground, my arms wrapped tight around my body. Maybe the embrace of a friend or a lover could ward off the pain pulsing within me. Maybe such warmth and compassion could hold the shattered pieces of my soul together. But there is no one.

Even after I got out of the hospital, no one ran up to hug me. No one held me tight and said they were glad I was all right. They stared right through me into their own grief and loss, they looked at me as if I had stolen Desmond's final life breath for myself. I'm so tired. All I want to do is sleep forever.

As beautiful as this place is, I am alone. The tears burst out. I can't stop them. I no longer try. They pour down my cheeks as if the wounds were newly made.

The worst part is that no matter how much they hate me, I hate myself more. A good man is dead because of me. He might forgive me, but they won't. And I will never forgive myself.

CHAPTER 3

I wake some time later. My eyes are crusted with sleep and tears, and my head is thick as if I have taken sleeping pills, my heart pulsing and my mind ill at ease as if I had a nightmare. But I didn't take sleeping pills and I can't remember the nightmare. Still...this heaviness...it's in my mouth as well, an unfamiliar taste. Like salt and copper.

Somehow I fell asleep in the middle of sobbing like a child. I had also apparently moved over to the tree as I now lie beside the arched branch. I don't remember any of that.

But I am still in this place, and somehow it doesn't seem so empty and vacant as my own house. Even with my thick head and foul bad taste, I feel more at ease. It smells better too. My house smelled like canned vegetable soup, close air, and musty laundry. This room...I couldn't place it before but I recognize it now. It smells faintly of gardenias, freesia, fresh-brewed green tea, and oatmeal raisin cookies.

Slowly I sit up. From the quality of the warm yellow light, it's well past three o' clock. Oddly I don't feel much pain or even stiffness. It's hard to believe it is so late. Time flies here.

Even though I shouldn't, I check my phone. I can't help it. Half a dozen more texts, scolding me, chiding me for not letting Lydia or any of them in. Reminding me that I had to be at the memorial.

I don't text anyone back. For the first time in a long while, my living alone seems like a good thing. They won't know I'm gone until I don't show up for the memorial tomorrow. Right now, as far as they know, I'm locked up in the house. The garage is locked too. Nothing will be any different.

Who knows? Maybe I'll even come back before the memorial. Hmm...no...I shake my head at myself. The memorial is the day before the full moon.

That excuse isn't likely to convince any of them, but it's enough for me.

Everything is so quiet. I loop my arms around my knees and stare absently at the wall. My thoughts drift.

They're unpleasant. Even awake, I can remember the scent of that fire. See his eyes. See the helplessness. Feel the heat. Feel my own ineptitude.

The doctor said I should go to a psychologist. A grief counselor. Something like that. But I already know what would happen. She'd listen and nod with wise understanding, offer me Kleenex, and ask me how I feel. Then she'd make some notes. Probably prescribe more pills. Tell me I have to forgive myself but then go home and judge me over a glass of chardonnay. No. I am done with that. This cabin is the best medicine there is.

My gaze drifts around the room again. I'm so tired even after waking. My eyes burn. Sleep without nightmares would be good. But that's pretty much impossible without sleeping aides. Even if I can't remember the nightmares, I feel them like I do now.

Once I posted on Facebook about how I couldn't sleep with all the nightmares. A lot of people said that was part of my punishment. Mona said nightmares are a sign of a guilty conscience.

"I don't know what they want me to do." I stop, realizing that I said that out loud.

The room is so still right now. My own voice sounds too loud.

I wish there was someone else with me here.

Standing, I pace around the room. The calm is heavy. Like an enormous blanket. I can't hear anything inside or out. Even my own breaths are muted.

Turning, I see the tree branch once again. It's remarkable that it could be here like this. How can it survive? Perhaps it's artificial?

No. Clearly not. There are the same globules of red-gold sap. It reminds me of blood. The sunlight catches one particularly large nodule in the crook of the branch.

Now that I'm looking at it, the tree doesn't look quite as healthy as I had once thought. This branch in particular is damaged. Some of the uppermost fingers are dying.

Kneeling, I examine it. It's thick and branches off in separate leader branches. I could easily sit in the deepest of the curves without bending it. But someone has been cutting at it. There are knife gouges here. Pocket knife perhaps. Half a heart carved beneath a knot. A broken heart actually. And up here...

Well, this is strange.

There's a long black stake in the crook of the branch. How did I not notice this? A dark oily substance is leeching off into the wood. I can smell it now. Ugh.

Like tar and alcohol and tobacco all in one.

What a stench!

Who would put such a thing in a tree? And why?

Carefully, I lift a section of bark nearest the dead portion of branches. The black liquid is seeping into the bark along veins. Water doesn't wash it out.

From the looks of the bark and this section of dead wood, the black liquid eats it. I've never seen anything quite like this though I have seen other diseases in trees.

I dig out one of my black cardigans, lay it out, and grasp the stake. It resists, clings, then — *snap*! It jolts free. The black liquid pools on the floor. It sizzles and hisses.

I dump the stake into the sink, and the medicine cabinet clicks open as if on cue.

It looks ordinary with contact-paper lined shelves, empty except for a long narrow saucer filled with the black liquid and a spike similar to the one stabbed in the tree and a silver dagger with a mother-of-pearl handle.

A wave of discomfort washes over me. I need a knife anyway to finish tending to the tree, but what is it doing in the medicine cabinet? And why is there another stake?

As I return to the tree, it strikes me again that it might be...alive. Are these the musings of a girl going mad? My eyes are heavy, and my body craves sleep...escape...

It's just one step to madness. I'm not that far away. But...

The knife rests heavy in my hand.

What if the tree is alive?

What if there is something more about it than a usual tree? Would it really hurt for me to say something?

"Listen...I can't believe I'm doing this." I run my fingers over my forehead. I'm hot and sweaty, my breath comes faster and tighter. "But I'm going to try to help you, all right? So...this might hurt, but it looks like that black stuff is eating the wood away. This part here is dead already, and if it keeps spreading, then it could kill you."

My words hang in the air.

Weird, Iscah. Weird, weird, weird.

But maybe it's because no one else has wanted my help in a long time. Not even the animal shelter. Maybe it's because I'm a pariah, and I want so much to mean something again. Maybe it's nothing. Maybe I'm going mad.

I kneel and begin my surgery.

My uncle was a tree doctor. He was the one who taught me how to climb and hide in those safe upper branches and how to diagnose everything from rot to termites. It had been a long time since I'd done anything similar to this.

It's amazing how easy some skills are to recall when they are needed again. My fingers seem to know what they're doing better than my mind. It comforts me as the sunshine warms my back. "It'll be all right," I whisper. Shavings of wood and bark fall away. The thick sap clots along the cuts. But it doesn't take too long for me to dig it out. It appears relatively slow acting.

But still...it bothers me why someone would do this.

Obviously it's just mean-spirited. It's cruel enough to carve initials into a living tree or to twist its branches. Of course, we use them to make paper and furniture. But I like to think that when we do that, they don't suffer as much because it is swift. Though...if I think of that too long, I'll feel worse.

"Do they do this to feel better about themselves?" I ask. I don't expect the tree to answer of course. I'm not completely crazy.

The fatigue is returning. I need coffee or some energy drinks or something.

Standing I clear away the mess. I don't want to go to sleep. I can't bear the thought of seeing Desmond again. And I'll dream of him and wake unrefreshed and sadder than before.

I'll go and see if there are any more spikes in the tree.

I start for the door, but a sharp pain snags my head. Oh. My hair's caught on one of the branches.

That's funny. I didn't think I was that close.

I tuck the dagger in my belt and hide it under my sweater.

If there are other spikes in the tree, I can remove those.

It feels good to be doing something productive. I slip the card and my phone into my pocket before letting the door drift shut behind me. It may be my imagination, but even though there is no wind and the tree itself is motionless, the shadows on the wall are moving.

THERE ARE FAR MORE rooms in this cabin than I anticipated. And even though I saw people — the snarky woman with the puffy coat, the mother and her teenage daughter, and the man in the sky-blue jacket who looked on the verge of crying — when I first arrived, I don't see anyone else now.

There's no one in the other rooms near the tree. Not at least that I can see. All of the rooms are actually quite like mine.

The first room holds nothing. Just more branches and quiet silhouettes on the wall. In the second room there are three stakes thrust into the tree. It takes a little longer to clean these up. The fourth room has one stake. The fifth room three.

Each stake I find I put in the makeshift bag I've made with my black cardigan. What sort of cabin hands these out? I have half a mind to call Claudia.

I go to the fourth floor and find much the same: a few black stakes thrust into this poor tree as if it is some sort of voodoo doll. The tree has been abused more in some rooms than others. A couple times I have to cut off strings from my cardigan to tie the bark back on.

"Why would someone do this?" I whisper.

The branches rustle ever so slightly. If trees could talk, perhaps that's what they would use for their voices.

On the first floor, the entirety of the oak's trunk is exposed. And...I frown.

There are seven separate stakes stabbed into the tree. How did I not notice this? They look as if they have been there for awhile. When I pull them out, they take chunks of blackened wood with them.

It takes longer to remove the damaged wood. Whole chunks are rotten. I take care to smooth down the splinters and the chunks. It's not commonly known, but if you leave a jagged cut in a tree or gouge out a section roughly, you can make the tree more susceptible to infection and further damage. All of this reminds me of the many hours I spent working with my uncle. I miss him. He always knew what to say when things were bad.

At last I step back.

All the dark marks in the tree make it look as if it has been savaged. The poor thing.

The globules of red-gold sap have filled in the holes. It's almost as if it's healing itself. Carefully I tie up the cardigan to seal the stakes in. I look up.

The dark marks in the tree have rearranged themselves. They say "run."

What? I blink several times and look back.

They're back to the way they were.

The foyer is still silent. No bootsteps, no laughter, no cries. It's a heavy silence like a library in a mausoleum. If there is such a thing.

The broad picture windows look out on an idyllic winter scene. Snow shrouded firs stand watch and glistening icicles cling to the overhang. Frost patterns adorn the corners of the windows, untouched by the sun's warmth.

There's no sign that anything is wrong. Maybe it's dyslexia. Or maybe...

Stepping closer, I place my finger along the outside of the first gouge.

It is somewhat in a straight line to the second. But there aren't enough to actually spell out the word "run."

Maybe they were sunspots? Maybe I looked at the sun and forgot...

My phone buzzes rapidly several times. It's like a nest of angry bees. I swipe the screen open. Over 73 missed messages.

No. I'm not dealing with it. Not right now. Why can't they leave me alone?

My chest locks with guilt, but I push it aside and walk.

It doesn't matter where. I just...I don't want any more of this.

My steps are swift, carrying me back up the polished staircase. But when I reach my room, I keep going. No. I have to keep moving. Keep moving. If I stop, I'm going to open my phone again. And if I see those messages glaring back at me...I...I don't know what I'll do.

So I keep walking. Straight down the hall. Straight past my room. Straight into whatever I may find.

CHAPTER 4

The hallway is empty. Only now do I realize how far it stretches out. I continue straight ahead, wondering how far it goes. I can't really see an end. It just fades from sight.

After a few minutes, the end of the hall is no closer. I've passed Elderberry 391, and still the hall stretches on. But now there's an opening and another hallway branches off in both directions.

No one is about. The air is still and quiet, and the hall stretches on and on. The doors here start at 300 again but have an E after the number. How is this possible? I'd seen the outside of the cabin, and there is no way it's this massive.

Another hallway opens up some distance further down. These doors have a C after the number. Maybe I should go back. Look for someone who maybe knows what to expect from this place.

No. Something tugs at me. I continue forward. It's pulling at my mind. I have to keep going.

Maybe I should think this is stranger than it is. Maybe...maybe I should...it's so hard to think. Walking is easier.

It's almost as if the path itself is guiding me. The long rugs lining the center of the halls have changed color. I don't seem to really notice them until they've all changed color. Sometimes to crimson, sometimes to cobalt, sometimes to pine, sometimes to gold, sometimes to snow.

Pictures hang on every wall, some oil colors, some watercolors, some prints, some pen and inks. They depict everything from a cat licking a snow cone to a woman surrounded by rabbits on sandstone stairs (possibly a depiction of Okunoshima?) to two old women peering out with mischievous light in their otherwise dull eyes. It's all rather random though the walls always remain the same. Ivory papered with walnut wainscoting. That was the same as before, right?

Wait.

That last painting.

The hairs on my arms lift up.

I fall back half a step and hinge my gaze toward it once more.

This oil painting depicts a stunning tree with black bark and turquoise leaves. But that isn't what I saw.

I saw...or at least I think I saw...a hollow-eyed woman, gaunt and pale, in clothing quite like mine. Except that she was staring at me, then she clapped her hand over her mouth, and vanished.

Slowly I lift my hand before the painting. It's a palette painting, and there is only the slightest of shine upon its surface. Not enough to create so vivid and striking an image.

Footsteps shuffle ahead.

Half-jumping, I turn. It's the man from outside. He's staring down at his phone, shuffling along, still in his jacket. He doesn't even look up as he passes me. Just continues on. There are tear stains on his cheeks and neck, and the red blotches remain on his face.

At least there's someone else here.

What is his story?

Perhaps we'll meet later.

The hall continues, and I follow it. The scare has passed. It must be my imagination. Or maybe it's a side effect from the painkillers. It's remarkable that I'm not nearly so stiff as I was. In fact, there's no pain at all.

Another painting catches my eye. It's a stunning picture of a green forest against a golden sky. A woman with long dark hair walks toward the forest, her hands outstretched. Hands reach for her from the forest itself, welcoming and kind. Her gown alone is a work of art, soft butter-yellow and rich yellow-gold. The train trails behind her, and her feet are bare. I can only see part of her face, but there is such joy and happiness I envy her and what she will find in that forest.

Maybe one day I'll find a place like that.

At last I tear myself away. It feels important that I learn how large this cabin really is. And that tugging call in my mind intensifies.

Every so often I catch glimpses of the other visitors. Few note me.

Sorrow saturates the air. A middle-aged woman crying into a velvet pillow in Melcherson 372K, her room's door half open. An old man with a limp in his left leg and an elaborately carved cane. He manages a faint sad smile as I pass, and he murmurs, "it really isn't the same." A man with a scarred left cheek and a grey glass-eye sitting on the floor outside Tamarisk 21H, his back to the wall. His only movement is the clenching and unclenching of his jaw, and he grips his jean-shirted elbow so tight his knuckles are white.

Pausing, I realize I don't want to pass him. My hand moves toward the door handle nearest me, and, before I can even think about it, I've stepped into another room all together.

A library.

My breath catches in my throat.

It's magnificent. Like something out of an old movie. The walls are lined from front to back with massive bookshelves. Many of the shelves bow under the weight of hard covered and leather-bound books, each one with elaborate title lettering. The room has an almost stifling quality to it, as if no one is supposed to be in here.

The air smells like old books, wood, and wool carpet. This carpet here is a heavy crimson wool, and it scrunches ever so slightly with each step.

This library is easily the size of my entire downstairs, and the ceiling is far higher than the hall's. It's almost as if the library doesn't belong here at all. Comfortable red arm chairs and high-backed sofas are arranged to form convenient seating nooks. A brass bar cart sits at the back with glistening goblets and six cut-glass decanters with dark liquid. A few of the wine glasses sit on one of the ornate round tables. There is no liquid nor any rings beneath the feet of the glasses. It is as if someone set them out and forgot about them.

But what draws my attention most is the secretary desk in the back corner. It is almost out of place. A decorative Greek key design of brass inlay lines the black wood, and the knobs and pulls of the various drawers and cubbies are brass as well. Like most secretary desks, the front can be pulled down to reveal further cubbies and a working space. But there is no stool or chair.

What could be inside?

As soon as I place my hand upon the lid, an odd surge of excitement

OF MASKS AND MAGIC

passes through me. It sounds silly, but I know that whatever is in this secretary desk will change my life.

All the sadness falls away and only curiosity remains.

The desk slides open. Unlike everything else in this library, the inside is layered with dust, and a scent like rotting leaves and branches wafts out. But then...a small man springs out.

He is no more than three inches tall with purple and green wings shaped like a dragonfly's. His wild mass of chestnut brown hair is further ruffled by a band of dark green fabric tied about his forehead. When he sees me, he tilts his head and leans back as if surprised. "Well now, what are you doing here? You certainly don't belong, now do you? Of all that I was expecting, you are certainly the last."

Leaping back, I stare in shock. "What in...how?" Is this some sort of computer trick? A holographic projection? Am I hallucinating? Maybe this is a side effect.

The little man crosses his arms. His features are remarkably delicate, but his vivid violet eyes sparkle with a brilliant energy. "You don't belong here, human." His voice is loud in my ears, even though he is tiny. "Get yourself together and go. This place is the anthu's feeding ground, and its paths are closing even as we speak."

His words make no sense. They aren't even connecting with my mind. I stare, my eyes wide, hands shaking. "You're...you're..."

"Oh, you aren't going to do well here if you don't get that under control, mon cher. Let me make it easier." He jumps forward, but as soon as he clears the desk, he becomes a man almost six feet tall.

A sharp gasp tears from my mouth. I feel sick to my stomach. "Wha..."

He grasps me by the shoulders, the wool of his fingerless gloves scratching my skin. "Hear me now, human child. You saved me, and for that, I'm grateful. I was to be trapped in there for the rest of my days if the king had had anything to do with it. And now I'm returning the favor and fulfilling my duty."

"Who are you?" I stammer.

"We fae are sent to close the traps and turn back visitors before anyone is caught, but we were too late this time. The rulers of this realm cannot kill us, but they can ensnare us, and that they did. I must find and free my brethren or else countless more will die. But as for you, you must go. The trap is sliding shut even as we speak. You have minutes before you are ensnared like all the other wretches. Get out now. All right?" He marches me toward the door.

His words still aren't registering. It's like so much noise and chaos. What on Earth is happening? I stumble, my foot catching on the carpet.

"Hey, hey!" He snaps his fingers in my face. "Sweet night, mortal children are dense." He grabs me by the arms and lifts me off the ground. "You don't understand a word I'm saying, do you? The minutes are falling, dear girl! When the clock strikes midnight, you'll be trapped here and the anthu will feed on your sorrow, your grief, and your soul. Do you hear me?"

The tightness in his grasp pinches me back to reality, and an ungodly panic stirs in my soul.

He plops me down in front of the door. "Do you understand?" he asks again, leaning closer. He smells like spruce and mountain air.

"Who are you?" I whisper faintly.

"Someone you will hopefully never see again because you will be too far from this cabin to ever look back. Once you escape, go and warn everyone you meet to stay away from this place." The fae points toward the door. "If you don't tarry, you can make it. Just keep turning to the right every time there is a hall, and you will wind up at the foyer. So long as you leave before midnight, no harm will come to you."

"What about the others?" I grab hold of his arm. "If the others aren't warned —"

"We'll get to them if we have time. But right now, you go. You look after you and leave the rest to me. If there's time, I'll get them out."

None of this makes much sense, but an even deeper fear sets in. If he's telling the truth, then that means I'll be the only survivor.

No! I can't leave everyone behind. There's still time. There was one man outside the door, and the grandfather clock in the corner reads only 4:15. The sun is still shining! Of course, there's time. There is enough time for everyone to get out.

Turning, I bolt back out into the hall. If there is even a chance that this is true, I'm not going to risk leaving them behind. "Hey!" I shout toward the scar-cheeked man with the glass-eye who was sitting on the floor by the door.

Except he isn't there anymore. Everything suddenly seems far darker now. "Hello!" I call out. "Is anyone out here? We've got to get out of here. Come on! Keep to the right."

"What are you doing?" The fae bounds out behind me, letting the library door slam shut. He glares at me fiercely. His purple eyes almost glow. "Just go! Don't waste time looking for the others."

"I can't leave them behind!"

"You don't even know them."

"That doesn't matter." Turning, I cup my hands around my mouth. "Hello! People in the cabin, we've got to get out of here!"

"I said go. There's just enough time for you to escape. It's almost midnight!" The fae shoves me down the hall.

"What are you talking about?" I whip out my phone and thrust it in his face. "It's 4:16 on a Tuesday. The full moon isn't until —"

"Look at the date." The fae grabs my phone and jabs his finger at the screen.

My eyes widen, and my knees buckle. It says February 24. But I came up here on the 21.

"You ate the food. It makes things happen first. There's no time to explain." He flings it against the wall. With a loud crack, the glass breaks, and the components fall apart. "The boundaries of our worlds are colliding, the portal is opening, and you are falling into the anthu's realm even as we speak. These are the paths of the fae and all our kind. Your laws of time, space, and matter do not apply, and if you do not go, you will be trapped. Now go!" With that, he gives me another firm shove and vanishes.

For a moment, I stare dumbfounded. Some small part of my mind insists this must be a dream. But if it's a dream, that means it's about to become terrible. Whether real or imagined, I don't want more people to die. At least I can start running the way he said and warn everyone I see.

Starting forward, I bang on the doors. "Everybody, run! We're going to be attacked. Everybody, get out of here! We're going to be trapped!"

My feet are heavy. It's getting darker. I'm moving slower. It's harder to breathe.

I knock on another door, my heart pounding from exertion. "Hello! Anyone in there? We've got to get out."

One of the doors opens, and an old woman with tortoiseshell spectacles hobbles out. "What is going on?" she demands.

I run up to her. My feet are sliding and slushing across the floor as if I have sunk into quicksand. "Come on," I gasp. "Something is happening. We have to get out of here!"

"Are you quite all right?" The woman scowls at me. "I have had quite a difficult day already, and I —"

"There's no time. Come on!" I seize her by the arm and drag her along with me. Though she gapes and protests, I refuse to let go. If I'm going to make it, so is she.

The light fades. Suddenly a clock I cannot see begins to chime. It's so loud it deafens me and feels like an earthquake all at once, a sound so strong I feel it right in the center of my body, reverberating through me and all around.

One...

The entire cabin jolts to the left. I crash into the wall, losing my grip on the woman.

Two...

The cabin rights itself, but the cobalt rug is now grass.

Three...

Another terrifying upset, this time as if we are dropping. Everything goes black.

Four...

Moonlight streams into the hall in thick silver swathes, but I can't see the moon through the ceiling. The old woman is screaming too now.

Five...

Another sickening lurch to the left and a fall. More screams now. Children. Men. Women. Even a dog howling. The din surrounds me.

Six...

The cabin shudders. Ivy and greenery spread across the walls, devouring the wallpaper, the end tables, and picture frames but leaving the pictures.

Seven...

Another horrifying drop. My stomach lurches with the movement. My head is spinning.

Eight...

The screams continue. But then a deep, blood-freezing, soul-piercing roar rises above it all.

Nine...

There's a shadow at the end of the hall. I can see — the cabin drops again and grates to the right.

Ten...

More screams. The cabin is becoming a forest! I fall against an ivy-covered wall, my limbs tangling in the thick wet greenery. Beetles and spiders skuttle about. I can't see the shadow!

Eleven...

Another violent drop with more screams and a roar. The roar is closer now. But where is the shadow? It's coming for us. I know it!

Twelve...

Everything settles, the entire cabin groaning and settling into place. I roll to the ground and struggle to free myself.

Whimpers and cries flow from all around me. I can't place any of them though except the old woman.

Horror still courses through me. I know what I saw. That shadow is evil, and it's coming for us now. Where is it? Is it the anthu?

I'm whimpering too, my breath twisting and lurching from my lungs in ragged gulps.

"What's happening?" someone calls out. I don't recognize the voice.

"Hello?" another voice cries, far more distant this time.

A guttural growl sounds up ahead.

No.

Slowly I turn my head.

The shadow has returned. Except it isn't a shadow this time. It's large and black with a form that is like smoke and silk floating in the air. Part of its form is vague, but the body...the body looks like a drenched sloth. A sloth as big as a Kodiak. It has three long claws on each of its distended paws, and its head is too small for its body. Beady red eyes shine in sunken sockets. The aura floats around it.

The old woman struggles to her feet as I fight to disentangle myself.

The creature slips closer. The floor creaks beneath its paws.

My mouth goes dry. My limbs flail. I try to point behind the woman, but only unintelligible syllables come from my mouth.

The old woman reaches for her cane. Her thinning blue-grey hair is mussed, and her dark floral dress is torn. She isn't listening to me! She isn't looking!

The creature slides up onto the wall. Gravity is irrelevant. The aura swirls about it. It's almost directly overhead.

Up. Look up! It isn't that hard of a phrase, but I can't say it. I can't force it out. My hands shake as I point.

The old woman is still muttering, smoothing down her dress, pushing at her hair, acting as if this is all one big bother in her day.

The creature arcs over her. It's even taller now that it's closer. More than nine feet in height.

"L-l-look!" I scream.

The old woman stares at me.

The creature slams its massive paw down on her and roars.

Someone's screaming. It's me I think. But I don't know. All I do is run.

It's a nightmare. The halls slant and twist at all angles. And with every step the creature gains on me. The floor shudders and cracks beneath it. With every step, I'm falling closer to its slavering maw. But I can't run faster. My legs feel like noodles.

All I can do is will myself to run faster.

CHAPTER 5

Run. Faster. Faster. I will my legs to move. The carpet is soft and squishy beneath my feet, like it's slowing me intentionally.

Someone else is screaming.

One of the doors flies open. A man, I can't see his face, bolts out. Small creatures with tattered wings pursue him. The air is ripe with stench and terror.

"Don't go that way!" I gasp.

But he's headed straight toward the monster.

The beast stops short.

The man skids to a halt, falling flat on his back. The tatter-winged creatures skitter and shriek around him, tugging at his hair and biting at his flesh. But he's motionless. Horror has transfixed his face in the perpetual rigor of terror.

My own voice locks in my throat. I have to help. But...

That hesitation is too long.

The creature roars. Its horrible voice booms and vibrates through me, the ivies and leaves encasing the hall bending with the strength of its lungs. It slashes with its heavy elongated paw, the claws glistening in the bands of moonlight. And he's gone. The tatter-winged creatures vanish with him.

What is this nightmare? I can't...I'm running again. I don't know

331

where. Everything is black and silver, dark green and brown. Shadows come alive. A mirror crashes in front of me. Somehow I leap over it.

Other people are shrieking and screaming. Sometimes they appear in front of me, sometimes behind. I crash into another hall, grabbing at the wall for support.

The old man with the cane is standing there, motionless. He's staring straight ahead as if he sees something he knows or as if he's resigned himself to some fate.

"Come on!" I reach for him.

"Keep going." He leans both hands on the derby handle cane.

"But there's —"

"I know." He keeps staring.

The creature roars again. The pictures are dancing now, the images spinning and shifting. The two old women are laughing maniacally, pointing toward us.

I'm running again. The heavy *thud thud* of the monster's footsteps slows only long enough for it to snatch up the old man. He doesn't make a sound.

Another door flings open. A bizarre creature, waxy-white and faceless, leaps out. It seizes me by the arms, pinning me to the floor. Shrieking, I writhe.

A sharp pain bites into my side. The dagger! I'd forgotten about it.

The faceless creature drags its jagged cleft hands along my side. Disembodied laughter swirls around. Words follow that I can't understand. Like some horrid incantation.

The faceless creature's weight pins me, but I wrestle my arm free. Black liquid seeps from its nails. My side explodes with pain as I wrench the blade up and into the faceless creature's chest. The blade slides through as if it's made of cotton.

The sloth monster thunders around the corner. Its claws gouge into the sides of the wall. Pictures crash and fall. I clamber away.

The faceless creature continues flailing on the filthy carpet. But the monster strikes it.

This is it. I struggle to my feet, my hands shaking. The dagger in my hands isn't going to do anything against a monster this size.

The monster slows. Those awful eyes burn into me.

My strength is almost spent. The adrenaline surges and courses, but my legs are too heavy to lift. All I can do is stagger back.

More laughter. More darkness. Those eyes keep burning.

Where else can I go? Desperation floods me. It's clenching, tightening my chest. I can't breathe.

There's a picture window behind me.

My last chance. I summon the last of my strength.

The dagger still in hand, I turn, run, and leap into it. The creature snorts and then bellows. The ground shakes as it starts forward.

The glass shatters around me. It gives way in a tinkling crackling chorus.

The ground strikes me. I roll and crash forward, the dagger falls from my grasp. Pain prickles and stabs across my body.

But I'm not outside! I'm in some sort of sitting room, half under a grand baby piano.

More glass breaks. A deep sniffing sound draws closer.

I crab-crawl backwards. My grip slips. My muscles and palms are burning. Blood flows from my side.

Suddenly, something snatches me up. Before I can even cry out, it twines its arms around me and thrust me against the wall. "Don't make a sound," a male voice says.

The monster in the window bellows again. I can feel that sound in my chest.

He throws the door open and then flings his body over mine. "Shh-hh..." He presses his hand over my mouth. His palm and fingers are unusually long, covering not only my mouth but the side of my face all the way to my neck. "Don't move."

Bits of glass and wood shatter as the monster slides through the window. A damp musky odor like old smoke, rotten leaves, and bile water creeps through.

I writhe, struggling to break free. We have to hide! We're out in the open.

He pushes his hand against my mouth harder, muffling my struggles. "Be quiet."

The monster is enormous. Even larger than I thought. It must smell us. Its black nose twitches, its eyes glittering with cruelty. The airy substance around it expands and contracts at intervals, gradually becoming larger each time. Almost as if...

Is it searching with an aura?

I don't move. I can't now. The stranger remains pressed against me, his one hand over my mouth, the other braced near my head. His body is motionless against mine.

The creature rears onto its hind legs and turns about slowly. A heavy sniffing follows and the aura grows. It merges with some of the shadows.

A sharp snort follows. Its head swivels toward us.

"Don't move."

A whimper rises in my throat. But it dies with my next breath. My heart thunders in my ribcage, blood rages in my veins.

The creature moves forward. Its long claws click and scrape across the floor as it comes closer.

The stranger's grip tightens on me. "Shhhh." His voice is directly in my ear.

Click. Click.

An even louder sniff.

I close my eyes. My entire body shakes.

The scent grows stronger as the creature looms over us. I can feel it even if I'm not looking. It's sniffing the air. Searching. The aura is expanding. It's like slimy feathers cold and slick.

The tension is terrible. It has to be worse than any bite or tearing of the flesh. I can't...I can't take it. My eyes clench even tighter.

What's it going to do? Why hasn't it seen us? We're right here. We're out in the open. Up against the wall. What —

Suddenly it's gone.

My eyes fly open. It's gone. The air seems lighter already.

The stranger slowly relaxes, his hand sliding away from my mouth. "It's gone for now, but it will come for you again."

"Wh— what was that?" I stammer.

"That was the anthu. The spirit of this place. It feasts on the souls of humans. Certain types of immortals as well if it can find them. That's how this place was created, but immortals are far harder to trap than you humans. You always walk in here so easily. So full of sadness and grief and all the things the anthu loves." He gives me a sad smile, resting his hand against my cheek. "But you're safe for now. It won't hurt you so long as you're with me."

It's only then that I realize how close the stranger still stands to me. His hand curves about my cheek, his fingertips grazing my hair. It's difficult to make out anything else about him as we're standing in one of the darkened patches, but... I swallow, trying to push down the butterflies rising in my stomach.

"Why did you do that?" I ask. "Why save me? There are others out there...it's going for them, isn't it?"

"Don't you remember me?" I hear the smile in his voice.

"No...I'm sorry. I...I'm...no." I bite the inside of my lip. "Who are you?"

"I used to have many names, but it's just Taomau now. You are called Iscah, yes?"

"Yes." I nod.

"Iscah." He repeats my name as if it is pleasant to say and then steps back. Crossing over, he shuts the door.

I'm still against the wall, my hands pressed to the embossed wallpaper. I still can't fully comprehend what has happened, and my mind is spinning in circles.

This entire room has become part of a forest while yet retaining all the attributes of its former purpose. This was a study. The chairs and the couch are there, but they are covered in moss and ivy with the occasional yellow, blue, or pink flower. The greenery has spread along all of the shelves, swarming the knick-knacks and the table legs. The baby grand piano has been mostly covered with moss.

"Can you tell me what happened?" I slide away from the wall. My head is still spinning and that foul taste remains, but curiosity compels me once again. "I think he was a fae, someone told me that this was a trap. That I had until midnight of the full moon's start. But that was a little after four, and then it was the wrong day. And then...then it was midnight, and the cabin was falling."

"Yes." The stranger returns to the picture window and fastens the shutters tight. The glass crunches beneath his feet. As the air stills, the stench fades, leaving behind only the scent of damp and wood. "The fae do all they can to prevent you poor creatures falling into this trap. The anthu is always hungry though, and your kind are so often sad. It's not hard for you to be lured in." He places the secondary bolt over the shutter. Moonlight still streams through the slats and from above even though the ceiling should block the light.

In the moonlight, I can at last see him. And for a moment, I am awed. He looks human and yet not. He's even taller than I thought despite being very lean, almost too lean for his height, he appears quite strong. His face is likewise thin with hollow cheeks and startlingly expressive green eyes, green as moss and new spring leaves. His red-brown hair flows all the way to the base of his back, shining beneath the moonlight. If his hair had been a great deal shorter, it might have curled. And even though he now stands quite still, there is an air of motion about him. His attire looks somewhat archaic, almost medieval, worn green wool and scuffed brown leather. And there is something...something strange about him. Perhaps in the curve of his mouth or the angle of his eyes or in the creases on his brow. I don't know.

No. I do. It's in his eyes. The eyes of a mourner who still wants to believe that the world can be good. Who continues to search for the good even though it wounds him. That's what sets him apart.

Taomau half-smiles. "Is everything all right?"

"What are you?" It feels so rude to ask, but such concerns are almost irrelevant now. I stammer over my words as I struggle to explain. "You keep saying 'you humans' as if you're not one. Are you...are you a fae?"

"Not at all. I am not nearly so swift nor clever as they. And they cannot die in this realm. I, on the other hand, I am as liable to death as you. Or at least I would be if the anthu could devour me. But it cannot. That's why it passed you over."

"So...what are you then?"

It's hard not to stare, and though I try to look away, I find myself returning. He isn't precisely beautiful to look at. Not that he is ugly. No. It's just that he's more fascinating than handsome, and whatever it is that is in his eyes, his life, his soul, his...light. I feel as if I somehow do know him. But I can't place him.

"Do you really not know me?" Taomau tilts his head. His hair slides forward, creating a mantle of red-brown around his face. "Truly?"

"I'm so sorry. It's...I'm not always good with faces. You seem familiar, but I can't..." I pick at my arm, my nerves returning. "I've been in a bad place."

"I'm afraid that your situation has not much improved. But I'm not offended. Only surprised." He smiles. It's gentle, almost soothing. "Fortunately, it does not matter. But you need medical attention." He motions toward my side.

Oh yes. I'd forgotten. There are streaks of blood flowing through my pale yellow tunic. The dagger blade didn't cut deep thankfully.

"There's water for now. It'll dry up when the full moon leaves this phase along with most other life." Taomau crosses to the piano and lifts the lid. He uses one of the goblets to scoop up clear shining water. The keys play softly, almost harp-like as he dips the goblet in. "Hold still."

He takes my hands and forearms, pouring the water onto them. The cold is sharp, but to my surprise, the pain evaporates as soon as the water touches my skin. Oddly enough, the red marks remain. He lifts my shirt enough to expose the wounds, taking care not to touch the broken skin and pours the water over my cuts and scrapes. He moves on to remove the bandages and does the same with the wounds from the car crash.

"The water is most potent right at the full moon. As more of it evaporates, what remains will lose its power. That's the way it is with everything in this place. And when the moon is gone, the water will be gone too. And if any remains, it will be poisonous."

"Thank you." My knees still feel wobbly, and now that the adrenaline has passed, I am shaky and weak. The pain is gone, but I feel weak. "I should —"

"You're going to get out of here," Taomau says. "I'm going to do everything I can to see that happen. But the anthu will return. It is searching this place for all like you. And if you do not have proper protection, it will devour you. We might get separated, so I want you to have this." He takes my dagger, gathers up his hair, and then cuts through it. As he does, he shudders, almost as if it wounds him. But taking the hair, he knots the ends together to form a necklace and places it around my neck.

"Wear this always, dearest Iscah. Nothing here will harm you so long as you wear it."

The hair is soft. The edges appear tipped in shimmering gold, but the glimmering fades when I look directly at it.

"Thank you. I don't really even know what to say." My fingers twine about the hair. It's magical and silken. I can feel it tingling against my fingertips.

"Just live. That's more than enough thanks for me." Taomau smiles and then takes my hand in his. "Now you should take your rest. You have a dangerous path ahead of you, and traveling in the day will be safer. At least what passes for day around here." He motions toward the couch. "Come and rest. I'll watch over you."

"I don't know..." I hesitate.

"There's no need to be afraid, my darling. Not even bad dreams will haunt you this night. And I promise, I mean you no ill. If I had intended to hurt you, I would have done so."

His voice is so gentle. Indeed, everything about him is soothing. For the first time in what feels like ages, I am comforted. The thoughts quiet in my mind as I let him draw me to the couch.

At first, I rest my head on the couch's arm, but Taomau guides me back so that I am resting on him. It's more intimate than I anticipate, but I don't refuse. It's...pleasant.

"Don't you need to rest?" I ask.

"I don't take sleep in the same way humans do," Taomau says. He strokes my hair, his long fingers sliding through my wavy dark curls without snagging even slightly. "How is it you came to this place?"

"I came to get away." Thoughts of Desmond return. All the accusing texts. My friends have probably sent me even more. A lump lodges in my throat. "I thought it was just a cabin."

"Most do. The king and queen have many ways of luring people to this place."

"Why do they do it?"

"To feed the anthu. The anthu maintains this place. You see...many years ago, the king and queen of this wretched place were exiled from the land of the fae. They had no wish to live within the mortal realm, and so they roused the spirit of the fallen eskudenine. They fed it the living bones of unicorns and two immortals whom they caught in their snares, and it became the anthu. That gave it sufficient strength to let it hollow out a realm between the fae and human realm. This cabin was constructed to set the boundaries of the realm and provide easier access to its gateways. They open from time to time, and the prey is lured inside."

"Only humans though." I murmur. His fingers in my hair are so soothing that I'm close to drifting away. I feel warm and...safe. It's as if we're talking about a story that doesn't affect us whatsoever. "What about the immortals? Do they get trapped here?" I whisper sleepily.

"Immortals are difficult to lure at the best of times. Unless cruel fate decrees otherwise, no more will be snared in this place. But humans are quite similar to immortals though it takes a great many more to sate the belly of this beast. And humans are so easily ensnared."

"So how did you wind up here?"

"They didn't intend to capture me, but they have kept me all the same."

"And the anthu can't actually eat you? Not even if it's starving?" I lift my head to look at him.

Taomau wears an expression of deep contemplation, a hopefulness mixed with sadness.

"My soul is not made of such things as the anthu enjoys. I am kept here only for their amusement."

"I'm sorry." I slip my hand over his. This is a cruel place. I can't imagine living here for any length of time.

"It's my life." He hesitates. Tears glisten in his eyes, but he wipes them away. "When I was small, my mother warned me of the unmarked paths.

She told me that ways and paths sometimes open between our realms and others, and she said that one so young as I could not discern which ones were good and which ones were dangerous and which were to be avoided at all costs. I should have listened."

"How long have you been here?"

"More years than I can count. I was very young when I passed through to this place."

I fold his hand between mine and kiss it. I don't really know what to say, but the loneliness in me recognizes the loneliness in him. I wish I could make it go away. "If you want, you can come through with me. There's room in my house."

Taomau laughs. It's a mournful sound, but that smile still reaches his eyes. "If only I could."

"What did you think you would find on the path you followed here?"

"That is another story, darling. Another story for another time. For now, you should sleep." He kisses the top of my head, and a wave of weariness passes over me. "Sleep well and without fear. I'll watch over you until you wake."

Everything becomes quite warm and dark as my eyes slide shut again. The air is close around me but pleasant, smelling like fresh blooming trees and sweet tinted flowers.

Then Taomau whispers again. His voice is like a sound far at the end of the hall. "Are you sleeping now?"

Sleep has lulled me to such stillness I cannot open my mouth. But I am aware of him.

Taomau leans down. His breath stirs my hair, and he kisses my cheek. "Sleep well, sweet one, and dream of me. If I could dream, I would dream of you."

CHAPTER 6

This sleep is peaceful. Gentle. Light. No dreams torment me. I'm only aware of rest. Sweet, blissful rest. I could stay in it forever.

Then there's a voice. It's whispering in my ear soft as the wind rustling in the leaves on a warm spring day. "Iscah. Iscah, you need to wake."

Slowly I find myself returning to consciousness. I find myself staring up into Taomau's eyes. They are so deep I think I could get lost in them as easily as in this sleep.

"I'm sorry to wake you," he says. His arm slides beneath my head as he helps me up. "But it's as close to day as it ever is here, and we have a long journey ahead of us."

"Thanks." I stretch. It's a deliciously indulgent one that makes me yawn so hard I'm almost afraid I'll pull a muscle. Surprisingly I am still pain free.

Taomau is already up. The bookshelves and cabinets have been built directly into the wall. He gives them a sharp tug. Loose strands of ivy and moss pull away, revealing damaged wood and fast growing blight. "We may get separated. If that happens, then remember to always go to the right whenever there is a hallway to choose from. And always go down the staircase. Unless you make it all the way to the sacred well. Then go up once and keep going to the right."

Taomau removes a mahogany box from the cabinet. With a swift click, he unlatches it. "The garland I gave you will protect you from the anthu and the other creatures of this place so long as you wear it. But it will not protect you from the king and queen or from their elite."

"And obviously I need to avoid them." My skin prickles. I shiver. It's colder than I realized. I miss being beside him.

"Yes. Here." He removes a thick black cloak from the box. Swirling it out, he places it on my shoulders, draws it up to my neck. His hands linger against my skin. "Keep your head down, and if anyone stops us, do not speak to them. And if I tell you to be quiet, you must be quiet."

There's something in the way he carries himself now. An anticipation, a fear, a wariness. It clings to him like the moss to the floor. "Are you going to get in trouble for helping me?"

Taomau forces a smile. It strains through his jaw. "That's my concern. Not yours. Now. I don't think there's anything suitable for humans to eat. The water is rich though. It will give you strength." He dips the goblet into the piano's housing. The same pleasant tones sound as he lifts it up.

The water is delicious. Cool and refreshing with sweet notes. Better than the mountain water I drank when I went hiking with Desmond and Nona and TJ and... A weight descends upon me. What they must think of me. No one is going to ever believe this. If I ever get out of this place, what will I tell them? If...

Taomau opens the door and peers out. Then he nods. He reaches for my hand, and we are off. Our quick and quiet pace lets me leave many of my thoughts behind, and the ones that nudge back into my conscious mind I thrust back.

There is a dull filtered white light that reaches through the ceiling. It never seems to care whether there is an opening for it to break through. It's as if the light is coming from some place entirely separate. But...as odd as it sounds, everything is a little brighter. As if someone has decided to lighten the ivies and the flowers and the paintings, turning the blacks charcoal and the burgundies soft red. The colors remain muted, but...it isn't so oppressive.

As we reach an intersection of the halls, small grey and silver creatures bound out. They look like ferrets but with bloodied backs and crooked wings sewn into their flesh. The wings on one poor creature droop painfully. The creatures stare at us with hungry eyes for a moment. Their bodies are so thin, I can see their ribs. Then they drop on all fours and scamper away. One pounces on a beetle and eats it whole.

"What have they done to those poor creatures," I whisper.

"This is hell. And if it isn't, they are treated as if it is. When night comes, you must not travel unless your life is at stake. That is when the most walk and when the greatest terrors are afoot. Right now, most are in the great room."

"Where is that?" I snuggle deeper into the cloak. It's enough to ward off the chill, but this is more to hide my own nervous energy. This is a terrible time to be developing feelings. I know that. I do. I promise I do. And it all makes such perfect sense psychologically...wait, I'm worrying about something making psychological sense when I'm in a cabin that has been dropped into another realm and there's a monster roaming the halls devouring people for their sadness. Please don't let me be crazy.

"The great room moves."

"Of course it does." I sigh.

"The king and queen place it wherever they feel they will have the most pleasure. Or create the most terror."

"This is a very confusing place," I say.

"Not so confusing if you assume everything here wishes to destroy you."

"How have you made it?" I marvel that anyone could survive here for a matter of days, let alone years.

"I didn't want to die. Some part of me hoped that I would find a way home, but by the time I was old enough to understand what needed to be done, my magic had waned. Otherwise, I would open a path for us now and take you to my realm. Truly, it is not often allowed, but I would break that law for you." His hand tightens around mine. For a moment, he glances at me, and my heart stammers forward. "So will you tell me more about why you are here, sweet one?"

"I..." My mouth goes dry. "I needed to get away from my friends. I let them down." Understatement, of course. But I can't bring myself to say any more. A knot forms in my throat.

He nods, but the look in his eye suggests he knows there's far more to it than that. "I'm sure you didn't."

He has no reason to lie to me. But he also doesn't know what I did. I try to swallow the lump in my throat.

"Who was Desmond?"

"How do you—" I snap my gaze back to his.

"You speak in your sleep."

"Oh." That's disconcerting. I wonder what all I've said. What all he knows. My cheeks warm. "I…Desmond was a friend."

"Did you love him?

"We...we were just friends." A loose strand of hair commands my attention, and I push it aside, avoiding Taomau's gaze. The lump in my throat is so large I can scarcely breathe around it. "What all lives here that isn't trapped?"

Taomau pauses for a time as if weighing my words, both spoken and not. At last he nods and says, "I'm afraid that this is a place where few choose to live of their own accord. Most in this place were trapped here. It's a wasteland. Those who do choose to live here are cruel beyond note."

I can believe that, and the tendrils of fear pull back the grief. We walk on. Our feet squish in the moss and grass covered carpet.

The paintings continue to move. Some of them seem to see us, and they gawk and stare, pointing with crooked fingers and watching us with mirky eyes that follow our every movement. But others are like windows. A child flashes by in one of them, a child in a cobalt parka and a red and yellow toboggan cap.

"Those paintings aren't what they seem," Taomau says when he realizes what has caught my attention. "The fae put some of these here to give glimpses into this realm and others to hopefully warn others away. But the king and queen used their magic to create their own hideous paintings as well, ones that leer and terrify. And they muddled the time. You can see into the other realms, but you never know which point in time you're looking at. Often it's your own, but not necessarily. And not always in the order you'd think."

I keep staring at the painting, hoping the child will come back.

"Come on." Taomau tugs me along. "Don't spend much time looking in the paintings. There was one man who escaped the anthu but who died before one of these. He couldn't tear himself away."

"He died there?"

"He withered away within a matter of days. None of the creatures attacked. Not even the king and queen. They just laughed at him. Thought it was funny. I always wondered what it was that he saw in that painting."

We fall silent, but we continue on. I wonder how far it is we have to go. There's little differentiation within the halls except in the paintings themselves, the odd shelf, and half shut doors. Most other doors are shut quite tightly. The air is close as well. Close but cold.

Beetles, roaches, and spiders crawl upon the walls. Sometimes all I can hear are their fast skittering or slow thrumming feet. But they're always there. Whether I see them or not.

"Whatever you do, don't eat them. You will die in horrible spasms," Taomau says.

"Them? You mean the bugs?" I arch an eyebrow. "I wasn't planning to." I hope I'm not here so long that those start looking good.

"Good. Even if you are starving, it wouldn't be worth it. The poison has no cure. I've seen warriors reduced to whimpering balls of agony after one bite."

"Do a lot of people get trapped here?"

"It's difficult to define a lot. I suppose less than a thousand have been trapped herebut far more than a hundred. To be honest...I have tried to ignore them recently. None of them have ever survived, no matter what I do. And sometimes...it hurts too much to try."

Somehow that didn't sound like him at all. There was more to it. "Why help me then?"

"Because..." He drops his gaze as if embarrassed. "Just because."

I thread my fingers through his. His hands are so warm against mine. His fingers are unusually long; mine only come to the first joint of his. It might have been offputting or alarming anywhere else, but now...it simply was. It's natural. Precisely him. "Thank you for helping me."

"I couldn't not help you. Even if you hadn't..." He pauses, his voice breaking. "This is all going so fast. Listen. If anyone does find you here, you must pretend that you do not know me, my dearest. They will hurt you, but they will hurt you more if they know that you have...you have..." He cannot speak. Tears flow down his cheeks.

"That I've what?"

"Nothing," Taomau says. He takes a deep breath. "It's nothing."

We keep walking. The floorboards creak ahead. One of the doors opens. I stand stock-still. Taomau stops as well.

A faceless creature, gaunt bodied yet sag bellied, creeps out of the room. It has cleft hands, the fingers a dull purple and the rest of the skin a sickly apricot tone. It staggers out, its long arms draping near the ground.

Taomau's hand tightens on mine.

He doesn't have to worry. I'm not going to say a word. That creature is beyond terrifying. What can it possibly be?

For a moment, the pale creature sniffs at the air. At first, I can't see the nostrils. Then I see the dark slit in its throat. A shudder courses through me.

The creature turns, then faces us. It moves forward, its steps halting.

Taomau puts his arm around me and pushes me behind him. "What are you doing out at this hour? Should you not be resting, friend?"

The creature bends forward. Its head rolls and lolls. Then a creaking voice speaks. "Entertain."

"Not now. Later. In the great room at the king and queen's pleasure."

The creature seizes him by the arm. It smells like rotten flesh. Taomau winces slightly. "Entertain," the creature says again.

"Later, my friend. You have my word."

The creature twists the thick nails on the ends of its fingers into his arm and then releases him with a huff of disgust. "Fool."

With a small gasp, Taomau straightens.

I wait until the creature vanishes around the corner to cross in front of Taomau. "What did he do to you?" I whisper.

"Nothing. It's fine." Taomau grimaces. He tries to pull his sleeve down, but the fabric is already darkening.

"Do we need to get some of the water?" I roll the fabric up. Amber blood swells from two black marks in his arm. The creature must have some sort of venom.

"No. It's fine." Taomau pulls free. "I heal quickly. That was simply a warning. The eltrines are not over friendly, and they do not like to be told no."

"Are you really going to have to stay here when I go," I ask. I'm not sure that I can leave him.

"I'm afraid so."

"Then maybe —"

"You cannot stay here," Taomau says firmly. He takes both my hands in his, brings them to his lips, kisses them. "And I cannot come with you to your world." He takes a deep breath as if his burden is increasing. "I should be stronger than this, but I'm not." The emotion twists in his face, his grip on my hands tightens. "And I was so lost and alone that my heart was ready to break even before you came. Now that you are here, I have to tell you that I love you."

I blink. What? I can't find the words. Disconnected syllables stammer from my mouth.

"Time is meaningless, Iscah. What is either is or it isn't. You humans need time to understand what is, but I don't. I know! I don't expect you to feel for me as I feel for you. Ah!" He cringes. "And I am such a fool. You must not tell anyone what I have said to you. Forgive me. We must keep moving."

His words leave me speechless, but he leaves me no time to process them. Instead, he pulls me along. We turn down another corridor. More bloody winged ferrets scamper away, and reams of beetles and spiders slide and scurry across the wall.

It's hard to think about what Taomau has said in light of all this. It's been a long time since I've been in a relationship of any kind. I don't deserve one, but...something in my heart stirs every time I look at Taomau. It's foolish I know. People don't fall in love this fast. It has to be infatuation and desperation on his part. Then again...I'm desperate too.

Day means that it is only a little less dark, but after awhile, I notice that the colors are darkening again and the shadows lengthening. Is there an end to this place? We have walked through hall after hall. Occasionally we come to a staircase, but it is always enclosed, the steps slick with moss, mud, and grass.

"Are we almost there?" I ask.

"No."

"But the size is all wrong," I whisper. "It's...it's —"

"Don't try to make it make sense with what you have seen." Taomau smiles slightly. "You'll just lose your mind. You'll need that when you get out."

He still holds my hand. I can feel the need from him, feel it within myself. If only it were another time, another place.

Down another staircase. Through more halls. It's making my head swim. Are we even moving? Sometimes I wonder. The only thing that's clearly changing is that it is getting darker.

Someone needs to say something, but I can't think of any good words. Each question I can think of, each thought that comes to my mind seems as if it would only cause Taomau pain or fuel the panic that is rising in me.

"I do have a question for you," Taomau asks.

I almost sigh with relief. "What is it?" My voice sounds so thin and small in this place.

"Why would you not do as Galban said?"

"Galban?"

"The fae you released from the secretary desk."

"How do you know about him?" I frown. "Was I sleep talking again?" No. That didn't make sense. I didn't know the fae's name to begin with.

"I know far more than you might guess." Taomau chuckles. "It seems that if you were told that you only had the time to escape if you left right away that you would leave and not try to rescue strangers."

I shrug. That event actually seems long ago. There are many different ways I could put this. I could talk about how important their lives are. How who I was was certainly not at all as important as them. But...in this heaviness, there's no need to restrain my words. It's all true, but one reason stands above all the others. "I don't think I could be the only survivor again. I had to rescue someone."

"I can understand that. Sometimes it's not as much a matter of who you save so long as you save someone." Taomau glances back at me. Our eyes meet again, and I feel that same sharp prickling and warming in my heart. "Not this time though," he says softly.

I should say something now. Anything.

Suddenly Taomau thrusts his arm out. "Wait..."

I can't hear it at first, but the tramp of feet soon becomes apparent. It's a dull thudding like a migraine. It draws closer and closer.

"Hide your face." Taomau pulls the hood of my cloak up. I cover my face with my hands and duck my chin down. The hood obscures most of my vision, but I can still see a little through my fingers.

Five men in elaborate armor march into the hall. Their armor is a dull grey with hints of yellow, like snail shells only much larger. The helmets curve over most of their faces, leaving only a thin visor in the bulbous top for them to see through. Their mouths and chins are exposed.

"And what are you doing about?" the leader asks. He steps forward. When he crosses his arms, the armor clinks and grates. It doesn't sound like it's made of metal.

"I'm simply enjoying the calm and the peace that the full moon brings. I suggest you do the same," Taomau says lightly.

"You weren't at the feast." The leader is so close to Taomau and me now that if he reaches out, he could touch me. But he doesn't seem aware of me. "The king and queen noticed."

"If they had wished to see me, they are always welcome to summon me. But it is wise never to overstay one's welcome. Otherwise what good am I?"

"You're never any good." The leader spits on the ground. "But it was noted. I'd have thought you'd have learned from the last time, but since you didn't learn from the times before that, well, it wouldn't surprise me if this time the king didn't just burn you."

The other soldiers laugh coldly.

Taomau forces a laugh as well, but the sound is strained. "Wouldn't that be a sight? Me all in flames. Somehow I don't think there would be much entertainment after I was set alight."

"You're not worth much as it is." The leader jabs his stained finger into Taomau's chest. "You'd best be watching yourself. The king and queen aren't amused, and if they're not amused, you know what happens next." He then claps his hand against the side of Taomau's head and strides on. "Forward."

The other soldiers file after him. One spits on Taomau. The others laugh.

I'm so angry, my hands shake. How can anyone be so cruel?

When they have passed, I look up and see the sadness in his face. My heart breaks all over again. "How can they treat you this way?"

"They do what pleases them." Taomau smiles faintly, but it does not reach his eyes this time. "Don't let it bother you. I'm used to it. Come now." He holds his hand out to me. "We need to keep going."

As I slide my hand into his, I cannot stop replaying what I saw. "Are you in danger? Are they going to burn you at the stake?"

"Burn me at the stake?" Taomau chuckles. He glances at me, forcing his smile to be larger. "Oh, no, there will be no stake burning."

He's not really answering my question. I feel the tension in his hand. But I can't press it further. I know he wants quiet now, and the words are too heavy for me to speak.

It's as if we are moving through a darkening palette. After an hour, maybe two, perhaps five, Taomau stops, looks about, and then presses open a door. "We should take shelter now. It's nearly night."

It's a bedroom, entirely overgrown with moss and close-growing plants. Ivies engulf three of the walls. The four-poster bed against the back wall has over a dozen rhubarb-like plants growing across the mattress. Several colonies of mushrooms cluster around the bed frame and dresser.

Taomau closes the door behind us and examines the room carefully. The drawers reveal a number of common household objects — a hair brush, hair pins, shoe lifts, and so on — encrusted with grime and moss. He opens the closet door. It's empty inside. "It will be safer if we sleep in here. We don't have to sleep in the same place if you don't want, but it would be safer."

"No," I say. "This is fine."

Taomau crawls into the closet and motions for me to join him. I slide in beneath his arm, he pulls the door mostly shut. Only a thin crack of silver light leaks through.

I glance up at him. He hasn't said a word about what happened earlier between us. And after all that he has endured this day alone...

I slide my hand up along his chest. His heart beats. Just like a human's. A steady paced *thrum thrum*. I can almost feel his grief through my fingertips. The loneliness. The aching. The cold. It's like I'm feeling my own heart.

"Taomau..." I whisper.

"Yes?" He rests his cheek against my head.

"What you said earlier...about loving me..." My voice trembles.

"Shhh." Taomau kisses the top of my head. A faint sigh escapes his lips. "It's all right, my darling. I don't expect you to feel the same."

"It's not that," I say. "It's just...I think I'm falling in love with you too." My breath catches.

Taomau makes a funny gasp in his throat. He pulls me closer, stroking my face and my shoulders. "I love you so much, Iscah," he whispers. His eyes shine with tears. "All this is worth it to be with you now. For whatever it is that comes or whatever it is that happens, I will always have this. This precious, precious time."

"You have to come with me. We'll find a way, Taomau." I kiss his hand. "I can't leave you here. I won't."

Taomau catches my face between his hands and turns it up to his. "Never forget that I love you, Iscah," he says. Then, curling down, he presses his lips to mine.

I lean up into the kiss. My eyes slide shut, and I twine my arms around his neck. It is beautiful. "I won't leave you behind, Taomau."

CHAPTER 7

"Wake up. Wake up, girl." A strange yet familiar voice jostles me from my sleep.

I wake with a start, still in the closet but no longer in Taomau's arms.

The fae who I released from the secretary desk stands over me. Galban, I think his name was. He's human-sized now, and a look of annoyance and panic mars his otherwise handsome features. His broad headband is askew. "Hurry up. I tried to save you once and you were too dense to listen. You will this time."

"Where's Taomau?" I ask.

Galban drags me to my feet. "He's been summoned. He wasn't there last night at the anthu's feast, and his absence was noted. And now that they have him, they're going to find out about you."

"I don't —"

"You don't have to do anything but run. This time I'm not letting go of you until we're there." The fae pulls me along.

My mind is still blurry from sleep. "Is he going to be all right?"

"We don't have time for that! Run!" The fae whips the door open and jerks me out.

Night has come to this cabin. Everything is coming alive.

Galban makes me move so fast I can barely focus. My feet strike the floor with a staggering beat, the damp moss-covered carpet squishing beneath me.

More of those waxy-fleshed creatures stagger out. Golems leer from the paintings. Strange laughter and cackling sounds all around. A black-scaled serpent slithers across the floor, diving beneath the moss.

My heart is beating so fast I can scarcely breathe. It's like a nightmare. Thousands of bizarre images pouring over me. Beetles and spiders spout out of a hole in the wall and skitter away.

"Don't touch the walls. Don't touch any of them. We can't know which ones are live," Galban says. He tugs harder, making me run faster.

We reach a staircase. It's blackened with rot, moss, and mold. My feet skid on it. Yelping, I grab for the banister. Galban doesn't stop. He flings his arm around my waist and takes the stairs at a run.

Wails and howls start up. They ripple through the cabin and tear across my mind. One of the bizarre cleft-handed creatures flings itself against the staircase. "Escape!" it croaks. "Escape!"

"Always to the right," Galban says. "Remember, always to the right."

"Is Taomau in danger?" I ask as we reach the bottom of the staircase.

"Yes." Galban jerks me forward. "But that doesn't matter. He wants you out of here, and I agree with him. This is no place for your kind!"

"No!" I shout. I dig my feet into the ground. For a moment, I slide along with Galban, unable to stop.

"You little fool!" Galban exclaims. "What are you thinking?"

I dodge him as he tries to get a better grip on me. "No, I'm not leaving without Taomau. Where is he? We have to help him!"

Galban's face twists with annoyance. But then his expression falls to fear.

We're surrounded. I don't even know where they came from. But all around us are soldiers in the same snail-shell armor. They carry tridents and maces.

Galban holds up his hands. "This woman is with me, under the protection of the fae and the trees. Do not harm —"

"Enough of you, fae." The leader strikes at him with his silver tipped mace.

Only the edge strikes Galban, but he flies backwards, an explosion of sparks flying from his chest. He shrinks back to his fae-size in the span of a breath, and then he vanishes.

"No!" I exclaim. "What did you do to him?"

"He's fine. His kind can't die here." The leader sets the tip of his mace against my chin. The metal buzzes with energy, stinging. "You aren't that lucky. So no trouble from you. You are summoned to the royal court."

They march me between them. The moonlight is full once again, and the entire cabin goes still. We go down three more halls, turn once to the left, twice to the right, three more times to the left, and then down another flight of stairs.

At the bottom of this staircase, it changes from the central hallway with hundreds of doors lining it to a freeform plan. This large space was a dining room of sorts. Silver moss hangs from the backs of the chairs, and ivy strangles the china.

Taomau told me not to let any of them know that I knew him. Did they hear what I said to Galban? My mind churns through this like the nausea in my stomach. Please let him be all right, I pray. Taomau has to be all right. What am I going to do?

The dining room opens up into a music room. Bizarrely discordant plucks come from the harp. One of the cleft-handed creatures hisses through its neck flap.

Past the music room, a foul odor rises, and the silver moonlight becomes more filtered and dull with yellow torchlight mingling among it. Shrieks and hoots flow from the room ahead. My heart beats faster, and my palms sweat.

Then suddenly, we're here. In the great room. The royal court of the king and queen of this ungodly place. It's more terrifying than anything I could ever imagine.

This great room is large and open with a slightly elevated dais. The couches, arm chairs, and coffee tables have all been thrust against the blackened ivy-covered walls. Torches with pale flames burn within elongated black sconces. All around the throne room skitter strange creatures and bizarre creations.

A woman without a face sits upon a couch. In her bony hands, she clutches a porcelain mask with living eyes. When those eyes see me, they narrow and redden.

A weasel with wings fastened into its back hobbles along. As we enter, it rears onto its hind legs, the leather stretched wings fluttering for a moment. It has the same bloody back as the ferrets. When he turns to scurry off, I catch sight of the bare muscle and tissue along his back as well as the raw wounds where the wings had been sewn on.

Everywhere I look there is more evidence of torture and agony. All manner of creatures, goblins perhaps, malformed monsters, who knows? They crowd around, snarling and hissing and hooting. One of the wax-skinned, cleft-handed creatures pulls at the strings of another harp. The discordant music barely rises above the chaos.

But even with all that, my attention is drawn to the dais. There is a door behind the thrones. The king sits on the throne on the left side. It has been carved from a single tree and set against a backdrop of oil-blackened tree engravings, polished so fiercely that they exude a dark light of their own. Two ravens perch upon the back of his throne, one by each of the carved serpent heads. They stare in separate directions, unmoving but for the slightest glimmer in their jet eyes.

But the king himself is even more terrifying. He has a gaunt and somber face that is both jaundiced and pale at once. Veins protrude from his hands, and his grey and amber beard is so long it has been braided and wound up over his shoulder, fastened in place with a silver serpent. Like the ravens, he stares unmoving, his left eye covered with a black metal patch. A massive black cloak encircles him.

The leader of the soldiers comes forward and bows. "We have found the last remaining human."

"At last." The king's eyes shift toward me. His gaze at once makes my skin crawl as if he is piercing into my soul and sizing it up to be butchered. "Won't my queen be pleased? She may yet win our little bet. All rise to greet her." He stands.

Two of the heralds blast upon dulled and twisted horns. The sound breaks out and silences all the chaos. Everyone stares at the second throne in anticipation.

The door behind the throne creaks open, and a woman steps out, her face at first obscured in the dim light. Her long purple gown is quite voluminous but pinched tight at the waist and dripping with silver embellishments. A silver crown sits upon her head, highlighted by the darkness of her short cut hair. She leans first to one side and then to the next, smiling demurely.

There's something familiar about her. For a moment, I feel as if I must know her. But that's ridiculous. Isn't it?

Then she looks at me. And I know her. Know those dark eyes, large and round, elongated, the length and angles exaggerated by eggplant eyeliner.

"Hello, Iscah," she says, smiling as she takes her seat. The king kisses her hand. She sits there with perfect poise and elegance. "What do you think of my cabin? Have you forgotten your troubles? It probably wasn't what you were expecting. Then again, it never is." Her smile becomes cruel. "But I would venture to say this is more or less what you deserve."

Claudia.

CHAPTER 8

I can scarcely breathe around the panic in my chest. Claudia. The woman who gave me access to the cabin. It all makes sense now. How could I have missed it before? Was I blind? I hadn't even thought about Claudia or who owned this cabin. My thoughts have been obsessed with escaping and Taomau and everything else.

Claudia smiles, pressing the edges of her gloved fingertips to her lips. The gloves she wears have silver tips on the ends, creating laced claws that go down an inch or so. "Oh come now, Iscah," she says. "Have you nothing else to say?"

I search for the words, but there's...there's... "Why?" I whisper. My voice is hoarse, it cracks. "Why did you do this?"

"Because my pet requires sorrow and grief to live, and you, dear girl, are ripe with it. But you have deeply inconvenienced me." Claudia leans back upon her throne. Her arms hang limp. "You see, it is always a bet which one of our captives will sate the anthu's appetite most. I had chosen you as the best choice, and because you were not there, I have lost."

The king chuckles. He pats her hand. "Not all is lost though."

"No." Claudia cuts her eyes back to me. "You may have failed in that regard, but you brought such superior entertainment in other ways. And you shall be rewarded."

I have no clue what she means. But the terror tightens.

The soldiers enter from a nearby room, a prisoner between them. A

CHAPTER 8

prisoner wrapped in silver chains bound so cruelly tight they are cutting into his flesh. A prisoner...my heart sinks. Taomau.

He's been beaten. Badly. The left side of his face is ragged and purple, seeping amber blood. His hands and forearms are bloodied and cut, and he limps, favoring his right leg. The instant he sees me, more pain washes over him, filling those gorgeous green eyes. His mouth is clamped shut. It seems so unnaturally tight, his breaths so shallow, that I wonder if sorcery has done it.

Oh Taomau.

I've failed again.

"Now before you deny it," Claudia says. "We know all about you two. And it was oh so very amusing. Love knows no time. It either is or it isn't." She clasps her hands in mock delight and then laughs. "And you even thinking you might love him too, you pathetic little human. Little saps the both of you. But at least you were entertaining. Though you really shouldn't think so highly of him, Iscah. His selfishness is the reason you're still here. You've been marked for the anthu. So nothing here was ever going to seriously hurt you except for it. Oh, some of the other creatures here do like to scare tidbits like you. Maybe nip at your heels. Bite off your fingers. Nothing you couldn't survive. But then he gave you that little garland there. So now not even the anthu can harm you. So truly, nothing here can harm you physically. But he still wanted his snuggles." She casts a withering look at Taomau. "If you really loved her, then you would have taken her straight to the entrance, but you never do, do you?"

Taomau avoids looking up. His cheeks appear flushed with shame. At least as flushed as they can be when he is this bloodied and beaten.

"You could have been out of here hours ago if he had been able to think of someone other than himself. But no, he had to lull you to sleep and hold you close and tell you his heart and speak his love. Oh!" She turns on Taomau. "Do you ever tire of this, you fool? How many times have you walked this path? And you know what comes next?" She's continues to look at Taomau, her eyes blazing dark and heated. She leans forward. "You'll never tire of it, will you, fool? But I'm getting tired of watching it. And now...you must be punished."

"No!" I cry. I feel like I don't understand everything she's saying. But I do know what I feel: terror, horror, pity, and fear. "Stop it. You've hurt him enough. Don't punish him for keeping me here longer."

"You think that's why he is to be punished?" Claudia exchanges a glance with the king, and then they and the court erupt in laughter.

356

"Because he was helping me then. Don't punish him for that. He did no harm," I say.

Claudia collects herself and smiles. "Oh no, my dear. He is not to be punished for helping you either. The fae do help many who come through this place. Or at least they try. Their ineptitude is always amusing. It keeps our soldiers sharp and the anthu entertained even if a few do manage to escape."

"Then what has he done wrong? Why are you punishing him? Why did you do this to him?" I cry. My voice is thick with tears and terror. I can barely look at him. The ravages of their torture is horrific.

"He broke the law," the king says.

"What law?"

"He fell in love." Claudia rises. She picks up a large silver and black scepter from beside the throne. She steps down from the dais between Taomau and me.

"You don't let people fall in love here?" I ask.

"No. Only he is forbidden from it."

"But why?"

Claudia smirks. "Because it hurts him."

"So you've beaten him because he fell in love with someone. I can't —"

"Because he fell in love with a human. More specifically you." Claudia's eyebrow arches.

My heart sinks. "I..." I don't know what to say. "He doesn't love me. No one falls in love that fast. He's just being kind. It was an act. He was only cold."

The king and queen exchange glances once more and then begin to laugh. Their voices are cold and hard, like steel knives against chalkboards.

"You do not understand how pathetic this one is," Claudia says. She strikes Taomau with the end of the scepter.

He turns his head so that only the edge grazes his face. The cut into his cheek oozes amber blood. But it's the look on his face that sears me the most. It's agony. Shame. Grief. I want to kiss those tears away and reassure him all will be well. But I don't dare move closer.

More laughter flows through this horrid court. I feel the heat of my own anger and fear. How can they be this cruel? Tears sting my eyes.

"Don't be too flattered," Claudia continues. "He falls in love at the slightest of smiles and lightest of caresses. We've had to deal with him before, but he just doesn't learn." She lashes at him again.

This time Taomau doesn't move fast enough. The blow strikes him fully. His flesh purples and yellows. He remains silent, not even crying out against the gag.

Tears blur my vision. I have to look away.

The king continues to study both Taomau and me. He fiddles with the thick silver rings on his right hand. "Taomau will rot here. He knows the punishment for his crime. But what of you?" He motions toward me with the air of one who already knows the answer. "You did not ask to be in this place. You did not ask him to fall in love with you. You did not know that love with him is forbidden. So perhaps..." The entire court leans forward in the pause, the air tightening with anticipation. "Perhaps you should be allowed a second chance."

Two faceless attendants step forward. They are both clad in the skintight wax-white garb. Not even a breath stirs within them. They carry a faded red pillow with a large silver battle-axe upon it. The pommel is the carved head of a screaming harpy, small rubies glittering in its eye sockets and jet in its mouth.

The king and queen rise. "This is a treacherous place. A young woman like yourself cannot hope to survive if you remain," the king says. As he speaks, Claudia weaves her hands through the darkness, muttering words under her breath I cannot understand. The king continues. "So if you wish to return to your world, you may do so. But you must create for yourself a bridge."

Claudia steps back. The air where she was gesturing continues to spin, darkening and shifting until it gleams like the finest polished jet. The fire-light reflects off it, and then the reflection expands. It becomes a mirror, and then it becomes a window, the reflection evaporating and the glass opening. On the other side, I see a tree. The oak from the foyer. Red-gold sap drips onto the floor. The exposed wood is a brilliant auburn red. A vague dread rises within me.

"Cut this tree down, and use the wood to build yourself a ladder. You will then be able to climb from this realm to your own," the king says.

My heart catches in my throat. The sinking sensation intensifies. I don't even reach for the axe. Everything comes clear in my mind. Now I know why he seems so familiar.

"Taomau..." When I look at him, I know for certain. "It's you. You're the spirit of the oak."

More tears roll down his cheeks, but he nods, ever so slightly.

The rest of the court erupts in harsh laughter. The sound grates in my ears, cacophonous and vulgar. I want it to stop.

The king and queen take great delight in all this. "Well, perhaps you aren't such a dullard after all," Claudia says. She sits back on her throne. As she leans back, she regards me with cold amusement. "It's unfortunate you never decided to do anything with yourself. You might have made a difference in the world. Desmond certainly would have."

"Indeed yes," the king agrees. "But now you're still here. You're yet alive." He lifts his arms as if this is something he's glad about. "Did you know that we have played this game so many times? Most of the time the woman never realizes what Taomau is until it's too late, and the other times, she doesn't care, and she tries to chop the tree down anyway." The king draws closer, an evil look in his murky brown eyes. "It's easy enough to separate the two. At least for humans. It's hard to conceive that there could be the spirit that looks and feels much like a man and yet recognize that that same spirit must have a separate physical anchor which is just as essential. Taomau is the spirit of the auburn oak. A prince once but now our lovelorn jester. One would think he might have given up, but you were so sweet and kind, pulling out the stakes, easing his pain, and sharing your own. He loves that, you know. Feeling as if he has some use beyond amusing us." More laughter and cruel jeers ripple out.

"There are no more like him in your world." The king circles closer to me, but my gaze can't rest on him. My intuition warns me to keep paying attention to Claudia. "They left long, long, long ago. Well...who knows. It's possible that some few remained. But you would know for certain if someone found one because they probably would have tried to chop one down. And do you know what happens if you try to cut, saw, or chop down a dryad's anchor? They will kill you. If you had chopped into that auburn oak, you would be bleeding out, impaled by the roots of one who claims he loves you."

Taomau turns his face away, ashamed. His shoulders slump as if the weight of the world presses down upon him.

"It's not as if he has a choice, of course," the king says. "It has been most delightful watching this play out again and again. It's almost enough punishment to make him see those he loves die because of him, but...what sort of message does it send if we do not enforce the law completely?"

Claudia continues to weave her fingers back and forth. Streams of darkness flow between them. It wavers and stretches, compresses and expands.

"Speak now, thing." The king makes a twisting motion with his hand, and Taomau's mouth is untwisted. "Have you suffered enough?"

"Do whatever you want with me," Taomau says, his voice steady and calm. "If you choose to kill me, then do it. But..."

"You aren't particularly good at this game," the king says dryly. "If you want us to spare her, you should pretend that it doesn't matter to you."

"Perhaps that's his game." Claudia strokes her cheek. "He wants us to think...no." She smiles. "He's not nearly clever enough for that."

"And he's not nearly entertaining enough to warrant such attention," the king says.

"She has survived your test." Taomau nods toward the portal. "Let her go free. The anthu needs no more sadness to sate him, and I can amuse you further. Imagine how entertaining it will be to see me grieve for someone who actually did love me and who I cannot have. Surely that would bring you much laughter."

"No," I whimper. "No. I can't leave you, Taomau. I can't leave you here."

"They're right. I did delay getting you out. I don't deserve your love. This is my lot in life. This is my life. I accept that. But it isn't your life. You don't belong here."

"Pfft." Claudia scoffs. "Let her go free?" She angles her head. "No one is ever released from this place by our accord. If the fae can save her, they may have her. If your kind wish to save her, they may have both of you. But they won't. No one has ever opened these portals to bring you home. And they never will."

"This bores me now." The king points toward me and crooks his finger forward. "You know now that chopping down a spirit tree will result in death, but did you know that these trees are not in fact immortal? You can paralyze them. The venom of our own eltrines is enough to allow us to use blades to pierce him. But those cannot kill him. Only sicken and weaken him." He picks up a torch.

My stomach knots. Something bad is about to happen. I feel it.

The entire court is watches intently, eyes glittering, claws clenching. I edge closer to Taomau.

Claudia lifts her hand. With a flick of her fingers, the chains and bonds fall from Taomau. They clatter to the ground and roll down the stairs. She then looks toward the spinning portal. The auburn oak is still on the other side. The bark starts to darken. Rain is falling on it. But from where?

The king grabs my chin. He is so close now I can smell the stink of his breath and see the yellowing of his ivory teeth. "There's only one way to kill an auburn oak and that's to burn him."

Within a blink, he flings the torch headlong through the portal. It strikes the auburn oak at the base of the trunk. With a sharp hiss that stinks of alcohol, the flames engulf the tree.

"No!" I scream.

The portal snaps shut, but the last thing I see is the blazing tree. Taomau is shrieking, writhing in agony.

The entire court is laughing. Pointing. Jeering. Mocking.

I don't know what to do. Terror grips me. Taomau's collapsing, flailing, convulsing, struggling to put out flames he cannot reach.

Lunging forward, I grab him and hold him close. He grabs onto me, screaming in pain. I don't know what to do. Don't know what to think. It's a nightmare. All I can do is hold him. As if somehow that can keep him alive. Save him. Heal him.

I don't know if it will work, but I can't let go. All I can smell is smoke and burning wood, and his screams of agony fill my ears and soul.

CHAPTER 9

It feels as if this horror goes on forever and ever. But Taomau's cries grow fainter, and the smell of smoke fades away. He at last collapses against me, limp.

I hold him to my chest, sobbing and gasping. My throat is raw, my eyes burn, and I can't let go of him.

Claudia at last stands and waves her fingers. The portal appears, opening up. There in the foyer is the auburn oak, burned almost entirely. The bark is gone, the branches withered, the floor torn up, the roots exposed. A great gaping wound lies in the heart of the tree, large enough for an adult to creep into. She smiles as if she's quite satisfied.

But I still hold Taomau in my arms. He's here. With me. Faint breaths stir from his chest.

"Taomau," I whisper. "Taomau, are you...are you..." I don't know what to ask. Is he alive? He's breathing. Is he going to be all right? His tree is dead. Is this a delay then? I don't even know what to think. His skin is blackened in some places as if by smoke and blistered in others, but it doesn't look as if he couldn't survive it. I feel so helpless. All I can do is shield him with my body.

The king rises. "I no longer find this amusing. Let's move the great room."

The many denizens of the court murmur and jeer as they finally depart. They take all but one of the torches. The night becomes closer and darker all around us.

Claudia picks up the last torch. She glides down beside me and shakes her head, her expression unbearably smug. "Oh what a shame. You only have four hours left before the full moon passes, Iscah. When the full moon's cycle ends, so does your chance to get home. And if you decide to save him, you probably won't be able to make it back in time. He will die, and you will be trapped here forever."

I jerk up, alert. "I can still save him?"

Claudia places her clawed fingers to her chest. "Isn't this delightful? You are relentless, aren't you, girl? Do you want to die? I think you must."

I clutch Taomau closer. His weak breaths wisp against my throat. "Please...tell me."

"It is possible to save him." She leans closer, the torch still in her hand. "But I'm not going to tell you how. If you want it badly enough, I'm sure you'll figure it out." Straightening, she flutters her fingers. "I'm sure we'll see you soon."

"Wait!" I reach out toward her, but my fingers grasp air. "Please!"

Claudia just laughs. "You couldn't save Desmond, and you won't be able to save Taomau. Maybe it's a good thing that soon you'll be dead." And with that, she is gone, vanishing into darkness.

My lips tremble. I cup my hand around Taomau's face, avoiding his broken and swollen left cheek and all the cuts and bruises as best I can. "Taomau, please, tell me how to save you. Taomau." I shake him as gently as I can.

It's then that I notice he's lighter. His body is not nearly as heavy as it was in the beginning, and I know what his weight should be. He's dimmer too as if he is fading. "Taomau! Please! Please if you love me, wake up and tell me how to save you."

Taomau's eyes flutter open. "Oh, sweet one," he whispers. "Please...you need to go." He tries to kiss my hand, but the motion pains him too much. His lips are cracked and bloody. "There's nothing you can do."

"No, no, she said that there was. Tell me! If you don't tell me, I'll stay here with you, and then we'll both be trapped here. Is that what you want? Is it?" I'm almost screaming now.

Taomau half-smiles. "If you had kept going, you would have —"

"I'm not leaving you behind, Taomau, and I'm certainly not leaving you here to die. Now tell me. Tell me now!"

Taomau at last nods. "Dryads can move from tree to tree. We can take physical form as I am now, but we need an anchor to survive. It can be any tree. Only a few have spirits. But there are no more trees here. If you take me to the sacred well and build me a temporary anchor, I may expend the last of my magic to call one last time to my people. This time...perhaps they will come, and if they do, they will find another anchor for my spirit."

"The sacred well. All right. Where is that?"

"On the lowest level." Taomau struggles up. His knees almost buckle, but he regains his balance, his one arm looped over my shoulders. "I shouldn't have kept you longer. I'm —"

"You don't have to apologize." I start forward. Most of his weight is on me. I don't care if he made me stay longer. I don't even want to think about it. "If they'd seen you taking me straight there, don't you think they would have intervened?"

Taomau nods wearily. His breathing is easier, and though he is far lighter than before, it is difficult to move with his body on me.

For now, there is only the sound of our own breathing and the skittering of bugs along the wall. Our footsteps seem loud, but that doesn't trouble me. Apparently nothing can hurt me here. My fear is easier to push away. All that matters is that I get to the lowest level.

Taomau struggles to make his legs move faster. "Promise me," he says, his voice tight. "Promise me that you'll run as fast as you can to the doorway. It will take you..." He gasps in another breath. "It will take you..."

"As soon as you're safe, I'll go." We are at a staircase now. I remember what Galban said. Don't touch the walls. Whatever is alive in them, I don't even want to imagine.

I grip the banister with one arm and ease us both down as quickly as we safely can. Taomau slides along with me. We can't rush it, or we'll crash down. Then where will we be? The rot makes the stairs so slick.

We move along as one, hitching and halting every few paces. The silence is painful. I want to fill it. "I don't mean this to sound bad," I say. "But...why don't you have burns on you? Your tree was destroyed."

"It doesn't work quite that way." Taomau winces. His gasps are coming faster now as if he's struggling to breathe. "I'm...I'm drawing from you. I'm sorry. I had to let go of the tree or it would have destroyed me. I felt it die, but it did not take me with it."

"You're drawing from me?"

"Your air. Yes. If I let go of you before the anchor is made, I will die." Taomau nods. "Forgive me."

"No. It's fine. It's not hurting me at all. But why are you gasping?" We are almost to the bottom of the stairs now. Two of the cleft-handed creatures stare at us. They jostle and chuckle before disappearing into a darkened room.

"I don't want to burden you, and even so you breathe so small. I had thousands of leaves. And I've been cut off from my reserves." Taomau places his hand on his heart.

We reach the bottom of the staircase. "If you die before we get there, what good is this?" I demand. I turn him to face me. "Take more air if you need it. I'll breathe for both of us."

He doesn't argue this time. Instead, he places both hands onto my neck, his palms and fingers sliding up along my face. Then he draws in a deep, deep breath.

All the air pulls from my lungs. My head spins, and for a moment, I am gasping as if I have held my breath beyond my natural capacity. But then he releases me, and I gulp in deep breaths.

"You're all right?" he asks, still leaning against me.

"Yes, yes, we can do this!" The room is still spinning a little, but it eases as I loop my arm around his neck and carry him farther.

And so we go. A little faster after he breathes, gradually slowing until the next breath. Sometimes my lungs feel as if they're going to burst. And still the seconds tick by. I don't know how to calculate time in this place. It's bizarre and unmanageable. But even this workaround that we have found is not working entirely. Though Taomau stops gasping as much and his breaths come easier, he is still lighter. He is fading even in my arms.

Nothing disturbs us as we make our way down the final staircase. We're running out of time. I feel it in my soul. I want to ask him how long he has left. But that seems like it would only make time vanish faster.

This staircase is longer than the others. It curves around and around and down into ever growing darkness. I'm afraid I soon won't be able to see at all, but as we keep going down, I find there's enough light.

Taomau sags against me again. "Hang on. We're almost there." I don't know that, but we have to be. "Hang on. Stay with me, Taomau."

His foot buckles. We almost fall, but I catch myself on the banister. It digs painfully into my wrist. We're still standing though.

"Taomau." I kiss his forehead. "Come on. We're almost there."

He nods numbly.

The air smells different down here, heavier and yet sweeter as if it has been perfumed. I hear running water. That's a good sign. That must be the sacred well. "What makes the clay and the water here so special?" I ask. My own mouth is dry, and the thought of water increases my thirst.

"It's connected to the other realms. Realms of life and hope," Taomau mumbles. His grip on me slackens. Then his legs collapse.

"Taomau!" I can't hold onto the staircase this time. We crash down the rest of the stairs, rolling and cracking against each stair. Somehow we hold onto one another. Aching spasms run along my back and ribs as I finally sit up, Taomau's hand tight in mine.

We're here. This has to be it. A broad river cuts across the floor lined with thick slabs of pale clay. They almost look as if they are waiting to be carved. The waters glow pale silver with undercurrents of gold, bubbling up from a circular well made from polished opals. "We made it, Taomau," I say. "We're here!" Hope floods my heart. We can make it.

There's no response.

I turn.

Taomau lies motionless, his face ashen, his hand cooling. "Taomau. Taomau!" I shake him, but he does not respond.

I can't give up on him. Not now. Grabbing him by the shoulders, I carry him to the river. He weighs next to nothing now. The cool waters slosh against me as I step in. There's no current to uproot me, and as soon as Taomau is mostly in, I grab his hands, thrust them against my neck, position his fingers as he set them, and give him my breath.

It works. But this time, there's only a faint gasp. His eyes open. He blinks. "Iscah..."

"Drink this." I cup the water in my hand and pour it into his parched mouth. Only a little bit at a time. I don't know if he can drown.

His face brightens but only a little, and he is still so light that any breeze might blow him away. "There isn't time." He swallows hard. "Go. I can —" He waves his hand.

"No." He'll die if I let go. I grab one of the blocks of clay with my free hand and draw it closer. "What does an anchor look like?"

Taomau leans over the clay. As the water sloshes against it, it softens. He pushes it weakly onto the bank and then begins carving with one hand. He's good. Better than I am with both hands. There's no more talking now. No more time. The clay slides beneath his hand, I remain at his side, helpless except to pull him along and pull up more clay when it's needed.

Slowly, too slowly for my liking, a form appears in the clay. I recognize his face and his eyes. Everything. It's him. The carved anchor looks precisely like him. He is incredible.

The sculpted figure soon rests beside the river, arms crossed over his chest. I don't like that he has carved himself this way. It looks like a funeral bier. But it's done. There's no time to suggest another form. Tears well up in my eyes. This is it.

Taomau stands shakily and slides his hands along my cheeks. "Don't forget me, sweet one," he says, his forehead pressed to mine.

I burst into tears. There's no time. I know it. But I can't help it. I don't want him to go, but he must. "I love you."

"I love you too, Iscah." He kisses me again. I feel the cold as soon as he pulls back.

Holding onto my hand, he steps into the living clay. His legs disappear in it. He's so weak, but he kisses my hand, caressing it once more. "I don't know if they will come," he says. "They haven't before, but in these last moments, it's said that our souls cry out the loudest. Maybe this time they will hear me."

"They will. They have to."

"Regardless...thank you." He leans forward to kiss me, and I cling to him this time. I can't let go. I have to. I don't want to. He's so frail in my arms now. Like a dream that's fading fast. His lips linger on mine. I pull back all at once, the taste of my own tears in my mouth. "Please live."

"If I can dream, I will dream of you, sweet one," Taomau says. He lies down on the anchor; his coloring and form merge with it.

My heart is breaking now. I cover my mouth, struggling to hold back the sobs, but I can't. They tear out of me. "And I will dream of you," I sob.

He smiles. His eyes close, and he releases my hand.

"Taomau?" I whisper. I search for some sign that his people have heard him. The waters continue to swirl and play along the banks, so quiet and soothing, unaware of our grief. There is only darkness and the water's glow. "Taomau?" I look at him. He isn't breathing. He isn't moving. I bend over him, but something rustles against my chest. I look down.

The garland of hair around my neck has turned to leaves.

CHAPTER 10

I stare at the leaves in horror. More tears come. No. Taomau's people have to hear his last call.

"Please!" I shout. "Please. Wherever you are, please!" Tears roll from my eyes onto Taomau. He looks as if he could wake at any moment. The wounds are gone. He's whole. But there's no breath.

I curl against him, resting my head on his chest. I've never heard such emptiness as the silence of his heart. "I can't lose you like this, Taomau," I sob. "Please, don't die. You can't be left behind. You can't stay here."

Suddenly a soft golden green light reaches my eyes. I sit up, tears streaming down my cheeks.

A small beam of light is opening. It expands with each breath, the circle widening until it is a shimmering golden portal in the base of the nearest wall. The scent of flowers and fresh air flows through, warm and refreshing. Cherry blossoms, orange flowers, apple blossoms, violets, and roses, lily-of-the-valley and honeysuckle. Through the golden portal, I can see the outlines of a great forest.

Four wolves stride through. They are even larger than timber wolves, but their fur is green and looks more like long grass than fur. Small white and blue flowers grow at intervals along their bodies. Flowers and clovers blossom beneath their feet with each step, and their faces are wise and intelligent.

They go to Taomau at once. The largest of the wolves nudges his arm and whines faintly. "We are too late," he says.

"No, please, don't say that. He's here. This is the living clay. You're here. Take him home!" I cover my mouth.

"His life has all but passed. We will bear his body back to his people, but by the time we cross the portal, all that remains of him will be gone." The lead wolf bows his head, and the others follow suit. Then, as if on some hidden signal, they throw their heads back and howl. It's the saddest sound I've ever heard. The plaintive wail of rescuers come too late.

"There has to be something you can do."

"We lack such healing powers in this place," the leader says. His tail hangs low, tucked between his legs, his ears drooping. "Your sorrow is ours."

A faint glimmer catches my eye. Looking down, I realize that there is still light gleaming in the leaves. They are tinged in gold that radiates along their edges and up their stems and branches. The magic lives. "Wait. What about this? He gave this to me. Will this help?" I lift it from my neck.

The wolves exchange glances. The leader nods slowly. "It might. But we'll have to move swiftly. Put him on our backs." The four wolves arrange themselves in pairs, standing close together, forming a living bier.

Taomau is so light now that it is no trouble to lift him. He is like air in my arms even with the living clay.

Once he is on their backs, I kiss his forehead and slip the garland from my neck. "Live, Taomau," I whisper. "Just live."

"I wish that we could take you with us," the lead wolf says. "But you are not of our kind and the portal will not permit you through."

I shake my head. It doesn't matter. This is where I belong anyway. "Just go."

The wolves bow their heads to me. And then they leave. Working as one, they carry him away into the green-gold light. Flowers and grass sprout beneath their feet and fade within moments of their passing.

I watch, heart still breaking but hoping. My gaze is focused on Taomau.

Wait.

Is that imagination? His chest? Did it stir? My heart catches in my throat. It was probably my imagination. I half expect him to sit up or open his eyes. Anything clear. But no.

The portal closes then. The green-gold light vanishes, and all is dim and dull again. Even the running waters of the sacred well are nothing. I am rooted to this spot, strengthless, weary, exhausted.

"So passes the auburn oak, prince of the dryads. At least that is what they might have said if he had not wandered off when he was so young. His people remember him as nothing more than a warning for other saplings. Those little leaves will do him no good. They only accepted them to placate a foolish human child."

The voice speaks behind me. Cold hands fold across my shoulders. My heart freezes and chills beneath the grasp. The king.

Claudia laughs behind me. "This is even better than I expected."

"His chest stirred," I say, my voice hoarse. "He's going to make it."

"I'm afraid not," the king says. "And you can trust that I would tell you. It would be so much more fun to let you rot here knowing that he had escaped and was never coming back for you."

I choke back more tears. Enough of all this crying. Taomau might live. But my heart says otherwise. I know what I wanted to see, and I know what I saw. Just the wind. He is gone. I've lost him too.

"You will be forgotten by your kind as well, human child," the king whispers. As he leans closer, his rank breath prickles against my ear and neck. "But do not fear. I have not forgotten you and neither has the spirit of my realm. At least in the end, you will serve some purpose."

Suddenly I smell something horribly familiar. I lift my head and find myself staring into the fiery eyes of the anthu. It glowers at me, drawing closer. Its aura expands. I can almost feel it touching me.

"Aren't you going to run, dear?" Claudia asks. "You might make it if you hurry. The portal to your world hasn't closed yet."

The anthu is only a few feet away. I know how fast it can move, this is only a game. A game I won't play. I'm too tired. Now I understand what the old man with the cane saw when he looked into the anthu's eyes and waited for it.

"No," I say. My heart quails with fear, but my body won't respond. I am motionless because I have nothing left.

The anthu snarls. It lifts its massive paw. The three long claws glisten. I don't look away. In this, I will be brave.

The great paw slashes down at me. I feel a great force against my body, and then I sink into darkness.

CHAPTER 11

I wake in darkness. Am I dead? I'm lying in some sort of thick liquid that smells like tar but feels more like...sticky, watery oatmeal. What — what is this? Did the anthu eat me? I am dead...

No, no. I quell the panic rising inside me. That's not it. It can't be. There's some other answer. The anthu wasn't this big, and what sort of afterlife would this be?

All my senses work. It's dark, but my eyes are slowly adjusting. Quiet sobs and soft wails rise around me.

Lifting my arm, I feel this substance pull at me. It's not letting me move easily, but ugh!

With great effort, I sit up.

Small dots of light dart about. There are six of us down here in the muck, waiting. Waiting for death most likely. I don't know how, only that it will come. Where did the anthu go? I can't imagine why it would leave us now unless that's part of its sick game. Maybe this is like a larder. It's dropped us here until it's hungry again.

I feel a dull satisfaction amid the fear in realizing I was right about myself. Some part of me always knew I would wind up in a place like this. Dark. Dank. Dire. It's as if the place I most deserve has been made for me.

If only death would come...

Whoa...I slide farther down into the mire. No, no. I flail my arms, whimpering. It isn't any good. Maybe I should die, but I don't want to go like this.

My wet hair clings to my back. The cold liquid squelches and tugs at me, but once again it stops.

Ok. No struggling. Apparently that's the key.

One of the green lights zips toward me. I recognize it, both surprised and a little ashamed. Galban.

Galban lands on my forehead. The faint glow that radiates from him highlights his square jaw and his bright purple eyes. He looks both stern and sad at once. "So you wound up here anyway?" His eyes become more sad than angry. His voice softens. "Do you even want to live, human child?"

Those words roll over me. I want to say yes, but...

"What's going to happen here? Can you get me out?" I ask. My voice comes in faint gasps. I've cried too long, and it's the hiccupping staggered breaths of someone who is out of strength.

"This is where the anthu drags its victims. It will return when it is hungry. I can't free you from here, and the incantation that the king and queen have placed on this wretched den of suffering prevents me from speaking plainly. So I am forced to use riddles. We all are."

"What's the riddle?" I ask.

"Remember everything that we have told you here and remember what the mushrooms said."

"Everything the mushrooms said? That's not a good riddle. What kind of riddle is that? That's not good at all."

"No, but we're running out of time. And it's the best we can do to go against the spells restricting our speech. The anthu is coming back soon. You still have time to get out of here. Once you're out of this, you must run up the stairs and keep turning to the right no matter how many halls open. Keep going until you see the foyer. But you must be there before the clock strikes midnight. The portal closes then, and we fae will be sent back to our realm, and you will be trapped here."

Galban flies up.

I can hear the bell-like voices of the other fae now. "Remember what the mushrooms said."

This is stupid. We're running out of time.

"You can get out," Galban says, darting down near my ear. "But you have to do it yourself."

This isn't making sense. It agitates me, welling up in my stomach, knotting inside me.

A shrieking wail vibrates through the chamber. Galban is knocked away. The other lights tumble aside. They vanish.

The anthu is coming. All right. Think, Iscah! What did the mushrooms say?

It was something about not having sorrow and sadness or otherwise staying forever. Something...I hadn't paid that much attention.

One of my fellow prisoners is sobbing. Her mournful cries mirror my own. "It's all his fault. If he hadn't been so selfish, I wouldn't be here."

Her outline sinks lower.

An idea pierces through the sludge in my mind. I sank when I was thinking about what I deserved. Could it be possible that these aren't coincidences?

I don't want to die.

There.

Breath clenched, I wait.

Nothing.

It figures. It really is my own fault I'm here. It's what I deserve.

Bloop. Bloop.

Down I sink, a little farther.

What the heck?

"I want to live." I say it out loud, softly at first. Then louder. Nothing. What is this?

The wailing snarl comes again. It screeches through the cavern and bounces off the rock walls.

The little lights return, pale purple and green.

I'm going to die here. I don't want to. I really don't. But...what's to be done...

I'm not sure how much fight is left in me. This cold muck holds me fast, and my very soul feels as if it is weighted down. There were so many things that I wanted to do. I wish...oh so much.

My thoughts drift all the way back to my uncle. I wish I could tell him I forgave him for leaving and not telling us. His landlord found a letter from him and forwarded it to me a few years ago. He said that he was so sorry. I don't hold it against him now. I forgive him for leaving —

Suddenly I'm moving forward. The muck sloshes back, and I am no longer trapped so deep!

In fact, I can even see the faint outline of a stone bank.

Sorrow. That's what the mushrooms said. But what makes me sad? Loss. Cruelty. Abandonment. I wrack my brain to try to put this together.

The fae zip down. They're continuing with their little chants, encouraging and calling.

We're running out of time. The portal will close soon. If we don't get out here in the next few minutes, we might as well never escape.

"I forgive Mal for leaving me," I say. Forward I lurch again. Yes! It's forgiveness. It's releasing the burdens of the soul.

"Yes, yes," Galban says, his voice brightening with excitement. "That's it."

"We have to forgive and release the sorrow," I call out.

"What do you mean?" a man shouts back.

"Whatever brought you here, whatever reason you're grieving, you have to forgive whoever did that to you and move on. Forgive everything!" I can say it even if the fae cannot. Their choruses of "yes" spur me on.

There are so many people to forgive. So many things I need to release. I start running through them all, listing the names and the offenses. It's not hard for me to think of those people I need to forgive. There's a lot of them. I'm desperate enough that it isn't hard to release them. Mona, Mik, TJ, Lydia, Rick...the list goes on.

My fellow prisoners are desperate to escape as well. They don't argue. The sloshing sucking of the escape from the mire continues amid declarations of release and forgiveness.

Suddenly the anthu appears. It lunges down, snaps up one of the prisoners, and disappears again. A sickening scream and crunch follow.

I gasp. I didn't even see it coming. It's too late for whoever that was. But there isn't even time to think about that.

The mother and her teenage daughter are almost to shore. The mother is now clambering out. Muck streams from her, but the daughter isn't moving anymore.

Her mother reaches out toward her. "Come on, sweetie," she says.

"I can't."

Her mother clambers back into the muck. She's starting to sink as well as the guilt reclaims her, but she flounders deeper and embraces her daughter.

Another distant roar sounds. The anthu must be nearly finished. That sounds like a warning. Does it know we're trying to escape?

The teenager is crying now. She's sinking farther down, her hand outstretched, her fingers twitching. "I'm sorry. I'm sorry!"

"Baby, it wasn't your fault. It wasn't your fault. Just say you forgive yourself. Please, baby. Maybe that's enough."

The teenager is blubbering. "But it was my fault. You loved each other before you had me. I was too —"

"No, no."

They're both sinking. And it hits me. "You have to forgive yourself," I call out. "Even if everyone knows it isn't your fault, you have to forgive yourself."

"I forgive myself for ruining your marriage," the daughter whispers.

The muck lurches and thrusts her forward. She's out! Her mother cries out with joy and says something I can't quite hear. Then she too escapes. They are in each other's arms, weeping and clinging.

The others in the cavern are making their way along. Half murmured whispers and cringing statements, slipping along. The mother and daughter run to the edge of the muck. "Come on. Hurry up," they call out. A man joins them. Then another woman in a thick coat.

The shore is only a few feet away. But I can't reach the outstretched arms of the others. I'm not moving any more. I wrack my brain. "I forgive Sasha for stabbing me in the back at the sweetheart dance."

I don't move.

Obviously that guilt or burden isn't holding me here.

There is one thing...

My mind returns to that night on the road...Desmond hanging from his seat, trapped...the flames creeping along the ground. They're moving toward him faster and faster. I have to save him. Need to. But I can't...I didn't do enough.

The muck rises around me. It's not stopping this time. My chest is crushed beneath the weight of this agony.

Galban lands on my forehead. "Come on, Iscah. You have to do this! You know what to do. You told them what it was."

"I forgive..." How can I say it?

I hear my friends' voices in my head. See the flames again. Smell the smoke and burning flesh. Oh the voices...

"How can you live with yourself?"

"It's the least you can do."

"He had his whole future ahead of him. What're you doing with yours?"

I'm sinking. The cold sucking muck pulls me back to the moment.

The anthu reenters the chamber. It creeps along the ceiling. Pebbles and silt pelt down.

Is this it? Is this what I want? No! But I can't — I can't move.

"Just do it!" the man in the sky-blue jacket calls out.

The others are clambering out as well.

"Just say the words."

Galban swoops down over my face. "You have seconds, Iscah. Seconds!"

Is this what I want? To die here. No! No. And I won't. I force the words up, my throat knotting with tears. "I forgive myself for not saving Desmond."

There's a great popping and lurching. Suddenly, I'm at the shore.

Galban returns to his human size. He grabs me around the waist and tugs me forward. The other escapees, the mom, the daughter, the man in the sky-blue jacket, the woman in the puffy coat, they all seize my arms, and pull.

The muck gives one more sickening squelch, and suddenly I'm loose.

The anthu roars. It lunges forward from its perch on the roof.

Galban strikes up a light in his hand and points ahead. "Run!"

There's a small doorway that cuts up a long staircase. We run toward it.

It's so dark that we can scarcely see anything. It's more movement and sensation than anything. I'm in the back. Galban runs alongside me.

The other fae dart in and out, shimmering and glowing. One flies to the front of the group. With all of the fae working together, there is enough light that we barely stumble as we race forward.

The entire cabin is alive now. The ivy and plants along the walls rustle. Beetles and spiders scurry out of the way. Cold air flushes down the stairs. The *tramp tramp* of our feet as we race ever upwards.

Suddenly a clock rings out. The great bong vibrates through me.

One...

Galban's face pales. "Keep going!"

We round the corner.

The plants are blackening and withering.

Two...

The teenager slides on the mushy floor. The man in the sky-blue jacket drags her up. Her mother grabs her arm. They keep running.

Three...

We're running down a single hallway now. A cleft-handed creature staggers out. We pummel past it.

Four...

Another turn to the right. More hallway! Where's the foyer? All of the plants are dying. Whatever insects and spiders are caught in the dying plants drop dead as well, legs twitching, bodies spasming.

Five...

"Galban, how much farther?"

Six...

It's darkening yet again. The moonlight is fading. The fae light dims too.

Seven...

"If you're not there before the portal closes —" Galban starts.

Eight...

"You can't go through —"

We turn right again.

Nine...

"Or else you'll die!"

We round the next corner. The foyer! It's wide open now, covered in ash-colored sand. Two stone sphinxes stand where the doors stood once. A narrow stone bridge now lies between them.

Ten...

"Faster!" the fae shout.

My chest aches, my lungs burn. I will myself to move faster. We're so close! The mother and teenager are almost at the threshold.

Eleven...

My feet strike the base of the narrow stone bridge.

Twelve...

The lights vanish, the fae disappear. All becomes silent. We halt.

Everything is dead in this place. It is all shades of black, charcoal, ash, and salt.

"What's happened?" the mother asks.

The man in the sky-blue jacket adjusts his sleeve. He looks faded, weary, and pale. Sniffing, he nods toward the sphinxes. "Home's on the other side of that."

"But the fae said not to cross it." The woman who I met in the foyer, the one in the puffy coat with the snarky attitude, she's standing at the edge of the bridge. "If we cross it, our bodies have to catch up with time."

"So what do we do?" the teenager asks. Her voice hiccups with strangled sobs. "Are we going to die?"

Her mother holds her close, shushing her. "It's going to be fine."

That's a lie. But the woman in the puffy coat continues. "We either risk it now or we wait until the next full moon when it opens again. That's what they said anyway."

"We can't wait that long. Look at this place!" the mother exclaims. "And if those things find us again..."

"Then we'd best go now," the man says. He points at the bridge. "If time catches up with us, then we need to go as fast as we can. Otherwise..."

We can see our world on the other side of the sphinxes.

"No." I shake my head. I didn't listen to the fae for most of the time I was here, and I had made things significantly more complicated. "No, we have to stay here. We might be able to make it. Time passes differently here. The last thing Galban said was not to cross it..."

The argument is becoming heated. It almost feels hopeless. My head aches, and I shiver.

"There's nothing to eat or drink here. Even if it takes one week for the next full moon because time is different in this place, we'll all be dead," the mother says.

"Yeah," the man in the sky-blue jacket nods. "Assuming there's nothing else here."

"We shouldn't." I cross my arms, struggling to get control of my emotions. "The fae have been right about everything, and they have been trying to save us. If it was certain death, Galban wouldn't have said for us to stay back."

But it's as if my words are not even spoken. No matter what I say, there's always another argument. And soon even the woman with the puffy coat has been persuaded that this is the only way.

They edge toward the bridge. It all looks so welcoming. The snow glistens on the other side of the opening. The trees cast faint shadows on the snow. Just a few dozen yards and then escape.

"Listen," the man says. "I'll go first. See if it's safe."

No one argues.

He steps up to the sphinxes. They are massive, becoming larger and larger as he draws near. And when he is between them, their eyes glow gold.

"Do you wish to pass?" they ask in a single voice. It is feminine and masculine at once, organic and mechanical.

"Yes." The man tightens his grip on his arm. "Please let me pass."

Our little group draws closer.

The eyes of the sphinxes intensify. "If you wish to leave, then so be it. But the consequences are upon your own head."

His face is sweating. The beads slide through the muck and mire. But he steps through. He crosses to the other side. Soon he's making footprints in the crisp fresh-fallen snow. "I'm through!" he shouts. "It's fine. I'm fine!"

I frown, surprised and relieved at once. What was Galban talking about then? Is it possible that there is some little bit of overlap? A sort of grace period? Taomau had been certain on this point as well. I don't understand how this is possible.

But the rest of the group is cheering with excitement. They cross over the bridge one by one. At last I am alone with the woman in the puffy coat.

"You should come," she says, her arms folded tight over her chest. "You won't survive here if you stay."

It's tempting. I want...I don't know...but deep down I can't shake the feeling that Galban is right. "I don't think we should. Galban is a fae. He knows the way this works. He's been trying to save us all this time. I can't believe he'd get something like this wrong. He was right about everything else. I...I can't."

"Suit yourself. I don't see anything dangerous out there. Certainly nothing worse than what's in here."

And that's it. She turns and crosses the bridge. Follows the same pattern as all the others.

Soon they're all together on the other side, and it's just me standing here in the darkness.

It's all right though. I hope for their sakes there's nothing wrong. But I have to stay.

Now that they are all together, they head toward the cars. I may even be able to see them walk away.

They reach the circle of mushrooms. The broad silver and gold caps are still free of all snow and frost. Almost at the same time, they step over.

A sharp wind strikes up. The snow swirls up around them with glinting silver dust. I hear groans and screams from the other side. What's happening?

My heart chills with horror. When the snow subsides, only the teenager and the woman in the puffy coat are standing there. And both of them are aged women, stooped and staggering. The others are no more than piles of dust.

I stare in horror, my mouth half-open. They're dead. Gone. Turned to dust.

The teenager and the woman in the puffy coat sob and pull at the piles of dust. They tug at their wrinkled flesh and now arthritic limbs, but it does no good. Time has passed indeed, and it has not been kind.

I turn my face away, clenching my eyes shut to block the image. All of their struggles were for nothing. I don't think I can even cry anymore. When I look up again, they are gone, and I am truly alone.

A faint growl sounds behind me. No…

CHAPTER 12

Slowly I turn, my heart hammering. Whatever it is, it cannot be worse than what has happened already.

The anthu. It stands beneath the archway, its fiery eyes glowing. Its aura stretches forward.

"What do you want?" I demand. "Isn't this enough for you? All of the tragedy and sorrow you have feasted on?" Sorrow fills my heart, and it weighs me down, but thankfully I don't feel guilty.

The anthu draws closer. I can smell its stench, see the wisping of its breath against the fine fur that covers its too-small head.

Where else can I run now? I stand my ground.

The anthu lifts its paw. The three long claws gleam over me. Then, down...

Nothing.

I look up.

The anthu stands before me still, its paw against its chest as if it struck me. It strikes again, but its paw passes through me. With a pathetic whimper, it twists its head to the side.

I understand. "You're a sad creature," I say. "But there is nothing left in me for you."

Then, like a shadow, the anthu vanishes.

Now I am truly alone. I turn to take in my surroundings. Who knows how long I will be here?

My heart staggers in my chest as I catch sight of something familiar.

The auburn oak. Taomau's former spirit anchor.

All that remains are blackened and gnarled branches and a half hollowed trunk. The roots are free of the floor, stretching up and out, reaching ever outward as if to some healing rest.

Tears prick my eyes. Apparently I can still cry. Oh Taomau. I wish you were alive. I wish so much...I miss you.

Reaching out, I place my hand upon the broken and charred trunk. Flecks of ash and soot rise and fall around it as if a wind I can neither see nor feel carries them in a constant current. The presence of his tree breaks my heart and soul in two. I lean against his trunk sorrowfully and let the tears roll down my cheeks.

TIME PASSES STRANGELY HERE. It feels as if it does not pass at all.

Everything is dead now. The ivies. The grass. The moss. The waters have dried up. The king and queen and their great room is gone as well.

Occasionally the anthu returns. It stalks about the ceiling and slides up behind me. But it cannot take me now.

Sometimes it sits beside me on the staircase or by the charred remains of Taomau's tree. I think it is as lonely as me. But it never stays. It always leaves.

I miss sunlight. I miss sitting outside with my eyes closed and that brilliant hot orange warmth against my eyelids. The longer I am here, the more distant my old life feels. Like a dream. An imagining meant to somehow comfort me.

There's no sky. I'm desperate for sky. Any sky will do. Heavy cobalt with thick marshmallow clouds. Pale watery blue with hints of grey. Even doom inspiring grey with massive swathes of angry thunderheads.

But there's nothing to be done. Sometimes I wander the halls, but I always return to Taomau's tree.

The paintings bring me some small comfort. When I look into them, sometimes I see beautiful images. Other times I see into the cabin as it once was or perhaps will be. One time when I looked through I saw a woman who looked just like me, staring inwards with sad eyes, tear crusted cheeks, her lips pressed in a straight line. Then I gasped and remembered it was me. I remembered the painting with the odd young woman. It was me. I watched myself dart away and wished I could call out to myself.

But what would I say?

I'm weary, cold, hungry, and thirsty. If only I could find that magical painting with the woman entering the forest, the sunlight glimmering on her thick dark hair, the long yellow train trailing behind her.

Perhaps that is what that fellow who died staring into the painting found. The perfect painting that captured his hope. A way to pass his final hours more pleasantly.

But search as I might, I cannot find it again. The paintings seem to rotate at random throughout the cabin. The ghouls and other atrocious beasts that inhabit some of the other paintings mock and point with silent cruelty, but they no longer bother me. Only time can harm me here.

It pains me to see more people entering the cabin. I see them through the paintings in brief moments of lucidity. They carry suitcases and trunks, backpacks and briefcases, their chest stuffed with sorrow and their souls burdened with guilt. Maybe these are past guests, maybe they are new. There's no way to tell.

I try to write warnings on the anthu's cavern walls and every other place I can. But something washes them away most times. The words "guilt" and "forgive" fade fastest of all. I hope a few will remain.

I have not seen Claudia or the king again. Perhaps they resent the fact that I live. More likely I hold no more entertainment for them. There isn't even the trace of chaos or a single back-wounded ferret or cleft-handed monster creeping about. Only the anthu and the paintings.

HUNGER PANGS COME in waves throughout the day — stronger, then weaker before fading to a dull empty ache and rising to a cavernous gnawing. It's bearable. At least more so than the thirst. That is constant. My tongue is thick, my throat dry, my lips cracked. It's almost enough to make me insane.

It's so cold. Shivering, I nestle into the hollow of the burned auburn oak. My mind drifts back to memories of Taomau holding me, his strong arms wrapped about me, keeping me safe and warm, his lips pressed to mine, his fingers in my hair.

I don't think I can hold on much longer. My fingertips are blue and white. My head spins if I move too fast, and all I want to do is lie here. Maybe if I don't move it will pass.

So this is what it all came to? What will happen to my friends? They'll continue with their lives. Desmond will continue on in memory, and I'll be forgotten. The curse on the fairy ring is true after all, but at least I am not devoured. My friends will —

Friends? No. They aren't that. Not anymore. I close my eyes. I don't want to go back to them anyway. And Desmond is in a better place now. If I could choose one person to be with right now, it would be Taomau.

Oh Taomau...I miss you.

If I don't breathe so deeply, it's easier to stay warm. It's funny. I wanted so much for the shadows and oblivion to swallow me up, and now it seems like it will. The darkness is deepening. The world, even the ground beneath me and the wood beneath my fingers, feels distant. Like I'm sliding into darkness.

Suddenly warm light shines on my face. It doesn't hurt, it pours into my cracking skin and aching soul.

"Are you sleeping, sweet one?" a familiar voice asks.

Slowly I open my eyes, confusion ruffling the edges of my mind. "Taomau?"

Taomau stands in front of me. He's whole, full color restored to his cheeks, the brightness returned to his eyes. He smiles. "Were you dreaming of me, sweet one?"

"I thought...I was afraid you were dead." Tears sting my eyes as I struggle to sit up. "Taomau..." They flow freely down my cheeks. Everything has dimmed except that which is in the path of the light. "You're...you're really alive?"

"More now than I have ever been. The magic you gave me was enough. I am alive thanks to you." Taomau holds out his hand. "Will you come with me, Iscah?"

"To where?"

"Home."

"My home isn't yours."

"It could be, darling. Just come with me." He leans lower, his hand inches from mine. "Take my hand."

I blink. The dullness remains in my mind. It's as if I'm still half-asleep. "I thought...I thought that the portal only worked for your kind...that...I couldn't..." Why is it so hard to speak? To think?

"Shhh." He crouches. His eyes are so gentle. It comforts me to look at him. "It's all right, Iscah. But this is a special portal, and I am stronger now. I have opened this one for you."

"How did you know I was here?"

"I just did."

I find myself smiling. There are still questions, but my eyes are fastened on his, and I know in my soul it's him. It's all right.

Reaching out, I slide my hand into his. His grasp becomes warm and tight as he lifts me to my feet. The heaviness and cold falls away.

"Are you frightened, Iscah?" he asks, staring down into my eyes. His arms are around my waist, holding me close.

"No." There's no more fear. No more pain. No more cold. Just beautiful elation.

"Then let's go." He kisses me softly on the forehead and together we walk into the soft golden light.

CHAPTER 13

The golden light encompasses us as we step into it. It's almost too bright to see and yet it does not hurt. All I know for certain is that Taomau is holding me and I him.

A few steps in though and I hear birdsong. It's light and delicate, a dozen or so gentle tunes floating through the wind. That soft fragrant scent of all manner of flowers and blossoms reaches me once again. Life fills my lungs, and the warmth reaches to my deepest core.

Vaguely I see forms, great trees surround us. We are walking down a path through a forest of all manner of trees. The path is soft and clear, a light chestnut brown with delicate velvet-petaled flowers and quad-leafed clovers. Wrens and orioles swoop about us. And there are people...no...tree spirits? All the light is soft and gold.

They are like Taomau, tall and slender with faces and manners so close to humans and yet so distinct. My heart beats faster, and I look about with increasing curiosity.

These men and women all look at us with delight shining in their faces. Some murmur and whisper to each other. I can't hear what they're saying, but my cheeks warm as if I am blushing.

"What is this?" I ask Taomau.

"You'll see." He smiles and nods his head forward as if to give me a clue.

Before I could not see what was directly ahead because the light was too strong, it was simply a gold mass. But now, it is lessening...or perhaps my eyes are adjusting. There is a man and a woman there. They have a wildness and a nobility about them that takes my breath away and there is something exceptionally familiar in their faces and in their bearing.

I almost feel underdressed. But as I glance down at myself, expecting to feel shame, I realize that no longer wear the ragged, muck soaked garments as before. Somehow my clothing has been transformed. My body is clean, my hands no longer bloodied and mud stained. I wear a long yellow gown with a tapered waistline and loose flowing skirt that trails in the back, leaving my bare feet free and cool. I look as if I belong here.

The woman steps forward. She could not be more stunning if she had been painted. Her thick loose auburn curls coil about her bared shoulders, and her lavender gown flows about her with great elegance and ease. There are crow's feet around her eyes and small lines upon her forehead, and small strands of silver streak her hair. But her eyes are what stop me. They are similar to Taomau's. Green but with flecks of gold and blue about the pupil.

I inhale sharply, realizing who she is, who the man is.

"Is this her, my son?" Taomau's mother asks. "Is this the one who sent you back to us after all these years?"

"This is she." Taomau says. "Her name is Iscah." He kisses my fingertips. "The portal to her realm has closed, and she cannot remain there any longer. I know that it is not our custom to allow those who are not our kind to live in our world, but, after all that has happened, I believe that an exception can be made."

The queen of the trees looks at me and then to the king. He inclines his head forward ever so slightly. "Do you wish to remain here, child?" the queen asks. "Would you not be happier with your own kind?"

"No." I shake my head.

"And what of those who will be captured in this land between the realms where the anthu stalks?" she asks. "More prisoners will be taken. Are you willing to leave that place now?"

For a moment, I hesitate. The impulse returns. Taomau's grip tightens on my hand. I duck my head slightly. Galban and the fae will return. I have carved what warnings I can into the walls and on the floor. My part is finished. I can accept that. I am at peace. "Yes...I have done all I can."

Taomau breathes with relief. And even his parents smile.

"Then consider this your home," the queen says.

The king lifts his arms. "And let our celebration begin, for on this day our son and more have been returned to us."

The tree people shout and cheer, and it's a sound like laughter in the wind, rustling in the leaves, and bending of branches. Taomau sweeps me into a deep embrace. I wrap my arms around his neck. The happiness is so much, I feel as if I could burst.

"I can't believe you came back for me," I whisper.

He kisses my head and pulls back. "How could I not, sweet one? I love you, Iscah."

I can't stop smiling.

As the music strikes up in a jubilant song and great urns of sparkling rich water are passed about, I feel happiness unlike anything I have ever felt. "And I love you, Taomau." I never thought it was possible for me to feel so good again.

He holds me tight. The music plays and sings about us, and an elm tree bard begins a ballad, but all I can see is Taomau.

We dance and waltz around the clearing. There's laughter, crying, and talking. It all blurs together in my mind. So beautiful and so perfect. It carries on for hours without waning.

At one point in the crowd, I think I catch a sight of Desmond. My heart catches in my throat. He's only there for a moment, smiling, lifting his hand as if to wish me well. But when I look back, it looks like another dryad. It might have been my imagination. I barely have time to smile back before Taomau spins me about and Desmond is gone.

It's the one final blessing to crown this day. There's nothing I can do but celebrate and delight in this new chapter and close the old forever. At last I am at peace. At last I am free. At last I am home.

THIS STORY IS SET in the same world as the Fae Bride Series. If you want to see more of what happens to Taomau and Iscah, make sure to check out Fae Rose Bride and follow her at her website jmbutlerauthor.com.

ABOUT JESSICA M. BUTLER

Jessica M. Butler is an adventurer, author, and attorney who never outgrew her love for telling stories and playing in imaginary worlds. She is the author of the epic fantasy romance series *Tue-Rah Chronicles* including *Identity Revealed, Enemy Known,* and *Princess Reviled, Wilderness Untamed,* and *Shifter Untamed* along with independent novellas *Locked, Cursed,* and *Alone,* set in the same world. She has also written numerous fantasy tales such as *Escaping Red Eye, Mermaid Bride, Little Scapegoat, Through the Paintings Dimly, Why Yes, Bluebeard, I'd Love To,* and more. For the most part, she writes speculative fiction with a heavy focus on multi-cultural high fantasy and suspenseful adventures and passionate romances. She lives with her husband and law partner, James Fry, in rural Indiana where they are quite happy with their five cats: Thor, Loptr, Fenrir, Hela, and Herne.

Made in the USA
Columbia, SC
11 January 2024

969a1249-3e7b-4bd0-be2d-476f73061d09R02